Rodman took two quick steps toward his visitor and straight-armed a right hand to his neck, pulling him back and down, cracking his shoulders on the desk top, Rodman's grip tight on his throat. Their breaths kissed.

Rodman's words came out in fitful spurts of restraint: "What the *fuck* do you think you're doing here?"

"What? You didn't like my letter?"

Rodman felt ambushed, his breathing irregular. "I can't believe you have the balls to come *here*—and looking like this! What the fuck happened to you? What were you thinking coming here?"

"I was thinking we needed to push things up a bit. The letter's, like, yesterday's news. I need acceleration."

"I *paid*," Rodman snarled. "I *paid* you already. You left last time with the condition that—"

He smacked Rodman hard across the face. "So, like, I'm *back*!"

ALIBIS

Robert DiChiara

FAWCETT GOLD MEDAL • NEW YORK

A Fawcett Gold Medal Book
Published by Ballantine Books
Copyright © 1996 by Robert DiChiara

All rights reserved under International and Pan-American Copyright Conventions. Published in the United States by Ballantine Books, a division of Random House, Inc., New York, and simultaneously in Canada by Random House of Canada Limited, Toronto.

Library of Congress Catalog Card Number: 95-90725

ISBN 0-449-14945-5

Printed in Canada

First Edition: March 1996

10 9 8 7 6 5 4 3 2 1

To Elaine & Katie—
my perfect alibis for not writing

Do it!

—JERRY RUBIN

What have you done, you there
Weeping without cease,
Tell me, yes you, what have you done
With all your youth?

—PAUL VERLAINE

PART I

1

REALLY, IT WAS after the sun introduced itself through his bedroom curtains as though rising from a dark graceful bow and demurely touched his face with the new day's heat. It was after the tiny wave and smile his wife gave him as he leaned in baggy red clown-pajamas over the kitchen sink, waiting for the rushing tap water to get cold in order to brew up his jolt of caffeine, and she, like an arcing, flying flow of curves, dove into the chilly pool.

It was really after the tartness of the grapefruit and the delicate ring of the portable phone and the dirty joke Howard told over it (Howard had gotten the gag via a client who worked on Wall Street) and after the laugh. Certainly after the laugh.

It was after the hot beating of the shower massage and the crisp feel of the collar on his neck as he tightened the knot of his Ralph Lauren silk tie, the tickle on the apple, and the last fresh handkerchief triangulating from his breast pocket like a badge of class.

It was after the chlorinated taste of Delia's have-a-good-day lips, and the assuring grip of his attaché case, and the cool round smoothness of the front doorknob.

Really after the grip of the doorknob, the hard grip, the sudden exhale of air through his nose, the tightened brow, the thump of his head against the door and another dizzying exhale, the pushing the door with his forehead, holding the knob, trembling, holding the knob—after the house, his wife, his *life*—

Really after his sudden springing up, straight as a switch-blade, and swinging his briefcase, cursing, striking, toppling a table lamp, did Carl Rodman finally decide—Yes. He had to murder a man.

There was nothing more to it.

Resolve had overtaken routine. New plans of death had destroyed old paths of life. He took deep breaths and peered out through the brass peephole, seeing only a distorted world outside. The whole of his mind now moved toward the kill, toward the person who wrote the letter.

It was the letter last night, after all, that started it again, Rodman thumbing through the mail as an afterthought. "Come to bed. It's late," came Delia's muted shout from the upstairs bedroom. "I need a toe warmer."

"My loins are busy!" he shouted back with a laugh and an easy resignation. "I'll be right up."

Rodman had pictured his wife's highly arched feet, always with a red blush about them, and always twenty degrees lower than the outside thermometer reading. She liked to bend back and nestle her well-honed rump into his receptive belly, and as though tucking for one of her classy dives, draw up her legs so that her feet slid between his thighs. He liked it, too, the sensation of nurturing ten nearly frozen wiggling buds, in spite of his recurring protestations. This bedtime tableau over the years had lost most of its sexual implications, a more protective instinct taking over, at times sadly desperate, especially since Eric's death.

Rodman had come to a particular envelope in the stack, which aside from being dully white and thereby less colorful than the advertising mail, was less crisp as well, almost soiled, crinkled from inception and not from postal abuse. There was something unclean about handling it, like having to use a secondhand napkin.

Carl Rodman's moistened finger had stopped at his own all-capped name in black ink on the envelope's front. (He later felt that if his mind wasn't in that twilight-filled drift before hitting the pillow, he would have recognized the arrested, childlike hand, even after all this time, and would have burned the letter unopened in the stone barbecue pit outside.)

But he read it, blank-faced. It was not unlike the last one. The money was up to $35,000 this time. But it wasn't the money. The money meant nothing. The phrase "child killer" was used more than once, not as a direct threat, but more so as a sick running gag, a joke only the teller found funny . . . and profitable.

After Rodman had torn up the missive over the trash bin, he climbed upstairs and slipped under the blue bed sheets, a bar of tension resting above hot eyes. Their heat radiated with even more intensity closed, and his constricted heart searched out another body.

Delia felt Carl's dark embrace from behind but she did not pull up into her accustomed posture. She wordlessly turned in place within his muscularity and guided his head into her breasts, her cool brown-freckled hands on the taut wires that were the back of his neck. They slackened when embraced.

Delia drove out all thoughts of what this entwining was calling back to her, the times best forgotten. She never felt comfortable having to give solace to Carl, or to any man in her past, for that matter. Not that she didn't appreciate the fact that Carl wasn't ashamed to cry in front of her during their times of grief, especially over Eric. However, any weakness Carl demonstrated seemed to reawaken those she herself had submerged. She did not want her husband to be a mirror of her fears set before her, but the model of what she wanted to be for herself. Carl often tried to fulfill the latter, consciously or not, but now his pained embrace was too close a reminder of what never should have happened. Never.

She stroked the back of Carl's head for as long as she could before drifting off. Rodman eased into sleep as well, duping himself that the letter would become lost in the seemingly infinite oblivion night has to offer.

But this morning it had come back on him. It always came back on him, like the brackish, murky water that reformed in the pool every year and had to be poisoned out. His son was two years dead now. It took two years awash in tears and self-loathing to try to reestablish the rich landscape of the life he led, to repaint his pastoral over a canvas of foul-mouthed graffiti. He tried to maintain the painting, this life, this *perfect* life—the edges of his teeth sucked in pain at the mind's mouthing of the words, *perfect life*—it was serene, green, one to be looked at, admired. (People politely ignored the one missing sacrifical lamb in the family's foreground.) And this morning's regal offerings—the poolside smile, the crisp white collar, the firm grip on his case—all were once more being violated by the letter's veiled threats of exposure.

Rodman realized all this while taut and readied against the front door, aiming a reflective stare at his favorite rural painting which hung on the opposing wall.

He heard the pad of bare feet on the paneled wood floor, and Delia appeared from the main hall. Her squared shoulders, though softened by a pilly white poolside robe, carried forth her dampened head with exacting balance and grace, as though it were being served as a sweet and dappled morning melon.

"You still here, hon?" she asked, concern in her voice. Then she spotted the felled lamp. "What's going on?" She restored the lamp to its appropriate place and took two tentative steps toward the intensely still figure at the door.

"Got a little dizzy and tripped, that's all," he said. "Woozy headache."

Rodman's eyes were the only parts of his body that moved, a pupillary float toward her face.

It was a lovely face, he thought, and a face he loved. Her pinkish white body, too. As he had watched her before at the pool, framed in the small kitchen window, he felt, as always, as though he were watching an old home movie, Delia the high school swimming champ, her youth refurbished, refreshed by the onset of water, the blossoming encircling wave, liquid petals, her head bobbing up at the flower's core. The constant sun had deepened her freckles while lightening her hair to a berry red. He worried about her skin, though, born fair from her half-Irish blood, worried about the possibility of cancer, the possibility of another death festering inside his house. That blackmail letter was like another death festering—

"That's too bad," Delia said. She sensed Carl's dark drifting and started to feel scared and worried, staring at the oozing scrape on his forehead. "Here," she said, handing him a tissue from her robe pocket. He nodded and blotted the wound.

"You take anything for it?" she asked.

"Took a Motrin."

"You use milk?"

He nodded. "I'd better get moving. Don't want to be *too* late."

Rodman straightened up from his slant against the door, shifting his sizable shoulders. Delia bit her lip as she watched her husband try to reassemble himself for business.

Neither was going to mention last night and Rodman's shriveling embrace, nor reenact the circumstances. Their love was as unspoken as their loss, like a diamond whose brilliance needed no words but whose flaw betrayed its crystalline surface. Lately, they always tried to let the events of the day work things through.

Of course, Delia had supposed their unspoken loss was that of their son to the shadowy hit-and-run driver, while in fact Rodman's loss at the moment was that of his freedom to the provocating demand that he kill a man to kill a memory.

Rodman drew the knot of his tie back to his neck. Delia fanned out some envelopes before him. "Could you mail these in town?" Without looking, he took them. Delia helped with the stubborn stiffness of his collar, and nodded her approval at his appearance when she was through.

"Thanks," he said, then he glanced at the top envelope, addressed to St. Luke's Hospital in Point Crescent. "A get-well card? Who's sick?" The name Mary Dorlack on the envelope meant nothing to him.

"Oh . . . just one of the patrons for the Leukemia Fund. A steady donator, a real help at our functions."

"A politic move, too?" Rodman coaxed himself to smile in order to see Delia return the favor. She responded with a chuckle. She was also cautiously relieved to see her husband's eyes refocused on the tangible world and not hopelessly adrift.

"I actually *like* this one. Mary has a lot more heart than the rest, who do their part only because it gets them out of the housekeeper's way back at the mansion."

Delia touched a damp hand to Carl's neck and kissed his cheek lightly. "Love you. Hope your headache goes away."

"It will," he said.

Permanently, he thought.

When Rodman left, Delia turned and started back toward her abandoned croissant in the kitchen. She was walking at a thoughtful, slow pace when she stopped and glanced at the painting she had watched Carl staring at for what seemed like years before she made herself visible. She had barely noticed the painting anymore, as most people over time never really notice furnishings once in place. It was a piece Carl had brought from his parents' house, a work conceived by an amateur artist, a mysterious "friend of the family." The painter had obviously tried his best to imitate Monet in style if not in substance, yet never really pulling it off. Not that Delia was a fan of the Impressionists anyway. Her tastes leaned toward Edward Hopper, the urban browns, the hard-edged nights.

This painting was bright, bold and ethereal, some green undulant field streaked by sun and shadow, with a benign shepherd hunkered at the twisty base of an ancient-looking tree. He watches his neighbors tend a garden on the hilly emerald slope beyond, while his own family of sorts, three fulsome sheep, grazes before him. Two of the sheep cuddle shaky-limbed lambs at their sides.

Delia shook her head and flipped her wet hair behind her like a whip to her back. The painting was making her terribly sad, and she hated it even more. She never understood what Carl saw in it from the outset, and certainly not this morning. It was far too unreal for her—a false ideal, at best; at worst, a debilitating dream.

2

ALONG THE HOLLOWSPORT shoreline a determined wind came skimming over the ocean and sprayed its heavy mist into the faces of the construction workers on Riller's Beach. It made the dark water dance in white-nippled peaks. It didn't make Louis Dembo dance, except in a slow dour stomp, left-foot-up, then down, right-foot-up, then down, all in place, knees springy, hands dug into his jacket pockets, fighting off the morning chill, the daily two-step waiting for Marty and the damned coffee.

Only thing to warm his insides right now was the suck of smoke from his cigarette. The grinding racket from the dinosaurlike machines seemed to echo in the low ceiling of clouds as though boxed in, and the noise hurt his sensitized ears almost as much as the biting wind. Dawn wasn't his *thing*, he would say. But by ten o'clock sharp (it was hormonal instinct that made him suddenly flash at his watch), Louis would stop everything and take in the girls that marched along the boardwalk like a sweet parade of fuckability. They all unloaded from the same bus, trotting along, talking, each pretty from his distance, and best of all, when they arrived at Mariner's Restaurant, they brought the sun.

The first seaside rays would inevitably fan out along their tender calves and brightly intensify the tight white fullness of their short waitressing dresses; those same rays stroked his own body, warming his sore joints from yesterday's dig, stoking him up. The sun connected the girls and him that way with a special heat. He watched the half-dozen peach-shaped rumps disappear inside, yet as usual, he picked out the straight-haired blonde as his focus. Best of the lot. Pussy-plus. The more gen-

9

erally populated daily peep show on the beach had been well over since Labor Day, so the restaurant's tasty frills would have to do. Besides, technically, the stretch of sand from here to a thousand yards on either side was closed for repair.

"Do we need more support here, Lou, or what?"

It was Marty, Louis Dembo's younger brother, interrupting his foreman's morning mantra. When the girls were out of sight, Louis turned and squinted into the sun at the stretch of cable and the tarnished yellow crane it reeled out from.

"Nah," he said, pruning his face. "You give it some slack, you got plenty." His brother nodded and played the thankful apprentice because Lou relished being master. "Like the last piling, Marty. Same rigamarole. No difference."

"Gotcha," Marty said. Then his eyes became impish. "You ever going to talk to them?" he asked, referring to the waitresses.

Louis spoke in earnest seriousness. "They don't know it but I'm working on them, don't think otherwise. I'm making them aware of me unconsciously. I got my eye working."

Marty sneered, then took it back, thinking maybe his brother was really being straight, then he sneered again. "Bull-*shit*!" he said, and when Louis gave him a closed-mouth smile, he broke into a laugh. Marty's braces lit up in a glare of sunlight.

Although he was twenty-two, Marty Dembo was determined to right at least one wrong his parents bequeathed his face. Unluckily, he had managed to compile each ill-fitting feature of the Dembo genetic line—from his mother's poorly aligned nose to eyes the size and hue and bulge of walnuts, courtesy of Dad. Even a dead old goat of a grandfather everybody thought was pure shit contributed a dark patch like a minute kidney, the mark resting just below his jawline. (Of course, his silver-wired teeth in the short run added a grotesque note to what was a symphony of quirky features.)

His skin was more ivory than flesh-toned. Everybody in his family could tan but him—what good was being Italian if you couldn't tan? No question, he was Louis's pale shadow in more ways than one. In fact, whether Marty realized it or not, part of his admiration for Louis stemmed, not just from Louis's greater experience dealing with the ins and outs of construction and the extracurricular muscle-money, but from Louis's handsomely brutish features.

Really, the only things the Dembo brothers had in common, besides their matching blue corduroy baseball caps, were a love of violent release and bad teeth.

As the afternoon approached, Louis grew anxious about his post-lunch highlight. He ate quickly beside his brother, the other laborers camped in twos and threes, looking too grubby and greased for such a beach party picnic. Louis then stood up, out from the shade beneath the fenced-off decrepitude of the pier, and happily saw two of his girlies on their break, as always, sitting at the edge of the elevated boardwalk, swinging their legs in the sea breeze.

One was a kinky-haired brunette, sipping a soda, with too much meat in the thigh but more than ample bosom to compensate. Her legs were full, brown, and their muscles bulged forcefully even in her idle kicks. She looked too much like one of his chunky ginzo cousins on his aunt Maria's side. The brunette kept up her end of the conversation even with a pair of earphones straddling her head, forcing it to bop.

But if the brunette was the entrée, Louis would rather just nibble, thanks, and hit the dessert. The sweet-faced straight-haired blonde was beside her, eyes closed, head tilted back, absorbing the brunette's prattle and the caress of the sun. Her straw-yellow hair, normally dancing just above the shoulders when upright, was behind her, clean and golden. Her face was serene and tan and had an aristocratic nose poking upward like the singular well-chiseled peak on a smooth, soft, vulnerable surface. Her tender legs were crossed at the ankles and swaying gently, the white dress riding up seemingly beyond her lower thigh, up beyond thought, giving the impression of an even longer leg and line to her entire body. She was delicate and chocolate-brown, and Louis just wanted to touch her and smell her and snap a piece off her and let it melt in his mouth.

Louis heard his little brother's signature chuckle at his back as he strode toward the two girls, his eyes fixed on their out-of-sync pendular limbs. He stopped just alongside the pair, on their blind side, if you will, what with the straight-haired blonde in a serene dreamy passivity and her friend turned toward her, talking. Louis was facing the back of the brunette's head, wanting to step in front of them in a single bold move, to establish perfect position: close enough to smell the blonde, to see if she wore any fragrance or even tanning butter; angled enough to work his hard vision between her supple upper thighs. Louis felt that his experience told him where he could move, how close he could get. He was grateful the sun was at his back, outlining his strength, darkening his rippled arms, arms he had since exposed in a sleeveless tee shirt for the noon-hour heat.

He came into the brunette's view immediately, but it was the tinge of coolness from his shadow on the lower portion of the blonde's legs that raised her baking eyelids. She squinted toward the older man before her, trying to make out the black-and-blue mark that seemed to stain his chest above the dip of his red tee.

Louis peered in at the conch-shaped name tag above the blonde's left bosom. Her name was Barbara. Just for reference, the other one was Lynn.

"Sorry about the view, girls," he said, pointing back at the reconstruction work being done on the small pier. "I know you two like to sit here on break and look at the ocean and all. I guess we're in your way."

Lynn just thought, You can say that again, and shifted over a few inches to see past the big-muscled thing eclipsing her. Barbara nodded and used her easy-to-surface politeness. "It's okay."

She straightened up and raised her hand to shield her eyes. It was a tattoo, she realized, the scaly pate of some creature's head trying to rise out of this guy's undershirt, a thing she had no desire to see the rest of.

Louis was pleased it was Barbara who had responded, and it gave him impetus to take charge. "We're gonna make it come out real nice, though. The pier. Just like the old days, lotta stalls with junk to buy. You know. Be a nice place to take a walk on at night with a date or something."

He nodded and gave Barbara his closed-mouth smile. She nodded, too.

"You the foreman over there?" Barbara asked, actually curious. Louis felt a blush coming on, and it fed whatever blood was rising into his cock. He realized she must have noticed him before, son of a bitch, and here she was, a dick length's away. His eye had been out and working for sure.

"Oh, yeah, I'm in charge," he said, as though it were obvious. He used the opportunity briefly to touch Barbara's leg as an indication she should look precisely where he was about to point. It made her push her bottom back a notch and pull her dress down in a subtle motion.

"See there?" Louis said. "I'm responsible for digging out the dry rot pilings and replacing every one. There's a bunch of them, too. It's real dangerous up there now, why's we closed it off. Lots of rot up top, too. It's slow work, but don't worry, we make our way. And the machines—you see . . . ?"

Louis pointed again, touched her leg again. Barbara wondered why he kept answering questions never asked.

"You see how big those babies are? Those are beauties. Those are my toys. I can work them all, I hadda. I could rebuild the whole damn thing over myself, you gave me enough time. That's why I'm in charge."

Louis didn't even look back at Barbara for a reaction, for what he hoped was a gaze of glassy-eyed awe at his empowerment. Instead he kept looking at the idle crane, at the heavy-plated bulldozer, at the ground drill. Those *were* his toys, and the men were included in that definition. He moved the workers and metal contraptions around as though flexing his muscles. He liked the way the machines manipulated the earth, manipulated *things*. Unbeknownst to him, however, he was also smiling as he took in and embraced his behemoth equipment, a relaxed open smile, not the tight-lipped, controlled one he forced himself to hand out to the girls and others.

Barbara watched Louis with apprehensive wonder. She figured him to be in his late thirties easy, with a Romanesque profile, sexy black-and-bushy eyebrows over amber eyes and a hard body. There was no doubt he wasn't like the boys she met at Easterly College, not like Danny, either, and at first she actually had let her afternoon itch of desire tingle at his appearance.

But it was the toothy smile that drained her, that revealed the scary skull beneath the rugged flesh. Like Marty's, each of Louis's teeth retained its tombstonelike individuality amid a fetid border of gums. They were also discolored by years of smoking nonfilter cigarettes since he was nine, and every third one seemed black with rot or holes of utter decay. His hidden smile unmasked, his nearness now made Barbara frightened. She sensed her skin bubble with sweat in his shade.

She glanced at Lynn, who was too busy bopping to her head music and looking the other way; easy for *her*, she wasn't being focused on, pinned down. Barbara couldn't push herself back any farther as Louis had improvised himself between her and Lynn, his right hand just behind her ass, his left hand pointing so that his arm was like a brown bar blocking her way ahead.

"That one there," he said, indicating the large bit that made the holes in the sand into which the thick wood pilings would be driven. "We call that one the Big Screw."

"Oh," she said, not accepting the renewed closed-mouth smile Louis offered along with his clumsy innuendo. His voice took on a serious just-between-us register.

"You like music? Your friend seems to."

Barbara just nodded, her throat tight. Positioned off to the side of her buttery legs, Louis settled for trying to look down the top of her white dress, smell her neck, her golden hair, maybe closer—

"You like hard rock? Maybe a little Bee Gees Saturday night dancing, some fever." His head swaggered to his own beat. "A little Sinatra for romance?" He suddenly sang, "Strangers in the night . . ."

This made even Lynn glare over at Barbara and raise the right side of her lip as though it were snagged by a fishhook and wonder what the hell decade did *this* jerk come from. Barbara thought Louis was getting beyond weird. She tried squirming away without too much fuss or show of fear. Then Lynn hopped off the planking onto the beach and started walking the sandy yards toward the trash barrel to deposit her drink container. Barbara started looking around the beach and literally around Louis, trying to look through him.

"When you get off?" he asked, sensing something had slipped.

"I gotta go," Barbara said.

"Hey, come on, what's the big deal?" Louis started to feel embarrassed. He could hurt this one, he thought.

"No big deal, I have to go back in."

"I don't get it. I'm just asking a question." Louis was almost on top of her. He could smell her now; her skin smelled like lemon and butter and that sweet dollop of fear.

"Please," Barbara said firmly. She felt as though she were blocked in.

"What? You gotta boyfriend? He rate a satisfactory in your book?"

Barbara suddenly pulled class, her tone announcing she was educated: she was future management, he was forever labor. "I don't *think* that's any of your business."

Yeah, he could manipulate this one good. His face was turning red; it was always like this with this *type*. He closed in and pincered her thigh with his fingers, a good hard squeeze. She stiffened, shuddered. "Don't soil your panties, sweetheart," he whispered.

Then he heard hard-soled thumps on the boardwalk, felt the footfalls under his right hand even at such a distance. He glanced unnoticed over the blonde's shoulder.

"I gotta go," he said, out of nowhere. "Catch you tomorrow." He winked and moved away. Gone. Barbara sat there and felt her breath leave her, stunned at the suddenness of his disappearance.

Lynn moseyed back beside her friend. "Guess you blew him off good," she cracked. She watched Barbara stand up, a pensive expression on her face.

"Yeah," Barbara said unenthusiastically. She remained momentarily uneasy because she didn't think she had much to do with his retreat and because she didn't feel totally free.

She was right on both counts.

Sam Ryan always had to carry his great height and reputation with him wherever he went. After all, his nickname was Beanpole and he operated a sports bar of the same name. He was the local high school basketball all-star some forty years ago—before the African tribes took over, he would say. A bum ankle put the stutter-step fake and lefty hook shot he had perfected like a dream to a halt; the third fracture was the charm. No college would touch him after that.

Ryan resented having to live out bygone Hollowsport days,

the Owls, the silver and yellow colors on the cheerleading Owlettes shaking their teenage behinds in front of the bench, because basically he felt stuck in Hollowsport ever since, felt stuck in this beachfront bar ever since Cole put up the money and had him front the place when it was at first just a seaweed-odored dive for East Coast surfer boys and their underage dates, felt stuck no matter how successful it had now become, especially on game nights, the large screen videos lighting up almost as fast as the digital cash registers. He felt stuck with his high school rep and unfulfilled future and his aging six-foot-eleven frame, good for nothing except accelerating arthritis and reminding people who he was.

He hated the guy who would recognize him and used it as an excuse to show him the silver-and-yellow card in his wallet as if it were a two-tone abstract photo of his firstborn, a card that meant he contributed major bucks to the Owl Silver and Yellow Fund, to Hollowsport High forever. Then Ryan would always want to show what *he* contributed to Hollowsport High by slipping his trousers and underpants down his legs and gripping his balls in the flesh of his hand.

Ryan slammed the door on the liquid-lunch crowd behind him as he stepped out onto the boardwalk and breathed the sun-drenched air. He gazed out at the renovation project, a project pushed through the county board by the right people, people whose restaurant and sports bar he would make a lot of money for, and take his minuscule piece. He listened to the whining machinery gearing up again alongside the dilapidated pier, caught the eye of Marty Dembo and motioned for him.

Ryan's second gaze, this time down the boardwalk, produced a less welcome sight. He marched forward with heavy, loping steps until he was noticed, then he stopped and waited, as all people in command do, for others to come to them. For all his bodily dissatisfaction, Ryan knew how to use his stature as a threat; no matter how lanky he was, he was big, and his shoulders appeared to have a cross beam shoved between them with a somber head in the middle and two large hard knobs at the ends.

When Louis Dembo finally arrived a good ten inches below him, Ryan peered down with a snarl and glanced over at the two young waitresses who were trotting back inside Mariner's Restaurant, Beanpole's companion eatery.

"*Look* ..." Ryan said to Louis, "but *don't* ... *touch*." He eyed Louis intensely. "We've been through that one before."

"Right," Louis said, sloughing him off, the same way he had the year and five months jail time. Marty Dembo approached from below the boardwalk and stayed there to listen, staring up from the sand.

"So, Sam, what's the word on the garbage talks?" Louis asked to head off any more tedious lectures. "My cousin just got in sanitation, you know. He's worried. They really talking wildcat?"

"Doesn't look good," Ryan sniffed, with the burden of having to be the authority on every fucking thing. "Definite possibility of a job action, the talks don't get better at the table." Ryan had associates in the local labor front he tried not to see too often, other fifty-year-old homegrowners who went into politics and liked having their pet athlete around. Ryan made the best of the connection through favors.

"If the wildcat goes down," Ryan went on, "I got a lead on a truck from Point Crescent, or Densfield even. I need a driver and a few boys for some county dump runs; otherwise, a day or two of the crap we throw out from the restaurant alone is going to stink away my business. You interested?"

Louis looked incredulous. "What? Scabbing on my cousin?"

"It's money," Ryan said.

"It's my *cousin*."

"Never mind," Ryan said in disgust. "Don't make a big deal out of it. I got you down for something else anyway. More in your line."

"Ac-*tion*," Marty said, sprouting a quirky grin.

"With control," Ryan added as he peered down at that little loser, pointing.

"What is it?" Louis asked.

"It's a talk ... with something extra," Ryan said. "I've informed one of my clients that he should come up with the money owed plus our agreed-upon interest. He needs to be better informed because I want him to take me more seriously."

Louis held in a smile. Beanpole always wanted, *begged*, to be taken seriously, which was just why Louis never obliged.

"So when do we give him this message?"

"Tonight. You talk to him tonight. Speed up his delivery time. He needs to be Federally Expressed."

"Same pay?" Marty asked, to assert himself a bit.

"Same pay," Ryan said.

Louis shook his head. "Not the same pay."

Ryan spread his long hands. "What now? You want a cost-of-living raise for roughing a guy?"

"Hey," Louis said, "if you're looking at us like we're garbagemen, oh-fucking-kay, 'cause we're taking care of *your* personal garbage, right? We're pulling the heavy load here. If you're sharking, we want a stake. We're regular with you—we do your dirty work, we want a cut of what's owed."

Ryan was dumbfounded. "A cut!?"

"Yeah," Louis said, crossing his chunky forearms. "We should take a—a—a eight percent cut—" It sounded good. Eight was a good number. His mother had eight knife wounds in her when they found her body. He looked with a shrug to Marty, whose brows were elevated in astonishment. "—you know, from what we recover. The bigger bundle you stand to lose, the more *we* stand to gain—" Louis moved up closer to Ryan and talked intimately with his lapel. "—the harder we do our job, right? I mean, get with the times, Sam. We're talking incentive here."

"All right, all right," Ryan said, trying to shoo Louis away like a greasy fly. "No big deal. Don't make such a big deal about it."

Louis clapped Ryan on the chest with his open palm twice, then winked at Marty, who tucked in his right arm and pulled an imaginary chain with his fist, but only a fraction so as not to be noticed celebrating.

Ryan just shook his head, watching Louis jump down to the sand with his brother to go back to work. It didn't matter anymore, he thought, jigaboo tribes, sanitation men, and losers like the Dembos were going to take over the world anyway. Let's get it over with.

"That's *tonight*," he asserted. "And, hey! Listen!" The Dembos finally paid attention. *"Don't . . . play!"* Ryan enunciated.

The Dembos shot each other a sober peek, then looked to

Ryan and nodded, only with big, broad smiles on their faces. Marty's braces gleamed. Louis's teeth offered tarnished lemons.

The silver and yellow, Ryan thought. There was no escaping fucking Hollowsport.

3

ALERTED, DELIA RODMAN saw what was coming, in more ways than one. The click-thump had been a loud enough warning all summer with the windows open, and as always it amazed her how swiftly her neighbor Hallie Fouche could stutter down the sidewalk though burdened with her disability. Hallie's foot had been badly deformed at birth. Now encased in a prosthesis it was a harsh constant in her life. Yet, according to Hallie, from the time she was a willowy teen she had promised herself she was going to make certain that the rest of her existence was going to be beautiful—a beautiful home, beautiful daughter, beautiful clothes, a beautifully wealthy husband, which was close enough if she wanted the former things as badly as she did. And she did. Delia admired Hallie's physical determination; it was the motivational force behind Hallie's ability for which Delia had little tolerance.

"I'm here to snoop," Hallie announced at the screen door.

And proud of it, thought Delia, as though being honest ameliorated the intent. Delia let her in, accompanied by the stinging smell of hair spray layered with a dose of perfume administered by a heavy hand. But then Hallie was forever the mistress of the overdone. Even now she was dressed to the nines for a neighborly pop-in, as though it were the 1950s—the high-necked green dress, pleated to just below the knees, belted in the middle, the pearls and matching earrings, and the single emerald high heel on her healthy foot. She reminded Delia of Donna Reed with a nineties snout for rutting up dirt. Unfortunately, most often it was accurate dirt, which also made Hallie a little bit dangerous despite being a visual anachronism. In fact, unknown to Delia, the true reason for

Hallie's appearance today was to uncover who would be at the Rodmans' party for State Senator McMann this Sunday. And maybe even to uncover that *special* who.

"I can't chat long," Delia said, letting her in. "I'm—I'm expecting a phone call." She cursed herself at the hitch in her statement, intolerant of her brief show of weakness. Yet it started spilling out, like jiggling a much-too-full glass. "I don't know, I guess business is taking me in more directions than I thought it would. And things at home now, I can't seem to get my mind focused somehow today."

"Trying to accomplish too many things at the same time." Hallie nodded in understanding. "Don't I know the feeling."

Delia dropped herself down on the puffy white sofa while Hallie placed herself at the center of a lounge chair cushion, a graceful descent embellished by a graceful smile. She leaned over. "I'm excited about your affair," she confided in a girlish voice.

"My what?" Delia said, taken off guard.

"Your affair for the most prominent Senator McMann, Delia. Come *on*!"

"It's not an *affair*," Delia said. "It's a party. Just a proper 'thank you' for his support. He deserves it for what he's done—and is still doing."

"For Carl, you mean . . ."

"For Carl, sure, but also, you know, mainly *my* projects, is what it's about, really. The Leukemia Fund and other charities. Not to mention his financial contributions, the people he's introduced me to—"

"Oh, so who's coming then?" Hallie interrupted, eyes widened. "Anybody I don't know?"

Delia felt herself rattling, being too out front and vulnerable. She should never have let Hallie in. Not now. "Well, it's hard to remember people off the top of my head. I'm sure you know—" Then Delia's head flicked right as though she heard something. "Was that . . . ?" But, no. She didn't finish what she was going to say. Instead she pulled her legs up under her, rolled into herself, a protective retreat.

Hallie stared with disapproval at Delia's bare feet poking out from beneath her buttocks. The posture was bad enough, but she didn't think Delia's constant lack of footwear to be attractive. She felt Delia was getting away with something, feeling the earth hum directly under her feet while, in the name of what's true to proper womanhood, Hallie had to distance herself three inches of heel away.

Delia was a bit on the masculine side anyway, she reflected. Always in a variant of pants, like now, in short, baggy yellow pantaloons, and what looked like one of her husband's shirts, sleeves rolled. Everything loosey-goosey. (And wasn't that what was wrong with the world?) But even Delia's billowy cotton shirt could not hide her wide shoulders, her hard-angled jaw. Not to say she wasn't attractive, but she had a muscular boldness that wasn't in keeping with the social strata she was in now.

Her husband Carl was a different story altogether. At least Delia used social decorum, if not sartorial. There was a shell of discretion to Delia that Hallie wanted to penetrate and see under; she wanted to be her mother confessor. The poor girl must need one. She should have a caring eye kept on her for the sake of her well-being, with her having had to weather Carl Rodman as a husband, and with, of course, the *tragedy*.

Hallie thought Rodman's "drying out" at the rehabilitation center in Allsbury should have been a juicy slice of gossip for the right people, like herself, to suck upon, not something to be served to the local newspapers, feeding the undeserved general community just for cheap sympathy. Hollowsport's upper strata had a right to share such disgrace and chew it around among themselves, sort of the equivalent to only blacks being allowed to call themselves "niggers." Then, of course, the death of his young son Eric garnered Rodman a public outpouring of emotion so richly undeserved. Where was there justice?

Hallie broke the mutually pensive silence. "You were saying? The guest list?" Then the phone jangled, and Delia became unconsciously stiff and so composed as to be overly formal. "I'll take it in the bedroom, you can relax out here, though . . . I may be a long while. There's a business snafu—"

"No, no," Hallie insisted, chin down with deference. "If it's important, I'll just get out of your way. No cause for concern." She hobbled toward the screen door.

Delia spoke abruptly. "Okay, 'bye." Then she trotted into the kitchen and snatched up the portable phone.

"See you Sunday!" Hallie sang out as she released the screen and with fervent determination swiftly and steadily pulled her sickly foot up the slope as though racing the electronic impulses buzzing along the wires. She cursed her burden during these times when God had denied her inherent grace and natural speed and she had to manufacture both out of a tenacious female will.

She slapped back her front door and caned her daughter's yellow pest of a cat out of the way. It leaped and bleated a sorrowful mew. She snatched up her own portable phone and fumbled with the antenna, telescoping it fully, then pushed the set up to her ear in an awkward crouch, her cane beneath her armpit, a posture reminiscent of a hump-backed pirate. The first sound she heard was masculine to be sure, but distant and riddled with static and unrecognizable as *anybody*, but definitely a masculine voice. Delia's was clearer, just a coating of fuzz in the transmission, however, with intermittent dropouts.

"It'll be awkward, but . . . if I . . . I know I can get lost . . . not be missed right away . . . and what about . . . no, I *must* . . . we . . . talk Sunday . . . what?"

Suddenly the line was dead. Hallie looked at her portable phone with suspicion, then reached under the ottoman's cushion and felt for the nestled binoculars. She steadied them at eye level and saw Delia step down into the living room from the kitchen, still on the phone, and start pacing. Delia must have switched signal channels on the portable's control pad. Hallie looked once more at her own phone, but suspicion had turned to repulsion. Her husband, Bert, must have bought a cheaper model. She had no such switching ability, no such expectant facility to keep up with Delia, to keep up with the world, *her* world. (Wasn't she crippled enough?)

Her face flushed in anger at her husband, then stemmed just as fast when she thought once more of Delia, of shoulder-swaggering, bare-footing, loosey-goosey Delia. So brazen, Hallie thought with a wicked smile, her painted red lips elongated across her face, cracking like a dry rubber band being too far stretched. Sunday's party should prove intriguing. A lovers' tryst taken amid the artichoke salad and sun hats. Hallie knew that Bert wouldn't care; and her daughter would listen but never really wanted to *know*, her young blond sweetness somehow without the necessary capacity for the bitter, for things tart and tasty.

Hallie took another glance through the binoculars, but the shade had been drawn, and she chuckled deep in her throat. The curtain would rise soon; it always did.

She gave an unmindful shrug and looked away from the window. She settled into her cozy ottoman. Perfect timing: *The Young and the Restless* was just coming on television.

4

I T WAS NEARLY midnight, so the ball game beamed in from the West Coast was live. Most of the crowd inside the bar had something at stake, depending who won—a friendly bet, a not-so-friendly bet, even some over-the-long-haul wagers with both money and management abilities on the line. That would be your rotisserie baseball freaks, those yups from the downtown business district over in the next booth who mainline on stats and form phony teams from real ballplayers and pool lots of cash so that at the end of the season they see who possessed the brains of Branch Rickey. Sonny Vance preferred the balls of George Steinbrenner; besides, he couldn't stomach the tedious number crunching and any bets that sat for months on end—too long for a payoff.

Sonny Vance would plug himself into the "not-so-friendly bet" category if given the choices. He and the house were always at odds, often long odds, with him hoping for the big jackpot. Though the house always took its role in the transaction way too seriously, always acted as though the money actually *meant* something. Whether he was down a few big bills or up some—hell, if he was in the hole for a dozen Swiss bank accounts or just won the equivalent of one day's collective casino take from Atlantic City, he'd still be laying another sweet wager on a tip or just on a tingle from his nuts, still scoring some blow for a nonstop flight a few feet above his skull, still having a few laughs on everyone because it was a goof, a fucking lark.

Life was a goof, Vance believed, sometimes more than now, with his last hit wearing thin, making his nerves bunch up, and one of the yups whining over his having traded Fred McGriff in the off-season for two prime relievers who both just went on the DL. He would like to shut that yup up with compound interest, but Vance tossed the rest of his vodka and soda down his throat to compensate. He widened his eyes as though stretching them, an optic yawn of fatigue. *Man*, was he coming down.

The sports bar seemed darker to him now, the descent a little faster than he liked, rougher, like hitting the rocky sides of a hole during the fall. He watched the video screen that he and the yuppie brigade shared, part of a vast array of nearly personal miniscreens that hung throughout Beanpole's, dangling at every other green-upholstered booth.

At the moment all the screens glowed with Tony Gwynn at the plate; in fact, what looked like dozens of Tony Gwynns, his bunched black arm muscles swinging a bat in unison from every corner of the bar, then filling the tumultuous room with a crack of wood and sudden running, fleet legs in a choreographed video dance. Big and small images cheered on, every screen, every*one* in eerie sync, except Vance, feeling out of step, left out, wavering ever so slightly, sweating ever so intensely. He felt as though he were being watched. The synchronized baseball ballet was a front, a diversion; not all eyes were on the screen. He saw a baseball cap facing him from across the bar, the bill of that cap bearing down on him in accusation. He couldn't see eyes. He felt the sweat under his ass, the sticky seat of polyester.

Then the screen that hung before him suffered a brief lightning bolt and resettled. Only now its picture wasn't the same as everybody else's picture. It was a three-foot-high face in extreme close-up. Then a recognized face, one that dropped immediate fear and resentful laughter into Vance's gut.

"Holy shit!" Vance barked in disgust. It was Beanpole Ryan's face, drawn and craggy, with a stolid expression pulling his bloodless lips down into the shape of flattened caulking. This one stonelike head amid a fleet of Gwynns rounding second.

"Jesus, man," Vance said to the stunned yuppie party next door. "Didn't know their cable company got the Ugly Channel." He turned to a mousse-slicked turk behind him. "It must be like, I don't know, Puke-per-View," Vance confided. "Cost them extra, too, I bet."

Ryan's electronically charged image spoke in a deep, pointed voice. "Outside," it said.

Then lightning struck twice, the horizontal twist and blip, and Tom Glavine of the Braves was facing the next San Diego batter with Gwynn on third and only one out, the same as everywhere else.

The yups all began reciprocating stares and saying, "Fuck was that," while Vance knew damn well what *that* was, what a goof *that* was, and, man, he needed another hit if he was going to stand this shit down. He needed to pull this plane out of its spin, yank that stick hard, get his nose up and fill it with flight.

Vance rose quickly, looked around, adjusted his thin reptilian belt with hyper fingers. His radar determined the baseball cap had been shunted aside, no longer honed in. He moved with alacrity toward the neon-signed BAT BOYS, opposite the BALL GIRLS, both humming a pinkish-white. He kicked open the men's room door, his hands too busy flexing. A middle-aged patron with hair like waves of snow was at one urinal, but Vance hit the sink first and splashed his face once or twice with frigid tap water, his shoulder-length blond hair catching the stray droplets. The sound of hot steaming pee could be heard from the other side of the tiled partition amid the noise of the pro–San Diego crowd exhorting the team for a run, yet another monitor hanging on the wall opposite the urinals. The sound of urination made Vance feel safe, alone for the moment.

Vance then pulled a Vicks nasal inhaler from his calf-high boot, a little drugstore item he saved over the years and felt attached to like an artifact of the past, a talisman that brought on highs that linked previous highs and collapsed time into one big party-ass float. He sniffed hard up each nostril, desperate, nostalgic. But not much was left; his sinuses puckered. It was like trying to suck in moisture from a sand dune.

Vance dropped the inhaler back down the side of his boot and joined the man at the row of urinals, still at it. Vance unzipped his pants and relieved himself to the trumpeting escalation of scales from an organ and a loud cry of "Charge!"

from behind. He glanced up at the wall-length ruler-shaped mirror that rested at a forty-five-degree angle from the ceiling to the tiles, providing all chronic urinators uninterrupted, if not disorienting, baseball, where lefties were righties and batters ran to third.

Vance chuckled to himself, letting whatever remaining charge he had inhaled spark his cranial engines. He always thought the urinal mirrors would be a better idea in conjunction with an inverted excerpt of a Jim Morrison lyric or William Blake poem hung behind you, so you could let ideas, feelings, and fluids flow at the same time.

Then his elderly bathroom partner zipped up, flushed, and strode out, made perhaps a little wary by the giggling longhair who had planted himself right beside him while ignoring the half-dozen basins that shone white and free down the row. Not a few moments after he left, however, Vance heard the lightning crack again, the ball game perish, and a sudden echoing silence take hold, actually enabling him to hear the drip-drip-drip of the faucet he failed to squeeze tight. He knew what he'd see when he tilted his eyes upward. It was Ryan's long, cold, gray face again.

Vance stifled the fear that started to quiver in his stomach like budding worms. He made himself think about the absurd mechanics of this nightmare, how Ryan had to be sitting in his office in front of some video camera, like an actor forcing up emotions to a machine. His voice bounced throughout the bright facility with more resonating authority than before: *"Out . . . side!"*

Then the rest room door was banged open by a short, well-built man in a blue corduroy baseball cap and was pushed shut. Vance gazed up at the mirror coolly, his patented smirk curling his lips. He watched Marty Dembo swagger up to him from behind, a chalkish white-skinned little man with a mean look and compact muscles. This guinea had a head full of features all out of whack, Vance thought, as if God had tried designing his face by fucking around with the knobs on an Etch-A-Sketch or something.

"Why you gotta make the man in charge play 'go fetch'?" Marty said, shaking his head. Vance just kept smirking in the mirror at the what? Twenty-year-old? And was that, like, *orthodontia*? *Jee*-sus, man! He started zipping his fly up slowly.

"Let's *go*!" Marty said, Beanpole's face still hovering over the little man's shoulder like an angry moon.

"Hey, man," Vance said, "don't wanna zip too fast, you know? You start singing an aria from *La Castrada*." Marty's brows sunk together in puzzlement.

Then Sam Ryan's face zapped off the screen, and a blast of noise from a crowd-hooting home run boomed from the tube. As though cued, Vance timed his sudden bend, then a backward side-footed kick to the shot of sound, and struck Marty in his groin. Dembo's cry was no louder than the ones from the television or from the distantly muffled bar area.

"See? You know the tune," Vance said. Marty collapsed upon himself to the floor, unable to catch his breath, clutching his pants, gasping, as Vance, his blood rushing through him like liquid fire, jumped to the white metal trash can shaped like an oversized bullet. He awkwardly raised it to his chest then heaved it out toward the small frosted window, shattering it.

Vance scurried through the opening, but the remaining glass, like jutting teeth from a square jawbone, drew a searing line of blood along his shin making him curse. The smart-ass jokes, the goof of it all, caught in his throat, started to suffocate him, as the adrenaline of fear and drug-induced frenzy took over.

He ran in some pain, half hobbling, along the boardwalk, but only for a few dozen yards, when he saw a large, dark figure slash through the moonlight from the slamming bar door and shoot out like a fist toward him.

Vance's chest tightened; his heart stuttered. He stood stunned for a moment thinking that the short guy he folded over wearing the blue baseball cap suddenly grew, molded himself a real jaw and good looks, gave himself focused eyes of death—like he cracked himself out of a cocoon and sprouted wings of fucking fury, for shit's sake!

His mind spun and he scrambled out toward the ocean. He suddenly realized he was out on the wide, rickety pier, the land-based segment leading to the water, and the beating he focused on was not the ocean against the pillars but the dulled pulse of feet on damp wood, gaining from behind. A glance back, he saw Louis Dembo loping toward him. In an instant of crystalline thought, Vance took two measured, quick steps to the edge and hopped off toward the sand below. A moment later he managed a deft half turn midair, and as his chest approached pier level, his outstretched arms slapped down on the planking and hung on. His legs swung up like a pendulum underneath the pier from the force of the fall, then steadied to a dangle. Vance listened and heard Louis Dembo's thud on the sandy beach—he had taken the bait. Thinking Vance had leapt off the decrepit structure, Dembo had leapt off the boardwalk, so as to track his prey down in the pier's cold lunar shadow.

On just the strength of his singularly thin arms, Vance pulled himself back atop the pier with great effort and lay flat for a moment to listen some more. A scattering of orange-painted storage barrels from the construction crew provided some cover as he strained to hear. The tide was slowly coming in, and its lapping thrusts into the weakened pillars made everything vibrate slightly, made everything around him seem alive and dangerous. His insides shook, too, and he wanted to vomit, but he stemmed the convulsions. Still, he heard nothing from below.

Vance rose slowly, gingerly, as though realizing the warped and weakened wood beneath him was doing him a favor by supporting his weight. He wondered how he got out this far on the pier in his blind run from the bar. He moved two quiet steps to the right and two toward the mouth of the pier, then crouched behind a barrel, almost tumbling out of wooziness, and listened again, swiveling his head like a megawatt lighthouse, the lamp burning inside his brain. His old Daytona— *think!*—his Daytona was parked just on the other side of the boardwalk, past the restaurant, yet in the haze of the moon it was a far-off duned planet, precarious to cross.

He listened again. Nothing to do, he thought, but to make a run for the car lot and swear out a few God damns to himself as a form of prayer that the fragile path wouldn't open up and suck him down to the muscle beast below. He rose fast, his head swirled, and he bolted straight ahead, striding as swiftly as he could, considering his fused-out balance and shin gash.

Then ahead to his left he saw the smaller thug, the one whose nuts he'd chimed, angle out of the bathroom window.

Fuck! Vance grimaced and took three, four more of what he hoped were even faster strides forward, now desperate to beat Marty Dembo to the pier's opening, when suddenly a fisted arm, hard and upright, smashed through a rotted-out piece of planking no more than twelve feet ahead as though belonging to an underworld demon breaking free the confines of earth. Vance ran on, too mesmerized by this living thing stretching out, now below him as he leaped over it, but not quite—the sighted hand snatched the loose-fitting pants by the calf. Then as Vance toppled face first, watching the splintery wood rise up flat and gray and hard into his face, the hand snatched again, this time gripping the top of his bad shin, squeezing the pain up into his eyes and pulling him into the hole.

Vance screamed out, but his left leg was still being eaten and scraped by the hole while his right leg was angled flush on the pier's surface, and the rest of the body and scrabbling arms were trying to pull his limb away from the hands, the tugging, vicious hands below the wood.

Louis Dembo steadied himself underneath the pier, his thighs straddled around the diagonally set beam he had climbed up and waited on, one of the sturdier bracing logs he had recently watched his men set in and secure. One of his arms wrapped itself around Vance's spasmodic leg, the other drew up a fist, a physical commodity in plentiful supply throughout his life, and punched out into Vance's groin.

Vance cried out and went limp, the side of his face hitting the woody surface smelling of the sea over time—foul, decaying, dead inside. Then one pained look with his left eye saw a smiling Marty Dembo approach with a quick light-footedness. There was in swift succession flashes of a glinting vengeful mouth, a few timed striding steps, and a devastating sneaker swat to his face. Darkness shut down all senses. Then, after a well-balanced follow-through, Marty shot up both his arms, a mock display signaling he had just kicked the winning field goal.

When Vance came to, the first thing he sensed was that his lips and left jaw were set off and throbbing, growing a life form of their own like a pain-giving parasite. Two of his bottom left incisors were just about out, too, a nerve thread from detachment. He was afraid of swallowing them in the grainy lavalike tide of blood that slowly made his throat sore and thick.

Strangely, his body felt encased and yet floating at the same time, not mentally floating from the blows but experiencing actual physical flight, or more precisely, suspension, a sense of being aloft and yet . . . constrained. The harsh sea breeze whistled through his facial cuts, throughout his bound loftiness, and his arms were bent back. Cable wire, that was it, cable wire was cutting through his pulled-back arms, wrapped around his waist and chest and legs and ankles. The entire back portion of his body from head to calves felt as though dulled blades were set at regular intervals pressing up against him, binding him tight. His eyes finally opened, focused, the moon a dull spotlight. He looked down a few feet at Marty Dembo, then felt Marty's fist smack his mouth one more time.

Louis Dembo's voice came from behind Vance, cautionary: "Don't let's lose his consciousness again! . . . Marty!"

Marty nodded, though his head was thumping to an adrenalized beat and he shadow-boxed, laughing, looking at the drooping Sonny Vance hanging there like a gob of grease on a screw. Which in fact was almost the literal truth. The Dembos had dragged Vance's unconscious body along the side of the pier, hoisted him up onto the prehistoric monster of a hole driller and, with available wire, securely bound him to the oversized bit, a twisted stake in the night. At the moment, the bit's point was barely nuzzled into the soft wet sand a few dozen feet above the churning tide.

Marty's gnarled grin shone with accomplishment. The sight of Vance's groggy, blood-spotted body pleased him, especially the dental work. At every opportunity Marty would aim his fist at a victim's teeth, subliminally trying to make everyone a part of the Dembo clan, someone like him, someone beaten from birth, or so he felt. Unknown to Marty, Louis had immediately resented Marty's braces along the same unconscious lines, that in some strange way the orthodontia was a kind of movement to disassociate their kinship, to unembrace Marty from what he was. Besides, Louis liked to work the body.

No matter, Louis felt pleased as well, sitting there in the driller's cabin, his palm running along the smooth, black knob of the rotation gear with a sensual delight. He was about to play with his big mechanical toy, or more precisely, his toy was about to play with Sonny Vance.

It was only the figure on the boardwalk, the lanky shadow of Beanpole Ryan, who was none too thrilled with the bizarre sight. He had told them this afternoon—didn't he tell them this afternoon?—no Romper Room roughhousing. No toying. No playing. But despite his annoyance, Ryan held back for now. Get it out of their systems, he rationalized; then he took another long drag from his Marlboro. The world was lacking in good listeners anyway, and the Dembos were deaf and not-so-dumb and heard only their own music, followed their own heartless beat, regardless.

"Man," Vance mumbled, his voice a raspy note of sorrow. "Hey, man." A pinkish dribble of spit and blood puddled within a crease cut into his soiled bomber jacket. "Please, man."

Marty was unmoved. He pulled off his blue cap, revealing a severe brush cut, and swiped his sweat-beaded brow with a sandy forearm. "Fuck that—let's *party!*" he shouted, and pointed to the man at the controls.

"You got it, baby brother," Louis replied. "Ow!" He crushed down the sticky gear pedal and engaged the drill. Vance started to rotate in a slow clockwise motion, a steady spiraling ride, fast enough for him to feel the nauseous tug of centrifugal pressures and dizzying vision, yet slow enough for his onlookers to watch his progressive decline. The grotesque apparatus became a revolving flip-card projector, Vance's color and well-being diminishing with each rotation.

Louis yelled: "Who's that flyin' up there? Is it a bird?"

Marty sucked up the sea air and released a mighty "Nooo!"

Vance's eyes squeezing shut didn't cut off the swirl of dots from growing larger, from relentlessly pulling his mind to a cyclonic knot.

"Is it a plane?" Louis yelled once more.

"Nooo!"

Vance felt his stomach suck up tight against his throat, gagging him. He was about to explode.

"Is it a twister?"

"Yeaaaah!"

A whoosh of innards rose up Vance's gut, uprooted like a tree in the fist of a whirlwind.

"Let's twist again," Louis sang, "like we did last summer . . ."

His cap set askew, Marty began to dance, looking demented and rubbery, a bulgy-eyed jester twisting the night away. That's when Vance croaked and spewed vomit like a vile sprinkler head, scattershot bits of the night's vodka, underdone burger, bun, fries, and two and a half bowls of salted peanuts flecking Marty's corduroy bill, his left shoulder, and both arms.

"Shit!" Marty cried, quickly backpedaling out of his dance, but too fast and falling on his rump. "Fucking gross—sonuvabitch!"

Louis abruptly stopped wailing and jerked the gear back, shutting down the machine. He peered over at his little brother flicking his hands of belly crud and cursing, then saw the brownish mulch caking Vance's shirt front, his floppy long hair hung down over his face, his head fallen forward like a spineless doll. Louis was overtaken with anger, with the insult his younger brother had sustained, as if having to be Marty Dembo wasn't insult enough. Louis cranked the gear shift back with gritted teeth and pushed the lowering device forward in gleeful anger. The drill began spinning, only much slower this time as it nosed itself into the smooth grains, drawn down by its own profound weight and the fleshy resistance attached to it, until it began to screw itself into the earth with each shuttering, grinding, deliberate rotation.

It whined and ground, and Vance, conscious enough to know what was happening, splayed his bound feet so that his ankles wouldn't bend and crack in descent. But the force was great, and he felt as though his calves were being pried from each bone and his shins scoured raw. He tried to ply himself as flat as he could against the steel ridges flush to his back. He pressed his eyes shut, absorbing the force as best he could, stifling yet another swell of fluids as best he could, while screaming out his painful torment.

Ryan had turned away, shutting out Vance's pleas. The scene appeared ridiculous to him, like a life-sized political cartoon from the sixties: a hard hat drilling a hippie into the ground with his heavy machinery and the caption: *Screw you, long-hair!*

It so happens Ryan had turned away in time to see two bluish figures jogging toward him, their tattoo on the sand like the steady beat of the brush on a snare drum. In spite of the late hour, the two runners were an injection of rhythm and harmony, a melody to combat the shrieking cacophony of the postmodern jazz sounds accompanying Vance's descent into the underworld.

The joggers ran one behind the other, both in powder-blue jogging suits with white stripes that picked up whatever moonlight fused through the clouds and traced a body scar down their sides. A tall, lean, bald man with a matching blue headband led the way, followed by a shorter determined-faced elder with a good build for his age and goggles wrapped around his head. This one was graced with a shiny silver bloom of hair, which was allowed to fly free in the sea breeze, affording him the aspect of lunatic regality.

They both trotted under the pier and out the other side, and were about to simply pass the spectacle when the older gentleman permitted his head to tilt right, and looked more at Ryan than at the mangle of noise and pain behind him. Ryan stared back at the gentleman and, after a brief locking of eyes, nodded once. The jogger's face remained unaffected, and still in stride, constant as a heartbeat, he returned his gaze forward to his partner.

When the two runners were merged by distance into a small four-footed smudge of blue, Ryan heard the machine stop, and Vance let out one discordant dying groan of agony. Ryan knew he was ready to talk.

Vance's head, braced up against the very top of the bit joint, was all that could be seen above the ground. Sonny was deathly afraid of suffocation now, as his constricted lungs worked hard to suck in whatever seaweed-sour air he could. He was nearly in tears. The earth was sitting on his chest after trying to twist out his shoulders from their sockets. A few ligaments were surely torn; the left arm felt dislocated.

But remarkably, what upset him most was being ten inches tall, raising his eyes, coated with a layer of moist granules, and seeing these brutal forms tower above him, speak down to him like a speck of dirt, a pitiless piece of nothing.

Ryan had his hands jammed into the pockets of his soiled mac, and his black oxfords on. He looked down with some pity at the tousled lanks of hair streaking Vance's upturned face, but his empathy was slowly being thwarted by the sand seeping between his nylon socks and the leather sides of his *good shoes*, damn it.

"You should have come to the office as requested," Ryan began, leaning into Vance's pallid face. "Do you hear me?"

"Gotcha," Vance said, wincing from the set of his jaw. Below his neck felt numb, nonexistent. "The Big Brother number on the tube. I heard you the first time."

"You heard me," Ryan said with a schoolmarm's tone, "but you didn't listen, did you?" He paused. "A lot of people don't listen." The latter was obliquely directed at the Dembos, who let the comment sail over their caps and out to sea. "So this is what it comes down to."

Vance blinked slowly, the sand flung from the drill's activity sticking to his sweat, his itchy nose, his teeth, his lids. "I'm all ears," he rasped.

"You're overdue," Ryan said. "Did I have to tell you that? I had to actually *tell* you that? Why did I have to tell you that? I mean, I lend you good money, and you do what you want with it—no business of mine—but then due date comes and you're not around to make payment. Okay, so I wait. I wait some more. A week. Then two—"

Vance forced his words through the throbbing thicket that was his voice box. "I was trying to get some cash from sources out of town. I—"

"—then you sit in my bar three nights straight and you *still* don't come to me."

"I was putting together some things, then—then I was going to come see you, man, honest. I figured everything was cool, I—"

"Cool? So how is it you give my associates such a hard time tonight when I want to see you?"

Ryan stared at Vance, who stared back with a mix of resentment and misplaced pride, all the while remaining silent. Ryan knew the answer. Any form of authority Vance confronted was mulched through that hippie rot of a brain and processed out as pig sausage, fascist meat to be discarded as unhealthy to your well-being. Bosses, cops, loan sharks, parents, presidents, and stoplights all fit the description of things that had told Sonny Vance what to do, and fuck 'em if they couldn't take a joke.

The only real satisfaction Ryan got from seeing this cocky shit planted in the surf was it forced him to be in one spot long enough to cast a shadow. Ryan had always distrusted Vance's rootlessness; he was dangerous in his sudden movements. He was a restless roach who you knew was into lots of things, *your* things—your food, your personal belongings—but who, like all roaches, never stayed long enough to catch, to smash. The Dembos were dangerous, too, sure, but their restless nature had boundaries. Their roots kept them in Hollowsport; they'd *die* for Hollowsport. The outside world held no interest to their parochial instincts. In some ways he wouldn't admit, Ryan also envied Vance's rootlessness. Vance would never allow himself to feel stuck to *things*, as he would. Certainly not to a bar and restaurant. Or to a boss as powerful as Braxton Cole. Not even to a payment deadline from a pissed-off loan shark.

"You got a story to go with your overdue remittance?" Ryan asked.

Vance raised a sandy eyebrow. "You really want to hear it or is this just the floor show before you kill me?"

Ryan was losing patience. "Look, jerkoff, if I wanted you dead, I'd have had Fred and Barney here lose you in the ocean bedrock somewhere six feet under, okay?"

Louis had climbed down from his machine and was standing with his arms folded, a disinterested glaze to his eyes. Not for only eight percent of the cut, he thought.

"I want my money," Ryan continued to Vance. "I want the interest *to* my money, so I want to know how you plan to get the payoff to me, just in case I need to see to its recovery myself."

Vance spoke quickly but with great effort. The sand hole was suppressing his diaphragm, so he seemed short-breathed. "Okay . . . okay, man. This is how, I *swear*, it's coming down. No shit. I invested the money, man. It was like, from the blue, I got a tip on some prime blow. Like a real Christmas surprise, man, when out of nowhere, you get snow. You know what I mean? I get two kilos worth. Cheap, too. I never got cocaine at Kmart prices like that, not good cocaine anyway like that. The dealer was jammed up for cash, so the haggling was a joke."

Vance took a hard swallow, and Ryan deemed to look at him again, his interest perked by the drug connection, a sure sell in this town. If Vance didn't have the money, Ryan knew friends-of-friends who knew acquaintances who would buy the dope outright and take care of the short coke supply in Jersey he had heard about.

"You sell it yourself or you still got it?" Ryan asked.

Vance was trying to gather enough spittle to shape more words, his tongue dense and dried out, so he shook his head, no.

"You got someone else to sell it," Ryan said.

Vance nodded.

"So you *got* the friggin' money!"

Vance shook his head.

"That a *no*?" Ryan blinked. "You said *no*?"

Vance recovered some vocal flexibility. "I got hung up a little, that's all. It's no earthshaking—"

"You piss it away in Atlantic City, scumbag? A pass through town for the bankroll? Don't bullshit me with dope transactions, dick-face—"

Vance shook his head vehemently, then sputtered, "No way. No way, man. Just listen up, will you?" The frenzy in Ryan's voice had stirred the idle Dembos into a pair of slow-pacing Dobermans awaiting a silent command. "I gave the whole supply to a guy I do business with. I've done business with him for, like, a long, long time, man. He's got a powerful distribution system, I know, from experience. I mean, I *know*."

"Don't tell me you're telling me you didn't get the money up front?"

"I'm *telling* you, Ryan, with this guy—reputable as shit, man—with him, you don't take it all up front. What happens is, this way, the way *he* plays it, he slices you a bigger cut on the way back. All right? It's better like this. He's done it with me before. He's doing it again. He gets it done. I swear. Okay?

He doesn't skip. He's got a pricey clientele pays way over the norm because they don't want to soil their soft leather slip-ons on slum street corners, man. He's one of *them*, man. His ass doesn't bulge like you and me."

Ryan looked perplexed. Vance was going to slip into his theory of how the poorer a guy is, the thicker his wallet from small bills, the more it juts out in his back pocket. It's the rich whose pants stay flat, whose line stays sleek, whose forward progress suffers no wind resistance through any doorway or golden opportunity.

"My dealer's well-off, what I'm trying to say," Vance continued. "You see? He deals it out, he collects the payment, he doles my cut, I hand whatever I owe to you. That's the whole shot. It's just—he's in the process, he's *doing*."

Vance thought he saw Ryan's expression soften up, Vance's words massaging the right angles, smoothing the right edges like deft verbal fingers. "Then I get my cut, and you get what's yours. If I come out the short man after all this, so be it, you know?"

But Ryan's soft face betrayed not acquiescence, but a dumbstruck disbelief, and his words broke hard: "Tuesday night, asshole."

Vance thought he didn't quite hear, as he was distracted anyway by a sheet of approaching water, the liquid finger of a large devouring animal slowly moving closer to him, testing to see if it were safe to touch him before the kill.

"What's that?" Vance choked out.

"I said you have until Tuesday night. That's your deadline."

"But that's not—not—viable, man." Vance was straining, stretching his neck out at Ryan. "He's working on the process. I *told* you that. It comes off slow and easy."

Ryan was shaking his head, almost laughing. "Well, I play hard and fast, how's that?" Just like any lazy worker, wants the world to take its time for *him*, he thought, and let the brass polish their balls and wait. "No chance I'm waiting on your friend to distribute on whatever timetable he sets up. I have my own timetable, mister. The bottom line is, you have the complete loan payment—principle, interest, *and* apology for your bullshit tardiness—on Tuesday night."

Ryan stopped himself, his gaze lost in speculation. "If not,

we might as well just keep screwing you into the ground another few feet and save you moving expenses."

Vance was struck speechless. His glance at the self-satisfied
Dembos dropped a fist of acid into his stomach.

"And if by Tuesday night, I don't get the money from *you*,"
Ryan continued, then squatted down eye-level to Vance, "I
want the money from your distributor. You see, technically,
then, I'm financing this deal, this dirty deal with drugs, which
I *hate* by the way—I don't use, I don't like users—but it's a
commodity, I can see that. Like milk, cotton, and steel, it's
product. I'm aware. And so, I need to see my investment
through. I need your distributor's name and where he holes up
. . . in case."

Vance started shaking his head in small, fast vibrations, but
like a struck pitchfork, they became slower and lengthier. "No,
man. No way. I can't."

"What do you think?" Ryan asked. "I'm going to cut into
this deal now and not wait until Tuesday? Is that what you're
afraid of?"

Vance appeared to not be listening, now mumbling. "No
way. Just . . . no . . . way."

"The last thing I want or fucking need is for your dealer to
mess up his end of things, if things are *doing*, like you said. I
need you in these remaining days to go to him to speed the
process so the money is ready. Because by Tuesday, I want the
money. By Wednesday, I'll take the dope. But by Tuesday, I'd
rather have the money. You know what I'm saying?"

"No fucking way, man," Vance was continually chanting.

"Are you paying attention to me, jerkoff!!?" The shout suddenly stifled Vance like a lid on a trash fire. All that remained
were two white-hot embers—Vance's defiant eyes. Ryan broke
off his stare, surrendering. He pushed himself up from his
squat, his sciatic back tweaking. With every ounce of middle
age upon him like some dead-ass weight hung about his collar,
he looked over to the Dembos. This was his life in its essence:
the gradual dependence on the younger, stronger, dumber. He
raised an eyebrow. Louis Dembo, pleased to be asked advice,
tossed his head back toward the machine. Ryan stayed motionless for a moment, then silently sighed through his nose and

closed his eyes. Louis hopped back into the drill's cabin; he knew a *yes* when he saw one.

The pin joints in Vance's upper jaw tensed with the realization, with the machine-induced shimmy buzzing down his sore spine. *"Come on, man!"* he screamed, shutting his eyes and pulling back his lips. "Come on with this *bullshit!*"

Vance told Ryan his distributor's name and address and the machine stopped its preparatory hum.

"Good," Ryan said, then added for encouragement, "Look. You got what? One, two, three . . . this is Wednesday now, after midnight, yeah. You got six whole days to get your friend to shake his booty. You're in good shape." He bent all the way forward and patted Vance's head with sincerity. "Just don't let Tuesday night slip by, because then we go the extra foot."

Ryan looked satisfied for the moment, an expression that took Louis by surprise, a smile as rare on Ryan as a cool cotton tee shirt, even on his day off. Ryan walked back toward the bar, his shoulders seesawing his mac with each stride in the sand. Vance was straining to see where the Dembos were behind him.

Louis waited for Ryan to reenter the side door at Beanpole's. "Helluva night," Dembo said, nodding, after searching out the sweeping night sky. "This kind of moon, peekabooing and shit, in and out of the clouds, in and out. Gives me a hard-on."

Marty laughed. "Yeah, right. The *moon.* You get a hard-on taking a dump in the morning."

Louis swiveled and forced a chuckle. "Well, fuck you, Mighty Mouse. The only way you get your dick swollen is when you soak it in the tub with your rubber ducky."

Marty didn't laugh anymore. "Yeah, sure," was the best retort he could come up with. Louis had felt remorse the minute he spat out his put-down. He didn't like competing in a prick-measuring contest with his brother. Marty relied on scraps, what could you say. Through the years of "raising" Marty on his own, Louis shared his pussy with his brother, whether she be drunk or paid-for or reluctant, and he always would. He gave himself his own word about that.

Louis looked at his brother kicking sand into Vance's left ear, a void that needed filling. Louis explained: "I'm just saying I'm revved, that's all. It's a Peeping Tom moon and I'm revved."

Marty stopped his little game and stared at Vance, whose eyes reopened reluctantly. "I see a nice mouth," Marty said, after watching Vance try to lick his lips.

"I'm not *that* revved," Louis remarked, and snatched Marty by the arm. Got too strong a taste for it in the joint, Louis thought. Queered a piece of him.

Louis gave Marty another shove, harder this time, toward the boardwalk. Marty flipped his shoulder away from his older brother in anger. Then they heard Vance scratch out words from his throat.

"Hey. Get . . . me out. . . . I told, I *told*."

Louis bent over toward the unraveled ball stuck in the sand with all this stringy stuff coming out of its top. "Yeah, we're getting you out. On union hours tomorrow morning. I can't work the equipment more than two hours overtime. It's in the contract. Better hope high tide's not until afternoon. Rest up, chump."

Louis pressed out a tight-lipped grin and tramped through humps of sand back to his brother. Marty purposely didn't look at him, just fell into step on their ascent to the bar. That's when Vance found a wrenched and driven power from his loosened bowels and sung out some indecipherable cry—all fear, all pain, pushing it out, out past the pier, past the shoreline, out into the dark, shimmering ocean, an ocean that heard his crying and reached out ever closer to offer its watery bosom.

When Barbara came out of the restaurant after a depleting double shift, the stinging sea breeze enveloped her like a field of energy. She crossed both arms and slid her hands up and down the slender shanks above her elbows. She shook her luminescent hair so that some of the yellow-blond locks covered her shoulders like a silken warmth, a scarf of shiny gold. Leaning on the boardwalk banister, head-on into the wind, she waited for Danny to come on his motorcycle to pick her up.

The restaurant had been light on customers that night, but that didn't make it feel any less restrictive, her hair pulled up under a pink cap, her miniskirted uniform a tightly woven shackle of polyester. She appreciated nights like this, a bursting out from kitchen heat to sharp bracing relief. The night appreciated her as well, darkening her skin from all its absorption of sunlight, as though the wafts of moonglow deepened her beauty.

Barbara always carried her beauty as one would carry a finely wrought sculpture—she held it before her in the cradle of her arms and displayed it naturally, watching people recognize it. She learned to do that from her mother as a means of survival in the world, what little she had seen of it.

Barbara knew that her mother's deformity made her all the more demanding that her daughter use her natural appeal to full advantage, to warrant her the best school, snare the best man, cull the best that beauty can buy or, more precisely, that can be bought for her by others: the tease of the lure, the stab of the hook. As a young girl, just watching the way her mother was forced to walk because of her disability amplified her life's lessons: first the dainty step of the left foot, a ladies' step, a feminine toe apologetically tickling the ground; then the leaden clomp of the prosthesis, the crush of earth, the stamp of revenge. That's what Barbara really thought about much of her mom-to-daughter talks. The point was revenge. Barbara didn't think her mother married Bertram Fouche out of love. It was to get back at Barbara's father and subsequently to torture the next in line. One man represented all men. Wound one and they all bleed. Her mother wanted her to be prepared early, land the low blow in the first round, not the second.

So Barbara put up the props needed for her "comely belle" routine, a stage set of sorority ponytails and honor society dates with future Ivy League candidates. It was a convincing show, but if it wasn't to please Hallie, she would have dropped the pretense long ago out of sheer depression over people's gullibility.

Barbara found the imagination beautiful. To her, on this night, the moon was the wizened face of a prophet, the ocean an ancient teardrop of joy fallen from his eyes. (That was why tears and oceans both tasted salty, she thought as a child, and wrote her first poem.) She wanted to be a writer, maybe study religions, explore what people believed and why—psychology, then? Barbara was confused the way a college sophomore ought to be, but she knew she did not want to be a polished piece of porcelain, glass-encased for her own good by some husband. The waitressing job? Well—consider it a first flash of independence, money without her mother's imprint, a public way to lower her own pedestal by degrees. Being with Danny was another way.

Barbara felt the wildness of the wind stir her body, her mind, her dress, cotton white and loose whipping behind her. She watched two merging shadows jog across the length of beach and under the pier, one behind the other, the tall one in front like the strapping proud stallion pulling the other in a chariot, its rider wearing a silver helmet of hair, more weary from the journey than his slavish horse. The wind howled at their heels, a comic sight at this magical hour.

But there was suddenly something stark and jarring in that howl, perceptible only through her sudden concentration on the sound. She peered, then closed her eyes to make it out— something dying, something dead but still grieving its demise. Barbara slipped off her black ballet flats, bent down, and hopped off the boardwalk toward the water, toward the spiky shadows that came off the pier. The cry grew more distinct. It was torn and full of fear, but just a sound, not a word; the wind kept it elusive. The sand on her bare feet was cold and damp. It made her feel vulnerable.

She turned instinctively to her right and thought she saw someone drop among the pilings, but there was no further motion she could make out. She glanced up at the moon, and it was no longer wise, but uncomfortably attentive, peering, hungry. Still, the pain that threaded through the wind kept her moving farther down the beach, made her approach the oil-smelling flanks of metal that made up the army of construction machinery just this side of the pier.

Then she saw the source of the cry, or at least she thought she did. It looked like a rock at this distance, abutted against the arm of one piece of machinery, only this rock shuddered and moaned and moaned louder still. Layers of seaweed slung on top of it were shaking with the rock, especially when a sheet of water drifted up the sand from a breaking wave and surrounded it like an isolated boulder. It would cry out especially loud then.

Barbara shot a look to the right again, hearing the crunch of sand. One crunch and then nothing revealed by her gaze. She was afraid to go on and afraid to go back. She felt stranded on a strip of land, the pounding ocean and screaming rock before her and something, something behind her now.

She spun on her heels and flinched. Louis Dembo was standing there, his head angled down so that his eyes peered just across his brow at her with mock suspicion.

"Looking for someone . . . ?"

Barbara slung her arms across her small breasts as a reaction to a resurgent gust of wind off the water, but really it was a protective move, her chilled nipples like hard candy. But the gesture only brought out the creamy brown allure of her limbs in contrast to the vivid whiteness of her dress, and the slenderness of her crossed forearms made her look all the more fragile.

"Me, maybe?" Dembo's gaze drifted up and down her body without a stir of motion from any part of his.

"No, God, I—" She was looking away from his eyes, couldn't look.

"*Has* to be me." Dembo chuckled and took a step toward her. "I'm the only one you know works out here. I'm not working now. I should be home hitting the pillow, but maybe you—I don't know—maybe you were thinking about me and conjured me up or something."

Barbara engaged him with a weak smile, a sliver of fear icing her spine, the magic of the night having turned black and out of control. "No!" She didn't mean to sound so insistent. "No, I just came out—I heard something—" She tried to angle the corner of her eye to see what was behind her but still yards away, a hissing of sand.

"What?"

"I heard a voice—"

"A voice." His face kept disappearing into the dark void under his cap every time the moon decided it didn't want to witness what she feared, no, *knew* what was going on here, what was going to happen if she didn't—

"Like a howl . . ." she said, backtracking, seeing the only way out was sideways, under the pier and past, maybe those joggers, that stupid chariot. She felt tears surge up to her eyes, her stomach ache. The runners were long gone. She was alone.

Dembo matched her step for step, kept the distance the same, close enough to breathe her in as wind blew through her from behind, gathering her sweat and pussy essence and pushing it into his face like a perfumed pillow.

"Well, you know, I can throw my voice," he said offhandedly. "Yeah. I learned it by sending away, one of those ads in the back of comic books as a kid. *Superman* or something, I don't remember. Never lost the talent. I was throwing my voice to scare you. You scared?" It wasn't a question; it was wish fulfillment.

Barbara was breathing through her mouth now, trying to catch her breath, trying to hug herself into nothing and disappear. She took a step to her right.

Dembo took a step to her right. "You're not answering me." A tinge of anger in his voice.

The wind was driving her mad, the sound of that *thing* out there in pain—

"God!" she shouted, a plea. "What's that moaning out there?"

Louis pouted his lips and shrugged. "Could it be . . . ? You and me five minutes from now?"

Barbara heard a thud. She turned and saw an ugly kid, about her age, in the same baseball cap as the man fronting her, saw him kick at the rock again and then once more, *thud, thud.* The scraggly rock didn't budge from the blows; it no longer howled, either.

Barbara bolted toward the pilings and let out a shout for help. Dembo dove and snatched at her leg, laughing. He caught her at the ankle, but his grip was all at the tips of fingers, not in the meat of the hand, and she fell forward but slipped free, retrieving her foot and, picking herself up with another shout, ran some more.

Marty started churning up sand, angling toward her, but she ducked behind a bulldozer and crawled between its jawlike shovel and the tank threads, a tunnel from which she watched Marty scamper past. She heard louder muffled footfalls, brushes of sand, moving the other way. She couldn't believe there were *two* of them. Or were they really the same? It was as though the handsome stature of the older one was but a shell, and it was this inner deformity that had split off from him and was running the show, a boy beast throwing his voice into a manly beauty: the lure of the howl, the thrust of the hook.

Barbara controlled her sobs and listened to nothing but a whistle of breeze through the bulldozer's teeth. She felt swallowed up within this metal pocket, sucked on by the dampness. She shivered and scuffled out of her hole and past two pilings and stopped. She stood flat against it with her back. She peeked out and thought she saw a piece of darkness dance, then another, from one piling to another, dodging, but approaching. She lost track of one of the shadows—maybe there was only one to begin with back there, and the other was— *where?* She heard the one from behind giggling. They were playing with her, toying with her; she didn't have a chance.

Barbara gave up and ran blindly now toward the boardwalk, but a figure jumped out at her from the dark recess under the pier and grabbed her. Her mouth widened with her eyes to let out a scream, to feel the smack of a hand, the ram of the hips. The shadow shook her and called her name.

Barbara suddenly refocused, the shadow gained substance, it was her boyfriend. It was Danny. She encircled him with her arms and began to cry, his gray nylon jacket a haven for release. She had forgotten he was coming, had forgotten the world beyond the howling wind.

Danny was stunned. "What's going on? What happened?"

Barbara quickly looked up at him, stroking the front of his shoulder. "Nothing. Nothing. Let's go. Now. Let's go." She leaned on him with extra force, entreating him away from the beach, the rock, the menacing machines.

Danny trusted Barbara, knew his own difficulties of expression, especially when primal or wired to the heart. He never pushed to open her up, and in her crazed state, he wouldn't now. He merely swung his arm about her and started to lead her back to his motorbike when she offered: "I hate my mother."

The well-honed sculpture she was carrying was becoming heavy, the props dangerous. Danny remained silent, as did she, both moving down the boardwalk wedded together, toward Danny's motorbike. Then Danny said: "There it is. Almost home."

But Barbara, when she looked up, perceptibly shuddered. Louis Dembo was leaning against the Mariner's Restaurant sign, adjacent the Yamaha, looking around nonchalantly, as though waiting for his own ride. His idle gaze then purposefully fixed itself upon the approaching couple. Barbara began stiffening in Danny's arms.

"Still cold?" Danny asked, squeezing harder. If anything, she was hot; she was going to explode heat; she was dripping molten liquid.

Dembo, however, was really not looking at Barbara, but at Danny, this guy who was what? Twenty-four, maybe. Decent build, but didn't work out or nothing. No ripples. No body discipline—Dembo could tell that right through Danny's zippered jacket. The kicker was the small gold ball in his earlobe—fag-ga-*roo*!—and his *face*—a real pretty boy, sensitive eyes and all that shit—brother!—*double* fag-ga-roo!

Barbara envisioned nothing, her mind burned blank as they started to walk by, knew Danny would be no match in a fight with the sinewy forearms entwined above Dembo's chest; Dembo watching the lovers draw even to him—no match, even with ample warning. But there was no need for a warning. They passed untouched. Dembo just started to hum, then sing low in his best Sinatra: "I got her . . . under my skin . . ."

Danny, about to straddle his bike, stopped and glanced back at the closed-lip smile of Louis Dembo, who then nodded. Danny remained motionless, then nodded back. He must have said, I got *you* . . . Danny thought, putting on his helmet, and he and Barbara cycled off out of the parking lot and into the empty early morning streets of Hollowsport.

At Danny's studio apartment they made love almost the minute they shoved through the stuck door, swollen with humidity. The used waterbed was set in violent motion by the storm of their bodies. Their passion for each other was not unusual; they were always free with their sexuality, even early in their relationship, wondrously so to Danny. Barbara used to be, after all, the alluring ice maiden who froze a new beau to her arm down every high school hallway he could remember. Still, one surprise tonight was that Barbara was the aggressor. No quiet glasses of cheap Chablis accompanied by talk of the day and Eric Clapton on the CD player as a preliminary. Tonight it was a sudden wanton tongue encircling his nipples and a surgent sucking of his scrotal sac then penis, a performance where in its finale he was on his back receiving her thrusts, his hands holding on to her cool buttocks, more as tactile appreciators of their firm smooth texture and not as grappling pushers, coaxers of deeper penetration. Any deeper or stronger and he would need CPR, he thought.

He laughed to himself when they, or really *she*, was done. Barbara saw his chuckle and joined in, holding back whatever fear she hadn't exorcised in her ravishment. This was the only means by which she would inform him about what had happened earlier tonight.

"*That* was out of character," he said jokingly, though really wanting to probe.

Barbara flicked her hair away from her face and rested her cheek on his bare chest, her nakedness rubbing against his side. "Didn't you like it?"

"Yeah, of course," Danny said, "I always enjoy making love to you."

"How are the stooges doing?" Barbara said, deflecting, referring to the three chest hairs her fingers began brushing up and back. When she had first discovered Danny's unclothed body, his overall hairlessness was as unique as it was exciting. The bones of his upper rib cage seemed like sharp exposed rock trying to jut out of a grassless slope of skin—except for three hairs near his right pectoral, two straight and a spiraled one. She called them Moe, Larry, and Curly, respectively.

"This a way of getting back at your mother?" Danny said.

Barbara flipped her head over so that she could look at Danny. "I don't get it."

"I don't know, I guess I suddenly realized it was a weeknight. We usually do it on a weekend, when all's safe during the day, your folks thinking we're at the beach or something. Tonight you insisted on coming here from work. Knowing your mom, she's probably freaking out thinking my bike fell into the ocean."

"I'll call her," Barbara said.

Even *that* was a surprise; she was full of them tonight. "That mean you're staying over?"

Barbara turned her head away from him again, cheek on chest. "Would you like that?" Her hand ran down his stomach and into his pubic hairs.

"As long as you can deal with the aftermath," Danny said, trying not to let his stirring overpower what he knew would happen with her parents. His balls were tightening, tingling; they hurt from too-recent restimulation.

"How about this?" she said, rubbing his testicles harder. "I deal with them, you deal with the party Sunday."

"What the hell . . . ?"

She slid her head down his abdomen and licked the top of his half-grown penis. "Deal?"

"Come on, Barbara," Danny said, raising himself off the pillow. "How many ways is this a blowjob?"

Barbara stopped her caress. "Don't make it sound cheap."

"Sounds like a swap meet to me," Danny said. "Jesus." He pulled his legs up, forcing Barbara to lift her torso and rest her bottom on her childlike feet. "You're confusing the shit out of me tonight, Barb. I swear."

She looked sorry. "I don't mean to."

Danny didn't respond, so Barbara met his eyes and continued. "It would just be nice maybe for both of us to relate with our parents head-on."

Danny snapped, "I've had that collision, thanks."

"Let me finish," Barbara snapped back. "I think—" She paused thoughtfully. "—I think if we want this relationship to happen, to last, we both have some work to do."

Now Barbara started surprising even herself. She hoped it wasn't just the grim fear at the beach doing the talking, the night having turned nightmare, a grasping at the magical in order to hold it as long as possible.

Danny shook his head but listened. Mrs. Fouche didn't care for him, but who did? he thought. Other than his own mother. Barbara looked at him sympathetically. Barbara had inherited her mother's need for a man, a steady, a thing to color coordinate with her fashionable facade. But she also garnered her father's affection for the afflicted. (Casey Winston, Hallie's first husband, was a vet who would cry louder at *Bambi* than his little daughter, would perfect and publish techniques for animal organ transplants, and would die of heart failure at the age of forty-eight.) Barbara often thought Danny one of the afflicted her father would have pulled into his care.

She knew Danny had a drug problem in his early teens, stole and cheated and lied for years before he straightened out after nearly dying of an overdose of PCP behind the Craft & Sons Bank building along with two dropouts from Hollowsport High who were dealing for street money. Danny would tell her that his father would beat the crap out of him with every lie of promised rehab, every stolen house appliance hocked for vial money. The trouble was even after rehab, his father still beat the crap out of him psychologically, never forgave him, and ultimately went into substance abuse himself. It was a weird reversal—the son passing on his addiction to the father. It was even weirder that it was Carl Rodman, a man as straight-looking as a Brooks Brothers suit. Unless there was something else going on with him or with his father's past that Danny didn't talk about, and Danny *never* talked about it.

The only other thing she knew about Danny's father was that Danny bought a circular table for his studio apartment, not a square one, deliberately. He said at home his father used to sit at the head of the dinner table, and Danny wanted to make sure he got one that had no head. Maybe this was some assurance his father would never come over; he wouldn't know where to put himself, wouldn't know his place.

In all, Barbara's keen emotional awareness caused her to believe that Carl and Danny Rodman were versions of the same person. They shared the same handsome facial features, yet they would look at each other as though from different sides of a dense glass barrier, a barrier that acted more like a mirror, and each didn't like the self that he saw.

"I want my mother to accept us as everything we are," Barbara continued. "That includes being lovers. But I also want you to deal with who your parents are, my parents, that world we're both from whether we like it or—"

"It's not *my* world," Danny insisted.

"I don't think it's mine either, anymore. I'm not sure. I just don't want us to kick it out of our lives so fast." Barbara grabbed Danny's hand. "For your mother's sake." Danny knew Barbara would make a run at that tender spot. "This party is for her and her organization as much as it's for your father's business."

"Political piggies . . . I don't like rolling in that kind of mud." Danny was protesting, but with a lilt of defeat.

"We go there as a couple," Barbara said. "A grand statement of our being together that *nobody* will dare comment on. We watch them have to hold it in like . . . like a touch of gas." Danny snickered at that one. "Tonight will give them one message. Sunday we make it public."

They argued a bit more, though Danny's position was less adamant, just leftover resentment, a dribbling out of remaining bile. Barbara finally had him play his guitar, an aged wooden instrument, darkened by time and wistful melodies that he could evoke so well, his fingers in an agile dance along the frets. She allowed herself to think him serenading her, with songs written just *for* her, even when he played more generic tunes of the open road or love's decline. She thought she loved him for this, for his music, his round table, her dream of the wounded knight. She could still dream, and felt good about Sunday and felt warm under light blue sheets on his bed as he sang in the spare cloister of his room.

After he played and they caressed and slept, Danny dreamed, too, only it was a disturbing one, full of fits and twitchings of his leg, his foot a stuck fish poking out the unwashed sheets. Danny's baby brother Eric was wearing his gray jacket and playing outside in the shroud of night. A car was coming that was invisible except for its growl and its headlights with beams that crazily crossed and recrossed each other as it raced forward. Then he was Eric, was where Eric was, standing in the middle of the road blinded by light and noise and fear. He ducked and felt something pass, only to see the car from the rear bearing down on Eric again, who was now yards ahead in the street.

Danny found he could become Eric again, and he did, but he was not afraid this time as the headlights crossed and ignited into one beam targeting him. He closed his eyes but again the car seemed to pass within him, the cold chill of death sifting through and out and once more heading for the small figure of Eric down the road a short distance.

Danny made himself take Eric's place yet again, wishing

death, wishing a final hit, but knowing the car would bypass him as though he were living vapor, nothing more. So he turned and with the car at his back and gaining, roaring, he ran toward the figure of Eric, yards away down the road, standing as numb and uninvolved as before. He leaped at his little brother, engulfed him with his arms and tumbled with him out of the car's path, only to roll off the side of a sudden cliff and fall.

As they fell weightlessly, endlessly, Danny discovered he was clutching, not Eric, but his father, who looked at him with as little recognition as his brother did. Danny gazed intently into his father's uncaring eyes and, as though willed, they changed into Eric's. It was Eric. He was holding Eric.

Suddenly, Eric and he were standing at the bottom of the drop looking up. The only thing falling was rain into their eyes. Eric was still a tousle-haired zombie beside him, but then Danny directed his eyes downward and saw the broken body of Carl Rodman, a sprawl of bones on the ground, his body decimated by the fall.

Though there were times he had resented his little brother, Danny still nodded in affirmation. He liked the trade.

5

IT WAS THE art of personal and financial attainment, the strategic transaction as flawless craft using money, influence, and prime positioning, whether the deal was about real estate or firearms. Land and guns!—Rodman laughed to himself, lost in thought—the legacy of America! Sounded like the hippie radical in him floating back, a weird mix, Hell no, we won't escrow!

Rodman's chuckle became unintentionally vocal and startled the keen-eyed men around the black boardroom table. Thomas Brennan, Senior Vice-President, stopped formulating his thesis on the Braxton Cole situation until Rodman straightened up a few inches and shook his head at the sallow-eyed Brennan, indicating it was nothing. Brennan licked his dried lips before he continued, his arched gaze lingering on Rodman.

"Evidently in his attempt to secure the Aquarius property with tax-free bonds, Cole is using his influence with members of the state senate? Is that right?"

Rodman nodded slowly, too slowly, so Dennis Whipp, the young head accountant, picked up the lead and said, "Yes. That's right. But that's why Carl is talking to State Senator McMann on Sunday. We *all* are. At the party." Whipp glanced at Rodman, who had never stopped nodding, his head somehow trapped in a heavier density than the rest of the room.

"We're close to him. He's on our side. I have it all worked out." The staccato sentences were spoken without emotional involvement, as though from a robotic entity.

The deal was well-crafted, Rodman thought, the art was in the doing, always in the attempt at the ideal, land and guns, all worked out. Yesterday afternoon Rodman had bought the gun

with which he was going to kill. He had contacted Eddie
Lebrand, a liquor retailer he always purchased his wine from
at wholesale prices, the pick of the prime crates right off the
docks from southern France. Rodman invested some of Eddie's
money in promising real estate limited partnerships as compensation. Rodman knew Eddie had a cousin who had been in
prison for a variety of charges, mostly for trafficking illegal
weapons. Rodman told Eddie's cousin he wanted a gun for his
cabin as a security measure but off the books. Eddie's cousin
asked no questions and put in a call.

The meeting took place at a large motor inn adjacent to the
Bollard Country Club, where clusters of pink-polyester pants
and pastel knits shirts wove in and out of the rooms, attendees
for the annual Hollowsport Amateur Tournament. When Rodman knocked on door 7C, he was greeted by an older puffy
man who had rolled himself in the same color palette as the
rest. Rodman couldn't meet the man's eyes, just shook his
hand coolly, stared at the embroidered emblem of sword-
crossed drivers on the man's flabby chest during the whole
deal or at the straw hat cocked on his head, the kind only Bing
Crosby used to wear. Eddie's cousin was jokey, even as he
rummaged deep into a lightly clubbed golf bag and pulled out
a fistful of pistols, laid them on the bed like ties he was choos-
ing from for dinner. Rodman shook his head, tried not to let
the sweat show, the ignorance, the fear of firearms, their power
intimidating him; then he pointed at one.

Good one, the man had said. Right, Rodman had sneered at
himself—the man would have said the same thing if he had
pointed to his dick. He paid the money in cash without shaking. The man put the guns back into his half-full golf bag and
shoved it under the bed, then took his real set of clubs, which
Rodman suddenly noticed had been resting against the side of
the headboard, and slung them over his shoulder. He told Rodman to wait ten minutes before he left and to wish him good
luck on his round.

"Good luck," Rodman had said with what was probably
faint enthusiasm at best. And you, too, bud, Eddie's cousin replied, then left the room, his full bag heard chinking down the
hall to the elevator. Then Rodman drove straight home and hid

the gun in a private place, treating it like a talisman only he could empower.

Still, Rodman had felt like the unskilled laborer in that deal, felt as though he were holding an awkward armful of hammers and screwdrivers and thumbs—land and guns. He was better at land. That's what the murder was about: reestablishing his land, the territory called his memory, making it his own again by blotting out with a bullet what he didn't want to remember. He had to protect and preserve the property known as family, *his* family, at all costs.

Rodman suddenly came alive at the dark rectangular table, became a muscular impulse.

"The fix is in, gentlemen!" he announced, gathering strength from the land. He then explained what Braxton Cole was attempting, and how he, Rodman, would counter. Everyone's focus bore on Rodman, Whipp especially welcoming the resurgence.

There were 157 acres of land at stake for the Triumph Real Estate Investment Corp., land now used for a dying dog-racing business, the Aquarius track, up for sale and development, and Braxton Cole and his entrepreneurial machine was vying for the same piece of property. Rodman had pushed his team into a plan that called for the tract to contain a middle-class spate of houses with a lucrative commercial strip fronting Sax Road. Yet Rodman's spiritual investment in the area was the building of a drug and alcohol rehab center, a personal promise he gave to himself and to Delia one day as they nestled against each other on the porch ottoman discussing the land's recent availability. It was one way he wanted to edify, literally, his change, his "clean" life. He wanted Delia to love and respect him again. Delia even set up a fund-raiser, through a network of her Leukemia Fund connections, which would help establish the private facility. The area-wide publicity didn't hurt Triumph Corp.'s chances at purchasing the Aquarius track, either, and local pols like McMann embraced the idea.

Braxton Cole, however, in keeping with his history, had other visions, and means to fulfill them. What little Rodman's espionage forces could gather was that Cole had been proposing a vast array of pricey town houses encircling a man-made mini-lake, an upscale venture similar to his Riller's Beach reclamation projects. Some corporate branch offices of major firms would straddle the town-house property and be the lure, for the young up-and-C.U.M.-mers (the Corporate Upwardly Mobile) with families to purchase the nearby housing.

What scared Rodman was the rumor of Cole's money-raising tactics through tax-free bonds. And although the land was housing a dog track, and a coming law said no tax-free bonds could be applied to gambling facilities, a bill was being introduced by Senator Willbury in the state senate, a "grandfather clause" to the new law, that would exempt the Aquarius Dog Track from its restrictions, allowing Cole his bond application.

"That's why Senator McMann, who is chairing the commission reviewing this new grandfather clause, is vital to our cause." Rodman scanned the rapt faces around the table. "We should be able to get a good read about his position at my house Sunday and be able to mold it to *our* position. Whipp will be there. I was hoping you would come, Thomas."

Brennan, though petrified with age, reacted with surprise at Rodman's statement. He never saw his younger member in the same way since "that alcohol affair"—the chink in a man's armor, to Brennan, went past the breastplate and scarred the soul. Rodman was aware of his conciliatory gesture to the elder partner, and when Brennan nodded his acceptance, the blurred collage of heads in the black table softened its surface, placated the hard stone slab. Smiles outshone its darkness. Whipp raised one eyebrow Rodman's way, his highest form of salute. The meeting was adjourned.

But like the handgun, nestled in its own secret niche, so too were doubts about the deal, about Cole, doubts that Rodman's grandstanding had not allowed to come forward. Cole was a man of mystery; some had him tied to underworld forces, some merely to local toughs. Nor was there proof, as yet, of Cole's influence on the passing of the "grandfather clause." Yet intrigue was part of the game, and keeping Rodman's own plans with McMann locked airtight in the boardroom and uncontaminated by Cole was essential. Kiki, Rodman's administrative assistant, had even reminded him that the "bug sweepers" were coming that day after hours, instead of this morning, because of equipment failure, the routine countersurveillance techniques being just that—routine—and necessary. The only secrets they couldn't bug were the one's kept in our hearts, Rodman thought, impervious to rehab shrinks and shared only with the dead or soon-to-be.

He smiled down at Kiki, a chunky and most efficient little brunette with overly made-up violet eyes Rodman suspected were contacts, and tossed the microcassette from his recorder on her desk. "Could you please type up the transcript of the meeting? Make sure you number our copies and give it to the designated board members by corresponding numbers. No extras!" This was old news to Kiki, but she listened attentively as though it were a virginal command.

"Oh," she then remembered. "Mr. Zimmerman is here for you. He says he has an appointment, though I—"

"Who? I don't remember a Zi—" A billow of laughter from across the alignment of cubicles distracted him, a singular warbling touching an empty spot within. Four women were adhering to a fifth, encircling her and engaging her humor. Kiki craned to see who the lunch crowd had brought home as a prize and saw it was Patricia Dokes. Kiki cast a furtive look at her boss to see his reaction; clearly, he too had seen her.

Pat was a refined-looking woman, middle-aged but firm and shining with health. She had full breasts and a baby-maker's set of hips; still, she was childless. Husbandless, too, widowed for six years now, four years after taking the job of Rodman's executive assistant. Many suspected her long professional relationship with Rodman turned incredibly personal over that ten-year span, though there were no concrete sightings, no substantial confirmations. If the talk were true, a *fling* would be too jovial a word to describe it; everyone sensed something deeper had formed. Maybe it was just a strong friendship. Maybe it was something else, something actually too deep. She left suddenly just three weeks ago, no reason given, at least not any the secretarial pool could tease out of any one of their executive sources.

Kiki was one of the questioners intrigued by Pat's departure, but for Kiki it was a question left unpursued, not so much because she saw Rodman as her superior, but because Patricia Dokes's quick departure thrust Kiki into Pat's position. At this salaried altitude, questions would be counterproductive, though if truth be known, Rodman had his questions, too, all left un-answered.

An inquiring melancholy graced his expression as he gazed toward the clot of females at the end of the room. Compared to her business contemporaries at the office, Pat always dressed young, thought young. A wide flowered belt cinched her white cottony one-piece, exaggerating her bust and hips. (She once played Mae West at an office costume bash.) A matching flowered band embraced her streaking gray hair, pulling it back, thereby projecting her soft face, her laugh.

Rodman saw her eye catch his, then retreat, toss it back. One in her group noticed the contact and spoke with her, Pat already sidestepping out of the light, eyes downcast, wedging toward the opaque half wall of a nearby cubicle. He thought he read her lips: "I don't want to see him." She gave the group a tiny wave and backed up two steps, another fleeting glance at Rodman, then flipped open the door and disappeared into the hall.

Why'd he keep losing people, Rodman thought, why'd they disappear on him?

Kiki was mid-sentence when Rodman decided to resurface: ". . . had an appointment."

"Who was that again? For what?"

"He didn't say," Kiki responded. "A Mr. Zimmerman." She pointed toward the man who was now exiting the office bath-room, approaching Rodman with a smile. Kiki didn't look at his bruised face this time, out of politeness.

"Carl, did you forget me?" he said, jutting out a hand.

Rodman paused momentarily, fixing his eyes on Zimmer-man's appearance, and finally shook hands. "I'm sorry, no, of course not. It's been a busy day, big meeting. Mr. Zimmerman, of course."

"Call me Bob."

"Right, Bob. Go right into my office."

Kiki looked up at her boss, bugging out her flowery eyes, sweeping her hand over her empty appointment book, but Rod-man shook his head and spoke to her in a voiced whisper while Zimmerman went inside. "My fault. He's part of this Cole business. I've been—off somewhere lately, I don't know. I need a day away from here, I think." He gave a smile his luminescent best, and she responded in spite of its diminished wattage.

"You should do it, Mr. Rodman," Kiki agreed. "They work you too hard." He nodded over his shoulder as he stepped into his office and quietly clicked the door shut behind him. He looked toward Zimmerman, who stood grinning at the gold-framed college diploma that hung beside built-in mahogany bookshelves.

"I'm impressed," Zimmerman said.

Rodman took two quick steps toward his visitor and straight-armed a right hand to his neck, pulling him back and down, cracking his shoulders on the desktop, Rodman's grip tight on his throat. Their breaths kissed.

Rodman's words came out in fitful spurts of restraint: "What the *fuck* you think you're doing, coming here, Sonny?"

Sonny Vance seemed unperturbed, his mind removed from his prone, bent back body. This was a day at the beach compared to his day at the beach. "What a goof, you hanging your diploma up, Jesus! What do you think . . . maybe, twenty years ago, you would have wiped your ass with it to show what you learned? I didn't know you went for this kind of thing. Where's the fucking framed first dollar bill?"

Rodman wasn't listening; he examined the still puffy skin and amorphous blue bruise that discolored the turn of Vance's jaw and the puckered crease of his right eye. He also noticed two back upper incisors missing during Vance's little commentary. Rodman couldn't surmise, however, Vance's previously dislocated shoulder which, upon release from his imprisoning hole, he had set back in himself by flinging his body down on the beach and pushing, thrusting his shoulders back, crying, flopping around the damp dune like a landed fish, all to the brutal amusement of the Dembo brothers. When his bone clicked back in, his arm muscle shuddering in its finality, he yelped in relief and sweat burst past the pain, soaking and draining his torso at the same time. Two days of bed rest brought him back to life, yet even now, his chest still felt scraped smooth, and he could swear he still tongued sandy grit from his teeth when he talked.

"What? You didn't like my letter?"

Rodman felt ambushed, his breathing irregular. He dazedly

let Vance up a bit. "I can't believe you have the balls to come *here*—and looking like this! What the fuck happened to you? What were you thinking, coming here?"

"I was thinking we needed to push things up a bit. The letter's, like, yesterday's news. I need acceleration."

Rodman removed his weight from Vance completely now and backed off. Things needed acceleration? Things were going too fast as it was—the fast track to the grave. "What do you mean?"

Vance raised himself up, pulled down the lapel on his dated poplin sport jacket, straightened his knit navy-blue tie, its back tongue tucked between the buttons of a faded pink dress shirt. Whenever Vance tried to dress up, appear modestly officious, the best he could muster was the look of a novice salesman at a Macy's Action shop. Even the long hair pulled back and twined into a ponytail was less an influence of *GQ* and more a function of uncleanliness, its greasy sheen the result of no hot water in the room he was renting by the day on Kalter Avenue.

"Your secretary buy the Zimmerman routine, you think?" Vance said, smiling, circling the room as though assessing its weight, its power, so high up in the building, in the world of money, prestige. "You didn't guess it was me right away, did you? With *that* kind of clue, too. Man, you're getting slow."

"You think every time I deal with somebody named Zimmerman, I think of Bob Dylan?"

"And then when you think of Dylan, you'd think of me. Sure thing."

"No," Rodman said, "not a sure thing."

Vance shook his head in disappointment. "The Batman would have figured it out. The old Rod-man would have, too." Pronounced just like my father, Rodman thought; Vance knew it all, up and down, always did, childhood through now, the dangerous now.

"I'm not the old Rod-man anymore," he said.

Vance dipped his mouth in a frown. "So your silk suit says. I don't buy in, though. Some things run so deep, things you can't shake. 'Like a Rolling Stone' was our anthem, man. Our song. Fuck it for our generation, I'm talking you and me. And why? 'Cause we gathered no moss, no shit, no fuzz, no permanent babes—some on temporary loan, maybe, right?" The flash of a leer, coming closer. "No family, no home—" Vance's meander finally wound up behind the wide glass desk with Rodman. "—sure as hell no gold pen and pencil sets in marble, no leather office chairs and fucking perky secretaries with bad eyeliner jobs. Just good drugs, good times . . . good money." Vance bellied up to Rodman, who began to seethe.

"I *paid*," he snarled. "I *paid* you already. You left last time with the conditions that—"

Vance smacked Rodman hard across the face. "So, like, I'm *back*!" he spat. "And I didn't appreciate the hello, good buddy."

It was a lightning shot, just as hot across the cheek, just as seeringly quick, just as improbable. Vance had never struck Rodman before, not even playfully when they were both teen rowdies in Catholic school. Rodman was bigger, for one; for another, Vance kept cross-country drug-selling and bodily violence on two separate ethical planes; one was business, the other a usually unnecessary ego orgasm. Still, Vance couldn't help but grin at what he had done to his dumbstruck friend, much like what he had done to the runt in the baseball cap at the urinals. Vance always knew it wasn't a bad high, could always see why the Nixonites dug it, the ultraviolence, though the mano-a-mano bayoneting of gooks made a lot more sense, getting-off-wise, than the impersonal push-button bullshit of flashing radar blips glowing brighter on direct hits.

Rodman just shook, holding his cheek, holding his rage in check, almost ready to kill him now, but not now! Thy will be done, motherfucker, but not now!

"I'm just trying to prevent people from finding out about you," Vance said with earnest sympathy.

"That right," Rodman mumbled.

"That's fuckin'-A right," Vance said, moving away again, then swiveling back. "Hey, man . . . nobody loves a child killer. You *remember* that." Vance felt in command now.

First, the physical blow, Rodman thought, then the psychological one—Vance had learned a great deal from the nuns, in spite of his rebellious nature. The ruler blow, then the sin exposed, but always first the ruler. Sometimes even the innocent were hit. That was okay by the black-robed sisters. If we didn't sin that time, we would be sinning at another, they said, leaving Rodman's knuckles red and numbed. Life would get evened out, they said. We were all sinners anyway, past and present, and the sisters were all too right. It had already got evened out for Rodman; now Rodman would get even.

"What do you want?" Rodman asked, knowing it to be the most ludicrous rhetorical question of his life.

"I need money and I need it by Tuesday. No delays. No bullshit. Tuesday."

"What for this time? A coke deal go sour? Or is Las Vegas calling your pockets to empty themselves?"

Vance had lied to Sam Ryan three nights ago about the delayed drug sale and most everything else, and he could easily lie to Rodman. Lies were where he lived. Where *did* that money go? And why was that so important anyway? It was used, drained, exchanged for, vanished. Only people like Rodman and Ryan wanted the means over the end. Money was meant to be invisible, especially in your wallet. Pleasure without tender—the ideal anarchy.

Rodman watched Vance sit nonchalantly at the edge of the desk, watched his misshapen face ease into memory. "You remember how we couldn't get our hands on enough tabs of acid when we hit Oregon and Washington that time, selling like freaky fast—man! It was Bullwinkle big then. You know I had the same kind of run there a couple of months ago? And you know who's the big seller now? Beavis and Butt-Head. I mean, I was like the post office dealing those stamps by the shitload, and it was fucking great acid, too, but here's the grab-ass: I think some of those jerkoff kids thought I was selling, like, 'collectibles' for their sticker books or some shit, gonna be *worth something* someday." Vance shook his head with mocking raised eyebrows. "Fuckin' Yuppie-Land U.S.A. is here to stay, man."

"So how much?" Rodman asked, hating more than ever the trademark rambles.

"And right after that," Vance continued, "I actually did a stretch in Tullburn County Prison for possession. The goof was: I wasn't holding. They planted the shit. I didn't have a Beavis to my name, fuckin' Broderick Ten-Four Crawford, Mr. Highway Patrol, dumps a bag of Afghani red in my backseat.

What would you say, man? You know me. What? Ninety-nine percent of my life, I'm holding. The six-friggin' minutes I'm clean, I get nailed." Vance smacked his hand down on the desk, but immediately laughed doing it.

"But it follows my philosophy of paradox," he preened. "You want to face reality, get wasted. You want long-term security, get short-term big bucks. You want life to go nice-and-slow, play it loose-and-fast." He suddenly focused intensely on Rodman. "You want to keep living clean, you got to keep getting dirty."

Rodman, having absorbed the crash, let the silence hang there awhile as they looked at each other, neither face betraying any emotion. "How . . . much?" Rodman said, more pointedly this time.

"Thirty-five thousand. By Tuesday. That's it."

"And that would make you go away forever," Rodman said sarcastically, ". . . like the last time."

"That's right," Vance snickered. "I'd go away forever. Like the last time."

To Rodman, the money amount at this shakedown was just a point of curiosity, no cash was going to exchange hands, no more payments were forthcoming. He pondered whether he wanted to vocalize the "act," let it out into the air, let it drift like a gray, looming cloud over Vance.

"And what if . . . what if I just kill you?" Rodman muttered.

Vance's eyelid twitched for an instant, the slender line of him a wily shadow from the past, motionless, thoughtful. Then a grin secreted across his face and a mocking laugh broke loose. "Oh, *man*!" he said. "You forget your Socrates or what? Know thy-fucking-self, man. Do you see where you put yourself and where I put myself and you think you could kill me? Baby, you never had the balls to cut free, I mean, *really* free. You couldn't stay out of these tunnels, man, these, like middle-class narrow-walled tunnels. Now you're going to what? Shoot your way out? See some light by puttin' a hole in your tunnel? Puttin' a fucking hole in *me*? Stab me, maybe? Do a Polonius number. Right? I'll go behind your drapes and make it easy for you. No way. No way you'd be risking all this, this goodie bag life of yours, by doing me. Besides . . ." Vance soberly added, waiting until he was on the other side of the desk before he finished, "I'm not a little kid so easily wasted."

Rodman snatched at him furiously, Vance dodging like a boxer unnecessarily to further emphasize the distance between Rodman's wild stab and his own jeering expression. Rodman took a truculent first step to circumvent the desk.

"Back off, fucker!" Vance commanded, hands out, trying not to laugh. Rodman stopped and looked away. "Jesus, I got you jumpy, man. I never knew you to be so jumpy. Chill a sec, all right? I just want another slice of pie, Mommy, and I'll go out and play. It's 'cause you got so much to lose, you got so much to give."

"More philosophy?"

"You remember," Vance said. "My best subject at St. Joe's."

"I remember."

"So, look, it'll be easy. Like last time. You pick the drop. I got the impression you don't want me back here," Vance said, indicating Rodman's office.

Acceleration, Rodman thought, he had been planning for days now, just moving faster now, a downhill slide to the bottom, the dark receptacle.

"Early morning then, Tuesday, four A.M.," Rodman said in a businesslike monotone. "Let's make it, I don't know, there's a dumpy-looking lot on Easton Road. On the other side of town. Next to the clothing factory. You know what I'm talking about?"

"Skidmore Clothes. I know it."

"I'll give you the money there. I have to catch a train at five. The station is close. I have some out-of-town business. Just as well you need the money fast."

Vance nodded confidently and gave Rodman the thumbs-up from across the shiny desk. "See? Okay. Great. The lot on Easton. Then you catch a train, maybe I catch a plane, we don't see each other again. No sweat."

"Good," Rodman said, and thought, Good. The locale, the meeting place, he had chosen it already, the night after the letter. The lot on Easton was a given, preordained. Vance didn't know that, didn't see his body in a Dumpster as Rodman had while drifting into a dreamy consciousness beside Delia, didn't see the precise green-metal grave, the precise stretch of erupting concrete and bottle-strewn weedy grass, the patch of land Vance would bleed on once shot, a well-thought-out place. Land and guns again. Land was definitely his strength.

Guns would come . . . in time.

6

O N SUNDAY THE weather was not nearly as convivial and engaging as the gathering that attended the Rodman function, the flashy centerpiece of which was Senator Thomas McMann, a chesty man in his late forties whose rust-hued eyebrows fluctuated in precise time to his crisply formed speech.

"The law will remain intact during its passage," he assured the overly servile Dennis Whipp, who was leaning into every phrase. "Any attempt to dilute its impact with a grandfather clause should be met with failure. I believe I have the swing votes I need." McMann smiled and nodded his head at the elderly Thomas Brennan, who sat a few feet across from him in an embroidered antique armchair. Brennan nodded back, the old king of one kind of kingdom to the youthful prince of another, though he wondered if Braxton Cole knew of these swing-vote senators and had his own unseen forces influencing them.

Hallie Fouche stood nearby, absorbing the handsome aura of the special guest as much as she could while equally disengaging herself from her husband Bertram. An overweight, dignified-looking man, born in France but raised in Canada, he puckered his lips so at each sip of bubbly, his slim moustache would disappear beneath his nose. His eyes kept seeking out the hostess while his head remained still.

Rodman, meanwhile, stood upright and primed at the imaginary center of the bow window which arced behind him like a natural majestic backdrop. He felt in complete control of the peopled array. Yes, there was the inexorable slide toward the murder, unstoppable now, a fatal fated meeting of bullet and bone, but within that uncontrollable descent, he believed he had a fisted grip on each moment, each directed step, ever since Vance bound them both to the time and place, this coming Tuesday morning, four A.M., on Easton Road. Reclamation, Rodman thought. His eyes rested upon the bucolic landscape painting once more—the stable greens, the graceful roll of the land, the sure-footed sunshine stepping among the shepherd and his flock (missing one—Stop it!). First Vance's death, then reclamation, his life restored. It was definitely his favorite painting.

"Did you know Senator McMann was an outdoorsman?" Rodman announced to the gathering, establishing the opening toward his alibi. The men buzzed and ahhed, while the senator produced a blush and nodded.

"Well, Carl, I hear you're going to your cabin tomorrow. Nice to get away awhile."

Rodman smiled to himself. Alibis were the misaligned signposts directing others to a different snakelike trail, away from the steeply sloping path that pulls us to our sins. "Yes, up and out early Monday morn. Be back late Tuesday. Howard's coming as well. The two city slickers—"

"Hey, any excuse to tear Carl, here, away from his business for once," Howard Bernbaum said, then continued in a between-you-and-me hush, ". . . away from his wife, too, for a while—favor to her." Bernbaum, a professional tease and one of Rodman's oldest acquaintances, mugged and winked openly at Delia, who was approaching. She forced a brief smile, the rest of her face betraying a troubled expectation, while everybody chuckled.

"Ahh, the beautiful hostess!" exclaimed Bertram Fouche. He sidled beside her, his large left hand nonchalantly massaging her back, and having a good time, Rodman reflected, considering Fouche's face-filling grin.

The same couldn't be said for Jack Able, Delia's older brother, whose sour demeanor was quite evident now that the conversation had turned away from senate machinations and power alignments to shotgun gauges and steel-jawed traps, though Rodman himself always recognized the metaphoric similarities. His brother-in-law viewed the discussion as some sort of campfire summit straight out of *American Sportsman*, *Wild Kingdom*, whatever the hell it was. After all, Jack Able had political aspirations—the only real reason he came down to this affair, aside from the family obligation, which in truth had the pull of a five-and-dime magnet. He wanted to schmooze with the senator, see what opportunities could befall him. A member of the massive firm of Winetraub, Dryer and Magee, he didn't plan, as he would put it, "to have his caseload sink him into his grave." He had a vision for himself, had it since high school.

Rodman had seen the pictures Delia would display for him from her yearbook when she was only a freshman and Jack was a senior. He had run for school president and, having the most meticulously planned program, he should have won, according to his proud sister, but it was Jack's "toady" look that did him in—the horn-rimmed glasses, the untreated pimples that flecked his long and horselike face like putrid constellations, the black double-knit pants that shone in the neon-lit hallways as he walked, his pale yellow socks peekabooing above humpbacked leather shoes.

That was now no longer an accurate depiction of the middle-aged man stifling his air of superiority toward the present conversation. This Jack Able had perfectly tinted contact lenses of sea-blue, a white linen suit with matching vest, alligator shoes, and, yes, pale yellow socks, though now they were quite fashionable. He still had that long, horselike face, but it was neatly bearded, his trim facial hair complemented with brush strokes of gray, giving him an air of austere authority, of someone who could not be dismissed. It helped him in the courtroom; it elevated him into the community of his rich clients; it would be invaluable to him alongside the right political connections.

Rodman had teased Delia that everyone, especially Hollowsport High grads, would bow to the transformed Jack yet, because when he finally attained his pinnacle of political power, Jack would then look down upon his followers, reach into his dapper pocket, and whip on a pair of thick black horn-rims to reveal his true soul: Jack Curtis Able, LLD, newly elected official and avenging nerd. Delia had giggled at Carl's aberrant vision of the future and playfully smacked him on the side of the head for such brotherly blaspheming.

Rodman smiled to himself, felt Delia's love kindle warmth

inside his cool controlling heart, but her azure eyes seemed so mournful now, a fissured pair of gemstones, as though expecting a loss. Maybe it was just nerves, party pressures. She said her lower disks suffered a slight pull the other day on one of her dives and she'd had some powerful muscle relaxants prescribed. (Now *there* was serendipity! An easy aid to further his alibi.)

Delia stepped away from Bertram Fouche's hold. She stared at Rodman an instant too long before she spoke, and Rodman almost reached into her hesitation, as though attempting to catch a ball about to be thrown from an indecisive child.

"Your trip," Delia finally said. "You realize I have an appointment for my car on Monday morning. The inspection date is up and it needs work."

It was a strange remark, and its strangeness was not lost on the guests. Rodman replied, "I guess you'll have to arrange a ride. I won't be here." Delia nodded back, but as if she were affirming no particular question or compromise. Though the general talk flowed back into outdoorsmanship, Rodman felt a greater concern for his distracted wife.

"Just wanted to remind you about it," she said, as lightly as she could.

Rodman embraced her arm to bolster, to question, but she drew away as though she had become suddenly liquid through his fingers. Rodman sensed a spiritual retreat, too, a forced smile. Did his touch expose his controlling power? His shadowy machinations?

In fact, her backpedaling had little to do with Rodman's internal storm: the doorbell had rung above the din and there were guests at the door. Important guests. *Her* guests. Her *son*. Rodman squinted over at the domed alcove where Danny and Barbara stood before the hired maid, both awkwardly awaiting Delia's urgent reception.

"You in check?" Barbara murmured to Danny, whose head bobbed in time with his nerves.

"Everything's nailed down as tight as I can manage." He shrugged. "It'll be cool."

Delia's open-armed welcome for Danny didn't surprise Rodman. Danny's attendance did, but not Delia's overabundant love for the leftover child. Rodman took special notice of this overcompensating affection she had been lavishing toward Danny of late. Certainly, it never had reached this intensity when Eric was alive. If anything, Danny was forced to share her attentions and getting less than he thought he deserved. Maybe Delia didn't have the time with a younger boy around hoarding her feelings; maybe it was the unconscious shifting of affection toward the baby of the house, thinking the older sibling more stable, secure. In Danny's case, such an assumption proved disastrous. When Danny started using and lying, Delia doled her emotion out in disciplined doses. Tough love, the pundits would label it. When he gave in to rehabilitation and completed it, Delia treated him with respect. She always admired strength in a man, and Danny proved to her he had it, deserved her devotion again, deserved her love. After Eric's death, Danny got all her love back with interest, even some of Rodman's, at least that's what Carl had believed.

Rodman watched Delia at the doorway squeeze Danny to her, a little too hard, too desperate, Danny responding in kind, always willing to accommodate his mother, though Danny still appeared ill at ease being here. And so he should. A dark part of Rodman still felt Danny didn't deserve the right, didn't deserve Delia's precious, just warmth for what he did to the family, for what Danny was when he was on drugs, for what he reminded Rodman of.

"I *thought* you would come despite your protests," Delia told Danny assuredly.

Danny laughed to himself as he let go the hug. His mother always made last night's long shot sound like a sure thing the next day. "Don't be so smug," he responded. "It was Barbara's idea."

"And whose idea was it to come together?" Delia asked.

Danny bent his head toward Barbara. "Two for two."

Delia faced Barbara and awarded her with a welcoming embrace and some newfound respect. Delia often had thought of Barbara as Hallie's hologram, her projected perfected image— not that she wasn't a nice girl, but that was just it—she was a *nice* girl, with all the flatness and acquiescence the label implied. Barbara's appearance here with her son was a brazen act for such a girl. Her physical appearance—her hair, ponytailed; her attire, a cottony yellow dress with daisy-embroidered hose and sun-colored heels—even Barbara would admit, was not only a decorous nod to Delia but also a large concession to Hallie. Barbara believed that a surprise named Danny attached to her hip would be quite enough of a weight to drop on her mother for today.

"I want to introduce you," Delia told the couple, and led them inside.

Danny came prepared for just such an ordeal. He had a small buzz on, having taken a few tokes from a stash of marijuana he had hidden from Barbara in the deep hollow he had cut out of the complete works of W. B. Yeats. Yes, it was a toe-step off the wagon, and Dr. Walford at the clinic would not be proud and Barbara possibly tearful, but by and large, his indulgence was a makeshift, fuzzy wall of defense and a slap at Daddy. *And* unnoticeable, a condition he most treasured, like knowing you have that "something" in your pocket somebody else is frantically looking for.

Delia took the young couple around the room, and people both known and unknown to them offered their greetings. Barbara, as always, walked with a natural affection for things, her body open to people's caresses. The senator was clearly taken with her, and Barbara's stepfather enlisted the same grip on Barbara he had had on Delia.

"She's a living doll, isn't she?" Bertram Fouche said. Barbara was blushing.

"Without doubt," the senator replied.

"Paws off," Hallie said in a loud whisper, smacking Bert's hands away from her daughter. "You're wilting her." Then she proceeded to put her own paws on: poking at Barbara's hair, pulling at the shoulder of her dress, a manic artist dabbing incessantly at a painting that never seemed finished. Barbara turned to stone—a beauteous sculpture to be sure, but stone just the same—and let her mother do what she did.

Danny, meanwhile, had turned away, unable to watch the spectacle that was Barbara's mother, and after a few meaningless handshakes to strangers, he seemed pleased to grip the palm of his uncle Jack. Jack Able responded in kind, his drawn-down face lifting itself up into a welcoming expression. Jack flicked Danny's tie. "What's this?"

Danny shrugged. "A leftover from Catholic school."

"*That* the girl?" Able asked. "I can see how you had such a crush. She's prettier than you said."

"I think we're beyond the crush stage," Danny replied, and with his pleasant high drifting down, settling snugly upon him, he added softly, "I think—I think she's really good for me." Able and Danny shared a smile, a smile of masculine understanding, then Jack planted a few chuckle-inducing words into Danny's ear that Rodman couldn't make out although he stood only a few feet away.

Rodman felt his grip on the room's control knobs slipping now—he was trying to listen to the senator compliment Delia on their son and Barbara; trying to understand how his brother-in-law now possessed a bond with Danny that he himself had lost years ago, or how his older son attracted such a sweet girl, or how his younger son was dragged nearly a block like a battered fallen muffler, or how he himself was going to make it through a death tomorrow in this tensed and sober condition—

Delia pulled Danny from her brother to introduce him to the senator, and also to approach his own father. "Hi, Dad," Danny said, wearing an invisible smirk supplied by the intoxicating weed. Then he offered his hand, which Rodman took without hesitation.

But in the grip of the handshake, Danny's buzz vaporized and he suddenly wanted something more. His defenses fell as tactile memories flooded his veins. That hand that locked onto his in mock arm wrestles and let him win most of the time even at the age of four, that hand that pulled him up from the tangle of his two-wheeler after yet another curbside crash when he was an imbalanced six-year-old, that hand that congratulated him on winning the talent show in the seventh grade for playing "Tiny Dancer" on his new birthday guitar, that hand became the conduit for Danny's emotions—he gripped his father with a kind of hopeful thrust, a pull.

Although Rodman's face was one of paternal pride on public display, his hand bespoke his heart. It was damp and dead, stiff like a moist baseball mitt and nearly as leathery from the sun. There was nothing for Danny in that hand, and Danny cursed himself for even a moment of missing the emotional endowment that was once there for him.

"Barbara needs me to save her from her mother," Danny

said as he quickly excused himself, feeling guilty and lost and angry, and moved away.

What Danny didn't know was the sudden shame that Rodman felt at denying his son, the shame for the murder that was killing his own heart. He thought he had sensed Danny's vulnerability, the child exposed, the one he used to love, thought he saw it in his eyes, felt it, felt it really in his hand, but Rodman's fingers were numbed. They would not obey this time out of guilt. He was too withdrawn into himself and the murder to come. Rodman saw his wife look at him with hopelessness before turning back to the senator, where brother Jack was making his political moves. Rodman stuck his worthless hands in his pockets, his numb hands, wondering: What happened to the control? Where were the knobs? Who shut down his feelings?

"Where are you *taking* me?" Barbara said as she was quietly being led into a narrow storage room upstairs.

"In here," Danny said, throwing her ahead of him and shutting the door behind. Barbara turned and inspected her captor, who wore a sly grin. Danny had already yanked the knot of his schoolboy tie askew, away from his neck, and opened his collar. Breathing slowly but heavily, he looked like a man who had just escaped a hanging and was too preoccupied to remove the noose.

"Where's here?" she asked.

Danny paused a second. "My observatory."

"And here I thought you were leading me up to your old bedroom," Barbara teased.

Danny's eyebrows danced upward. "Disappointed?" he said, and he charged into her, Barbara crying out in laughter at his uncharacteristically rough hug. Then he kissed her. She responded open-mouthed, her tongue reaching out to taste his, the cavity of her hips naturally drawn into the thrust of his solid thigh. She suddenly thought she detected the bitter bite of marijuana, a hollowing fear of loss beginning to drain her passion, but she blotted all doubts from her mind. At least for today. Let's get him through today.

When they parted from the kiss, they continued to hold each other by the waist. Barbara's eyes began measuring the crowded room in her mind. "This looks more like a closet of some kind," she said.

And she was right. Even at twelve by eight, its floor-to-ceiling shelves, bursting and dangling with paraphernalia, constricted the tunnel-like "room" even more. The light at the end of it, literally, was opposite the door: a chin-high octagonal window that now revealed a late day sun whose orangey light imbued Danny's face with a beatific glow. It also eerily illumed the shelves' contents: stacks and stacks of record albums; disembodied sets of clothes; hats; marbled-cover notebooks; newspapers which were orange with age to begin with; out-of-date texts from a spectrum of college courses; and paperbacks, both literary and trash, the spines of which, like the rings of trees, had deep-set crease lines from which you could tell how old they were.

"My father's junk," Danny said, now sifting through a few pungent newspapers, dampened and delicate. CHICAGO 7 ON TRIAL, announced one tabloid headline, and he snickered. "His little corner of the sixties."

From a rough-hewn wooden crate Barbara popped out a battered and bent stovepipe hat made of green felt with a polka-dot ribbon for a band that was bowed in the front. She was tempted to put it on for fun, except that it was musty and the brush of the moist material made it feel alive.

"Was he at Woodstock?"

Danny made a face. "What soulless, fart-nosed businessman past forty has ever admitted he wasn't?"

Barbara put the hat back down delicately, as she would one of her mother's china vases. "Well, I can't imagine your father as a freak."

"You never noticed? He *is* a freak. In search of a sideshow."

Barbara could tell by Danny's tone where this was going. "So I'm in a closet, so you can talk about your father."

He then surprised her by producing an eased expression. "No. You're here to see my observatory." And he walked toward the latticed octagonal window that could neither open nor close, the greater heat of the sun feeling good on his face. Barbara snuggled beside him, looking out, sharing the warmth.

"I don't get it," she said. "You looked at the stars from here? Weren't there better windows than this?"

Danny exaggerated his head shake. "Not to see what *I* wanted to see." He pointed down, and only when Barbara got on her tiptoes was she able to angle her view toward the Rodman built-in pool just below. The large liver-shaped basin radiated a deep blue and was bordered at one curvature by a small, semicircular colonnade of white Vermont marble. She saw Hallie plodding around behind a few of the columns, no doubt looking for her. "Hi, Mom," Barbara chortled to herself.

"You wanted to see the pool," she responded, backing away, making sure her face was not visible to the eyes below.

"Only on late nights. Hot late nights." A secretive, loving smile brushed across Danny's face. Barbara was slowly starting to catch on.

"You see, on most summer nights," Danny continued, "when she was restless and hot, there was this girl from next door. A young, beautiful, shapely girl. An untouchable girl, who used to come to the pool—was invited to come, really, any time she wanted by the lady of the house. She would come down the slope from next door holding her white towel. She usually wore a pink one-piece, went way high on the thigh, and a diamond cutout to show her belly button like it was something to see." Barbara laughed and squeezed his hand. "Then she'd stand at the side of the pool and step into the water slowly. She wouldn't dive, this girl. Too radical—"

"You're going to get it!"

"—too intense a change for someone so delicate, so proper." Danny paused; his face appeared less playful, more sincere. "But I couldn't show my face to this . . . beauty, splashing in the moonlit water. So . . ." He let go of Barbara's hand and reached down behind the left-hand shelf. He slid out a mirror, a perfectly round mirror approximately two feet in diameter, a mirror that would have been used more as a decorative wall hanging than as a means to a practical reflection, because upon it, in yellow, was painted a peace symbol. Yellow enamel, a good two inches thick, bordered the circumference, and "the topsy-turvy crooked cross" or "the chickenlike footprint" (depending on your political viewpoint) intersected it and occupied its middle, equally yellow.

" . . . I would watch you this way." Danny held the mirror up with both hands just above his head, the reflective surface angled toward the water. "I could see you perfectly, watch you bob around, see you dry yourself off, rub yourself all over beneath the pool lights. Your skin was so—I—I loved your hair—" He was speechless. Barbara's eyes grew. The symbol on the mirror had disappeared because the sun's rays were enveloping the shiny circle and making it glow and burn orange, as though Danny were raising up the vibrant sun itself, holding a giant wafer of light in honor of their love. Her dark and sensitive knight lowered the glowing orb and it became just a kitschy mirror once more. He leaned it up against the wall below the window, and seemed to be deliberately avoiding looking at her.

Barbara said softly, "You never told me this."

She saw Danny shrug from behind. "For some reason it was hard to. Especially since I was so fucked up with drugs . . ."

"I mean, now. Since you went clean. Since *us*. You never said—"

Barbara finally got him to turn around, and held him, but his gaze was still pitched downward as he spoke. "I haven't said a lot of things I feel for you." He corrected himself. "I *felt* for you, then, even." He shook his head. "You intimidate the crap out of me, you know. You're too good for me."

"Stop it," Barbara warned. She hated that.

"You *are*."

"I don't want to hear that stuff," she said more loudly than intended. "You want to be like my mother or my lover?"

"I want to be what will please you. I'm just not always sure I'll be able to do that."

"Be whatever you want. *Tell* me whatever you want." Barbara put her head to his chest, heard his heart patter like a puppy's. "Okay?"

"Okay," he said finally, though to his ears, his voice lacked conviction. Danny still wouldn't dare tell her that most of the time after watching her at the pool, he would coke up bigtime—snort a few lines on that very same "peace" mirror and then masturbate on his bed with her image still floating and wet in his daydreams. It was his fucked-up mind-set back then and he hated himself for it, but he wasn't going to shatter his romantic tale of the past with anything as dirty as the truth, no matter what she said about revealing all.

"I love you, Danny," she whispered.

"And I'm crazy about you," he said. His arms encircled her, and that embrace, that affection of love, was the truth, too, a vivid truth, a *now* truth, and it was even more than her ephemeral image in the mirror had ever promised. His hands began to slide from her back and roamed down her thighs and then up to her breasts as their lips met. He wanted to be shot through with her, absorbed by her smooth, fresh skin. He became hard and pulled her buttocks to him.

Barbara broke their kiss with a shaking of her head. "We can't do it here. No—"

"Why not?" Danny said, still rubbing, now working his finger underneath her cotton bra cup like a worm stimulating the stem of an apple.

"No, Danny, no," Barbara said calmly, though she was pulling her passion in with great difficulty. "I don't want it like it's some kind of revenge on our parents. Doing it here. At the party. In your father's whatever." Danny stopped his probing and looked thoughtfully at her. "Please," she said.

Danny closed his eyes as though doing it were a means of shutting down his genital engines. "Okay," he conceded, then cuddled her. "But how about we just go make out in my old bedroom? Didn't you really want to see it? I'll be good, honest, mostly. You can trust me. I'll show you my old baseball cards and everything." His expression was one of innocence to the nth degree.

Barbara wore a sly look. "Sure. You got an old stereo there, too?"

"You know it."

Barbara reached past Danny and at random grabbed a handful of albums, ten records thick, from the eight-foot-wide stack on the shelf behind him. Following suit, Danny spun around and grabbed a similar handful, leaving a dark tunnel of space behind with a shiny center that caught his attention.

Then the door squealed open with a forceful rush, and the stern face of Carl Rodman swung in right after. There was a moment of theatrical stillness until Rodman saw what Danny was holding. "What the hell are you doing?" he said, clearly shaken, almost panicked. "This isn't your house anymore. This wasn't even your room when this *was* your house."

Danny dipped his head down to Barbara for a vocal aside. "I forgot to tell you this was off limits. This is, like, my father's closet of secrets. At least he acted like it was. Still does, I guess. I just see a bunch of old records and shit."

Danny reached out and was about to widen the gap on the shelf by grabbing hold of another handful of albums, but Rodman's right hand beat him there, palm down flat on the sides of the records so they couldn't be slid out.

"Well, they're my old records and my old shit and that's all you need to know." Rodman noticed Barbara's troubled concern and felt badly. "Sorry, Barbara."

"Yeah, me too, Barb," Danny injected. "For you ever getting involved with the boy next door." Thwarted by his father at the shelf, he took hold of the stack of records that was in Barbara's possession. "Think these scratchy things are worth something at the flea markets?" he asked nobody in particular. Then both hands let go, allowing the records to drop as one to the floor.

Rodman's face twitched with the cracking sound the neat pile made when it landed at their feet, still erect. He just wanted them out of the room.

"You're as far away from the boy next door as you can get," Rodman said.

Again, Danny in an aside to Barbara: "He's right, you know. I'm a deviate. I ride a motorcycle. I like reading and playing guitar better than holding a steady job. I don't buy and sell land or some crap under people's noses—"

"Don't you goddamn stick your secondhand ideals in my face! I know from ideals. I had plenty. I suffered for having them. I cherished them—"

"Listen to yourself, will you please?" Danny shouted back. "You're Mr. Past Tense. This room is past tense. What you were in the sixties doesn't pull dick in the nineties, Daddy."

Rodman thought, He doesn't know, it wasn't *that*, it wasn't free love and peace and causes and all *that*, not just *that*, there were the bomb-crazy SDS's and the wasted thousands and the dirt and depression and smells of sweet oil and sweat, and the aimless air of "fuck it" in the streets, and there were the Vances, there were me and the Vances. . . . But Rodman said, "I went through hell because of you and your bullshit drugs."

"And tell me about after that," Danny shot back. "After you went through hell to straighten me out and then had to get straightened out yourself. What happened then? *You* got the pat on the back, the kiss on the cheek, nice work, you beat it today, let's stare it down tomorrow, you're a better man for kicking it, you've seen the worst, now be the best—I know the lyrics to that tune, you know?—'cause I kicked it, too, remember?"

Danny leaned over, now feeling as though he were in a coffin, a toxic time capsule, buried deep and better left unopened. He hissed into his stiffened father's ear, "But what did *I* get for straightening out? Where's *my* pat on the back? What have *you* given me?"

Rodman couldn't answer, and Danny never gave him the chance. He marched out the door and Barbara followed, averting her eyes away from the blank-faced man in the closet. Rodman had wanted them out, but he didn't mean for it to go that far. Why did he always go too far? He stood motionless for a time, seconds on end, then he turned somberly and, remaining inside, grabbed hold of the brass knob and pushed the tomb door shut.

Hallie cursed to herself. Delia was gone. She had lost her. That Delia would disappear mid-toast was odd, and even more evidence of some sort of concealed assignation, a meeting set perhaps by a preordained time. It was seven on the button when the bubbly was offered in tribute. Maybe seven was the destined moment Delia was to rendezvous. But now, alone, near the pool, Hallie felt she had lost track of everybody, not just Delia. Where was Bertram, her foolish husband? And the senator was no longer seen being crassly schmoozed within the glass patio as he had been before, unless he was back in the living room again. But it was Delia! *She* was the honey; *she* was the prime attraction. To meet her secret caller, her out-of-town dalliance, here, now, at such an affair? How could Hallie miss this moment? Where *was* Delia?

Steadfast and peering about, Hallie plunked her way past the edge of the pool and began gloating to herself at the way she reacted to Barbara's dragging along that going-nowhere Rodman boy to Delia's most-important social occasion; which is to say, Hallie didn't react at all. Her goat not gotten, her hackles flatly unraised. Hallie was not about to give Barbara the satisfaction of a tantrum. Besides, a public scolding wouldn't be perpetrated by anybody with even a chromosome's worth of class. Barbara would realize soon enough she didn't need that unprofitable loser of a boy. Then she heard it.

Hallie moved as best she could, as fast as she could, toward the west corner of the vast Rodman property, where the stone barbecue pit was located. She swore she had heard a short cry, really more like a suffocated bleat of pain. She heard it just beyond the hedges near the pool house, but as she turned onto the stone pathway, she nearly ran down a wobbly figure coming through the green arch of ivy.

"Delia!" Hallie gasped, though the near-collision barely registered in Delia's demeanor. She looked thoroughly drained, and the fading daylight made the tears she was shedding seem all the more sharply etched on her cheeks. "What's wrong?" Hallie asked in a hush. "What happened?"

Hallie watched Delia try to recover quickly, the backs of her hands blotting her face as best she could. "Nothing," she said harshly, then, as though she had to let some of it out before it tore through her, "I just . . . I just know something now, I thought I wanted to know, that's all." Delia pushed by the crippled older woman easily, her broad shoulders moving forward, back to the party.

Hallie had no time for conundrums, let alone the physical ability to give chase, so she did the next best thing and hobbled, with all due haste, into a grassy area, well-hedged, that had only a few access points. She checked the clasp on the gate door leading to Miller Lane, and sure enough, the shank of metal hadn't caught the latch all the way, so maybe whoever it was was sloppy about leaving, or in a hurry. He could then have easily walked around by now and through the front door again as though nothing had happened. But what *did* happen? What made the stoic and strong Delia cry so?

A wisp of smoke from the Italian stone barbecue pit brought her closer. Among the coals there were two sheets of charred paper, just burned—Hallie saw the ashen stick match beside it, smelled the sulfur. One sheet was absolutely black and flaked to the touch; the other had remnants of white, and Hallie made a two-finger stab at it, catching it by its white, wanting to keep it white. She flicked it onto the grass and laid her hard boot on it with a thump, extinguishing any remaining embers. When she picked it up again, no writing remained on the unburned portion, which was near what seemed to be the bottom. It was probably some kind of personal stationery, she surmised—more in hope, since the paper stock gave no clue—maybe even a love letter. What she *did* see was what looked like an X in ink. Part of a name? All of a kiss?

Hallie let the paper drift back into the dark of the pit. She felt saddened. She had just missed what she loved to watch most: the end of an affair.

He had wanted them out of the room, but didn't mean for it to go that far. Yet it had. As it always did.

Rodman picked up from the floor the stack of dropped records that leaned like a lopsided set of stairs. He always meant to throw this sixties menagerie out. Delia had certainly wanted to, the minute they moved in, when he claimed this anomalous area of their new home as his own. She wanted a "real" storage room, where you store "things you need." She had no patience for the past, *his* past really, especially anything pre-*them*. "I wouldn't have given you the time of day if I met you back then," Delia would say. The truth was, back then he was often so wasted on hashish or downers, he wouldn't have *known* the time of day. At least, that condition would apply to the latter phases of his freakhood, when he and Vance did their cross-country dealing, their version of *Easy Rider* minus star-spangled bikes and a chance encounter with a young Jack Nicholson and a pork chop.

Rodman sifted through the records in his hands; it was the Bob Dylan pile—the bootlegs, the early acoustic folk and the burgeoning electric folk. He hadn't followed Dylan later on, down Dylan's meandering religious path, musically or philosophically. In fact, it was because it *was* the Dylan pile, Rodman had wanted them out of the room, though he didn't mean for it to go that far.

Rodman thought of Danny's music, again felt Danny's grip in his own, the hard finger calluses scratching his palm. Rodman loved the music, loved hearing his son play—that was before Delia's surprise pregnancy with Eric, the unexpected gift of a new baby. Danny had always played for the family before Eric came along to turn the household around, and Rodman always marveled at Danny's talent, always wanted to be that good himself. Rodman's love of music had come before the teenage drugs. He recalled hiding a transistor radio under his pillow at night so that his dad wouldn't catch him listening. The music *was* his drug for a while, not that the music ever brought on the drugs, no cause and effect, no matter what Spiro Agnew had said about *Sgt. Pepper's*. The drugs had become enhancement, the enhancement led to blockage. First blocking out the past, then the present—I didn't know what I was doing. . . .

He had wanted them out of his room, but he didn't mean for it to go that far. Rodman looked into the dark gap left by the removed stack of Dylan albums and reached back into it toward the shiny object behind. He felt the butt of his chrome revolver still securely nestled next to the wall, the rest of the gun concealed by the adjoining parade of oldies in front of it. The gun felt warm to the touch. The box of bullets was behind the Grateful Dead. Rodman replaced the Dylan records, pushing the others down, tightening the formation, strengthening the wall.

Rodman had wanted them out of his room, out of his past, but most of all he wanted to protect his son from the taint of his own approaching sin.

PART II

PART II

7

THE NEXT DAY, predawn Monday morning, Rodman gave his wife a prolonged, thoughtful look as he put on his light flannel shirt and stood pantless at the foot of the bed. He was quiet in his preparation, and she was deep in sleep, her red hair having fallen down the side of her face like wavy rivulets. His fingertips lovingly touched her sculptured cheek and brushed the wayward strands across it to the cradle behind her ear. Last night she had gone upstairs before him, her face somehow full of sad anticipation, the way his own eyes must have looked, Rodman thought. Maybe last night was just a reflection of his own intensifying dread. Maybe she just couldn't get herself to tell him something.

He finished performing his usual cabin-trip routine except for two deviations: he confiscated a handful of Delia's muscle relaxants from the bathroom and he recovered his chrome gun from the back of the Dylan collection. These two sidebars were carried out with steady everydayness, only allowing himself—that other self, the detached one—an internal joke when at his record collection he stuck the pistol in his pouch and thought about Vance being number one with a bullet.

Rodman drove to his office, using his executive set of keys to enter the dark rooms. He picked up his unattended mail and report files that Kiki had laid out on his desk on Friday. He pocketed his microcassette recorder for good measure should any ideas hit him while on the road. (You're going to *kill* a man. What the fuck ideas are you going to— Shut it *down!*) He checked the "hidden" compartment on the satchel for the emergency money he kept there. Then he drove due northwest through Hollowsport's developing outskirts and two hours toward Mandrake Road, the lesser-used byway up to Janus Mountain, the eastern half, and its small, fish-laden lakes.

Two-thirds of the trip up the rock-hugging road, Rodman stopped at Wesley Koontz's gas station/general store, really a one-story, wooden frame box of a house Koontz had built himself. Koontz used the front section to sell his small sampling of food supplies and minimal fishing and hunting equipment. The back of the house contained the three modest rooms he and his wife Roberta actually lived in. Two gas pumps filled with fuel of dubious quality stood out front like bright red sentries at the ready, handles in salute; the only pieces of his property Koontz repainted with any regularity.

Rodman pulled into the station next to Koontz's rust-pocked pickup, and before he could swing out his door, Koontz had swung out of his, wiping his hand with a checkered towel and chewing on something that was maybe breakfast. He squinted at his customer as though the sun bathing the mountainside had gathered up into Rodman's propped-up smile.

"Wes! It's me!"

"Hey, there," Koontz said, his face bearing no expression in particular. "Mr. Moth, how you fairin'?"

"Just great, Wes, just great. Finally getting away, just need a few supplies. Here for only an overnight, really."

"Mr. Moth on an overnight . . ." Koontz nodded and scratched his nose, a craggy formation, not unlike his home turf. "Well . . ." He shrugged, after a strange pause, then gestured for Rodman to follow with a wave of his little towel. Koontz had little to say and even less in common with the younger changeling, younger by his seventy-two-year-old standards, in spite of the fact that he and Rodman's father were friends and fellow professional outdoorsmen.

And that "Mr. Moth" business all the time. Koontz knew Rodman as a boy when Blaine Rodman took his son Carl up to the cabin from the Catholic boarding school in the then burgeoning city of Hollowsport. Then he knew Rodman as the hippie living in his late father's cabin, living with similar scrungy friends, one of whom was Sonny Vance, doing Lord-knows-what, but it was none of his business, and his crustaceous nose kept its distance. Rodman figured that, to Koontz, this must have been his "fuzzy caterpillar" stage, he and his freaky friends just a singular creature all arms and legs and too much hair. Then Koontz knew Rodman as the clean-cut entrepreneur, the mousse-riven, sharp-suited young man who came back to the wild to sell it. At least the western half, the *other* side of Janus Mountain. It was there that Rodman had first gotten involved with real estate, used his innate business talents (no matter how hard he wished for musical ones), and made his first legitimate buck, his first post–Sonny Vance drugselling buck, which was to be the first buck of many.

The prefab cabins and panoramic condos sprouted like profit-bearing buds, a blossoming of wealth in Rodman's landgrabbing seventies. Rodman, out of deference to his dead father, had offered Koontz a piece of "the other side," for almost nothing. But Koontz said no, with no reason given. Thus it was this latter persona—the transmutated hippie into the successful businessman—that spawned the "Mr. Moth" appellation from Koontz's lips.

Rodman was never particularly comfortable with the name, but told himself that "Mr. Butterfly" would have sounded too insulting to someone like Koontz, too fey a labeling, when in fact Koontz thought of a moth as an indiscriminate eater of other people's property. It was as simple as that.

Following a few perfunctory purchases (after all, this was but another concrete layer in the foundation of his alibi), Rodman was about to leave, when Koontz remembered something. "Won't be here for a few days starting this evening. Closing up a few days on account my wife's sister is sick in Dallingsford. Got to take her there. You need gas for the way back, better get some now."

Rodman shook his head. "That's okay, Wes. I'm tanked pretty good. Take care."

Back on the road, Rodman regretted the stop. Koontz's face had the markings of his father—the hard tracings of authority, expertise, and the guts to respect the harshness of life and nature—and Rodman sunk into the morass of memory.

Carl's father was a professional fishing guide for the Janus Mountain region. He could also match his hunting expertise with some of the best trackers in the area. Yet the lake was his calling, and the freshwater bass his primary prey. Leading some weekend "fly-swatter"—as his father would call the stock amateur fisherman who came to him and had all the casting grace of a bear at a tree pawing for honey—was just his excuse for making money while sitting in his boat and idly bobbing his life away. Blaine Rodman had no conversational gifts. His demeanor was for the most part surly to the hairless bipeds he shared the species name with. He never received a joke well or listened all that attentively to the excited tales such primal surroundings provoked his clients into telling, tales of former wilderness conquests, or else he would have had a greater circle of customers, something Blaine Rodman couldn't care less about. Still, his father's skills at fly-making and his uncanny sense of where in the lake, within what precise circumference of water, one could angle a line into a converging intersection of fish, eased clients past his sour aspect and into his roughened hands as regulars.

Rodman was Blaine's first and only child, as Carl's mother Maureen had died during his birth; the fetus rebelling against the womb, destroying it—*that* should have been Rodman's first unforgettable warning as clearly as it was Rodman's first unforgivable mistake. His father could not cope with raising a son alone, in spite of all the help Aunt Lucy, Maureen's older sister, would give. In truth, Blaine Rodman resented her presence, her filling needs he could barely acknowledge. So the older Carl grew, the less his father allowed Aunt Lucy to be around and the more Carl found himself spending boyhood nights alone, hiding in bowers near Sepian Creek to keep away from his father's nighttime rages, sometimes alcohol fueled. The bristling pines gave Rodman succor and allowed him to dream green and air-pure dreams. Still, there were times he would purposely defile his verdant nest. One summer he foolishly started small, but potentially serious, fires in sun-drenched clearings, fires that drove his father mad with frustration at not being able to find the perpetrator. Carl's continual goal had been to see the back of his father's neck pull taut and flash red, so that its tendons were like the tension wires on a bridge.

When Rodman was thirteen, Aunt Lucy suddenly died, and his father said, "See that? She dropped us, too," somehow failing to remember the occasions he would openly demean her, sometimes even physically provoking her to leave.

"Dropped us? She dropped *dead!*" Rodman had angrily shouted back, and he was smacked hard across the face for the remark. Somehow people were responsible, not only for their own lives, but for their own deaths—or so his father had impressed upon him. It was at these times that so misshapen a logic made Rodman believe he was not responsible for his mother's fatal blood loss, that his *mother* was somehow at fault, that she somehow left them deliberately. At other times, his father silently vilified him as the deadly cause, made him feel the poor substitute, the slack end of a poor trade—wife for child at the child's wailing insistence, its *having* to come out, its *having* to live at any cost.

Shortly, Carl was sent to a Catholic boarding school in town, where whatever guilt he had accumulated during his brief life, like sand quietly building up in one's shoes, was compounded and solidified, codified and graced by "God's will" and by the good sisters of St. Joseph's. (Sins were sins, unconsciously committed or not, and God's retribution was to come, here or hereafter, but weren't we still paying for Adam's fall even though we ourselves never tasted one sweet drop of the apple?)

Blaine Rodman put little stock in la-di-da religion or the looming threat of hellfire, but it was his unknowing way of giving Carl a mother figure in the form of the Catholic Church, the spiritual house at which his wife Maureen had worshiped and was baptized in. And even better, these women supplied the staunch discipline Blaine so much appreciated, the callused hands of nuns swatting the cheeks of young offenders, those little motes in God's all-seeing eye. It didn't matter that the sisters struck innocent and guilty alike, the punishment coming before the questioning, or even that Carl was more often innocent than not. At least, at first. For it was there that he met Sonny Vance, and so it was there where the root of the tree truly began to blacken and fester, and finally threaten its inevitable fall, Eric being its most precious, precious fruit.

Rodman reached the cabin in a somber mood, but lightened his expression upon seeing Howard poke out his curly-cued head and offer a smile from the bedroom door. Howard was dressed for fishing, overdressed really, always insisting on caricaturelike proportions. "I beat you here," he gloated, his bulky beige sleeveless jacket and floppy hat wielding a plethora of flies, as though he were a human porcupine with a shield of stainless steel prickles.

Even in college he would come to dorm poker sessions dressed akin to a riverboat gambler, and at one recent party arrived as W.C. Fields so as to constantly solicit in adenoidal tones the curvaceous Pat Dokes as Mae West. (Howard always had a thing for Pat, and Rodman often wondered if he ever out-and-out propositioned her for real. If so, Pat had never divulged it.)

Rodman dumped his bag in the long-timbered bedroom he himself had added on to this now sprawling structure, nostalgically called a "cabin."

Then they gathered their rods and packs and marched out to the adjunct clearing where the tarp-covered rowboat lay resting on concrete blocks, hull side up, like the shaved-off hump of a black whale. Howard was chattering away about the party Sunday as though it were a sports recap, the hits, the errors, the plays of the week. "Your brother-in-law was making his move on the senator," he remarked, a note of admiration in his tone. "The man's quiet, but quick."

"Did you notice Delia in a funny mood?" Rodman asked.

Howard shook his head. "No, not really." Rodman felt he could always talk about Delia with Howard now, after all these years, the ups-and-downs of marriage you shared with any good friend, especially one who could turn connubial turmoil into a gag. Rodman never sensed any lingering jealousy over Delia, and yet in this instance he thought he perceived a bite to Howard's answer.

With a singular grunt they lifted their faithful boat over their heads and carried it in a syncopated walk, like two men in a horse suit, down the well-trodden pathway along Sepian Creek toward Thorpe Lake. They sat out in the boat for hours, the sky cloudless, the sun relentless, the lake flat, seamless, a drifting here, a pull there. Howard wasn't as talkative as usual, even after reeling in a four-pounder or two, while Carl sat anxiously waiting, not for nibbles, but for the deep and breathless dark of night.

"You're going to wear it out that way," Howard said, out of nowhere, then indicated what Carl's left hand was doing. His fingers were unconsciously rubbing one of the pins that dotted the front of his timeless denim jacket, more white with wear than blue. A Boston Red Sox badge from the collapsed 1978 pennant drive, a St. Joseph's school tie tack bearing a crucifix diagonally crossed by a ruler, and others, were all superceded by the one pin Rodman now finally let go of to inspect—Eric's math achievement award from the first grade. He often found himself stroking it the way he would his boy's minor bruises caused by a day's rambunctiousness.

Made aware of his nerve-induced habit, Rodman held the pin by the tips of his fingers with a tenderness and near tearfulness. Howard was right: the ROD from ERIC RODMAN was starting to fade down to its auric base. Even the pin itself was endangered, dangling, flapping against an enlarging hole caused by his manipulations.

Eric had given him the pin on a humid Father's Day, just after the school year ended. He was alive with a boy's passion for summer, bright impatient eyes anticipating his dad's incredulous look when Rodman lifted his own faded denim jacket from a gift-wrapped Macy's box.

"What's this?" Rodman asked. "I believe in this environmental business, but they teaching you to recycle *presents* at school, too?" Delia had stayed mum, her lips suppressing a smile.

"What's new?" Eric bounced up and down on his sneakered heels, a short-billed white bicycle cap slid backward on his head. "Don't you see somethin' new?"

The name-painted gold pin in the shape of a right-angled triangle easily outshone the sun-worn paraphernalia festooning the jacket's front. Rodman felt as though *he* were the one being awarded, and he hugged his son. Later that morning, he teased Eric about the pin being so glittering he could use it as a light source for night fishing, or as the most sparklingly magnetic of fishing lures.

"You really think it could work?" Eric asked. "Let's try it next time at the lake, okay, Dad? Promise, please, next time."

Rodman laughed at Eric's enthusiasm. "Okay, next time."

But there would be no next time. Rodman's own cocaine and alcoholic indulgences were nearing an apex by then, the family fortunate he was on a temporary upswing that June weekend, a perky high before another fall. There would be no fishing in Rodman's immediate future. And all too soon there would be no Eric, either. Only repentance. And with Vance's death, goddamned redemption.

Rodman thought of the gun back at the cabin, tucked into his travel pouch along with his office papers. He never did move it to a place of concealment within his bedroom, but it wasn't as though Howard was a snoop.

From a distance Rodman could see the small peninsula his father used as a natural shooting range. Blaine Rodman had a long-barreled .45, only just recently acknowledged as lost in a box or a trunk somewhere, a relic of a piece, and on his son's holiday visits from St. Joseph's, Blaine would take Carl out there on that flat, scrubby thumb of land, set up a few empty Del Monte vegetable and syrupy fruit cans on a small boulder and blast away, Rodman flinching at every shot his father squeezed off. Blaine Rodman always punctured those cans, then stood with the crease of a half smile on his face, a yellow-tinted cigarette in one hand, his pistol in the other, his hip out like a lazy tart.

Blaine had stuck the gun in Rodman's hands once when Carl was only ten, as though handing him a turkey leg to eat, told him to "put holes in them things," and flailed a hand toward the tin cans. Rodman could barely lift the archaic weapon, his father helping him grip it with both hands out away from him, growing impatient, Carl shaking, trying to steady his eye down the long slick barrel to the nub at the end.

"Come on!" his father said, the cigarette dancing up and down between his lips as he talked. In disgust, he pulled the stained Chesterfield from his mouth. "Shoot it!"

Carl tried to pull the trigger, just as at the same time he tried to pull his face in, to flatten it back inside his head, in fear of the blast.

"Don't tighten. Let the blood do it!" his father shouted. And the shot rang out, the bullet arced up and wide and out toward the serene lake, and Carl was thrown back as though an animal had pushed forward with thrusting paws and jumped from his hands onto his chest. Blaine Rodman laughed a laugh of disgust—a short snort for the boy who was butt-deep in the mud of the patchy shoreline grass. "Jesus," he said, "you'll never be a Rod-man that way," which maybe was the only time his father ever made a conscious joke, let alone a pun, but maybe not. He always pronounced it Rod-man, and never once alluded to the fact that it was the perfect name for a fishing guide.

Years later, his father well in the grave, Rodman brought his two boys to the same finger of land. Danny was in the middle of his addiction, and Rodman literally threw him into the car one dim cool morning, grabbed Eric, and drove to Janus Mountain. At least up here there wasn't too much Danny could slip under his leather jacket to hock, none of Delia's jewelry or Rodman's Bang & Olufsen audio equipment to fence. What Danny *did* find was his grandfather's ancient pistol in working order, and he wanted to see how it shot, almost daring his father to try it out again.

Rodman demurred, but let Danny have a crack at an empty milk carton he fished from the Hefty garbage bag in the kitchen. There were still some bullets in the barrel's chambers, and Rodman could still clearly remember Danny drilling a hole through the carton on that same boulder; and when being physically stimulated by the kick of the shot, his firing off a second; and Eric, just a tot, squealing at the reverberant sound, the crack of the bullets echoing over the lakefront; and himself, forever flinching, once, twice, until Danny, having made a pair of hollow eyes in Mr. Low-Fat Skim, flipped the gun to the ground with a flourish and gave his father a don't-fuck-with-me smile.

When Rodman and Howard oared back to shore, Howard took the lead in the kitchen, where he expertly gutted and sliced the slippery trove that filled his netted sack, and cooked with a verve all his own. He was great with his hands. His deft and delicate touch made him accomplished with fishing flies, for more than once Howard would hold up a new whatchamabob, a hook disguised as a burlesque dancer, and announce, "A thing with feathers." And it fit. Because Howard was good with hope, too—ever so. He once hoped to be a comedian, but his comedy was usually confined to entertaining the brokers and clients at Intercounty Investments Corp.

Howard's feathery hope had especially extended to the search for the perfect girl, whom he had thought he had found in Delia. When Rodman had first become acquainted with his bespectacled fellow freshman at Acker State University, they were both dateless wonders, and so became fast friends. After buddying for two years, Howard and he both toured Europe their sophomore summer on a budget the size of a hitchhiker's thumb.

But that fall of 1967, Howard left for a private school on a transfer scholarship, while Rodman never went back to Acker when his father died that September of a stroke. Carl simply stayed in Hollowsport after the funeral, alone, sad, angry, and vulnerable, taking over the mountain cabin, and having a reunion of sorts with his fellow hometown hippie and St. Joe rad grad, Sonny Vance.

It wasn't until after—after the tour, the drugged-out, nationwide, draft-dodging, substance-selling, brain-abusing, soul-squashing tour—that Rodman, having left Vance to his travels and to the broken rib he had given him as a farewell, returned to Hollowsport once more and ran into Howard Bernbaum, of all people, manning a booth at a careers convention in the local sports complex. There he was introduced to Howard's beautifully regal and strong-boned assistant with feathery crimson hair haloing her freckled head, and azure eyes that bore in on you, tested you and teased you, Howard's girlfriend, in fact; his hope-to-be-wife, his "thing with feathers," Delia Able.

Rodman had no intention of stealing this dynamically willed woman from his friend; it just turned out that way. She was with the Frankel Sports Arena people at that time, helping to book conventions, set up booths, and the following week she would call Rodman for lunch, having surreptitiously fished his number from Howard's Filofax one office visit. Rodman could have not accepted, of course, but that would have meant he had not accepted the reciprocating attraction that had been obvious from the moment they shook hands over the convention table, that he denied the hard kernel of fire in his genitals Delia so strikingly acknowledged and fanned with the athletic grace of her firm body, a simple leggy stretch from her seat, and a "Hello." And he also soon discovered that she cared for Howard but felt immersed by him, surrounded, that he pushed too fast for things like security and the steady road to a future already tarred and leveled and cooled and set. She saw a loving light in Howard, but no heat.

Rodman always felt Delia had been attracted to the dark bolt of ambition that shot through him at that time of his life, an ambition and strength of purpose that ran counter to all of his father's years of rooted placidity and resentment. Rodman used his manic counterculture self, his protester, experimenter, mind-journeyer, and squeezed it into a new mold, one in which aggressiveness was equated with success, in which an energetic pitch need not sell a high, but a high rise. It was all a matter of reshaping. He acted no more like a freak than he looked. He was a groomed young man now in his early twenties, his suits from the proper European tailors, his shoes the shine of a moonlit Mediterranean night. He was taking college courses after work—he was dabbling in real estate, law, business management—and always looking into opportunities, prospects, any opening that would dare present itself to the imposing pile of drug money he had accumulated. That was when Janus Mountain loomed before him as the land coup it soon became. But only because of Howard's help.

After the initial jolt and acrimonious break-off, Howard seemed to take Delia's leaving him in stride, though Rodman was to this day unaware of Howard's group therapy sessions that lasted over five years. Delia always had Howard's heart at the end of her polished fingernail, balanced there like a juggler's pin, always afraid to let it fall, yet not wanting such a responsibility. She didn't want to use him or hurt him any further. It was with great hesitation that she asked Howard to have Rodman be part of the Janus deal, work the finances, since Rodman was still a novice in land development maneuvers. Howard agreed, made his money, made his punch lines, made Rodman's reputation, kept him as a friend, fellow cabin mate and sometimes business partner, but mostly Howard basked in the grateful green light of Delia's eyes for his true reward. It has ever been that way, Rodman thought, rocking there in the cabin's living room after dinner, sipping nervously at a small glass of Chablis, watching Howard reflect and draw warmth from his affection for Delia as a loved and loving old flame, as he now spoke about her, asking Carl to get the recipe from Delia for that "unreal" avocado salad dressing she served at the party.

"Speaking of recipes . . ." Carl said, rising in order to move to the kitchen and make the mint cocoa he had promised Howard, a lifetime chocoholic. On the way, Rodman fiddled in his jeans for Delia's painkillers. They felt like the little creek pebbles he would collect as a boy, worn smooth and round, only to be unpocketed in a plucking inside-out maneuver by Aunt Lucy every time she wanted to do a wash. The fingertip feel of the pills comforted him in the same way the pebbles had.

Howard was still cozying at the fireplace sipping his wine as Rodman prepared the cocoa as quick as he could, but without clumsiness as a by-product of his haste. Howard being a notoriously light sleeper in the country stillness, Rodman needed him totally unconscious while he tended to Sonny. He fisted the five spherical hits of Noctec, when he caught a whiff of air, warmed by the sour pungency of Chablis, and glanced over his shoulder. Howard was stretched out in the door frame like a long-armed monkey. Now, Carl knew he couldn't take a chance that Howard might spot a secretive move, or hear an incongruous plop. Especially in the sudden silence.

"You know, I've been meaning to ask," Howard said with a serious expression. "You ever find out what the deal was with Pat Dokes?"

Rodman tried not to tense. Where did *this* come from? "What do you mean?"

"I mean, why she left your company in a heartbeat two weeks ago. I was, you know, looking forward to seeing her at the bash. You didn't invite her?"

"Sure," Rodman said. "She knew about it weeks ago. I guess, I don't know. She never replied. She could have come."

"Isn't that a little strange . . . ?"

"Yes—"

"I mean, the whole thing. You say you don't know why she quit. She doesn't come to an important party. Doesn't it bother you?"

"*Yes,*" Rodman said, more forcefully than he realized, the topic and his task at hand both pressuring him too hard. The Noctec was getting tacky in his fist from the sweat.

"Yes," he repeated with a breathy laugh, a shucking, "of

course it does. She never told me anything, no whys. . . . She didn't quit in order to avoid seeing you, if that's what you're thinking." But even Rodman's quip had no effect on Howard's browful of thought.

"It had to be something, though," he remarked. "It's real curious."

The friends looked at each other for a moment straight-faced. Then Rodman turned back to the cup of cocoa without a word, his stomach grinding.

"Hey, I just remembered," Howard blurted, as though breaking through a watery surface from submersion. "I brought some things for you to read at some point about the Crogin Towers project. Take a second. And, oh!—something about Braxton Cole."

Rodman stirred. "What about him?"

"No, nothing earth-shattering to pin the bastard. Just a long article in *V.I.P. Weekly*. Pictures and stuff like that."

Rodman's eyes brightened. "Hey, you think you could put the magazine and Crogin Towers material in my room so I don't forget it tomorrow?"

"Sure," Howard said, and in a blink the door frame was freed. So, too, were the red, now pinkish, pills, their ruddy dye staining Rodman's palm by the mix with its sweaty film. In a tumbling rush down his open hand, they fell into the rich, hot liquid. He stirred them in methodically to make sure they were disintegrated.

"Done," Howard said, reappearing.

"Well . . . thanks for thinking of me," Carl said. "I really want to read that article now that you brought it. You know I met the man about a month ago, for about two seconds, at a mayoral luncheon. Shook hands. That was it."

"All nicey, nicey."

"Oh, yeah. Wears these big-mother glasses, like out to his ears with the lenses."

Howard produced a tiny smile. "A blind man, huh?"

"Makes him look like a *frog* man."

Howard laughed. "Well, I figured you'd like to see the article. It's more of a puff piece than anything, but whatever. I know from experience. You have to know all you can about a rival, am I right?"

The cup in Rodman's hand seemed even heavier, as though burdened by the portent of Howard's question, and a paranoiac flow of heat burned through him, rushed to his head. There was something knowing about Howard's little grin, not a happy grin, his strange remark—Was it strange? Was it a challenge? Rodman pushed down hard on his emotions and brought the ice of reason to bear on his inflamed mind. What better time to be distrustful, he thought, to hear the subtle whisper of innuendo, to see smiles as scythe-shaped threats, than when you are slipping one of your best friends a kick-ass killer of a mickey.

"Right," Rodman said, and he handed Howard the mug.

Howard raised it nose-level, just to witness with pleasure its sinewy trail of vapor, to breathe in a minty facial. "Smells great. Let's see if it lives up to its potential."

Rodman nodded. "Let's." Then Howard took his first big gulp.

It was now just after midnight, and Rodman, understandably anxious, checked to confirm the reality of his gun. He dragged the travel pouch toward him on the bedsheet, already feeling the heft of the weapon in his effort. He reached inside and took out the unopened envelopes and office reports, the magazine and minicassette recorder, finally removing the silver pistol, and held it for a moment, looking at it as though wondering if it was going to cooperate.

After placing it back into the throat of the bag, Rodman thumbed through the magazine, trying to steer his thoughts, his *being*, away from his deed, just for a while, a little peace for a while. He began to read the Braxton Cole article, to learn once more about Cole's privileged upbringing and his Yale scholarship and his monied-self-made-manhood (the paradox wherein someone starts with two million in inheritance and *then* gets rich) and his state capitol old-boy networking and all that other P.R. prattle. Rodman read how Cole loved American Revolution artifacts, mile-long jogs on the beach, and every Gary Cooper movie ever made, read how the scope of his business acumen—and then Rodman jolted from a singular thought, a late arrival: Howard had put this magazine in his pouch—could Howard have seen the gun?

Rodman's face flushed, and he cursed his own stupidity. He rose up, angry, thinking in a blur. But if Howard saw it, wouldn't he have said something? Rodman didn't normally carry a weapon, not even to the lonely starkness of a Janus Mountain retreat; there wasn't even the proverbial shotgun over the mantelpiece. Rodman started shoveling the papers, the letters, the memos, magazine, tape recorder, scooping it all and thrusting it into the travel sack. He had to go. He had to start the procedure. He couldn't wait. He'd wait in the lot. He'd sit in the muck and rusty bed of pipes and debris, and feel his purpose, not this panic. He had to feel his purpose.

He moved with speed and without sound toward the other end of the cabin and listened. The susurrous sounds of steady breathing from the guest room were good omens, and a light-footed dip of the head within revealed a bundled blanket and Howard facing away, sleeping.

Rodman jumped into his car, his pistol tucked into his belt, the safety on—the safety was on?—the safety was on, and he sped off down Mandrake Road. He felt dizzy, but that wasn't quite it . . . tilted was more like it, top-heavy, leaning, and within a quarter of a descendant mile Rodman realized it wasn't him. It *was* him, but not *just* him—it was the fucking car. He stopped along a scraggly embankment and jumped out again into the cold bite of darkness. He bent over under his headlights and stared, disbelieving, blinking, numbing. He had a flat.

Rodman blinked some more, a tic of circumstance. It was a joke. It was worse than a joke; it was fucking absurd. Immediately his hands were all over the tire, feeling it, and within seconds he spotted the culprit, a bent-up nail head, and in the utter silence of the roadside he could now hear the hiss of venomous air. Jesus!

Rodman knew he didn't have a spare; who the fuck remembers to replace spares after you use them? There *was* a repair kit. Rodman's fingers fumbled with the kit's sticky compound, pulled the nail, applied the sealant. Even when he was done, shivering from the cold, a cold assisted by fear, anticipation— What time was it? Thank God, he started early—he knew he needed air.

He hurried back into the car and drove the half mile down

the road to the gas station. He eased up around the steep bend, knowing Koontz's place was just past a familiar crescent of rock, and killed the lights, then took his foot off the gas. He rolled silently toward one of the red sentrylike gas tanks, making sure Koontz wasn't at home, that he and his wife did, in fact, go to comfort a convalescent sister-in-law. As hoped, Koontz's pickup was nowhere to be seen, the store and back windows dark. Rodman slowed the car near the battered air pump.

The high-pitched *ping*, sounding out at measured intervals while Rodman held the hose to the fluted nipple of the tire, was like a misplaced clock chime singing out weakly in the black of night, marking the hour, trying to draw distinct lines in the indistinct darkness surrounding him. He looked at his watch; the hands glowed a few minutes after one. The air pump's final chime disagreed. Fourteen o'clock it said before it stopped. Rodman concurred with the latter—he was somewhere adrift, out of real time.

Rodman parked two short blocks from the designated lot at approximately three-thirty, his car abutting a headless parking meter. He was still early, which was good. He walked down the sidewalks, broken with eruptions of concrete and shimmering with specks of finely ground glass, sidewalks like solid waves in a storm-wrenched ocean, glittering from the light of hunching streetlamps. The few former three-story residential apartment buildings he passed were beaten in, many sightless without windows, and reminded him of the time his father took him through this strip, even then well-decayed, to show his son what World War II towns looked like when he was on recon after an Allied bombing. It was a good place to have a death.

Then Rodman passed a playground that stretched out adjacent to the Bundridge grammar school, a dark chocolate-brown box of a structure with catcher's masklike bars on the windows and barbed wire on the fence encasing the play area. He had forgotten about this place, felt an abdominal hollow form, not just because of this playground; *any* playground, *all* playgrounds. . . . He quickened his pace.

Rodman seated himself up against the south wall of the Skidmore factory, let it tower behind him, let it become his backbone. He positioned himself in such a way as to see over the calf-high parabolas of weeds to every side of the lot's perimeter. In this knees-to-chin posture, he waited for Vance.

It was ten after four when Rodman spied someone entering the far end of the debris-ridden plot. He knew it was Vance from over a block's distance, the way he moved, that shoulder-to-shoulder sway, not so much a swagger, but a dragging of his spatulate bones through dense air, one at a time, like a two-paddled oar. Vance's long hair was down now, riding free, unlike last week. Now it was the way Rodman was used to it, lanky and brown—thinning rapidly, he noticed. Aging finally strikes Sonny Vance, he thought.

Still, Vance seemed fresh and ready for business at four in the morning, Vance's prime time. He wore his clawed-looking bomber jacket over a gray ALCATRAZ: UNLISTED NUMBER tee shirt, and shrunken blue jeans with the fly missing a button. His spotty calfskin boots still had high enough heels to give him a sense of stature, no matter how artificial.

Vance stopped short when he saw Rodman on the ground and he chuckled snidely, almost losing the half-smoked cigarette dipping from his lips. Vance threw it to the ground anyway, and toed it into the dirt, able now to vocalize his laugh.

"What's with the squat?" he said. "Looks like you're taking a crap." His eyes quick-scanned the surroundings. "Though in this place . . . we're talking improvement."

Rodman stayed silent and lifted himself up. He glanced over, down the length of the wall, almost forgetting to check, though he had checked on Friday before going home—the garbage Dumpster, the ten-by-five green metal container on wheels, just below a first floor ledge, its lid open and waiting, its contents putrefying, the bin still used because the cavernous first floor of the clothes factory was also still used by various city departments as an all-purpose storage facility, a.k.a. universal dumping grounds.

"Yeah . . ." Vance pooched his lips, nodding, as though engaged in an actual conversation. "Remember how we were going to, like, take one of these holes—" His fingers indicated any number of dilapidated, abandoned walk-ups across the street. "—and kind of set it up? I mean, make it Freak Headquarters, U.S.A.? Make it like the cornerstone for a true Pig-

Free Zone, No Rules Allowed. Remember that? We were going to out-Haight-Ashbury Haight-Ashbury. That was to be *after* our major joyride across the states, after we saved up some major bucks from the shit we were selling. . . ." Vance wouldn't stop nodding and yammering. "Guess we spent our money on different things, huh? I mean, after you busted me up and split on me—*you* wound up buying the other side of the tracks with your savings, the *good* side. You started your mountain, your Shangri-la Condo thing, for all the rich folk with *your* savings. I didn't pull that kind of shit with my savings." Vance peered at his friend with one eye. "You know why?"

Rodman didn't answer.

"I didn't *have* any friggin' savings, that's why." Vance cut a quick laugh. "Spent it all on the *now*, man. I mean, you know. That's all we ever have. You never caught on. You have to screw 'em while your dick is *hard*—it's gonna go down someday. You hear what I'm saying?"

Rodman still didn't answer. He was stiff, his throat pulsing.

Vance finally shut up, finally shut off that bullshit-machine of his, a little wired from the so-so powder he had finessed over the weekend in a corner booth at the Black Hole Club from two teenage metal heads. His meandering gaze gradually centered on Rodman's short denim jacket replete with pins, on his Red Sox baseball cap dotted with flies.

"Whoa," Vance said, taking a step back, "Marlin Fucking Perkins, man."

And again he laughed, and again Rodman stayed silent. It didn't matter that Marlin F. Perkins had almost everything to do with *Wild Kingdom* and almost nothing to do with lake fishing, but it was just Vance regurgitating pieces of old *Tonight* shows he had watched, mostly while blasted and sometimes while getting laid. It was the only thing Vance would ever claim he had in common with Middle America: he had fucked at his best during Carson monologues. Then Vance finally, *finally*, became aware of the vacuumlike silence. "So what's going on? . . . Where's the money?"

Rodman had been waiting for that silence, for that still, empty air, for a space minus anything between them, minus talk, minus hope, minus life, knew he couldn't do it in the noise, the entropic chatter of sounds from Vance's mouth, like verbal obstacles to his thinking straight, his keeping himself focused, keeping himself from being sucked into the past, into the rationalization of things, the rationalization of death, drugs, of having no responsibility *to* or *for* anything but your own fat ass in the name of self-righteous freedom. Rodman had needed a clear-headed stasis point before he could reach into the tuck of his belt and gingerly draw out the shiny silver revolver. It glinted even in the embracing darkness, reflecting the mesh of muted light the cloud-hidden moon offered.

Rodman's breathing seemed as though it had stopped, as when an important person has entered the room and you are in awe, stunned by his or her dominant presence. Vance was motionless, too. He looked at the gun, trying to identify what it was, then tried to place it with who was holding it, both the pistol and the man pointing it at him not signifying, this picture pattern not holding in his brain, tearing; the channels must be mixed, the head was wrong, the gun not real—

Then came an unexpected moment for Rodman, the utter dread on Vance's face. His innate wiliness seemed blunted; his bagged eyes became enlarged, terrified and pitiable; his mouth quavered. Rodman allowed the gun to dip a few degrees from the weight of what he saw. There was nothing "fresh" here, nothing four-in-the-morning vital, except the freshly healing bruises suffered last Tuesday, their fading purple rejuvenated with Vance's blush of fear. Mostly, there was a withering of skin, an abuse of body, bone and brain, all of which formed what was in fact an old shit-ass hippie blackmailer, someone who—in the words of Rodman's father—needed a man's haircut and a damn long bath.

The other twist to the moment came from Vance's body as well. It screwed itself around, awkward, stumbling. And, shock-propelled, he started to run away. Vance's pitiful appearance and his flight for his life left Rodman dumbfounded, unprepared. Still—he raised the gun once again and aimed down the sight at Vance's back, no more than fifteen feet from him. . . . Still—he was unable to shoot. Rodman had expected anything—Vance standing him down, mocking him, mocking his determination, laughing at him, even charging him—*any*thing but this terror, this stunned belief in his own death at Rodman's hands.

So Rodman ran, too, ran after him as he would a dog gotten loose from a leash, Vance's hair flopping wildly, his breath short, his feet hitting the uneven ground at ankle-bending angles, the V-creased beer cans kicking up at him, the concrete chunks stubbing him, the winding, bending reinforced wires branching up from trashy mounds stabbing him, slashing him, the world was against him, the fucking world was against him, and he fell, head first, arms braced, into the weedy patch of ground, dislodging some soured milk cartons and rotten fruit rinds in the tumble, then spun around, looked at his patsy, his buddy, his killer, and crabbed backward for a few seconds, before bonging his head against an oil drum that angled out of the dirt like some ocean liner's smokestack. Delirious, Vance sat there and closed his eyes, heard the footfalls stop before him, kept the darkness within him for a while as Rodman watched the cornered animal's anemic-looking belly bellow in and out, and so raised his gun again, and so shook just as hard as before, not sure about it, not sure about anything.

They posed there for a while, the two former revelers, travelers, dealers, twenty years ago their paths forking away from each other, yet imperceptibly arcing inward, unwittingly angling toward a convergence, their movement circular with the passage of time, and now they were nothing but a gut-sucking breath apart from the completion of that vicious circle. And Rodman wasn't sure about what to do or how to do it.

But then Vance pulled himself taut, his eyelids popping open like a lizard's. He gave Rodman an up-from-under look of contempt, a smile-cut scowl, and he began to laugh. Rodman just stood, aiming, wavering.

"Asshole!" Vance shouted. "You just want to kill the messenger. Everybody always kills the fucking messenger." He shook his head in disgust. "But the message lives on. The message *lives on, jerkoff!* It never dies. Truth'll always be there," Vance pounded his chest once, "whether or not I let it out for you."

Rodman was only half listening, didn't want to listen—

"So what are you fucking afraid of? What is it you're unwilling to pay your poor hippie-dippie friend not to say, not to *tell the stinking world!*" Vance laughed again, felt in charge again, desperately so.

—and yet Rodman *did* want to listen, for this was more like it, this was what he wanted to kill—Rodman's finger curled, his palm more firmly readied—that *fuck-it* face, that *life's-a-goof, dipshit!* sneer—his eye burned down the barrel—wanted to wipe it clean, cleanse it with blood, *let the blood do it,* Eric's blood, the blood of Christ—his hands trembled violently, his finger trying to pull—He died for your sins—*Pull it!*—Eric died for your sins!

"Child killer!" Vance shouted out, edging up the oil drum, his knees almost buckling, now steadied. "You got that, everybody?" Vance spat out another laugh, climbing, nearly standing. *"Carl Rodman is a child k—"*

Rodman fired, though his eyes were all but clenched shut. The first shot caught Vance in the upper chest, closer to his shoulder than his heart, and Vance crashed back against the rot-encrusted barrel, then he let out a scream and charged Rodman. He flung himself, his arms, in a catapultlike lunge, his hands just reaching Rodman's neck when the second shot, its blast muted because of the embrace of bodies, caught Vance full in the stomach, like a screw boring through his intestines. Vance clawed his way down Rodman's heaving, shaking chest, tearing at his jacket, Vance's hands finally two defiant fists, as were his red-webbed eyes, and he fell at Rodman's feet, Rodman taking two dizzy steps back, amazed, aghast at what he had finally done, yet alert in his withdrawal, not wanting any blood to stain his clothes, wanting to stay clean, just like what this act was, a cleaning.

Rodman's hands and lower arms were quaking as though electrically charged. He sucked in lungfuls of air to stay standing, stay clear-headed and purposeful. Dump him, dump him, dump him—like a drumbeat on each long breath—came from his head—or was it his chest?—then Rodman sprang forward, retucking the gun in his belt, and he forklifted Vance from behind by the armpits. He dragged him over the abusive terrain, Rodman scanning the area as he grunted with each sharp, elongated pull, alert for the unlikely stray onlooker—a homeless wanderer, a hophead who couldn't sleep—though any witnesses at this hour and in this neighborhood were not known by authorities to be the most reliable or the most likely to invite the police to look into something suspicious.

When he reached the green rectangular garbage bin, Rodman gave Vance one final hoist from behind, letting Vance's chest and head flop over the inside wall of the Dumpster. Then Rodman flipped Vance's lower body over, and the stinking mattress-thick odor from the refuse seemed to cushion the thrown body's impact. Only Vance's left arm thunking the metal side gave Rodman a start.

"Damn it!" Rodman verbalized to himself, watching his hands as though he were a frightened onlooker as they still twitched involuntarily, unwilling to be unplugged. Suddenly, Rodman found himself running in order to unjangle the muscled cords, all knotty and jittering, up and down his spine, his legs; in order to unthink what he had just done and what would be done; to unthink how the sanitation truck driver would appear with his mammoth L-armed hoist and slide its shafts of iron through the sides of the Dumpster and raise the heavy bin up and up and over his cab's roof, and toss the smeared newspapers and colored cardboard scraps and foam containers and chunks of unidentifiable foodstuffs and lifeless body into the voluminous receptacle of waste behind him while tapping the beat of a Janet Jackson tune in his head on the steering wheel, all this at five-thirty this Tuesday morning, the scheduled pickup time.

Rodman had chosen this spot for just that reason, had investigated garbage bin pickup times at the Department of Sanitation under the pretense of future building purchases, knew this desolate area well, knew of its isolation, found out about the truck's early collection at the clothes factory lot, and the exact days, envisioned Vance's body being sloughed from the truck, embedded within tons of waste, layered amid the fetid mounds at the county dump. And even if the body were ever found later—a day, a week—who was to say from where the corpse appeared, from what truck, from which pickup point?

Rodman reached his car, out of breath, panting. He slung open the door, dropped himself into the seat, slammed the door behind, and sat there a moment. Then he leaned his forehead on the leather-wrapped steering wheel, bracing himself, still trying to unthink everything, keeping his heart hard, pressurized, like a jag of coal pressed to diamond density. Yet for all the unthinking he was trying to do, there was one clean, brutal conclusion that overwhelmed his burning brain: that whatever else the sixties were, they were finally— determinedly—unquestionably—irrevocably—*dead*.

Howard Bernbaum's face was a pale mask of morning, drained of sunshine, as chalky-toned as the clouds that gathered over the lake. "Jesus, I feel like shit and a half."

"You look about that, too," Rodman remarked, sitting hunched over the back of a pinewood kitchen chair, sipping black coffee, watching his friend shuffle his feet toward the counter for the orange juice container. Howard picked it up and inspected it.

"You sleep all night?" Rodman asked.

"Mm—what?" Howard looked away from the juice, distracted. "Oh! Oh, yeah, I did. I can't believe it. I slept like I was dead or something, *that's* a first!" He shook his head. "But I woke up . . ." Howard began to rub his abdomen as though feeling for foreign objects. "You think this OJ is too acidic for a big-time bad stomach?" Howard looked like an overgrown baby teetering there: his glasses slipping down his nose; his hairy firm chest bare, as were his feet; his underwear briefs saggy and off-white from unbleached washings. Rodman pulled an exaggerated face of uncertainty, while his mind steadily raced ahead for excuses. "Maybe. Didn't sit so well with me. My stomach's doing a number, too, this morning. It was probably our extra helpings of sour cream on the baked potatoes. Could have been turning, you know?"

Howard shrugged then placed the plastic cap back on the container. "Maybe it was your *cocoa*," he said in a half-kidding, half-accusatory tone.

Rodman remained stoic, his voice one of reason. "But I didn't have any, so how could I have the same upset stomach? It had to be something we *both* ate."

Howard, leaning from the open refrigerator door, raised an eyebrow, then nodded at the logic. He grabbed a milk carton and brought it to the table, where he reviewed his friend more closely. "*You* actually don't look so great, now that I see you," he said, sitting down. "Did *you* sleep all night?"

Rodman took another swallow from his black brew. "Of course. You would have heard me if I made a sound and been up with me."

"True."

"No, I slept fine. Overwork's just catching up to me."

"True."

Rodman breathed out a quiet laugh, and Howard smiled at him, blearily, though Carl's amusement was not caused by Howard's tease, but by the fact that nothing about this moment was close to true. What was true was not sitting in this kitchen sipping at a cup of Kenyan roast after a serene nocturnal slumber. What was true was sitting in his BMW flooring the pedal, peeling away from that scrapyard of a neighborhood after he had added one more dead soul to it. It was his then stopping at a twenty-four-hour liquor store and finishing off at least a third of a bottle of scotch with throat-blazing gulps, before he drove from the parking lot. Off the wagon? What the fuck—he was off the *planet*, off the *scale*, over the *edge*—he had just killed a man, for God's sake, and he had to quiet those hands, those quaking fingery things, all knocking knobs of bone and plunking tendons, that just wouldn't *stop*, wouldn't let him drive. He couldn't concern himself about falling off now, about breaking the vows to himself and family. All he cared about was its mind-dulling effects, its strength in quelling tides of emotion to a foggy yawn. He always remembered liking it, of course; liking it too much, really. This was a short-term thing, he had assured himself, a medicinal treatment of the moment, the benefits of which he immediately felt. His hands gradually steadied, his heartbeat slowed. He headed up Mandrake Road with thickening fatigue. Still, he knew the road by instinct, knew it from youth, from moon-blind nights of pitch-darkness.

Rodman had pulled his car into the loose bluestone driveway at just about six-thirty, record time, by his account, the dawn seeming merely a lighter shade of night. Once inside the cabin, he made one more breath-holding venture by Howard's room to assure himself his friend was asleep. Then he disrobed quickly and brushed his teeth, making certain any bitter wisp of booze was minted over. When he finished and stared at himself in the bathroom mirror, he began to see Danny. He thought of how Danny's face would look upon him now with such pathetic disdain, how he would relish seeing his father's blatant need to suck "the fat tit of Mother Alcohol." The remark would hurt him, as it did now, though it was one of those remarks Rodman remembered, not because the remark was actually said in real life, but because it was said in one of his imagined internal arguments, those made-up cathartic fights we have that bear such vividness, such scarring verity, they become part of your interpersonal history, your relationship. They *become* true.

"I'll tell you what's also true, buddy," Howard said, then winced with another tummy grab. "No way I can stay up here for the rest of the day."

"You feel that bad," Rodman said.

"Yeah, well, if it *was* the sour cream, I had more of it than you—"

"You don't have to run excuses by me," Rodman interrupted, flashing on how Howard often needed to defend his manhood in silly ways. "You should go. I should stay. The only way for me to not overwork is to not *go* to work. I'll treat my stomach here and not at the office."

Howard nodded his agreement, though his face belied another twinge of pain.

The lake that morning proved a bit rugged as a moist wind brushed through the tall parade of pines and agitated the waters. Rodman didn't notice it much, didn't care, either. The plank-board boat was his point of isolation, his cradle. There in the slate-gray water, within the mountainous surroundings, he slept, weary, lightly rocking, his head on a seat cushion against the stern. The scotch had imbued him in warmth, as he decided on a few more swigs before he ambled down to the shore, his denim jacket picking up the country dampness, as though it had swelled, alive with fresh air and sweat and bass and dew. Rodman awoke when splashes of afternoon sunlight heated his face, insulated the length of his body. He was drying out, both externally and internally, as his first thoughts were of the remaining quarter bottle of golden liquid left on shore, propped up next to the gardening shed, and of how he would avoid that path when he rowed back.

He stood and stretched, felt woozy, and sat back down. He

hesitated before opening up the fishing tackle box, just looked at it awhile, then let his head clear a bit more and embraced the green serenity of the woods, the bird songs, the natural aliveness of things. Of course, he thought of his mother.

As a boy, whenever he was frequently alone on the lake or in a shade-dark bower or atop a pyramid of rocks lording over a dip of pasture, Carl would share the moment with her, would *be* with her—with her voice, anyway—and even that wasn't so, having never heard her speak. It was his aunt Lucy's voice telling him about her, about Maureen Rodman, Maureen Barney before she married, and the sisters' lives together on a farm just north of Janus Mountain in Stroller Valley where they and his grandparents raised sheep and goats as well as grew a panoply of crops. Your mother lived for the land, Aunt Lucy would tell him, your father just lives *on* it as though it were his right, as though the fish weren't God's creatures, but *his*, as though the land itself weren't owned by the Lord.

(In light of Lucy's words, Rodman had often felt as duplicitous and divided as the mountain itself when it came to his later success stemming from its real estate potential. Half of him despised what the developed side of Janus Mountain had become because of his initial speculation and planning and ambition, yet his other half felt vindicated, felt it was flexing a muscle in his father's face.)

The young Rodman would hear all kinds of familial stories of the past exclusively at the small white Formica kitchen table while he waited for Aunt Lucy to prepare lunch. She was not able to go out for extensive periods in the rich sunlight to share the majesty of God's doings because of a cataract problem she never had the money to treat, so it would be her insistent, reedy voice that young Rodman took with him, and it would somehow transform into his mother's recitations.

His father may have taught him every angle about how to snare the lake-bound fish, but it was his mother's voice that made up stories about them, silly mythlike tales about how they got their scales or why God had put an eye on each side of their head and none in the middle, just as his mother would tell made-up stories to Aunt Lucy about the Kidd Family of goats—"Little Maureen, by sainted Jesus, there at the birthings, each and every one," while the older, but more timid,

Aunt Lucy couldn't stomach the thick-blooded ejaculation of the baby goat from its mother. Lucy would hide in the loft or pretend to be busy with a mop. Meanwhile, Rodman's mother would immediately give each kid a name and a set of predetermined character traits so that each could develop in her ongoing make-believe family saga. She did the same for the sheep and their fledgling lambs. These animals, these children of God were your mother's children, and they all grew up and prospered in her imagination, Rodman heard the voice say. Children allowed you to imagine a future.

You weren't supposed to kill them, he himself now added, and stopped his thoughts right *there*, as though corking a wine bottle with a flat-handed blow. His eyes moved from the landscape to the tackle box again, ready to do what he came out there to do. He opened the box but there were no sinkers, no flies—he hadn't even carried his rod on board. All that emerged was the silver gun clenched in his hand.

In his earlier plans, he envisioned himself at this final step, standing up between the oar rings, arching his back, his arms extending as though about to fling a discus, then letting fly, the gun spinning upward, a graceful, slow-motionlike flight, barrel over handle in a heaven-bound rise, then angling, accelerating downward, finally cutting through the water's surface like a streamlined waterfowl slashing through to the depths for its prey. It would glint no more, nestled in the sandy lake bottom.

But such an act now seemed far too aggrandizing a gesture. Rodman simply dangled the gun at his fingertips for an instant and let it dribble over the side like so much backwash. It plopped and vanished, and he sat there awhile immobile and waited, waited as though his turn was supposed to come up, his turn for some sense of true relief.

Rodman drove back home by late afternoon, hoping to catch the outskirts of Hollowsport by just past rush hour. He anticipated an easy ride, though someone didn't let his back muscles and neck tendons know. He thought about how he would go about convincing Delia to let her long fingers knead the bumpy length of his bow-tense spine. With him on his stomach, he wanted to feel her strength tonight, her lean thighs pressing his, squeezing him like a fleshy vise, as she sat on his bare buttocks atop the cool of a taut bedsheet. He could feel her hands unfold his muscles, slow and hard and unforgiving, and then he would detect a dampness, a tacky spot of wetness that would paint the upper part of the crevice between his cheeks, so that when he was ready, when he was rolled out like a ream of silk, smoothed, relaxed and stimulated simultaneously, he would turn over in place, still held in the carnal vise, and he would slide up her moistened lips, into the damp open source of the slick spot. He wanted to be ridden and pounded and taken by Delia, by the unyielding meat of her legs, the sucking grip of her vagina.

The heat rose to Ródman's cock and to his face, reddening it, then flashing red and he was braking sharply, a slight swerve, and a police unit's roof light threw another crimson flicker at his eyes as it passed by, speeding ahead, no siren, but too fast for—

Rodman realized he was in his neighborhood. His directional instinct had brought him through the city and into the adjacent suburb. He saw the patrol car, now not so much a car as two red taillights with a red flasher at the apex of the crimson triangle, the triangle floating, suspended far ahead in the dark of the tree-shrouded streets. Rodman's pulse was still racing from the patrol unit's sudden pass on the narrow residential road; then the red dots darted right, like three streaks of vanishing spray paint, turned at the corner where he was going to turn, and his pulse never slowed.

Rodman made the right as well and leaned closer to the windshield, pulling himself to the steering wheel as though he were bringing the front of the car up to his chin like a protective blanket. It was fast becoming dusk; he was having a hard time seeing, but somehow he did not want to put on his headlights. At the bend into his semicircular street, he was suddenly in a line of slowing cars, not many, three or four ahead, one behind. But rounding the curve, Rodman could see the same steady sweeps of red light that had struck him moments ago, this time striking a shingled garage up ahead, its source still unseen at this angle. His heart began to beat at the same rate the red light flashed, to thump at the concrete block inside him. Shit! he thought. Shit on me!

His mind could not comprehend this—it had to be something else, something ridiculous, something tragic, maybe both, maybe Hallie Fouche on a snooping sortie fell into his pool, her leaden foot propelling her down, cracking a few tiles as it thudded, keeping her erect like gurgling statuary. He thought of his gun. There was no way anyone could find that. He thought of Vance. Too soon for him, far too soon . . .

And it wasn't Hallie—yes, it was. The far end of the curve produced a hazy vision of his neighbor on her cement walkway between two manicured shrubs the size and shape of six-foot-high teardrops. She was talking to a young policeman, who kept nodding and nodding, and Rodman, trying to figure out what was going on, peered over the dashboard to see what looked like another patrol car, this one without a beating light, blocking the road from the other direction, forcing a single lane, and other cars facing the wrong way, official-looking cars parked, it seemed, and that's when Hallie caught sight of his slow-motion BMW and then his face. He had no idea what look he had revealed to her, but hers was clear. It was one of terrible recognition. She shouted and shouted and pointed at him emphatically, over and over, and the young police officer shot him a fierce glance and shouted as well. Another officer, older, a beer gut protruding before him, began trotting straight at Rodman from two cars up, his hand tapping his pistol holster.

Rodman felt every surge of his hard-thrusting blood drain from his head, his eyes. The line of cars were barely moving; he felt onstage, like something for sale rotating slowly on a display and about to be snatched up. He spun his head around to find an opening, then jerked the steering wheel to his right, screeching up the blacktop driveway of the Wainwrights' house, then cutting left, over the inlaid marble-block boarders of their lawn, and over the greener-than-green sod and built-in sprinkler system.

Rodman heard the older cop shout something that sounded like "Halt!" though he couldn't tell for sure. The officer angled to his left, cutting between a parked minivan on the street and a thick elm, with his gun, now in his hand. But the cop couldn't cut him off mid-lawn as Rodman pushed the gas pedal, veered away from the black Cadillac Seville in the adjacent driveway and swung right onto the sidewalk, barreling down the cementway, looking to cut back onto the road to his left at an opening wide enough for a sharp, fast turn, for an opening sans car, intruding tree, or narrow driveway ramp.

All the while, the while being all of eight seconds since Hallie's cry, since he bolted off the road, panicked—that's what he did, didn't he? He panicked!—still, all the while, these *seconds*, he expected a shot, like when out your city window you hear the screech of a brake, imagine a careening car, and internally brace yourself for the brittle-sounding crash, so too did Rodman brace himself after the policeman's warning shout for the crack of a bullet. So, as though he couldn't wait any longer, he briefly glanced back, an instant's head turn, left side, quick; what had he hoped to see with such a move? A sharp-eyed cop in his shooting stance? A silent, piercing shell enter his own brain? He saw nothing, that is, nothing you wouldn't ordinarily see from the sidewalk—cars, curb, leaves, garbage cans—flashing past. When he spun his head back forward, he saw the little girl.

She was immediately right *there*, blond braids, mouselike nose, thin arms dangling from a yellow jumper, a white blouse with yellow piping and embroidered teddy bear over the pocket, no more than four, squatting on the sidewalk, a piece of purple chalk in her hand, and she was frozen, looking at him at that placid moment just before the shock of fear locks in, hits your spine and tears at the unsuspecting serenity of your expression. The small girl's ivory-white face was about to tear before his eyes, and then again in a bloody rent of chrome and snapping bones. Rodman felt himself cry out even before the girl could rise halfway and open her lips.

With a knotty maple tree to his immediate left, Rodman's instincts yanked right, the BMW pitching up a steeply inclined lawn, its bank thick with vines, the left bumper just avoiding the frightened girl. Then suddenly the car was momentarily out of control, two right wheels in the air, and its body going into a roll. The left side of the car smashed itself flat and hard onto the sidewalk and began scraping, skidding, the frictional scream of heated door metal searing Rodman's shoulder, then, twenty-five feet later, sliding sideways into the next driveway, slamming into a Thunderbird convertible, and a spray of glass, a pounding jerk of his belted-in body, and

Rodman was finally motionless, a flaccid empty vessel, hardened at the center. There was a momentary silence, but only momentary. He was tipped over in a straight-ahead world. He was in the dark. He didn't see the ash-blond little girl suddenly become that much more valuable, that much more ephemeral, to the scooping, thankful arms of her stunned mother. But he didn't have to see it.

Two officers extracted him from his car as though he had fallen into a mine shaft. With the right door facing the evening sky, they had opened it like a hinged lid, and squinted down into the dim interior, a waft of new leather upholstery sweetening the burnt-rubber base to the air. Afterward, two EMS workers examined him and asked cursory questions which Rodman answered while sitting stoop-shouldered on a short brick wall that abutted an elevated flower bed. He just nodded to everything, he was fine, he was swell, he was dead inside and in the pink of health. He was also looking through the one medical assistant, as though he were tracing paper, at the outline of the real listeners, the real questioners, the two dark-suited gentlemen who not-all-that-patiently waited for their turn to get to him.

The scene was somewhat chaotic now with a cumbersome, squealing tow truck maneuvering into position; a shiny ambulance; police radio chatter; slowed traffic; gawkers; neighbors outside, leaning in to each other like conspirators; more throbbing red lights, some blue, in sharp syncopation, more beats of gaudy brightness than during a bad Iron Butterfly drum solo. *That* was it, Rodman thought, he felt almost stoned. He was so wasted and numb, everything outside of him, outside his skin, felt heightened, loud with purpose, while his visceral self and his humming mind remained inert. He kept touching the bandages on his neck and face that were applied to the glass cuts, kept squeezing his left wrist, which appeared to have been wrenched, all in order to feel sensations, any sensation, even pain would do, while the men, the dark-suited men, no hats, talked of murder, arrest, and Rodman's right to remain silent.

Just words, he thought, and what words, indeed. Indeed, what words would he say to Delia? What would he finally tell her? What was left after this? What could be hidden after this? Still, he was glad Delia hadn't been home to see the carnival of lights outside their house, to see his final descent to the sideshow.

Then he heard the word "evidence" spoken by the more intense of the detectives, his high forehead topping granule-small eyes that offered little sympathy. His moustache twitched in odd ways when he spoke, too, and his cheeks were dotted with divots of acne scars.

Rodman's fingers moved to dally autonomously with Eric's pin, only—Rodman dropped his eyes quickly—it was gone! It had been severed loose from its dangling threads, had somehow fallen off, was torn off . . . was pulled . . . and . . . and . . . it all came in on him, a weight of understanding quickly descended. *That* was their evidence, then. Vance, clutching at him—Rodman remembered—fingers like prongs trying to pull and scrape off Rodman's clothes, skin, as Vance slid down his chest, his thighs. Vance's fist was clenched finally, on the ground, clenched even when Rodman flipped his body over into the bin. But . . . that must be it. They found the body—with the pin—his name on it. Eric's full name on it. Rodman sat stunned. His *son* told them, he thought. A getting even. Another death for a death. His boy Eric knew everything and told them about it.

The word "body" was mentioned, thrown into one of the detective's sentences like a stone in a puddle, and Rodman raised his head at the awakening splash.

"Didn't think you'd find it so soon," Rodman interrupted, though it was barely a breath of words.

The small-eyed detective shut himself up and glanced at his broad-backed partner who stood with his arms crossed. Rodman was trying to figure out if that was his own voice he had just heard.

"Surprise, surprise," the partner said in a tone that made it unclear whether he was referring to the fact that they had found Vance so quickly or that Rodman was finally speaking. *Was* that him speaking?

The small-eyed detective leaned down now, close to Rodman's face, as though he could hear better with those tiny cold pupils than with his ears, his expression businesslike.

"Does that mean that you admit to murder?" he asked evenly. "You admit you did it?"

It *was* his own voice before, he was sure of it, and it was his own voice now. It sprouted like a stubborn green shoot that worms its way up to the surface of a concrete block and breaks through, life triumphant.

"I did it," his voice said.

The small-eyed detective shot an even sharper look at his partner before resuming with Rodman. "You willing to restate that fact on videotape—you know, answer some questions while being filmed?"

Rodman nodded, even though he knew whatever well-paid criminal lawyer Delia had her brother Jack find for him would not appreciate this cooperation with the authorities. But that little green twig of truth had to live, in spite of its roots being so buried and tangled and encased by the ponderous cement block in his chest.

The small-eyed detective rose and nodded. "Well, all right then, let's go."

Rodman was not quick to rise, and heard a wheeled stretcher squeak toward him as he uncoiled himself with effort to a standing position, watching the medical staffer approach.

"I don't need to go to the hospital," Rodman murmured, taking a long breath while dazedly holding his chest. "I'm okay."

The small-eyed detective seemed not to listen. "Uh-huh."

"I want to see my wife, but—"

"What?" The detective moved his feet from the path of the rumbling wheels of the low black gurney being pushed near him toward the medical wagon.

"I want to see my wife," Rodman repeated, attempting to be emphatic.

The cross-armed partner swung out his hands and stepped forward, appearing annoyed. "Sure," he snarled.

He then restrained the low black gurney with his fat-fingered left hand, and Rodman noticed now that this stretcher wasn't black and empty, but black and bulky, and with one deft motion the detective unzipped the top of the dark, shimmering sack and Delia's face appeared, jumped out at him, a face bursting out of a nightmare, a large white face driven up, unearthed from a dirt-dark grave, only it was *her* face, her strong, freckled face, his wife's beautiful, beautiful face and her hair, matted, dark red, streaking her fair cheek, but not hair, but dried jags of blood coming from a hole at the side of her head, her lifeless punctured head.

"You do nice work," the partner remarked icily and was about to zip the body bag back up when the hard, dense, fusion-driven block from inside Rodman's gut exploded into a thousand and one shards of disbelief and horrifying reality, a thousand and one hurts and sins, cutting through him, slashing every vein and nerve, and he screamed out in demented agony, screamed loud, fell to his knees, sucked for air, needing air, and embraced Delia, embraced the cold nothing that she was and screamed out again in an attempt to drown out the last scream, feeling again, feeling every fucking thing again and seeing everything he loved, now the last thing he loved, gone, ripped from him, lost forever, death for death, death for death. . . .

All told, it took the two detectives, the young cop, the ambulance driver, and a shot of chlorpromazine to subdue Rodman, flatten him to the street, meld him with the tar, fade him to black.

8

BARBARA CLOSED THE front door to the second-floor apartment behind them and sadly watched the shadow drift like an isolated cloud over to a scooped-out canvas chair—more appropriate for the outdoors, stolen from his parents' pool house, not missed, just another inconsequential thing like a bottle opener or a son—watched him settle in its valley, in its red-cloth palm, and remain dormant. She watched Danny with his jacket still on, her back against the door, in a timeless sort of duty, on guard, waiting, waiting for anything, a movement, a sound.

Danny hadn't said a word to her when he picked her up at the Mariner's, after he had called its kitchen pay phone from his parents' house to say simply that his father shot his mother, that she was dead, and he would be by the restaurant hours before her usual quitting time. She wasn't able to say anything much into the phone receiver, her throat paralyzed from the news, having thought it was going to be just one of those spur-of-the-moment "I've been thinking of you" calls from Danny that usually illicited a sexual aside from Tolly the cook and an envious nose twitch from her coworker Lynn. All Barbara had been able to choke out in response to the news of Danny's mom's death was a faint "Oh, my God," before he said, "I'm okay, so don't even ask, I'm just . . . okay," and after a moment's silence, he hung up. It sounded clumsy, the receiver rattling in its cradle.

Barbara tried to call the Rodman home from a tenuous memory of their exchange but got the wrong number twice; that, coupled with perturbed remarks from Lynn about two of Barb's impatient tables, forced her to stop trying to reach

Danny, broke her purpose. From then on her nerves jerked her around her assigned serving station. She was unable to think straight—a broiled trout went to a startled medium-well cheeseburger, a Coke to a huffy mineral water—her stifling sobs, not really understanding, the message, its reality, not sinking in, not wanting it to, not knowing who to call back, and then Judd, the floppy-haired new waiter told her that her mother was on the phone.

Barbara told him to say that he didn't think she was still at the restaurant, but Hallie didn't believe him and began yelling. Judd held the pay phone receiver out away from him as though it were something animal, something alive and squalling in his reluctant grasp. From a distance Barbara could hear Hallie's squeaky, mile-a-minute diatribe cum plea cum sermon, a Minnie Mouse gone mad and frantic. Strangely, the frenetic sound actually caused Barbara to calm down, a natural reaction from her of late, to feel and react the opposite of how her mother felt and reacted. It also caused her to realize fully the crime that took place; the world was being affected, her world, it actually happened, and her nerves released its taut net and she let the grief wash over her, let her face flush with the re-alization: Delia Rodman was dead.

A film of tears glazed over her eyes as she took the phone from Judd and said, "He's already told you, Mother. I'm gone."

Then she gently placed the receiver back on the pay phone's hook, its quiet click silencing the wire-crammed squeal. She hung onto the receiver's grip for a moment as though clinging to a spike on a rock face, but then she let go and prepared to leave.

She knew that her mother had been alternately pleading and demanding that she not see Danny, to flee any contact, to es-cape the circle of the Rodmans' influence, but to Barbara that would be a denial of their attraction, their bond. There was something deep and tragic about Danny's family. The Rod-mans had always somehow touched real life, Danny had en-dured real losses—his mind to drugs, his little brother to a hit-and-run driver, his self-respect to his father, and Danny had weathered it all, endured every scar, thickened his armor with-out sacrificing his caring, at least up to now, up to this horror which, Barbara feared, could produce the unhealing rent, Danny's emotional undoing.

Her own mother's losses, even the most serious and inescapable one, that of her foot, was Hallie's talisman to touch in order to hate the world. The Rodmans' losses were things to mourn over, to use as tests of self, to feel the essential vacuum behind the facade of daily living. Barbara was afraid of that vacuum, never named it as such, or rationalized it through as such, but like many people, she was viscerally fascinated by it, because the surface of things didn't seem as though it were enough. To Barbara, the back-from-college Barbara, that is, her house was but a doll's play set, her stepfather a pawing moneybags and human laugh track, and her mother a grotesque, something from a rejected fairy tale, not quite a witch, but someone who would be resentful she couldn't have at least *been* the witch. And her own life? So far, it had been closer to Barbie's, not hers.

She did miss her real father, her memory-enshrined "real life" father, and she felt comforted that at least she could share the growing emptiness with Danny when he came, or so she was thinking as she stood in the glass alcove of the Mariner's Restaurant that night. For a week now she had been doing her waiting for her ride home from Danny *inside*, not outside near the beach, ever since the incident with that bruiser, the dark-haired construction worker with a reptile in his skin. She had never told Danny about what happened under the pier, and she'd been having twisted dreams about it, especially the one where the muscled man with the puss-stained skyline of teeth actually penetrated her, ground her into the sand with his scaly penis, a nightmare that was *too* real. (Dreams, she felt, could take on emotional dimensions that surpassed those of life.) Of late, Barbara even avoided going out at lunchtime with Lynn, which was why her friend had her nose out of joint for the past few shifts.

Abruptly, the violent sputtering of Danny's approaching motorcycle jostled Barbara from her meditative state. When he stopped, he sat there without shutting down the engine, letting the machine between his legs idle loudly, a growl that imbued his stoic form with a shield of sound. He wore his blue-tinted aviator goggles but had no helmet, which was not unusual. His hair had been whipped through the night like an embattled flag, his handsome features worn by the wind. The weight of it all was already testing him. Danny kept looking straight ahead as Barbara walked up to the curb. She caressed his neck, kissed his temple, before straddling the back of the bike.

He then revved the motor and roared off, the back wheel churning street dust and sand, though not before Barbara spotted two dark familiar figures the moment before her and Danny's getaway. It was them—*him* especially—the two of them with caps, being talked to by Mr. Ryan, who ran the adjacent sports bar, the two of them with that kind of football-huddle stance, nodding their heads as they slouched, as though their upper back muscles were too bulked up to allow a straight spine—a Neanderthal stance, she thought.

Her eyes were peeking at them like tiny glowing suns just above a mountain range, which was the high gray crease at the back of Danny's jacket, her arms wrapped around his waist, the side of her head against him like a giant, peering over the slate peaks, hidden from view, watching evil, watching anger, as Sam Ryan, a giant of sorts himself, began to become incensed at the two cave dwellers. But that was all of the tale she could conjure, since the bike pulled away onto Dune Boulevard and brought them here to the one-room flat on Hawthorne Avenue above the used-record store where Danny worked most of the time and fixed guitars through word of mouth some of the time, while the time in between was for "figuring things out" and, more recently, for their newfound love.

Barbara silently sighed. She decided at least one of them should do something normal like remove a jacket. Then cat-quiet she crossed the room, watching the immobile presence on the canvas chair—Danny unstrung, as though his bones were merely adjacent and unattached within his fleshy sprawl. "You need anything?" she finally said, feeling it was an act of bravery to speak.

Danny kept staring straight ahead. "Oh, yeah, I need something all right," he mumbled. "I need it bad, too."

Barbara flushed and began to choke up again, struggling to retain her composure. "I won't get you any coke or—or a reefer or *anything*—not like that. So don't ask—"

"I'm not—"

"—I can't do that for you—not even now—I *won't*—"

"I'm not *asking!*" Danny shot back, looking away, raising a clenched fist to his face.

Barbara kneeled down to him, tried to appeal with her eyes to the back of his head. "I'm dying here, Danny . . . please . . . tell me what happened?"

His profile returned with a snap. She couldn't discern if his eyes had filled, though his cheek was red. "What's to tell? My father murdered my mother. Happens all the time. Don't you believe in statistics? Don't you read the newspapers . . . ?"

"Please, Danny—"

"Isn't this America the Beautiful? A chicken in every pot, a—a gun for every chickenshit, a pothead for every gun, *I* don't know . . . I just don't—fucking—*know*. . . ." He raked his long fingers through the sides of his scalp as though pulling his thickened thoughts through a strainer.

Then he set his right hand slowly onto Barbara's, caressing her small smooth fingers, and it was as though he had touched the release valve, letting free within her the pressurized air, the tenseness. She gave him a plaintive smile, which he turned toward finally, sorrowfully, then turned away again, yet not letting go the hand interlocking with his. They let the faint drone of the evening traffic on the commercial street below surround and isolate the room for a while, let it put them in a hum-and-rumble limbo, before Danny broke through his anger, allowed the grief to seep into his heart like tepid water.

"The UPS man found her," he said in monotone, his eyes fixed on a particularly unparticular spot on the blue wall between the soot-blown front windows. "Must have been getting one of her catalog deliveries, I guess . . . my mom was a catalog freak—not too many people knew that. The hot-shit catalogs and stuff. Gourmet kitchen utensils, pricey toys because they're supposed to be educational . . . like that."

Barbara thought she saw Danny's face ease, his eyes inwardly envisioning his mother in a familiar pose, maybe leafing through a mail-order array while with her free hand she hand-fed a young Danny a few neatly cut sandwich triangles of grilled cheese and talked to him about the practicality or ridiculousness of certain sale items, or helping him open her just-delivered box as though only they two were secretly sharing a Christmas every few weeks or so.

Danny continued: "The UPS man knew my mom. All those deliveries and he'd, like, linger sometimes to get invited inside for a cappuccino when she was in the mood. She'd give him some in a plastic cup and everything, a top, 'to *go*,' for Christ's sake—she could be too much. She gave to everybody. . . ." Danny shook his head. "So . . . I guess he must have been hoping for a handout and he came around the back, cops said—maybe she was swimming—and he saw her from outside the sink window right away, she was on the floor, laying there. So he runs to your mother's house and calls 911. . . . Anyway . . . they go in and find her dead in the kitchen, on the floor . . . dead for a while, they said. They first thought she maybe tripped on something. She was in her nightgown, so maybe she came down to the kitchen at night, stumbled in the dark—I don't know—cracked her head on the corner of something, you know—as she fell? Because there was blood on the floor beneath her, beneath her, her face, the side of her face, only . . . only when they pick her up, they see this . . . hole . . . in her head—" Danny ceased talking a moment to let his Adam's apple stop knifing his throat. "—a *bullet* hole. . . ."

Barbara was stroking Danny's hand in hers, while still looking intently at him, stroking it as though trying to encourage his words, to lead them out safely.

"Said . . . said I was lucky I didn't get to see it . . . the blood and the mess. Trouble is—I see it just fine, thank you." Danny squeezed his eyes shut, squeezed Barbara's hand tight, his jaw tight. "And the big joke, you see—I mean, how we used to tease her about how clean the kitchen had to be, how spotless." Barbara understood the "we" to be Danny and his father.

Danny pushed a small laugh through his nose, a sharp funnel of air at the painful mental image of his mother's blood oozing outward from a thickening red puddle beneath her mashed face like the deliberately moving extensions of an amoeba, staining the pristine white tile floor, a dense liquid flower of spreading burgundy petals.

Danny's eyes popped open to obliterate the scene. He exhaled and tried to recover. "They said they were going to look for signs of a break-in, but the back patio door was unlocked

to the pool, and . . . yeah, sure . . . you know . . . with my
mom, that spur-of-the-moment dip, when she couldn't sleep
even, she—she loved . . . she loved that pool, swimming. . . ."

Barbara realized Danny's train of thought was spiraling
down; he was losing it. She touched his lips with her fingertips
and he quieted. Still, she needed more, she needed to know
more, but gently so, so she whispered, "But . . . how did they
think it was your father that did it?"

The singular convulsive laugh startled Barbara, after which he
paused as a teardrop shimmered down his cheek. "He confessed," Danny said, gazing downward. "He fucking confessed."
Danny looked up at Barbara's incredulous frown and half
smiled. "Just like that."

"But why?" Barbara asked, astonished. "Why would he do
such a thing? Why would he . . . kill your mother?"

Danny searched Barbara's face for a place of comfort, but it
was too pure, too pretty, what he felt too dark, too horrible. He
turned away and let go of her hand, wanting the brown-black
smear of the walls again, the blurred indistinguishability of the
dim room, the open windows, the melting of colors. He
seemed to murmur something to the teary blur, but Barbara
wasn't going to pursue it. As he silently wept, she leaned in
and held him. She wouldn't ask more of him. Not now.

Soon after, she coaxed him out of his dusty jacket, then his
perspiration-wrought clothes, and they lay together in the dark,
he on his back staring, she on her side turned toward him, naked on his bed, her warm body nestled beside his, her blond
hair glowing in the angular splotch of a streetlamp, her hand
stroking his frozen moon-white face, the rivulets of silent tears
gathering in tiny droplets on her fingertips. Every few minutes
she would bring her fingers to her mouth and slowly lick them,
taste his grief, tenderly suck its salty flow, reminding her of the
ocean and its secrets, its depths. She hurt from his pain, life's
pain, but somewhere she embraced the bitter tang of his tears,
this tidal surge from his inner torment. It was more intimate to
her than semen, or even blood.

In the dream hours of the night, Danny sat up at the edge of
his bed for an immeasurable amount of time. His body felt
nonexistent, dispersed, so much so that barely a crest formed

on the water mattress when he finally rose. That was when the one fierce weight descended, the stroke of pain to his head, the throb at his temples. He shuffled clumsily, his eyes half shut, to a metal folding chair that fronted a makeshift desk consisting of an unpainted plywood door held up by old-fashioned weather-darkened milk crates that Josie, the store owner downstairs, had formerly implemented to display her used records and CDs.

It was being used as a repair worktable. Sure, there were papers and notebooks, some old college texts, a few ripe-smelling paperbacks that had fallen into an unknown brownish liquid that encrusted them along their borders, a cracked mug with pens and pencils, and a few nearly new guitar picks at the mug's bottom which Danny still thought were lost. But the clue to the area's purpose lay in the scattering of small tools, especially pliers—needlenose, square-jawed, small and big— some tacks, hammers, the loops of guitar wire. A fifteen-year-old, twelve-string acoustic instrument, the frets of which needed mending, was the giveaway. It was stretched out on its back like a helpless patient. It looked dead and without song since its strings had been removed. Danny felt sorry for it as he sat there dreamily.

He rubbed his eyes and let his tongue moisten the dried outer edges of his lips. He knew what he wanted, what his thumping head wanted. He thought about Laraby, his former supplier, envisioned his serene, broad face and mercurial eyes, as though this "Skel From Hell" (written across his black tee) had seen things you couldn't hope to see. Danny envisioned him at the Battery Acid Club mocking out a few of his tagalongs, pulling joints from his lackeys' mouths to toke on himself, always a cool expression, life was easy, take it easy, take some dope. Danny's tongue poked out again. He puckered his lips, could almost taste the powder, feel his heart thud with greater frequency with each nasal suck. It was a doper's daydream, a fucking, *non* coping breakdown—

Danny squeezed his hand into a fist, thought about putting his fist in the small vise attached to the corner of the worktable, take away the need with broken bones, break the hand that takes the coke, that feeds the need, that frees the head . . . that lives in the house that Dad built. Danny let out a small laugh, then heard himself, as though outside himself, and looked to Barbara. She slept, the naked curve of her back to him, like the sensual slope of a guitar on its side, her white rump, her gradually deepening brown from lower spine to shoulders, the delicate neck, that yellow thrust of silken straight hair like a tassel.

Then he remembered her questioning about the murder, the unanswerable "Why?" remembered his dreams, his thoughts, and all he could go over again and again was Eric's death. His mother was just killed and all he could think about was his little brother, a brother he sometimes resented while alive, sometimes wept for while dead, but most times missed as this fantasy adult, this man who would be with him, the two of them together, as brothers, as men, who would both understand things, talk about things, things that excluded their long-gone father—the new Rodman generation usurping the old.

But, instead, it was the old that was destroying the new, extinguishing his family, his father revealing himself as some kind of minister of decline, of death. And it was Eric who Danny couldn't forget tonight, who kept him up, got him up to the desk wanting a snort, who brought him little sleep, as though his baby brother were tugging at his sleeve the way he would some early afternoons at home, Danny still wearing yesterday's limp clothes, prone on his unkempt bed, Eric the innocent wake-up caller sent to Danny's room by his father to test the waters, see how hung over or dried out Danny was from his night's roaming.

Danny gazed at Barbara's slumbering form and thought about how she wasn't around when Eric was killed, how she was away at college, her first year, how she missed the show, the puzzling, disturbing, mysterious show, and most importantly, how he never told her the troubling details.

Not the specifics of how Eric was hit by the car, or how he must have looked having been dragged a half a block under the bumper, then shucked, scraped off by the parked Mustang convertible near the Hackworth's house like dogshit on your shoes. Like Barbara, Danny wasn't there for that, either. Only his mother was blessed to see that mangled sight, got to memorize it the way you memorize where your parents' gravestones stand in a sprawling cemetery because they *get* memorized whether you like it or not. Delia only heard a distant indistinct scream—of tires? of horror?—and the subsequent roar of a car straining to flee, as much as everyone else heard on that segment of the block, insulated by the humming cool of their collective central air systems on a humid July night. Delia never conveyed to Danny what Eric looked like when she ran out in the street in front of shocked and weeping neighbors, and Danny never asked.

He only saw Eric later at the hospital in intensive care, a thick plastic curtain smearing an outline of a fragile pulplike thing in gray-white bedsheets, head and torso bandages, and a dangle of tubes. They could have told him it was anybody. At the foot of the bed, peering down, he wished it *was* anybody, anybody *else*. The doctor said he had multiple fractures, including his skull. His right arm was nearly ripped off, his legs were fragmented, useless. His lungs looked healthy, but his kidneys were brutalized. He had little hope of living, and if he did live, he would be chair-ridden.

But as if to compensate for the dead future, for the comatose form that was her small boy, her baby, Delia Rodman was manic, bossy, asking preoccupied nurses questions in the strident tone of a skeptic, demanding their strength of purpose, their kinetic energy; as though such a fervor of attention and activity could revitalize his brother, make him sit up and ask for his skateboard or some ice cream money with laconic ease and chuckle at their feverish concern over him; as though Delia were realizing how collectively frail, how helpless, they all were in the face of such a void—the inert child, the dying egg. Danny had never seen his mother so out of control before or since.

He sat her down, suppressed her, to the relief of the bristling staff. She was in navy-blue shorts and barefoot, her lavender blouse half crooked, her mouth the same. It was as if she had run to the hospital breathless; her mind, her clothes, her life in dishevelment. Delia held Danny, tucked him to her, in a way he had never remembered before, or at least not since he was Eric's age, certainly not since the start of his compelling addiction. But he had been clean for over two years at the time of Eric's accident, having survived his two months in the Allerton rehab program, getting in past others on the waiting list with the help of his uncle Jack's client connections, regaining his mother's favors, her endorsement, her respect. It seemed Delia extended much more leeway with her sons than with her husband, the bond of blood bringing greater understanding than the bond of marriage. His mother forgave him, though she would never forget the family suffering he caused. His father could manage neither. All he could manage was to succumb to his own latent tendencies, his desperate need to handle things through intoxicants the way he had when he was young. Not even a month after Danny walked out of the Allerton Clinic, his sickness, like some kind of psychological virus, moved to his father. In some strange way, the relief of Danny giving in to professional help let down Carl's own guard, allowed him to inflict the ridicule he aimed at Danny all those years onto himself.

Soon Carl Rodman didn't come home for dinner very much. He had been overworked since his last promotion at the firm, was pressing, drinking heavily for business and for what some misname pleasure. He was suspected of an affair, but unquestioned by Delia. (Pat Dokes was not brought up in conversation by either party during this time.) He was put up with by Delia through strong will, a proof of her inner resolve to weather this, too. And put up with for the sake of Eric, who loved his father regardless of his absence, his erratic behavior, or his harsh, scotch-stale breath when he kissed him on the cheek in his bed at whatever hour Rodman fumbled home some nights.

So, in the intensive care ward when Danny asked his mom while holding hands, "Where's Dad?" it was no surprise for him to see a scowl cross her fatigued face.

"Is it a shock to tell you I have no idea?" Delia responded, a bit stunned that her husband was even brought up at this time. And yet she suddenly looked worried for him, too. In simple terms, Carl Rodman was not there for them, for Eric, at such a compelling time, and no one took it as a surprise, just as a reaffirmation of their family's inexorable decline.

Almost on cue, however, they heard footsteps approaching, masculine footsteps, the pace of which signaled a known destination, and Danny and his mother looked at each other. Danny had no expression, suppressing a sinking feeling; Delia tensed her jawbone and honed her sad eyes toward the door. When Danny's eyes hurriedly followed, in he came: a total stranger.

The unknown man gave a cursory look to either side of the medical unit and summed up quickly that he wanted Eric's bed, in spite of showing disappointment with something. He wore a lightweight beige trench coat over a well-tailored, yet out-of-date nylon suit, his tie a tasteful swirl of deep blues and greens on silky gray. He was clearly an old man, but with a sharpness to his movements one associated with the force of youth. His hair was in two parts; each formed a large cottony wisp above either ear like cirrus clouds, with a richly tanned bare scalp spread between. Add to that a white full moustache, and his aspect gave him intelligence and eccentricity. His eyes were heavily bagged, brown, and sympathetic as he stepped up to Delia. "Is this the young boy who was just brought in, struck by a car?" he asked, as delicate as he could make his voice.

"Yeah," Danny said, starting to stand. "What's it to *you*?"

The man ignored the rising body of anger to his right and readdressed the tousled lady. "My deepest sympathy," he said, taking Delia's unextended hand, ". . . Mrs. Rodman, is it? Mother of the poor boy. Have you seen young Eric's doctor? I just need a word—"

Delia had stiffened, though she allowed her hand to stay caressed in his. "Why? I don't understand. Who—"

"Don't concern yourself about me. Your son needs all of your concern right now." He patted her hand twice and released it, his eyes now looking for someone of authority.

Danny moved himself into the elderly man's face. "Hey . . . *sir!* My mother's concern is our concern, and right now—" Danny grabbed the floppy lapels of the raincoat. "—you concern *us*." With a steady thrust, he drove the man against the sound-retarding wall, jarring a few hanging fluid bottles on the way. "Now who the fuck *are* you?"

"Let go of me!" the old man shouted, not in fear, more in effrontery. His arms hung to his sides, noncombative.

"Danny!" Delia cried. "Danny, let him go!" She tried to grapple her son by his shoulder to turn him around.

The old man stayed defiant. "I'll call the security guard if you—"

"You shit, you'll call a *nurse*, man . . . !" Danny pulled forward on the lapels, then banged the man back against the wall, a dart of pain seizing the man's upper back. A nurse, unnoticed by the trio, had just trotted to the commotion and quietly ran for assistance.

Delia yanked at her son more successfully now, both hands peeling him away, nearly muscle by muscle. "Danny! No!" Those last words were almost directly into Danny's face. Reluctantly, his fingers sprung out and freed the jostled man, who twitched a little and breathed more easily, though rapidly. Then, as the elderly man was about to step away, Delia slid in front of him, restoring the bodily pin, unknowingly drawing back her full shoulders as if readying for a thrusting dive into the deep end. "Now . . ." she whispered, "who the fuck are you or *I'll* call the guard and make something up, something good, too."

With his head bowed, the man's eyes angled upward with suspicion. He gazed at the determined woman a second, then finally flashed the briefest of conciliatory smiles at her. "As you wish . . ." He dipped into his lining pocket and presented her with a business card, gold-embossed, finely scribed. It said: THEODORE MATTERA, ATTORNEY-AT-LAW and an address Delia didn't bother to read. She handed the card to Danny, her eyes drifting around maniacally, as though mimicking her thoughts, and she backed off. Mattera stepped free, straightening his coat collar.

He immediately reclaimed the bereft demeanor he came in with. "You have to understand, I had to come see the boy and his doctor. To find out firsthand about his condition. That's all for the moment."

"He sent you, didn't he?" Delia said.

"Excuse me?"

"The person who did this . . . *this!*" Her finger tried to point to Eric, faded behind the curtains, but it trembled too violently, lost its way in trauma. "To my boy, my son! You *work* for him . . . or her—*it!*"

"I represent a party who—"

"Who is it? Who is it, goddamn it! Who!? Who did this to him?"

"I cannot divulge—" Danny stood behind Delia, not quite understanding and somewhat stunned by his mother's fury. A black-bearded security guard was suddenly there, too, piping in, with a nurse in tow. "What's going on? Everything all right?"

There was a momentary dead spot, a realization of onlookers, then Delia hissed between her teeth, "You slimy son of a bitch," and struck out. She smacked Mattera hard across the face, full force, in front of security, in front of the world— What the hell could anything matter now?—cutting his thin peeling nose with one pass of her sweeping fingernails, the impact of the swat jarring his center of gravity onto his right foot, a slight sway, nearly toppling him.

The guard was readied to grab her, and Danny, instinctively, stepped toward him, when Mattera raised his hand, halting the uniformed worker. He caught his breath, holding everyone frozen in a position of near-action. "Everything's fine, sir," Mattera said, even-toned. "No real . . . concern."

The guard seemed unsure, glancing from Delia to Danny to Mattera. Still, he eased his lunging posture and let the silence calm things, as the snow-haired lawyer dabbed his nose with a monogrammed handkerchief, looking blankly at the wobbly, tearing woman who stared back and who hated him with an intensity his client would pay extra for.

Mattera then gruffly nodded and left the intensive care unit in as determined a stride as he'd entered. Afterward, Danny had to assure the nurse and guard there would be no more fisted theatrics, that the emotional edges were blunted, while Delia sat hunched in her chair and held Eric's limp hand as though none of the others were there.

Danny remembered still not quite understanding what had happened between Theodore Mattera and his mother, this "client" business—the old guy couldn't be working for a wanted criminal, a potential killer, and not be made to tell the police, could he? Well, yes, he could, as Uncle Jack later told the family in his capacity as their legal adviser. Able explained that whomever Mattera represented, that person, although ethically and legally obligated to reveal him- or herself as the hit-and-run driver and come forward, had no reason to fear being "turned in" by Mattera. Mattera being that person's lawyer, client-attorney privilege protected what was said between them, and if disclosing his client's identity would hurt his client legally, as it would in this instance, clearly Mattera was obligated to remain mum.

Danny recalled his uncle saying it just like that, "obligated to remain mum," straightforward, all business, even in the face of his distraught sister. But that was Uncle Jack, a man who never mixed the official with the emotional.

Delia had tried to see Mattera a few times after the hospital incident. In fact, just days after the funeral, she had bulled her way past snotty office secretaries and was removed by building guards. Another time she called under the pretense of representing a government agency. Once she had actually cornered Mattera on a downtown side street where, by luck, he solicited a passing police car and swore he would file harassment charges, this in spite of the fact that when finally face-to-face with him, Delia let loose sharp tears rather than ire toward the elderly attorney, begging for his sense of true justice.

Uncle Jack finally stopped her from continuing her futile badgering of the attorney. Theodore Mattera was no smalltimer, Able insisted. He was linked to some of the most influential people in the state, and whomever he represented was probably "no Joe Schmo, shit-shoveler."

"Isn't there any way," his mother asked, leaning over Uncle Jack's desk, her eyes having sunk deeper into her face, her face seemingly more lined, more bony, "*any* possible way, to find out who's pulling his strings? Who his client is? Then—Then at least we can accuse *some*one. Someone is to blame for this. Someone should *pay* for this. . . ."

Danny sat his mother back down at the black leather chair that fronted his uncle's broad oak desk while Able looked down at its blotter, not suffering his sister's tantrums very well, the fingertips of his spread hands touching. "Well," he ultimately conceded, "I suppose we could go the private investigator route. Though I hate the practice. Like throwing money into a bottomless hole. And I'd have to find someone who Mattera hasn't used. Or has something *on*, for that matter."

"Would it work?" Delia asked flatly.

"Maybe. Maybe ... whoever—could find out with time. But I think it would be safer to use somebody from out of town, just for the reasons I just gave before," Able surmised. "Mattera has a lot of influence in this area. What I could do is check with a few people I know up the coast who might offer us suggestions, some reputable investigative firms, or even solo operators ... but ... you realize, this guarantees nothing. And—well—it might prolong the grief."

"The grief is going to last my whole life, Jack," Delia said with glazed eyes. "I may not show it, I may not say it, I *will* go on with things, but it will last—*forever.*"

His uncle silently sighed through his nose and nodded his consent to the arrangement. He would hire the investigators in his name so as not to alert any of Hollowsport's big ears.

Danny recalled that, of course, his father wasn't there in that office for that crisis decision, either. At that time, he was confined to detox at Allerton Clinic, even had the same therapist as Danny did. Yes, his father chimed in with his support for the use of a private investigator, and after he had left the center and had come home cleaned out, he looked at the monthly reports from Barkley Investigations with seemingly the same dread and anguish that Delia did, for they showed nothing. Then a year or so later, after seeing Theodore Mattera leave his Hollowsport law practice to move a notch up in his career by joining a nationally known law firm in Chicago, and after consulting with the Barkley private investigators who had come up with few leads and many dead ends, it was suggested that the case be dropped.

Danny could still see his mother standing, shifting, with her arms tightly folded, her face a mask of anxiety, nodding in that disbelieving way we nod when we really don't agree at all, as if affirming—yes, everybody *is* fucked-up here, aren't they?

Uncle Jack disconsolately shrugged and said the Barkley investigators did all that they could. They certainly couldn't follow Mattera to Chicago; they saw no need, in fact. The case was closed. The police had given up long ago. It was time for the family to live with the little they knew.

"What do we *know*?" Delia said, gesturing to her brother in the soft light of her living room.

"He's dead," Carl Rodman said quietly from the sofa. "We

know he's dead. It doesn't matter anymore who did it. I'm sick of it. I can't live with it anymore."

"It doesn't matter?" Delia asked. "How can you say it doesn't matter?"

"Sometimes you have to say, 'Enough torture, enough lingering.' Sometimes you have to blot things out, things you can't—can't hope to know, and move on."

"But how can you possibly say it doesn't matter? He was our boy!" Delia began to breathe in fits of air and anger mingled. "He was our baby boy," she said more softly, sadly. Carl couldn't answer, his face reddened, the tears welling. He dropped his head into the cups of his hands for support.

"Let it *go*, Deel," Uncle Jack injected. "We're never *going* to know, unless—unless this person tells someone on his deathbed, for God's sake."

Then Delia turned to *him*, to Danny, her now only son, only *child*, who was called that night by his mother to come over as a moral support, as a surprise guest. "What do you think, Danny? Does it matter? Does it matter anymore?"

Danny knew this was a no-win question. It felt like a parental trap, a test, but before he could even say a word, his father raised his tearful face and muttered, "What an ex-druggie thinks matters even less." Danny thought the remark aimed at him, and of course, it was, but the dagger was also aimed inward and stuck in Rodman's own heart.

Danny had wanted to say something after his father's comment, but he couldn't, his crushing rage wouldn't let him, his sudden knowledge wouldn't, his sudden knowledge that it was the last time he would come into this fucking house if he could help it, and it *was* the last, before Barbara convinced him to attend that party—When was that? Sunday? Doomsday? *Some* day—Danny's mind swirled at the repair table—it didn't matter.

"So be it," his mother had finally said to the men in her gently lit living room, and then she clopped her sandaled way up to the master bedroom.

But even that scene, that pathetic family scene which closed out Eric's death, wasn't what was keeping Danny up this muggy night by its recollection. It was before, Danny thought, it was one of the scenes before, back at the hospital, the one right after the accident, in the intensive care ward, right after the confrontation with Mattera, the big-shot lawyer, after the appeasement of the guard and nursing staff. It was when his father finally decided to appear at the hospital, his intoxicated entrance and thereafter. *That* was it.

Carl Rodman had stepped into the darkened ward wide-eyed, his breath deep, nearly gasps, hard swallows. His bright tie was to one side of his neck; his suit jacket fell rumpled at the vents. He ran his fingers over his mouth as if wiping away sweat or drool or the taste of Cutty Sark. And for all that, his hair still looked miraculously slick. Then his voice came out slow and dense; it had body: "Thank God ... Thank ... God, he's still alive."

Delia didn't even look up at him, her concentration subsumed by Eric, by the lawyer's lingering rent to her passion, to her sense of right and wrong. The last thing she needed was a semidrunk husband, and yet in many ways she needed him desperately, needed Eric's *father*. Danny, however, just stared at Rodman from the other side of the bed, watching him perceptibly sway while trying to stand still, watching him trying to soak in what Eric looked like, to make it sober him, kick him, hurt him, burn him.

Rodman stumbled to his wife and fell to one knee clutching her legs. He swore at himself, he swore he would stop, stop everything, that he would seek help that week, the next day, he was done, this finished him, this killed him, this was the end, he couldn't live, couldn't live with this—this—

At that moment, Delia turned and held him, silencing him, except for his sobbing, then his head slipped up her body to her shoulder and, leaning into him from her chair, she let herself go, too. She believed him, had to believe him, was too shattered not to believe in him, believe in *something*.

And Danny just watched this scene with a sense of detachment, as though an outsider to the emotions before him. After all, how many times in his drug-filled despair did he wish himself dead and wonder if his parents would cry like this, hold onto each other like this, for *him*, the loser, the drifter.

And then while watching their embrace, the true moment came. His father's flush face rose up over Delia's shoulder as he held her, and for the first time since he had come into the ward, he looked directly at Danny. It was that look Danny remembered. It was pathetic and it was hateful all at the same time. Danny had always felt Rodman's antipathy because of his adolescent troubles, of his somehow copycatting his father's young recklessness, because he was regurgitating the dark side of the sixties for Rodman, but this time what Danny saw in his father's fiery-veined eyes was guilt, and *knew* Rodman felt responsible for what had just happened to Eric, felt responsible for the death of "the good one," and Rodman knew that Danny *saw* that look, that sense of responsibility, and it was for *that*, for seeing his sense of guilt, that his father never forgave him. . . .

Danny rose from the worktable, his knees cracking from sitting too long. He moved over to the open window to breathe in whatever lightness the summer air would offer amid its moist blanketing of the night. It was late. He wished that he at least had some more weed, that he hadn't used it all for that fucked party. No . . . not true . . . what he really wished, what he had always hated himself for, was he never had the guts to go out to the hospital's parking lot that night, that moment, to check the bumper of his father's car for any damage. That's what he *really* wished.

9

CARL RODMAN STEPPED up into the police transport vehicle through its two back doors and sat on the bench that was riveted to the van's cold gray interior. It was early the next morning and he was being taken to a holding cell where he would soon be called for his arraignment. The courthouse normally used in the adjacent building was undergoing an expansion, so all prisoners for the past several months had to be driven two blocks away to the temporary court facilities.

It became suddenly dark when the doors rattled shut, for the police transport was already in a poorly lit underground garage beneath the station house. He was uncuffed. His denim jacket hung damp and limp on him. He was quiet. He had had to be sedated for most of the night and kept in a separate cell from the small-time thieves who were caught pinching handbags and gold neck chains after a local outdoor concert in Fulsom Park. His cell was more of a hospital offshoot, with white plaster walls instead of cell blocks, and a male nurse at the right hand of the cops on guard. It was a time of nightmares, too, of visions both true and false, of praying he could exchange one for the other. Physically, Rodman was wrung dry of emotion. He had soaked the foam mattress with his grief and shuddering sweat. He had come through to the other side, past emptiness.

In between breakdowns, he had deliriously pointed to the folding leather holder, the business card, that of his lawyer, this when he flatly refused to videotape his confession as promised. By all accounts, the detectives looked less than pleased about Rodman's change of heart, irked that the camera would not, at least for the moment, be able to verify what Rodman had revealed to them, not allow him to hang himself with not only

140

his statement but the actual unfolding of the killing, the motive, all the step-by-step details a jury likes to listen to and believe since it's right there, on TV. But since Rodman had been immediately Mirandized, the detectives could at least testify to his criminal admission at the scene of the murder, so all was not as bitter as the twelfth precinct's muddy brew of coffee.

The suited dicks became further disgusted, however, after they actually phoned Rodman's attorney. "He offs his wife," the pea-eyed detective muttered, "this Able guy's sister, it turns out, and he expects his legal help. Jesus, even a lawyer's not *that* coldhearted." They couldn't quite understand Rodman's "big-time show" at seeing his wife's corpse, either. He wanted to see her, they show him, he *freaks*. It was beyond his really feeling bad, too. It was as if he didn't realize what he had done after saying he did it . . . ? Maybe the guy was a schizo, *but*— that might get him off, so fuck mentioning that.

Today, Rodman was thinking more clearly, which was a mixed blessing at best. It was true that the night before, his brother-in-law Jack had refused to help him find a criminal lawyer, which Rodman now understood, considering the supposed crime, and so a new lawyer was set up to meet him in the holding cell at the temporary facilities down the street just before the arraignment the next morning. *This* morning, he reminded himself, the darkness disorienting him.

The dark made the van feel like a coffin, cramped and spare, but he felt like a dead man anyway, so he wanted it to stay dark. The bile glazing his hollow stomach welled up to his throat as Delia's bloodless face came to him, the matted hair, the nothing that was her.

They had spoken to him earlier, when all the sedatives had passed out of his system like possessing spirits, and, in truth, he was amazed, even in the midst of such degradation, *amazed* at what he heard.

They said that they knew he wasn't at the cabin that night, at least not all night, as Rodman had told them, had *lied* to them after rescinding his confession. They knew that he had driven back to town in the early morning. It seemed that Wesley Koontz wasn't feeling so good himself late yesterday, "felt a bug droppin' through his system," and had his wife take the truck and drive herself down to her sister's to spend the night. Then in the middle of the night, groggy with sleep, Koontz's head lifted, having heard a doorbell his dawning consciousness knew he didn't have. ("When bare knuckles will do, nuts to electricity," was a Koontzism applied to many things.) The bell became more of a ring, a ding, a steady ding, and he scuffled out of bed to see Carl Rodman placing the air hose nozzle back on the pump and driving off down the road, back toward Hollowsport.

The police also told Rodman that the fingerprints on the murder weapon matched his; the only others were Delia's. His prints being on the small, white-handled .22 was no surprise. He had demonstrated to Delia how to hold it just recently (as if he knew something about technique—his father would have laughed). She had bought it at Regal Security and Arms, an upscale guns-and-ammo outlet where many of her friends got theirs. She wanted it for the bedroom; she was disturbed by the spate of robberies in the area of late. Rodman had told her there had always been robberies in the area, but he rarely denied Delia things, even if they happened to be firearms, for whenever she displayed a vulnerability, especially one usually associated, sexist or not, with females, he was quick to assert husbandly bravado. Delia was not one to own up to her weaknesses, after all.

To Rodman's way of thinking, a thief could have surprised her the other night, her with the gun in her grasp after hearing a noise. The thief could have been wearing gloves, which would explain his fingerprints not revealing themselves when the handle was powdered by investigators. That would have meant the thief overcame her while she held the weapon—he couldn't have found it, or knew where it was—and then used it on her. Had the detectives mentioned anything in the house was stolen? Why should they, when it seemed they had him tied up to the murder so neatly? Maybe the thief never had a chance to take anything. Maybe it wasn't a thief . . .

He remembered setting the safety on the gun himself (he knew *that* much) and, after his little demo for Delia, placing it under her side of the headboard. He then cajoled her about making sure she memorized the pitch of his shoe squeak so that when he tiptoed in the dark after a late night, he wouldn't get plugged.

"You know my waterlogged ears," she straight-faced. "Better play it safe and spend those late nights with me."

Now that she was dead, her statement held more tension than tease. Was she alluding to his alcoholism, to his dependency possibly returning? Was she suspecting an affair?

That was the other thing—his supposed motive. The cops said that they had reason to believe from questioning people close to Delia that she had a lover, and that Rodman killed her when he found out. At that point, amazement quickly became fury, puzzlement, disbelief, fear, all of the above and out of sequence and back again.

"Where the hell did you get that?" Rodman snapped at the bigger, thick-wristed detective, the smug one who enjoyed inflicting the verbal prod.

"*There's* that anger," he said. "Good. It would tick me off big-time, too, if my wife was doing it with some other schmo, but I wouldn't have shot her in her own kitchen."

Rodman pulled himself back again, let his mind take back his heart. The act disgusted him since it forced him to objectify Delia, yet it was a bitter necessity in order to cool himself down. "There was no affair," Rodman said with as much conviction as possible.

The cops shrugged it off. They were saving their sucker punch for last. They claimed to have a witness who could put Rodman inside his house at the time of the murder.

"*Who?*" Rodman said. "What witness?"

"That would be telling." Lieutenant Smug grinned.

"Your lawyer will know soon enough," the small-eyed one said, consternation curling his thin lips. "You should reconsider the videotape business when you see him, you know."

"You're cooked, baby," the other one said in farewell.

Rodman *felt* cooked, a fatty chop of meat in this steel steamer of a van, *dead* meat. What could he have said to the detectives? I wasn't there at the house murdering my wife, officers, because I was murdering someone else at about the same time. Rodman refused to believe that these eerily corresponding events were the deathly collision of random chance. His mind-set saw it as rightfully destined. Fate was coincidence made purposeful, he believed. He was caught in a fitting trap, a deserved punishment. Death for death. Rodman accepted it as one accepts the monthly electric bill—on trust. His inner world was forever filled with retribution. And yet in the pit of his soul he also wanted answers, wanted to know, *demanded* to know: *Who* could have killed Delia? *Was* there a thief? If not, who would have wanted her dead? The cold touch of an idea: Could it have been Vance? Why would he suddenly think of that?

Delia and Vance had never met. No way. Vance never existed in her life's circle, and she never knew of his existence in Rodman's. He never told her about it, him, the trip, the blackmail—never told her a lot of things. Delia knew Rodman's past vaguely, mostly through secondary sources, like Howard, but those times related were the pre- and post-Vance eras, the "straight" times. Her depth of information about his drug-selling days was surface, like a two-line synopsis to get you to watch a bad program on television, *Those Psychedelic Sixties*: "In tonight's episode, Carl tours the country with blood money, crabs, and one tee shirt before he crashes and comes to his senses." And like all good come-ons, even *that* wasn't particularly true. What *was* true was Delia never asked to hear the specifics, and that reluctance to face her husband at his worst, that need to shut his hedonistic persona up within him permanently, had locked it up way too tight. And only Vance held the skeleton key.

The logic wasn't clear, but Rodman felt he had to find out where Vance had been staying. Vance himself and possibly Eric's pin were yards deep, buried in a county compost heap, but Vance's room somewhere could be holding a clue, a sign, something that might show that Vance was at the house with Delia before Vance met him. Maybe Vance thought he could squeeze money from Delia *and* him. Maybe he just killed her out of spite, revenge, randomness, letting out the hatred he hid beneath the mask of a Merry Prankster with a coke habit.

Rodman suddenly felt even more cramped and confined. Then the sole guard who drove the prisoners to the temporary court facilities bounced into the cab of the van and started the whiny accelerator up. "We're off," he said, flipping his voice back through the steel mesh to Rodman, his tone that of a school bus driver taking kids on a class trip.

The van rumbled ahead up a ramp, out into traffic, and a

cloud-filtered light spread through the wide front windshield for a while, like when a door in a dark movie theater opens, allowing in the unasked-for glare of the lobby. Then there was a sharp turn at a narrow cobblestone street corner that a Hollowsport founding father once lived on, and a straightaway down the alleylike block between government buildings. Hovering construction cranes, naked beams in rust-colored rectangles upon rectangles, and the attack of pneumatic drills were to their left. "A quick trip," the officer assured his prisoner.

The van entered a granite archway that extended into a short, street-level tunnel, part of the main floor of the archaic county court building that was under siege by workers. The core of the van grew opaque again, and Rodman squeezed his hands, saw spots, visions, and almost prayed—when he heard the driver shout, "Geez . . . !" and Rodman instinctively braced himself. His stomach whooshed forward, his body lingered back, as the van swerved left and diagonally struck a dirt tractor that had trundled in front of the tunnel's exit a moment before the van emerged, and angled into it.

The front of the van collapsed on impact and, though the vehicle wasn't going all that fast, the officer, unbelted, was propelled through the windshield cleanly, almost comically, like a seal rising, hooking, and diving through a glass hoop. The van toppled to its side and Rodman's ribs smashed against the inner wall.

A spate of workers looked at each other, then laid down their equipment and began to trot to the steam-spewing van and to its driver, sprawled across the curled top of the tractor's scoop, bloody and loose-limbed. Many stopped at the gory sight and stood and stared at it in a momentary mix of shock, repugnance, and recognition. However, the diminutive tractor driver did not become such an onlooker, and instead leaped to the front of his machine and maneuvered himself toward the crumpled van, arms raised before his face in defense against the smoke and shooting radiator steam that penetrated to the sides of the tunnel opening. He was followed by a few other men, some in hard hats, a few in baseball caps, many shirtless, a good many tattooed. A muscling crowd was forming and enclosing the area. But by chance a batch of rookie officers was crossing the adjacent corner, and at the wave of their sergeant's raised arm, ran in front of the surging laborers now being joined by groups of passersby on their way to work.

In the meantime, once the van had toppled and Rodman had lain almost shoulder and head first, ass up, on his left side, and felt the trickle of his own blood creep down from the gash near his temple, all he could sense, all he could think of, was the rush of release. There, a few feet away, was a second source of light—weak, gray-muddy from the dull wash of the building's tunnel, but light just the same—and the right side of the van's back door, swaying open and closed, squeaking in complaint, still alive from the impact, and then dead. But the light stayed, the opening remained.

At this point Rodman's mind was a buzz of ratiocination without being rational. His arraignment, his impending bail and probable temporary freedom through the courts before the trial, was an irrelevancy. His mind was trying to figure out the why's and the who's of murder, not the intricacies of law and evidence. After all, evidence said he did it. And he *did* do it— just not the same "it." He realized his own safety was meaningless right now. His own life was outside the norm, outside the dull commute to work, the expense-account lunch, the flicking scan of the remote control after dinner, the simple taken-for-granted touching-base of a good-night kiss. He had things to do, life-straightening things. . . . Rodman bolted out the hanging van door.

Only two men managed to bull their way past the rookie force and suffer the steam that sprayed the arch's filthy decaying walls and the black smoke that puffed low and heavy from the burning engine, clouding the neck of the tunnel—the tractor driver and one of the baseball-capped men. However, the sergeant in charge spotted the encroaching duo and managed to slap a hand on the arm of the tractor driver as he was trying to climb up to the van's cab. The tractor driver gave the cop with jowls and three stripes on his arm a disdainful look and, from his loftier perch on the runner, kicked him sideways, flat-footed, straight in the face.

By the time the tractor driver hustled around to the back of the van, the baseball-capped man was coming out the unhinged back door, his eyes wide, wild. He peered hard toward the shimmer of cars and pedestrians passing by the other end of the tunnel. There was no sign of Rodman.

"Fuck!" Louis Dembo said aloud, and both he and Marty ran hard toward the bustling light.

Rodman had no ring or watch to hock. All his personal belongings, not to mention his wallet, were still imprisoned in a large manila envelope at the police station. So he begged, he lied, and he looked battered and destitute enough to back whatever plea he wanted to concoct. (The island of caked blood along the side of his head and splotched on his denim jacket clearly helped the effort, though he was unaware of it.) At every few blocks through the city toward his neighborhood, which was miles, hours away, he managed a few dimes, then a quarter, asking charity from people he was afraid would recognize him, not as an escaped murderer, but as a professional businessman gone sour, shamed more by poverty than crime, a curse of the nineties. Of course, the irony was soon not lost on Rodman that the sharply creased suits, the attaché-grippers, were not the ones who stopped and placed a coin or two in his hand and walked on. It was the working guy in a rayon orange short-sleeve shirt, the tennis-shoed fast-food counter woman, and the thirty cents that put him over the top was from a long-haired high-schooler wearing a vest but no shirt, wire-rimmed glasses, and black sneakers with checkerboard sides. He even said, "Peace, brother."

The dollar and a quarter Rodman collected got him the things he needed: a token and a transfer. It was a little over an hour later when he stepped down from the bus along Tapani Avenue and into the expansive lot of Home Port Car Care. The four-bay garage was wide open, and in the far right one, Benny DiLauro, head mechanic, was prone under a Saab tapping at something, a drop light illuminating his form, as though he were a saintly presence beneath an exhaust system.

Rodman glanced over at Benny's lazy cousin, Frank, who they called Tic-Tac because his mouth usually contained a breath mint to make sucking noises with. He was leaning back in a leftover dining room chair, the stuffing of which emerged from three slashes in the vinyl from a sharp object. Tic-Tac was snapping through a newspaper, not really reading it, some-

thing about a wildcat, a tiger, in the headlines, striking somebody? Hurting?—Rodman lightly kicked the soles of Benny's
work boot. "Ben? Carl Rodman."

"Ho!" Benny said, after wheeling out from below on his
dolly and recognizing the longtime regular. Delia had met
Benny through the Hollowsport Hospital Leukemia Society.
Benny's ten-year-old daughter was just starting treatment at the
time, and his service to that organization as well as to sickly
automobiles seemed to be as generous and knowing as his
heart (the only reason, many thought, his cousin Frank hadn't
been fired long ago). "How you doin'?" Benny performed a
slight double take at Rodman's less-than-perfect appearance.

Rodman nodded and propped a smile. On the bus he at least
had removed his encrusted jacket and was now holding it
rolled up like a ball and wedged under his right arm. He
couldn't do much about the gash at his temple except splash
some water on it from a drinking fountain at Reese Park near
the bus stop. Overall, his demeanor seemed flaccid, his normal
crispness sagged, though his eyes were vividly alive and had a
touch of madness in them.

"How's that project thing coming, Mrs. Rodman bent my
ear about?" Benny asked, wiping his hands on a matted green
towel. "You gonna build a rehab still?"

"Hope to . . . hope to. Politics doesn't get in my way. You
know how that is."

"Oh, yeah, I can guess. I wish you the best on it. I *mean*
that. You're one of the good guys."

"Thanks."

"So, listen, your wife's car is all set," Benny said, pointing
out past the bay door. "But let me show you something."

They strolled to the side of the lot where Delia's five-year-
old Mercedes sedan was parked beside other well-tended vehicles. Benny pulled the shop's transparent protective cover off
the driver's seat, told Rodman to sit, and handing him Delia's
keys, made Rodman test it out in front of him, a personal
touch Benny liked. He himself slipped into the passenger seat
on the other side.

"The ignition was giving up a little, scratching away. The
key was getting hard to turn, too, but I loosened it for her."
Benny then twisted his wrist, gesturing for Rodman to try it.

Rodman did and the engine hummed cleanly, as simultaneously the Blaupunkt radio sprung to life in low volume playing the end of a Hermans Hermits' song: "Something Tells Me I'm in for Something Good."

"Sorry," Benny said. "Wasting your battery. Have to have my music when I work, but only WGLD. Anything after the Beatles and the Stones, forget it—I can't get out of the sixties."

"I know what you mean," Rodman said. "Look, Ben, I forgot my credit card, so—"

"No problem, Mr. R., whatever. Your wife can come by during the week, she wants."

"Okay, thanks." Rodman patiently listened to Benny explain a few more things he should tell Delia, his dead beautiful Delia, what he had done to the car, Benny talking like a proud student explaining to the teacher exactly how he had completed his school project. Rodman tried to show normalcy, calm, no stress, nothing out of the ordinary happening; in doing so, he became unexpressive and remote.

Then, after a Crosby, Stills and Nash oldie, the radio station's local news headlines began to drift into the background of Benny's discourse, and Rodman felt his pulse speed, his cheeks blanch. ". . . strike in its third day. A shoreline bus accident kills eight passengers, injures twelve. The murder of a—"

"Enough," Benny interrupted himself, flicking the radio off, Rodman lunging at it a beat behind, then withdrawing his hand just as quickly and looking at Benny in a way that said his fearful spasm had never happened, or should be thought to have never happened in the name of decorum. Benny complied.

"I hate the news," Benny said, forcing a smile himself. "It's all bad." There was an awkward pause. "Are you—uh—okay, Mr. Rodman, I—"

"I'm fine, Benny. I'm . . . I'm great, I just have a lot on my mind. Work and all—"

"Okay, well, that's good . . . anyway, I'm glad you came by. When you and your wife, you know, dropped the car off so late Monday morning, I didn't think I would get it done on time, but then I called last night and nothing. Not even the tape machine—"

"Yes, right. Yeah. Forgot to set it. We were away. It's the damn work. Real estate planning's getting tougher these days—you know, recession—got some meetings this afternoon I have to get busy on—have to get changed—"

Benny took the hint, nodded, backed himself out the still open side door. "Oh! Yeah, okay, sure—uh—give my best to Mrs. Rodman, okay? Let her call me she doesn't understand what I told you."

"Wait!" Rodman suddenly said, his mind jarred. "I *don't* understand."

Benny's head popped down to the window again. "What about? The transmission stuff? I—"

"No, no, the stuff about dropping the car off. My wife dropped the car off, right?"

"Uh, yeah," Benny said slowly, feeling the conversation get even stranger.

"Well, you kind of implied that both of us dropped it off."

"You both did—no?"

"You saw me with her?"

"I—uh—I saw—no, not specifically—I mean, she came in with the keys and then went out to her ride. I figured it was you in the car, but—it wasn't you?"

Rodman's expression darkened. "No, it wasn't."

"This a problem?" Benny said. "I—uh—I don't mean to make like any problem or anything—or cause any—you know—because I couldn't see who—"

"No, no, don't be silly." Rodman conjured up his smile to go along with his lie, spread it out there for a shine. "I'm just trying to think when it was that she said she was going to meet her brother. It was probably her brother down for a visit."

Benny brightened. "The lawyer guy, she's spoken of him."

"Yeah, that's him, that's right. It was her brother. I forgot." Rodman shrugged and waved good-bye.

Rodman slowly circled to the front of the garage bays toward the exit, his mind abuzz with thoughts of adultery and motives for murder, when a second look at Tic-Tac made him pull up short.

"You finished with the paper?" Rodman said, his head jutting out the window. Benny's cousin had just closed the *Hollowsport Daily Post* and tossed it on the floor. If Rodman's picture was in it, Tic-Tac hadn't noticed. Then again, he hadn't noticed his fly was open, either.

"Sure," Frank said. He contorted himself in an abbreviated yawnlike stretch before handing the paper to Rodman. "It's yours. Benny won't be reading it. He hates the news."

Such a rigid philosophy was becoming very attractive to Rodman. The misunderstood headline from before shouted more clearly this time: WILDCAT STRIKE HURTS CITY. The smaller lead said: Sanitation Worker Walk-out Creates Possible Heath Hazard.

Rodman skimmed the rest: the garbage strike was in its third day; it started Monday morning; there were no pickups since then. Rodman dropped the paper on his lap and thought, thought quickly, had a shocking vision: Vance's body—not smothered beneath a faraway acre of debris—but still lying there in the Dumpster for two days like a hopeless drunk on a rancid bed. Rodman shot out of the service center lot. He had to go there. He had to search Vance's clothes, possibly get Eric's pin, get an idea, get a sense of any connection with Delia. In death as in life . . . the fucker just wouldn't go away.

The neighborhood didn't look all that less mordant and desolate during the day. The addition of one more dead body among the charnel house smells and brick-fallen walls of buildings meant nothing to a sun that simmered the slummy amalgam like a witch's brew. Except now it contained one bright, living thing: children.

As Rodman approached the lot, he once more saw the tip of the schoolyard and heard the ghostly voices of kids at recess beyond, shouting at each other, laughing, yelling for the ball, singing the song of double-dutch jump rope. Unseen around the bend, their spirits haunted the desolate lot he buried Vance in, and rightly so.

Getting closer, he suddenly saw a few stray grade-schoolers who had left the confines of the chain-link yard and dug and kicked at the lot's outskirts, pulling broken legs of a folding table from a pile of rubbish, mock-dueling, scaring the girls who dared to tag along. Rodman moved into a slow trot as three of the children—two white, one black, all in scruffy shorts and cloth sneakers—began to fool around in front of the Dumpster.

Then one of the white boys scuffled up onto it, waving his
stick like a pipsqueak pirate. "Let's put'm down the dungeon!"
Rodman thought he heard him shout, and the black boy
snatched at the smaller white one and caught him by his loose
polo shirt. He pulled him toward the Dumpster, his victim
starting to whine since he was losing the battle.

"Hey!" Rodman shouted, now at a run across the lot, "Get
away!" But the kids didn't hear him. The boy on the Dumpster
was encouraging the black boy, who finally got his arms
wrapped around the smaller one's waist from behind and
swung him toward the garbage bin, feet off the ground, forcing
him toward one end. The boy on top bent over and began to
pull that end of the bin's heavy lid open, when it slammed
down with an extra force and the old metal rang out, making
them all jump. Rodman kept his hands flat on the Dumpster's
lid and yelled, "I said, get the hell out of here!"

The kids scurried off without a second look at Rodman, except the head pirate. When he was far enough away, he swiveled mid-run, shot Rodman the bird, and turned forward again,
not missing a stride. Rodman watched the bunch hustle behind
the clothes factory toward their school, then he turned sharply
and let out some tremulous air. He hoisted himself on top of
the Dumpster, like the boy, feeling like a boy, and raised the
left side of the lid to see, smell—experience Vance, face-to-
face once more.

Rodman grew woozy, spotty-eyed; the stench was horrible,
the sight was worse. Blood drained from Rodman's cheeks.

Vance wasn't there.

Rodman looked up, amid his faintness, and glanced about,
as though momentarily thinking this wasn't the right bin, the
same lot, the correct planet, this wasn't his *real* life he was living. He couldn't orient himself. He dropped his gaze again to
the organic and inorganic mulch and hopped inside, sinking a
bit, consumed by the odor of decay, and hunkered down farther
into it, sucking it in—death was a part of him, rode him, liked
him, was part of his existence, he knew that, he finally accepted that—and soon he noticed signs of bleeding along the
corroded inner wall of the Dumpster. This *was* the Dumpster.
This *was* where he had placed Vance's body. Of that, he was
sure. He had to be sure about that, but . . . was it a *dead* body?

Could Vance still be alive . . . ? Part of himself physically convulsed at the thought. It stymied his heart. It was like realizing a part of you that you thought you had matured past, controlled, was possibly still within, only temporarily dormant, still potentially capable of destructively affecting your next action, next thought.

But Vance couldn't be—there was no possible way he could have gotten himself out of there, unless . . . maybe somebody found him and treated him, had taken him to a hospital. Somebody by chance? Had to be chance. Nobody knew of their meeting. But how could it be chance, either? How could they—whoever *they* were—how could they have found him alive? He was unconscious, he was *shot*, he was fucking *DEAD*!!

The last word was shouted aloud without his realizing, and, hyperventilating the Dumpster's acrid fumes for too long, Rodman twisted down, folding himself inward, down to his knees, and vomited.

It was a righteous puke 'cause it echoed—at least that's what the smudge-cheeked pirate told his rapt and giggling classmates about the boner-brain of a homeless guy he eyeballed from behind the factory who kinda like yelled to himself and chucked his cookies trying to make a smelly garbage bin his home. The laughter may have disrupted Mrs. Barr's history lesson, but clearly, Rodman had made the kid's day.

PART III

10

F ROM EARLY ON in life, reputation was going to become his
legacy, not children. That's what Jack Able had decided
in a most conscious way, for Jack Able was a most conscious
man, aware of his steps, his appearance—not "self-conscious"
in the usual sense, not the hidden inner loathing one associates
with the characteristic, but more "conscious of the self," the
intent, the purpose of things, how they are done and for what
gain. Children gained you little, cost you much, pained you
more. He'd seen it even in the happiest, even wealthiest, of
parents, young or seasoned, there at his law firm, not to mention within his sister's marital caldron. Emotional toll meant
something, and he had been hurt enough as a child, hated himself as a child—the clumsy outcast, the smarty schmuck—and
so he decided he didn't want any part of that child as an adult.
Who wants to reexperience one's childhood through one's own
children? It was a horrible and demeaning little journey the
first go-round; he'd pass on the return ticket.

And yet, this was not to say he did not take pleasure at the
usurpation of Carl Rodman's role in Danny's life, that he did
not relish to a degree the avuncular duties that superseded his
brother-in-law's status with his nephew, Carl's oldest son. In
fact, he felt masterful at this very moment with Danny, who
nodded amenably at the burial time Able had set with Mandrake & Sons parlor. Able believed his inner strength was
there to console and be strong for them both over the loss of
Delia. He had taken charge of the funeral arrangements, performed the proper functions that needed performing. He had
lost a sister. Danny had lost a mother. They would grow closer
still. Even now, Able felt Danny's needs radiate from him, as

they stood behind Able's triptych ebony desk with silver accessories and gazed out from the Gothic arched balcony window. They overlooked the private driveway, beyond which lay a woodsy thicket, and farther beyond, a pastoral spread that was the rest of Hamlet Hills Estates' exclusive grounds. This was as close as the richness of emotion and that of possessions could get in similarity.

Able gave Danny a single-armed hug, his nephew's forehead pressing his left shoulder for a moment. "This will be difficult," Able said quietly, sternly. "This has no place in our lives, this tragedy ... this *revulsion. . . .*"

Of course, he was thinking of Rodman, had always wondered about Rodman, about Rodman and Delia, more so. When he first met Carl—Delia all hyper and swaggering, telling the world she was in love by her every gesture—Able was distrustful, protective: Rodman was an up-and-comer, out of nowhere. Able was the steady plugger; he started and succeeded years before Rodman. The path was narrow and selective, and Able was loath to deviate from it. He could tell that Rodman was one whose path could never be wide enough, one whose swath cut large, was prone to wide turns, reckless swings, fatal trees.

Back in those days, Able knew, in spite of Carl's dapper appearance, that Rodman wasn't really this clean-cut type, saw the deviance in his remarks, his eyes, saw the past indiscretions. (Danny couldn't hide much in his expressions, either, come to think of it.) Able had tried probing for weaknesses on the one and only fiasco of a fishing excursion Rodman took them on at Janus Mountain. Able was never comfortable out-of-doors. The primal was an urge good for sex (which for him, considering his two embittered ex-wives, was losing *its* natural calling as well), and it had little to do with snaring a slimy-finned vertebrate or suffering a fertile dampness in every crevice of your clothes including your silk Italian undershorts. Rodman, of course, was content in his ubiquitous and crass denim jacket and flannel everything, and talked, and kidded, and tried to loosen his brother-in-law's screws while Able kept probing, not the lake with hooks, but with questions, baiting Rodman. Where was Carl all these years since college? *What* whirlwind trip?

All that was ultimately brought to the surface, however, was the fact that Rodman had been some kind of hippie wanderer and the sundry and sometimes conflicting associations that label conjured: Was he a peacenik? A doper? A dropout? A social activist? A longhair with no agenda but fashion and fashionable liberalism? A pseudo–"heavy" thinker whose philosophy gave him reason to be unkempt and uncivil? Or a little of each? Rodman never gave testimony that day. In truth, Able could confirm a drug-juiced link way back there somewhere only after Carl's headlong alcoholic fall of just a few years ago. And his sister certainly had suffered through that tumble.

What amazed Able was that Carl's binge and thrown-away past certainly could not have been what attracted Delia to him, for if all good little girls somewhere deep really wanted to marry their daddies, his sister certainly shot wide of the mark. Their father was a civil engineer, a creative man forced to be practical after the dreams of being a fiercely independent architect began to dissipate. Whitney Able gave this practicality to his son, but Jack gave it his own spin, used it as a service to ambition, not as an acceptance of what comes. His father was too accepting, Jack had thought; he gave up too easily. As a child, he saw the loss in his father's eyes firsthand, looked inside the man, exposed like his drafting easel, his plans as big and blue as the deepening sky; his white lines intersecting were like constellations, their stars connected like dots, projections in space, dream houses, fantastical museums. But his father had settled for stolid park playgrounds in concrete, a repair depot for municipal trains, all the gray, mundane physical forms, the practical forms of our everyday life.

Maybe that was it, Jack had thought, the tenuous similarity. Whitney Able and Carl Rodman were both builders of sorts, dreamers to be sure, though he could tell Rodman wore his dashed dreams like hurts, like visible wounds, very shoddy, very immature, the boy who didn't wipe his nose so that everyone could see he had gotten it bloodied. Whitney Able just put his dreams in a drawer. "That was their new place, that's all," he'd say. "They were still very fine dreams," he'd say.

Jack had different ideas. If his dream of political gain were thwarted for the moment, he wouldn't wear it broken as Rod-

man did, let alone indulge in intoxicants like a leftover pothead. And he wouldn't stick it in his sock drawer, like his father, either. He would merely endure the temporary setback
and find another way, a better way, *any* way, even an extrale-
gal way—after all, isn't that what knowing the lawful limits is
good for? To comprehend precisely where the line is drawn
so you can occasionally tread a toe beyond without leaving a
telling imprint? Able had already helped the current district
congressman on the Federal Trade Board with his wayward
son's bond holdings, which were unethically obtained, doing
so as a favor to Langston Weber, the oldest partner at the firm,
and such was the first advance in what he hoped was a knowing march up the capital steps—state, city—whichever would
hold out an incentive first. Dreams, unlike people, were not
born to die.

Jack Able now looked at his nephew Danny before him and
saw a bright kid, inheriting his father's boyish features without
the adolescent swagger Carl carried with him as an adult.

"Is that girl Barbara there for you?" Able asked.

Danny nodded, a serious aspect lining his face.

"Good, good. It's important."

Danny nodded again and hid a bud of skepticism. His uncle
had gone through two divorces and, as far as Danny knew, had
found little importance throughout his own life to be with a
woman, and yet—and Danny felt suddenly unsettled—it was
his uncle he had first told about Barbara. Not his own father.
Not even his mother, since she harbored such a silent, cold anger toward Hallie and, in kind, toward her Little Miss Perfect
of a daughter. It was as though Uncle Jack was always the
adult in his life, the benefactor, the one who gave him his
blessing.

Even in the hard times, the obsessive times, Danny had
never stolen from his uncle for a drug buy, never resented his
material wealth the way he had his own father's. Maybe it was
because throughout Danny's childhood, his uncle had shared
his special room with him, his "toys," his past, in a way Carl
Rodman never had.

This room they talked in now was a high-beamed study of
contemporary decor and old-style architecture, and the immac-
ulate largeness of it, the mix of blacks of metal lamps and

whites of pillow sofas, was a constant in Danny's mind. His uncle's place, his "identity," was this upper-story, open-air room, and even with Danny having grown up, it stayed as impressive and imposing to him as it was as a child. His uncle had one of the first personal home computers, and he would let Danny play whatever games came through the then primitive modem lines, would let him talk via the monitor to other children of privileged parents on the system. His uncle made him feel connected to the world.

Also, sprinkled about the room were block puzzles, wooden abstracts that through manipulation formed cubes, pyramids, parallelograms, and the young Danny would tackle these bits of challenge while timed by his uncle's Rolex, trying "to reshape anarchy into straight, true lines," his uncle would say. (And Danny thought, that was the law, too, wasn't it?) As a puzzle maven, Jack thought these blocks were as close as he had ever gotten to Whitney Able's love of solid structures.

Danny tipped the final icy tinkle of lemonade to his lips, then placed the empty glass on an enameled coaster. He took a steadying breath. The balcony's air was fresh; his heart was stale, worn-out, ready for rejuvenation through drugs, rage, speed—speed would be nice. A greenie or a fast rev on the Harley: you pick it. He also wanted to speed through what he sensed his uncle was there to tell him.

"What about my father? You said you knew something, or something?"

Uncle Jack smiled wanly at Danny's inarticulateness. He held his own tall glass of scotch and soda like a staff. "Yes. I wanted to tell you a few things I found out today. I wanted to tell you privately. In as comfortable a setting as possible. I hope you're always comfortable here, Danny...."

"Did they find him?"

"No, he's still at large, I'm afraid, which, of course, compounds his guilt, and *will* compound it with any jury they finally can muster out there, no matter how many times they may be told that his running is an irrelevance to the actual crime. But, regardless, I used some of my influences—I went over the evidence with the assistant D.A.'s right-hand man—and it all looks solid. Fingerprints, witness, the whole deal. I don't know what else I can do about it, what I can say to you.

It's why I can't defend your father ... you understand that, don't you, Danny? I just can't do it—"

Danny saw his uncle's Adam's apple jut out, choke off his voice, almost touch off an imbalance of emotion in what Danny knew to be a most guarded spirit.

"I don't need any excuses from you. I told you that." Danny touched his uncle on his forearm, then took his hand away, lowered his head as though shamed. His words came out sharply edged. "I wish he was dead. I wish they shot him escaping."

Able let that one slide by. "In any event, I also found out other things, tangential things. . . ."

"What things?"

Able shook his head as though he had wished he hadn't brought it up. "Look, you might find out anyway. It might be added to the indictments they already have on your father."

"What? What is it? What now?"

Able stopped his verbal wavering and sat on the curve of his desk. "Okay . . . okay. It's just that during their investigation, they came across some other evidence—and they wouldn't tell me what, seems really high-powered, or attached to somebody high-powered, I'm not sure—"

"What evidence? About what?" Danny was anxious now.

"It's about Eric, Danny," Able solemnly revealed. "They said they think they can even link Eric's death directly to your father. That it was his car ... that he was driving it at the time of the accident."

There was a silence between them, Able's brow furrowing, aiming down toward the unfazed, if only slightly bewildered-looking, aspect to Danny's face. Then Danny laughed to himself, then out loud, a breathy laugh that almost sounded like mockery. This sudden turn brought an equally sudden turn to Able's face—*he* now wore the bewildered expression.

Danny, it seemed, had been imagining the revelation to be some great looming doom, some absurdist link from nowhere, like his father was really a CIA traitor, or a serial killer who first married his victims, or a Vietnam War criminal in hiding, and not even those specific far-fetched acts, but something to do with the core of a more shapeless tragedy, a vague evil, something Danny finally couldn't hate enough, couldn't drug out enough, couldn't handle, finally couldn't laugh at. For in truth, all he really thought when his uncle told him about his father having killed Eric was, My God—for once—old fucking news.

11

ODMAN FIRST CHECKED the closest hospital, Hallap Medical Center, the one that served the bereft tenement dwellers of South Hollowsport, home to the fetid lot where Vance's body was supposed to be laying as dead and vile as the unpicked-up garbage. But clearly, it had since decided to move itself, walk away, maybe levitate—maybe the son of a bitch had been so high he floated the fuck away! However, there was nobody matching his description admitted to the emergency room two nights ago, or for that matter anybody at all with gunshot wounds. "Stabbings, we got a bunch from a bar fight, you want any," the nurse had told him, shuffling admittance papers as she spoke.

The other hospital, Hollowsport Central General, the big one, the better one, the rich one, was closer to the line between the burbs and the center of the city, and would have been much too far to drive to in Vance's condition. Even if somebody had driven him, why go there? Besides, Rodman thought he might be recognized at Central General should any staffers be about, his having joined Delia at the celebratory opening of a blood research lab there just a month ago.

No, Rodman thought, this was a false search. Vance could have easily been taken to a nearby doctor, some side-alley quack who specialized in law-ducking lowlifes. And yet— Rodman was still dizzy with the assumption—how could Vance still be alive? Two bullets gutted him. Rodman saw the blood, he *wore* it, like the sticky residue of red paint, only warm and horrifying. But Vance *had* to be alive, even if barely. Who would move a dead body?

Rodman decided it was time to backtrack, do what he

thought of doing before Vance's vanishing act. It was time to find out where Vance had been staying on this go-around, to find out which room-by-the-day-for-the-rest-of-your-life hotel he dropped his olive-drab satchel in. (Rodman was sure the Army-issue pouch would *be* in the room, could see it bulged on damp sheets, as he always had seen it, in other rooms, other times, filled with "goodies.")

Rodman began heading for Kalter Avenue, as an ember of memory had been burning through his mind's haze of loss and fear, and prodding him. Vance had mentioned a Kalter Avenue in some context at the last shakedown (the one after which he was never going to see him again), something—some *place* possibly to do with where Carl could get in touch with him—Rodman wasn't sure.

Yet the section of town that Kalter Avenue cut through heartened him; it had Vance's stamp on it. Rodman's, too, back when. It was just the type of neighborhood they both would crash in for a while on their Magical Mystery Tour when they weren't on the road sleeping in their van, the type that was close enough to possible drug sources and to delis for all-hour munch-outs, and yet far enough away from your potential points of sale—local schools, city parks, suburban borders (didn't want the middle-class "straights" having to drive *too* deep into the heart of darkness for their pharmaceutical pickup). Generally, the neighborhood they would choose was just Downtown U.S.A., an older section, busy, though actually run-down because of it, and spotted with transient hotels. A short north-south venue, Kalter Avenue had three such establishments.

Rodman parked in a public multistoried car park, a cavernous concrete structure primarily used by the people working for or attending the doings at the county courthouses nearby. Except for the first two floors filled with cars, accounting for night-shift jobs, the upper ramps were nearly empty, it being just past seven.

At the first transient hotel, the man at the desk was grizzled and somewhat cross-eyed, but he was friendly and shook his head in what seemed to be sympathy at not having a Sonny Vance or any hippie types around, though sometimes those "rock band fellas" would come stay a few nights, after playing the dingy basement clubs on the north side of town. He smiled a poorly dentured smile thinking about the "made-up" girls that usually came calling after a show.

The next hotel was seedier, and the heavily thighed man at the front desk far less friendly. He was in the middle of reading a *TV Guide* page by page, and Rodman felt the questions he had to ask were interrupting the man's ability to properly program his Friday night lineup.

"No Sonny Vance here," the man said curtly, scanning the one A.M. cable schedule.

"Can you *look*?" Rodman asked, about as nice as he could while clenching his teeth. The closed register book was being leaned on by the clerk's hefty arm, the one holding up the magazine.

The man flipped a page. "I don't look. I *know*."

His patience diminishing, Rodman then described Vance as quickly and as accurately as possible to the man.

"I couldn't tell you what the residents here look like," the man responded. "And I don't give two shits, either. I'm not paid to look. I couldn't even describe what *you* looked like."

The man was being truthful, considering he hadn't yet glanced up in the few minutes since Rodman's arrival. Rodman wasn't sure what to do, save try to somehow muscle the guy for a look at the register. He had no money to bribe the thick-butted slime—then a thought hit him.

"How about a Zimmerman?"

"What?"

"A Robert Zimmerman. Bob Zimmerman. *He* here?"

The torpor-filled man actually gazed directly at Rodman this time and snorted. "Bingo. Room 41."

Rodman didn't bother to ask if Mr. Zimmerman was in at the moment or not, let alone thank the slug, he simply moved swiftly up the darkened flight of stairs to the fourth floor then paused to take a breath at the landing, slowing himself, his metabolism.

As he walked noiselessly with measured steps through the barely lit hallway, checking door numbers—going down, 49, 48—it made Rodman feel as though he were also walking back through time. After all, these places didn't change. That which was in decay tended to stay in decay; once past bad, it never seemed to look much worse. But the familiar squalid surroundings did not revivify his youthful self. He felt much too aged with the burden of purpose and fear now, unlike then. Their staying in these ramshackle hotels was in their minds proof of the weakness of the physical world and its inability to imprison the young duo, proof of their power to bypass any confine—nothing could hold them in, tie them down. The drugs enhanced that sense, reinforced their innate superiority over those drudges who chose to be encased in fashion-proven rooms, well-furnished abodes, chained by their china and finery, fettered by their gleaming goods and tech toys. Vance and Rodman were kings in these shitholes, and their kingdom was the infinite height of any given infinite high.

They were all the way down now . . . 43 . . . 42. . . . The numbers had run out at the far door abutting the one hallway window: 41. Rodman stopped, though his heart continued even faster. What now? *(Knock, knock. "Mr. Zimmerman?" "Who is it?" "It's Jimi Hendrix." "So?" "So, I want to know how you came the fuck back from the dead so I can do it.")*

In spite of the flashing joke, Rodman prayed there was no answer, but he didn't have to pray very long. A touch of his hand confirmed the door's freedom of movement, attained from whoever had splintered the doorjamb. It swung back with nary a squeak. (And where was that person now?)

From the hall, the inside of the room was shadowed by a set of flipped-up blinds, hanging only partially down a single window which radiated a yellowish glow from the streetlamp outside. The yellow blanket of light remained completely still. All dark outlines of the bed, dresser, what looked like a drawer on the floor, were also still, as Rodman kept the door open with his left hand while standing motionless in the hall, his eyes working the room, scanning it, his nerves bunched. He waited to see if anything was going to flinch, breathe, blink.

Nothing.

He spotted a switch on the wall to his immediate right and flicked it without looking, still staring inside as though waiting for the leap, a thrust. . . . A light fixture with two splayed bulbs from the water-stained ceiling lit the room harshly and imbued the furnishings with a hard line, dark edges, as though their borders were gone over with an inky marker. Rodman closed the door behind him and surveyed the apartment with his back up against the wood. It was one room, no bath. An off-white, chipped sink jutted out of the far wall; the imperfect mirror above it showed his anguished look, diminutive from such a distance, as though he were witnessing it on television. The bed was unkempt, the dresser a cheesy Formica. One drawer was spit out on the planked flooring before it. Then there was the closet, its door shut, the last bastion for potential surprise.

Rodman walked toward it. He grabbed hold of the knob and held it firmly, then held it some more and listened to the quiet. He yanked the door open and something brushed him, his face, and he flinched, swatted at it backhanded, and he retreated a step, his lungs sucked in. It was a shirt. It had been hung inside on the closet door hook and its sleeve had swung into Rodman's face after his sharp pull. A closer inspection identified the colorful long-sleeve shirt as one of Vance's, to be sure. It was dated and worn white at the collar and had a doobie in the front chest pocket. Aside from accumulations of dust chains breezing along its floor, the closet was empty.

A large over-the-shoulder canvas bag was under the sink's exposed piping, and Rodman picked through it, through other shirts, a pair of black jeans, a patched-up denim jacket, and a mix of soiled and clean Jockey underwear. . . . This was his suitcase, Rodman thought, recognizing the kind of "luggage" Vance always used. The laugh was, the canvas bag looked more recently bought than most of the logo-fronted tee shirts Rodman was sifting through. There was nothing to note among the bag's apparel except the almost tactile stench of encrusted body odor from infrequent washings.

Rodman couldn't tell if the bed had been used recently, because it looked as though it had been wrestled as much as slept in, with its twisted sheets and kicked-over blanket. Vance's pouch lay halfway underneath the covers, poking out like a green lizard's snout. Rodman opened it, but it was uncharacteristically vacant—no product. Rodman's moistened finger ran along its insides, then was closely scrutinized, but no spill of powder, not a fleck, adorned its tip. Whoever broke in didn't get to rob Vance of any drugs because the S.O.B was dry, Rodman thought.

The gold-sparkled Formica dresser had a few imported beer

bottles on it, some dog-eared paperbacks, and a hardcover—a Carl Jung biography—overdue two years from a public library three states away. The upended dresser drawer had some audiocassettes spilled from it—Warren Zevon's *Excitable Boy*, a Led Zeppelin, a half-dozen others—and a portable tape player with headsets. Apparently, whoever searched the room was not looking for something to hock for spending money if they left that brand-new Sony cassette player on the floor.

Walking back to his car, Rodman established that if Vance were still alive, he sure as hell didn't go back to that place. There were no bloody bandages in the wastebasket, just candy bar wrappers and deli paper from sandwiches. Vance couldn't have left town, either, *wouldn't* have, not with his personal belongings, as meager as they were, still in the room.

The elevator at the car park didn't seem to be working, so Rodman used the stairs to head for the third-floor ramp. Then where was he? Rodman asked himself. Was somebody holding him? Caring for him? Threatening him? How could two bullets not have stopped him, not have drained his mean, petty heart? Then Rodman thought of Delia, the double wound in her head, and he became slightly unsteady on the stairs for a moment, his eyes spotting. He strained not to sob again, paused a moment, head down, then pushed on, determined, thinking. He had found no physcial link in Vance's room to Delia whatsoever. That still didn't rule out his killing her before he— Rodman raised his head.

An eerie cry, screechy, was echoing ever so distantly in Rodman's mind—or was it? No, it was . . . up. Rodman glanced up the final flight of stairs to the door that led to the third-floor ramp, and he now definitely discerned some—what else could he call it?—some *cry*. It was high-pitched, not continuous, but intermittent, faded then loud, louder, then nothing, then back again, almost circular. He marched, up, toward the door—the cry was more distinct now, more like a reverberating squeal—what the hell *was* it?

Rodman opened the metal door and stepped onto the concrete ramp. It sounded like tires—*that* was it—but they weren't echoing away and gone, silent, but away and back again, away and back again, accompanied by the steady rumble of an engine. The reverberant noise was piercing through him. He suddenly felt scared, dottings of sweat breaking from his forehead. A moist fall wind was blowing in from the gaps between the ramp floors, stirring the air, the invisible cry. The source of the frightening, nerve-grating noise was just past the bend where his car had been parked. The rest of the ramp had but one or two vehicles still awaiting their owners. The cavelike hollow of the car park offered only the harsh squeals for him to come to. He only had to take four or five tentative strides straight ahead to see it, and what he saw made no sense.

It was his car, Delia's car, the Mercedes, driving. It had no driver, but it was driving. It drove in a wide circle, over and over again, over empty white-bordered parking slots, missing the building's fortifying beams. The car had its own haunted space and screeched like chalk on a blackboard as it turned, the piercing sound worse up close, echoing in this empty concrete, hurtful to the ears. The sharp sound made him shiver. The sight of his driverless car made him freeze. The steady wind made him feel hollow. There was something ghostly about the vision, frightening, having the air of a runaway merry-go-round in a child's nightmare.

Then something banged anonymously above the shrill cry of tires. Rodman shot a look left to see the elevator door once more bang a red fire extinguisher, which had been put in the way, refusing to allow the elevator to close. The automatic door just recoiled back to its open position.

Then before Rodman could straighten his head forward, he was struck by a blow to his kidney. He gasped and sagged to one knee, his neck jerking up. A baseball-capped little man, holding something brown, was watching him from alongside a concrete beam about ten feet away and totally oblivious to the whirligig of a car shrieking just behind him, watching Rodman with such serious interest, like a scientist anxiously anticipating the findings of an experiment. A second blow struck Rodman from behind, and Marty Dembo's voice before him said, "Ooh, that sounded right," fist to internal organ obviously hitting the correct pitch for such a trained ear.

And before Rodman could fall completely forward, face first, Marty slid the flat piece of box-brown cardboard he was holding underneath Rodman's body, catching it flush. The cardboard didn't make Rodman's landing any less impact-absorbing, but it would serve its unique purpose. Rodman, still trying to catch his breath, to feel his lower spine at all, was then rolled onto his back and sat on by Louis Dembo, the kidney crusher. He pinned Rodman's arms with both his well-developed legs, hunched over his prey and smiled his sour-lemon-toothed smile very near Rodman's pallid countenance.

"Guess you didn't find nothing either, huh?" Louis said, matter-of-factly. Rodman stared at Dembo, trying to understand the question through the dull pain in his back.

"Wha . . . ? Who . . . ?"

"At Sonny Vance's little dump of a place. You paid him a visit. What were you wanting from him? Some more of our money, or what?"

Rodman caught his breath, shook his head. "*Your* money? I don't kn—ugh!" A bellow of air was forced out of Rodman's lungs, his chest having been strongly pressed upon by not one, but now two bodies, Marty Dembo's misaligned face sitting on his big brother's shoulder like a second smaller and much uglier head. Marty's upper body had bounced on his brother's back, and with a thrust of his black Reeboks on the concrete floor behind, slid the three of them a few feet forward. The tire squeal grew *that* much closer, the passing car's rumble just about fifteen, twenty feet away. The cardboard, it was for smoother movement, like a sled on snowless ground—Rodman thought, then rethought—more like a makeshift flume, logs to a fucking buzz saw. Oh, God . . .

Louis shifted himself, most of his weight on Rodman's abdomen now, his shins and knees on Rodman's lower arms; his hands were pinning Rodman at the shoulder. Rodman's skull was just beyond the cardboard, his head cold from its slide along the dank concrete and stuck out there like an exposed appendage.

"Try it this way," Louis said to his brother, feeling more comfortably away from harm. Marty gave another strong shove at Louis's shoulders and moved the cardboard a few more feet.

"That's good," Louis said. Now Rodman could almost feel a slight oily breeze brush the top layer of his hair from the circling, screaming car as it passed by every ten seconds or so on its dizzying route.

Gazing at Rodman, Louis looked pleased with himself, pleased at seeing such fright, such panic-stricken realizations flash before him on this uptown face like a good horror flick. Louis looked almost playful, then a phony, pouty sad. "This is not any easy ride you're taking—which, I know, is no news to you. I mean, a guy's head could get some serious squishing done on it. Like pumpkin-mashing time, you know what I mean?"

Rodman heard Marty laugh somewhere behind the hard weight of Louis Dembo, who leaned back into him, pressing. "But back to business—*our* money—you heard me right, your wheels haven't closed up your ears yet. You see, Mr. Sonny Vance was no longer part of the deal as of this past Tuesday. That was his deadline. So we're kinda taking over his account with you. We want either the money with the appropriate interest—which makes the amount roughly fifty thou give or take a few bucks—or we want the drugs Vance dropped on you."

"What drugs?" Rodman could barely force out. "I don't have any drugs."

Louis sat up halfway again and, above the screeching, peeled out one sharp whistle through his teeth. That cue brought another brotherly grunt and thrust and hissing cardboard slide, and Rodman's head another four feet closer to his renegade Mercedes. Rodman stiffened even more. He cocked his head back so that his eyes could catch an upside-down glimpse of the circling sounds made real, solid, made metal and deadly and totally disorienting. It was like slipping backward into traffic, unavoidably into traffic, like a dream, a bad dream, like a child, like *Eric* . . . !

"I *don't—have—drugs!*" he shouted with all the breath and volume he could summon on each word, but Dembo mashed his hand to Rodman's mouth, the back of his head thunking the gray floor, shutting him up.

Dembo leaned in, applying pressure with his hand, with his voice, forcing his loins into Rodman's as he would into a dumb bitch.

"We don't want to hear this *shit*, mister," he hissed. "We

should be getting your undying thanks, and we're getting your shit."

Under Dembo's hand, Rodman was shaking his head in short vibrations of confusion.

"We *sprung* you, dick-head!"

"Boing!" said the maniacal young face that suddenly popped alongside Louis's then disappeared again.

"Freed your butt from that tin-can cop-mobile. What did you think? It was a miracle? God or something? You think you're worth more than me? You think God *likes* you better . . . ?" Dembo strengthened the press of his hand on Rodman's mouth, not allowing an answer to filter through. Dembo's gold necklace had tumbled from under his shirt, and its crucifix swung before Rodman's eyes. Momentary self-preservation made Rodman's head follow the icon's movement side to side, no.

"*We* did it. Me and my brother. Schmucks you wouldn't even spit on. You escaping was our guarantee you didn't use Vance's money—"

"*Our* money," Marty's disembodied voice corrected.

"That's right, *our* money, to make bail, or maybe offer your dope connection to the cops for a plea or maybe reveal our boss's name. See, we don't know what Vance told you, so lots of things coulda happened if you'd have got your butt involved with a lawyer and all that court bullshit. We got lucky we could cut you loose like we did before you saw your new lawyer. Sloppy stuff that transfer, huh? Fat-tub, shit-for-brains, jail cops. We spilled you out like a prize from a Cracker Jack box. *But*—you got away from us, didn't you?"

Marty's voice sang, "You're baa-ack!"

Louis Dembo puckered up. "So tell us true, sweet lips, where's the stash or give us the cash. Stash or cash."

"Or *smash!*" Marty said, clapping his hands together.

Louis laughed and released a whoop of enthusiasm. "Ah-ow! Yeah! You got *that* right, bro. Or smash!" A slit-eyed peer at Rodman. "Hey, ass-wipe, ever hear a head pop?" Dembo hunkered down to murmur in Rodman's ear. "Newsflash. *I* have."

Then Dembo sat up again, quickly this time, and as though about to lead a steer herd, raised one arm and snapped it straight at the elbow. He cried out, "Ho!" in an extended yell,

a yell in which Marty joined with relish—"Ho-o-o-o-o-o!"—
and bulled with all his compact strength into this big brother,
shushing them and Rodman and the cardboard another four
feet, then another hard push, for another short slide. Rodman
didn't know if their adrenaline was going to stop, this rush
might push them, push *him*—the spinning tires were on top of
him now, the Mercedes just a few feet from him, blowing by,
its screech piercing his skull.

"I *swear!*" he cried out. "I don't *know* about a deal!"

The stop-and-start journey just stopped, and Dembo began
shaking his head in seething disappointment.

"These are not good answers here. You're not moving in a
real productive or healthy direction—you gettin' me on this!?"
Dembo's anger was building, was restless.

"I'd tell you if I—"

"He *named* you, asshole! We had Vance spinning like a top
at Riller's Beach, we had him dead and buried in the sand up
to his nasal hairs, he was gull food! Vance said *you* were his
big-shot coke seller. He gave you goods—you sold it. You
made money. We want it. Maybe you *couldn't* sell the goods.
You still *have* the goods. We want it. Either way—*we want it!*"

"The stash or the cash," Marty added in a calm note.

"This job is *important* to us, you know? We're moving into
your end on this one, executive class, part of the company
take. We get a cut on the return, we got a stake, a percentage
of the biz, we've turned fucking Japanese—can you believe
that shit? These are my incentive juices you're getting here!"

And Rodman could only come up with questions amid his
delirium, like wondering what kind of crap did Vance sell
these thugs to save his own neck? What new lies and deceit?
How many deaths did that hippie fuck bring down on his life?

The was another metallic bang, only muffled, near the fire
extinguisher, but not *from* the fire extinguisher. The Dembos'
heads turned as one and saw a middle-aged, double-breasted
suit of a man wearing large tortoiseshell glasses, holding a
black briefcase and, unknown to them, muttering to himself
about having to use the stairs. He had apparently slammed the
metal door behind him in a jolt of anger after spotting the fire
extinguisher that was blocking the elevator's operation.

But then the eerie, screeching reality set in. The toadlike ferocity on his face transformed into an instinctual fear from what his ears heard and mind sensed. Marty, having taken two steps back to crane his neck around the bend, just stared at the interloper with a pissed-off squint. Meanwhile, Louis sat up straighter still, arching back, as though his body was straining to hear what he couldn't see.

"What?" he said curtly.

Marty shrugged. "A guy."

Dembo snapped at his mesmerized brother. "Get him!"

Marty nodded in trancelike slowness, confirming what he was already thinking, and moved toward the stunned man. Slipping his right hand into his jacket pocket, he fingered his smooth metal knuckles, all the while still staring, honing in.

The man began to say something, but the sight of Marty's determined, narrow eyes stifled any question, even pleas. Releasing his report-laden case, he spun around and ran for the stairwell door, his hand slipping the knob once before managing a solid grip, turn, and yank. As the man disappeared, Marty trotted to the elevator and kicked away the fire extinguisher, pressed 1, and while the elevator closed, thought about whether the guy was going to say thank you when he opened the first-floor stairwell door for him like a real gent. He'd let his brass knuckles say you're welcome.

Meanwhile, Dembo, leaning back, had had his ears attuned above the tires' squall and managed to hear both doors—stairwell and elevator—shut, as though he were mentally keeping track of his lesser self, his younger brother. Simultaneously, Rodman had had the mental discipline to relax, in spite of the intermittent rush and rumble of the car behind him, to relax his muscles, his arms, their weighty burden lessened when Dembo had angled back; had begun showing filial concern, his gene-pricked anxiety—take advantage! Rodman screamed to himself, *take* him!—while calming his wrists, his forearms. They seemed to have gotten thinner within seconds, looser, possessed with a fraction of space, room to maneuver.

So just before Dembo's weight was to perform a nearly imperceptible shift back to applying full pressure, Rodman pulled at his arms with his shoulders as hard as he could, as though his trapped hands were pieces of meat at the end of sticks, and his arms shot free. By then Dembo was completing his head

turn, beginning his lean back in, just then sensing, acknowledging his knees' loss of their fleshy padding, acknowledging
the freeing of Rodman's arms and the sudden make-or-break
sit-up Rodman was performing.

Carl's chest was rising up, but his chin, his head, was tilted
down, and his hands grabbed out and snatched Dembo's jacket.
Suddenly Dembo was being forced to bend faster because of
the sudden pull forward, and the top of Carl's skull sped upward and butted Dembo squarely in the mouth. When Dembo's
head snapped back, Rodman quickly lay down again, rounded
his spine, and still holding Dembo's jacket lapels, rocked back,
lifting his legs, lifting Dembo up, and with a strength-inducing
grunt, flipped Dembo over behind him, though not before
Dembo's hands clawed at Carl's face during his airborne tumble, and when he landed hard on his pelvis, Dembo still had
the fingers of one hand locked under Carl's chin, gripping it,
forcing Rodman to remain prone.

Livid, Dembo pulled at Rodman's chin, using it like a ladder
rung, sliding himself forward on his chest from behind Rodman's flattened head. He managed both hands hooked below
Rodman's chin now and stared at him upside down, nearly
snapping Rodman's neck off backward, slowly, as Carl kicked
and flailed and tried to roll over. Rodman saw his killer's face
inches from him and his maniacal topsy-turvy grin, a bleeding
grin from the head butt, a blurry grin as Carl's mind was
swirling, feeling his consciousness start to slip, the blue dots
swirling.

Rodman was dead except for one thing. In the seconds that
accounted for Rodman's flipping Dembo and Dembo's recovery, both had forgotten the squeals. The grating noise had become commonplace, but the Mercedes was still holding its
course, and Dembo's body, sprawled out from the top of Rodman's head where he was applying his choke hold, was in its
path. To his credit, Dembo's antennae twisted his attention to
his right, and he spotted the circling car's approach. He immediately released Rodman's chin, his legs scrabbling, rolling, his
body rolling, then all limbs scrabbling forward, the tires carving into their turn and missing Dembo's calves and ankles by
inches.

Rodman, meantime, had pushed himself upright, then onto

his feet as fast as his malleable legs would allow. He saw Dembo stop rolling, start puffing, his hot breath catching the chill from the cusp of the city's wind and frosting it, cold clouds of dragon's fire, anger. Dembo's eyes showed animal ferocity under his richly dark eyebrows.

Dembo leaped, in Rodman's view, from all fours to upright in an instant, quadruped to bi- in one evolutionary flicker, hunted to hunter once more. Rodman broke toward the stairwell and Dembo moved ahead quickly to cut him off, knew he would easily, but then, so did Rodman. Carl had only feigned his route to the EXIT sign, having quickly realized Dembo's younger brother would probably be on the other side of the metal door, probably a flight or two away. Rodman merely wanted Dembo to commit himself in that direction so that he himself could stop and cut back, back to the screeching Mercedes, his only real hope for escape.

Rodman scurried to a point in the imaginary circle he thought he could meet the car at its right front door where the window had been opened. Dembo slipped in his backtracking and then hurled himself forward, readying to tackle Rodman flush in the back, and with any luck, into the oncoming car. But the Mercedes got to Rodman before Dembo could, and Carl threw his head and shoulders into the open window as best he could. His face and chest bounced on the leather passenger seat, his legs still exposed outside the vehicle. The driving, circling force of the car immediately tossed him over, and the base of his skull struck the gear shift as he squirmed to pull his buttocks down from the window and drag his legs inside. As he raised himself up, dizzy from both the struggle and the ride, he was then pitched sideways back into the door. He finally landed, sitting on the floor space in front of the passenger seat, scrunched up there and facing left toward the driver's side, his head abutting the passenger door. He also got to understand how his car came to be a weapon.

A cement block had been placed just far enough on the gas pedal to weigh it down halfway, and a makeshift hook was grappling the steering wheel and keeping it in a forty-five degree dip, the hook attached to one end of what looked like a modified tire jack locking things into place between the angled wheel and floor.

Rodman blew out a breath and awkwardly rose sideways into the passenger seat, the spinning car turning his stomach. As he leaned over to grip the jack pole and pull, a crazed yell shook his purpose, a force struck his back, and a forearm was shunted under his neck like the bolt to a lock. Louis Dembo had leaped into the same window and grabbed onto Rodman's head, and though most of his body was hanging outside, his feet up, knees against the outside of the passenger door, his support was the yanked-back body of Carl Rodman, slammed up against the passenger door like a brace, holding Dembo up, though by doing so, he was being strangled. Dembo hung tight and cursed in Rodman's ear, sweating, bleeding, riding this twister of an auto like he was in a rodeo.

"You fucker, you almost got my legs flattened, you—"

Rodman was pinned back, gagging, his fists striking backward blindly at the dense greasy head, pulling at the solid arms pinning his neck, then trying to poke at eyes, any eyes. One finger caught the corner of Dembo's left eye, and Dembo cursed again and bit down on Rodman's earlobe as hard as he could. Rodman gurgled a scream, then kicked out his legs. His eyes suddenly flashed in recognition: his feet were well beyond the steering column, the hooking jack.

Through the pain, Rodman shot out his right leg at the lower portion of the jack's stem. His foot beat against it again and again, and maybe it was just desperate hope, but he sensed its trunk slipping a fraction with each blow. Dembo spit out the rubberlike piece of Rodman's lobe from his mouth, feeling dizzy himself, but goddamn feeling alive, feeling the blood, *tasting* it, feeling him crushing life from the hot-shit scumbag caught in the joint of his arm like in a muscled-up nutcracker. It was a cowboy carnival ride, a tiltawhirl death rush. And Marty, it figures, was missing out, the stupid fuck.

The tires kept screaming, and Rodman let their screams be his screams, his thrusts, his kicks at the jack. It moved more that time! Then one final one—Carl prayed, Carl gritted his teeth and absorbed the screams—one final kick and the jack sprung out, its bottom flipping away, the hook losing its hold, the steering wheel starting to right itself with a sudden jerk, while the speed remained constant, the brick still applying its pressure, and that was just the way Rodman wanted it, hoped it.

Dembo felt the car adjust, nearly throwing him off, but he still hung onto his victim's neck as a hanger would a coatrack. But the car had lost its radius; it arced out now, more in a velocity-driven curve, and slammed straight into the short, open-air wall that overlooked the city. The sudden crash was too much for even Dembo's strength; it forced him to let go, flung him off the car door like a fly flicked from a wall. The side of his head and right shoulder was propelled into the low barrier, knocking him nearly unconscious and certainly defenseless.

Inside the car, Rodman had been thrown against the dashboard and landed on the floor again, his legs tangled in the steering wheel and stick shift. He scrambled upward, bleeding at the side of the head, at the ear, his throat thoroughly bruised and not fully expanded. He pulled the still-running car into reverse and, blurry-eyed, sped down the nearest ramp, skidding along the corkscrew concrete sideguards along the way, scraping paint, until the final opening, the streets spreading out before him, the end of the cyclonic ride at last.

Moments later, after Marty helped up his battered brother, Louis remained silent a few moments. Then he whirled and punched Marty flush in his left jaw and broke a silver-braced tooth. Louis yelled at him, furious for not getting his help. Marty held his mouth and whimpered into the blood filling his hands. Louis stared at his kin, forgetting the sympathy he had felt for Marty just minutes ago for not being able to take part in the joy of the kill, now blaming, displacing failure, like a mentally unbalanced mother eyeing her child, her burden.

12

HALLIE HAD FINALLY stopped pacing and sat, though not idly. The only times Hallie would ever be still was when caught in the glow of the bright thirty-two-inch television screen, snared by the plot, the romance, the richness of travel and experience that was not her present life. As she watched her shows, she was rooted, leaden. Unlike her husband Bertram, forever out-of-town, out-of-touch. Not that she wanted him under her feet (maybe her foot), but maybe now, maybe when there was death so close, so cold—next door, for heaven's sake!—he shouldn't have run back to Canada on business, not now!

She sat looking at the embroidered handmade spread that graced a rattan love seat, smoothing it with her hands, ironing it with her touch, as though making a perfect place to sit for someone. Barbara was coming, she thought; at least *she* will be here.

Then her anticipation got the better of her and she stood up, all nerves, her deformed foot's dormancy always made up for by the rest of her agitated body. The nineteenth century grandfather clock said eight-seventeen. Barbara was late, Barbara was being poorly influenced, rubbing elbows with—— Hallie censored the name even from herself. And rubbing God-knows-what-else!

Hallie paced past the den window and just missed seeing the dark face that had been frozen there for a moment, the shadow that outlined the filmy curtains. She moved to the living room and put on a Johnny Mathis CD just to soothe her conjecturing mind. No sooner did the music begin than the doorbell chimed.

"Barbara!" she cried out excitedly, hobbling to the vestibule.

"Where's your key, dear?" she shouted as she arrived at the door. Then doubt sprouted beneath her music. She paused, hearing an inquiring voice.

"What?"

"It's the police, Mrs. Fouche," said the male voice outside.

"Yes?"

"We're setting up a guard post next door, ma'am. Outside the house. We're wondering if we could use your yard as a lookout point as well. It's very well-located. We need your written permission, however."

"Very well," Hallie said, and she unlocked the door. The instant she began to open it, the impostor barged through before even the first glint of recognition could alight Hallie's face. She staggered back, nearly falling.

"God! Oh, God!" she cried out.

Rodman—his face streaked with splotches of blood, his clothes disheveled—glared at her for an instant.

"Shut up!" he said, then slammed the door behind him, locking it.

Hallie backed up a few more thumping steps and started screaming through the highly polished fingernails that had flown up to her mouth in surprise.

"Quiet!" Rodman yelled at her, but Hallie was hysterical, her brown eyes like jutting bulbs blazed with fright. She shook all over, felt violated all over—

"*Quiet!*" Rodman yelled again, then took two long strides toward her and struck her across the face, her fingers no shield to the force of his open hand. She took in one elongated gasp and cupped her own mouth, crying into it, her eyes just little sad slits with spider-leg lashes. She leaned against the wall sideways for support, sobbing, shaking.

Rodman was shaking, too, looking at her, pitying her. He wanted to say he wouldn't hurt her, but he just had. He sat on the arm of a striped sofa to settle himself down, his arms limp—watching her, wondering what his life had become, what *he* had become, grubbing through apartments of an apparent dead man, grappling with masochistic thugs, smacking crippled women. . . .

Even though he had cased the house from the outside, Rodman's eyes scanned the entrances to the living room; his ears

listened for noises above the strains of "Chances Are."
"Where's Bert?" he said.

Hallie's face grew red. She gurgled through her sobs, her burgeoning anger. "You're ... bleeding ... on my couch."

Rodman was taken aback by the non sequitur. He squinted at her, almost laughed, then touched his right ear, which was still dripping blood in slow intervals. He had the latent urge to collect a few fresh globules and write "Kill the pigs!" on one of the cushions.

Instead, he said, "I know it was you, Hallie."

Hallie shook her head and kept her cheek as close to the wall as she could get, wanting to go through it, wanting to get away and kill him both at the same time, wanting to unleash her leaden foot at him like a dog, lift and shoot it like a gun, screw it off and swing it like a sledgehammer.

"Don't shake your shitty little plastic perm job at me, you supercilious bitch. It was you."

"Are you—" Hallie was trying to catch her sobs, stifle her fear, raise her ire. "—are you ... a-accusing *me* ... of killing your wife?"

"No," Rodman said bluntly. "I mean, you accused *me*. To the police. *You're* the witness. I know. You had to be the one. I don't know why you were up at four A.M. and it doesn't matter, but you had your peep show going, and you said you saw something, and I want to know what."

Hallie turned her back to the wall now, facing Rodman, showing her defiance. "I saw *you*, that's who I saw. Who do you think I saw?"

Rodman stood suddenly and Hallie flinched. "How can you say that? How can you fucking say that?"

"You have no class," Hallie muttered, Rodman wondering if she was referring to his supposed wife-killing or his filthy mouth.

"I'm going to drip blood on your couch, your imported rugs—and it may not all be my own in a minute. Now what happened? Why did you lie to the police?"

"I don't lie," Hallie spat back, "not like some people. I have virtues. I saw what I saw. I—I couldn't sleep. I don't sleep well. I heard something next door. A noise. I looked out—"

"With or without your binoculars?" Rodman interjected.

Hallie stopped and felt herself blush. It was never out there, was always unspoken, and as long as it was unspoken, it maintained an aura of privacy, of privilege. Exposed, it seemed dirty.

"Without," she curtly answered.

"Go on."

"I saw you walking toward your house in the driveway."

"How'd you know it was me?"

"You know if you kill me, I still gave my sworn statement to the police. They'd still get you in court, they don't need my testimony in person—"

"Jesus! How'd you fucking know it was me, Hallie?" Rodman's shout shriveled her.

"Your jacket," she said. "You were wearing your jacket. That one."

"*This* jacket," Rodman repeated, holding out the bottom of the battle-soiled denim one he was wearing. "You saw me in this jacket—" Hallie nodded. "—but you didn't see my face, did you?"

Hallie didn't answer.

"*Did* you?"

"I didn't have to," she hissed.

"And that's it? That's all you saw or did?"

"I went back to bed. I thought maybe you had forgotten something for your trip or you came back early. I couldn't believe it when the police told me. . . ." Hallie's eyes started to drift off, and even her heavy-handed application of rouge couldn't keep the pallid hue from her cheeks. She began to weep for her friend Delia, and Rodman saw that her surging sorrow was real and deep-felt.

Rodman believed her tears, bonded to her because of their shared loss, in spite of his dislike for her petty power plays in the neighborhood, in her family—but what was he to make of the account she told the police? How could she have seen his jacket? Very easily. If she *wanted* to see him, she would say she did. So what *did* she see? A man? Somebody in blue? Maybe nobody at all. After all, her mind's eye was an active and elaborate one, a palette of colors in her paint–by–social class world.

"What was the noise?"

Hallie was wiping some tears, blackened by mascara. "What? What do you mean?"

"The noise you heard that brought you to the window. The noise you *said* you heard."

Hallie understood the implication. "I *heard* a—a sort of shout. Like you were calling her name. Sounded like 'Delia,' then you were banging the sliding door to the pool. . . . You remember shouting, don't you?" she added snidely.

"Why would I have shouted her name? Why bang?"

"You forgot your key. You were drunk again. There were a million reasons I could come up with—most of them displaying a lack of consideration or self-control."

"My best traits," Rodman said flatly.

"If the shoe fits . . ." Hallie said, her eyebrow arching bravely, while the rest of her still huddled in as close to a standing fetal position you can get while against a wall.

Rodman began to step toward Hallie, his body falling into shadow. "Now tell me the *other* fairy tale you told all the detectives with little pads to fill."

Hallie cowered. "Don't come near me! Don't . . . !"

Rodman stopped. "Tell me about the lover—"

"Don't hit me again!"

"I'm not here to hit you, damn it!" Rodman brought his arms in to his body, tried to settle himself. "I'm here—I'm here to find out what the hell is going *on*. I *didn't* kill Delia, I don't know a fucking thing about a lover, and I don't believe there *was* a lover. But just in case this isn't one of your crossover dreams from a soap opera, I want to know about this lover!"

Hallie didn't hear the subtle tone in Rodman's voice amid the demand, didn't hear the faint note of need, of pleading; she was too involved in her entrapment. She let her disdain buffer her meager sensitivities and told him what she knew gladly.

She told Rodman about Delia and her mysterious trips during the past year or so, her packing and unpacking of overnight bags when Rodman was away on business; about how Delia, when cordially asked, would tell her she was on a P.R. mission for the Leukemia Fund, but when Hallie would call their local chapter, the girls would tell her Delia wasn't there and should be home, the workers never mentioning any promotional mission or out-of-town business meeting. Hallie also told Rodman about the phone call Friday (though she pretended she had overheard excerpts from the living room while still visiting and not from her portable phone next door) and about the secret tryst at the party and the stone barbecue's burned love letter.

After a few minutes of Hallie's tale, Rodman began only half listening, not wanting to hear more, began denying it even more in spite of . . . Those trips, he knew about those trips. At least some of them. He thought they were usually downstate to Peabody for fund-raising seminars, but unlike Hallie, he never checked up on her. If anything, Delia would call *him* when he was away. He assumed she was calling from home, which most of the time she said she was. Or calling from Peabody when she had simultaneous fieldwork to do. Was he just being gullible? Innocent? He had just killed a man, at least tried to— *did*—and yet . . . he felt as naive as a child first coming to understand the disturbing mechanics of sex.

"You have no proof," Rodman interrupted in a monotone. "That's no proof. She ever mention a name?"

Hallie shook her head. "Delia and I shared things we didn't have to say. We knew."

"You a psychic?"

"I'm a *woman*." Hallie always resented the need to remind men, people, of that fact. "I also know how men operate on a double standard. How jealous you idiotic creatures get if you find out such a thing about your wife, but how easy—oh, how easy it is for you to do yourself. Like you and your former secretary Pat Dokes. Don't think *that* didn't look obvious to everybody."

Rodman sneered. "You think you know everything, don't you?"

"I know the type of man you are, the lowlife kind of family you come from, the lowlife kind of son you brought up. You're the ruination of this country, you people. You've killed this country like you killed your wife. That's what I know."

Rodman's face burned red. "Oh, yeah? And do you also *know* where your husband is?"

Hallie struggled to stand up straight, forthright, but the act wobbled in its conviction. "Where he *should* be," she said.

Rodman emitted the bark of a derisive laugh and nodded

and thought about where Bertram Fouche *shouldn't* be, about the sundry brothels in Quebec Province Bert would laugh and joke and brag about "vacationing" in to Rodman; thought about where certain *parts* of Bertram Fouche shouldn't be, too, like his fat hand on the soft cusp of Delia's lower back. And what else? Rodman thought and raged. And what else?

"And what else?" Rodman said aloud, his heart racing, his eyes pinning Hallie to the ivory-colored wall.

Approximately forty minutes later, Barbara Fouche used her key and walked in the front door. She thought she saw a shape, her mother, two rooms over, sitting alone at the head of the dining room table with her back to Barbara, but then it appeared to resemble more a flaccid, overweight manikin.

"Mom?" Barbara called.

The shout brought the puffy manikin to life, and now it was a squealing, unintelligible wind-up toy, gyrating and bouncing and going nowhere. A quick trot forward and she saw that her mother's arms were behind her back, tied up.

"Oh, my—" Barbara stopped and hurried back to the door she had closed behind her. She opened it and quickly spotted the hunched figure near the motorcycle, gazing down the street.

"Danny! Come in quick!"

Though startled, Danny responded instantly to his girlfriend's cry. He was supposed to be waiting outside while Barbara talked to her mother awhile about everything, then he was supposed to get a cue to come in, but this wasn't the cue he expected.

An urgent sprint into the dining room revealed Hallie bound up tight to the high-back oaken head chair, both legs and arms wrapped in gold-colored curtain cords. Her mouth was sealed shut with wide decorator tape of a pastel burgundy. Barbara tore off the swath of red at Hallie's mouth, which produced a ripping sound and a pain Hallie knew too well from getting her legs waxed.

"Oh, Jesus, oh, God, oh, Jesus . . . !" Hallie kept saying, seemingly out of breath.

Barbara's voice was raised, panicky. "What happened? Who did this? Were you robbed?"

"It was—oh, God—it was—" Only then did Hallie double-take and spot the person who freed her pulled-back hands. "It was *him*! His *father*!" She said it as though deliberately shouting out a four-letter word in the middle of a church service. Hallie's eyes enlarged and embraced her daughter's for sympathy. "He broke in. He hurt me. He rifled my purse for money. He—"

Danny felt his heart stutter and started to back off as if a madwoman were invoking some kind of evil spirit.

Barbara couldn't feel anything except assaulted by it all. "Mr. Rodman? He was here?"

"That's what I just said, didn't I?" Hallie snapped. "Don't you believe me?"

"Of course," Barbara said. "Of course, I do. I—" She put her cool hand on her mother who was still heated and gyrating, jumping in place on the chair even though free of her bonds. "—I was just shocked to *hear*—I didn't—"

"What's so shocking?" Hallie said. "My God, I didn't know *what* he was going to do! I was helpless. He could have killed *me*, too—"

Barbara squeezed her mother's forearm, hard, hoping to find the nerve ending that would quiet her; Barbara didn't want to hear this. The night, the day, was too dark as it was. "Don't talk. Calm down. We should call a doctor."

"Call the *police*, that's who!" Hallie said, trying to raise herself. "We should call—get me the phone!"

Barbara was nodding. "Okay, okay. And a doctor, too." Barbara turned to address Danny behind her. "We should call a doc—" Barbara stood up, felt an empty chill. "Danny?" she said.

But Danny was gone.

13

AFTER ABOUT TWENTY minutes, his tactile memories won. He could only lean back on the front door, regain the posture of last Friday, which seemed a millennium past, and again stare at the bucolic painting. The complete circle. Same headache. Two dead. This was the house of the dead.

Rodman wondered why he had never revealed to Delia that it was no "family friend" but, in fact, *he* who had painted the quaint pastoral, his best effort, really. Probably because he knew she didn't really care for it, that it was an accommodation to his taste, the one item in the room that didn't have her touch, her dynamic style.

Rodman had painted it while at the cabin with Vance and other so-called antiestablishment-oriented friends after his father had died and he had quit school. It was when many in his minicommune talked more about "real" change, about social revolution, political action, when they read *Mother Jones* and far more radical counterculture journals in between the smoke-swirling bongs and the acid parties. It was before Sonny Vance poisoned things, or maybe just tapped things, the things in Rodman that vortexed into drugs, the business of, the money in.

Now the half dark of the shut-up house deepened the painting's texture, dimming the greens, illuming the whites, the sheep's wool, and Rodman wondered why he did not give the one sheep its own lamb like the others, an obvious lacking. Was it a fated preknowledge of Eric's death? His own unconscious wish never to have been born? Never to have been the instrument of the first death, his mother's? Dime-store, he thought. Psych 101. He had more practical mysteries to solve, physical not spiritual ones.

Twenty minutes ago Rodman had broken in with an armor of determination to solve those mysteries, to *know*, had allowed his intent to lead him around blindly throughout his own home, like a sniffing, driven hound, nosing for any clue, any sign of the secret life that was his wife's. He stormed through things, appointment books, shopping lists, laundry hampers, barging past any associations it may have to her (Delia), to him (Eric), to people (dead)—they're dead—moving through items, files in her home office, looking quickly, making sure the ghosts wouldn't stick to him, wouldn't be there, as they always were there, for him, part of him. He ran through her medicine cabinet, her makeup; he avoided the mirror so as not to imagine her face there. And it was working. It *was*. At least for the first twenty minutes.

But eventually Rodman had to slow down or he was clearly going to miss something at this pace, this avoidance. His mind had to focus and steady itself and, in doing so, gamble, gamble with the possibility of infiltrating emotions. He tried to be more patterned. What he had sorted through haphazardly at that point was immaterial, known quantities. He needed surprises. He was looking for the surprise: any links with Vance, with somebody even as ridiculous as Bertram Fouche, with anybody, really, or any *thing* not consistent with what he knew about Delia's daily life. The first surprise came from himself. He decided to believe Hallie, or at least come at the search through her story. The lover. The phone calls. The overnights. The party.

And with that he was up and outside, quietly maneuvering through the expansive backyard, through the hedges, and approached the roughened stone barbecue. He fingered through the gray-powdered ash and remnants of coals and found the fragment Hallie had mentioned, noticed the X, the "kiss." He took the torn triangular piece inside and, using a flashlight fished from the hall closet, tried to discern a watermark, tried to determine if the piece was of a cloth bond and traceable somehow. But it was simply paper. Plain white paper. And *whose* paper? That is, was this *her* letter or her lover's? Her X or his? And why would they write letters if, according to Hallie, they were always talking on the phone?

At the time, that thought gave Rodman further strength to ward off the memories, though he purposely avoided the kitchen, avoided the outline, her outline, the scene, just glanced in once and saw dark stains, dark red—Blood? His eyes blotching?—he wasn't willing or ready to find out. What he wanted to find were the phones, concentrate on the phones.

The Rodman household had been the equivalent of a two-story phone bank between Delia managing most of her charitable concerns from her home office upstairs and Rodman being on the line every day to brokers, associates, Howard, government offices. There were five phones in all, three of which were portable and had recharging cradles strategically placed around the house. Thus Rodman began to punch the redial button on each receiver with the intent of tracking Delia's last call. Two phones dialed up the detective bureau, phones obviously used by the investigation squad after the murder. Two dialed up the foundation, Delia's staff. But one—

"Ollie's Tavern," said the older man's voice on the other end.

Rodman thought he was ready for anything, but this took him off guard. "Ollie's . . . Tavern?"

"That's the name. Sure you got the right number?"

"Uh, yeah, I was—uh—told I could find a Delia Rodman there, or somebody who knew her. You know her?"

"D. L. Ro . . . ?"

"*Delia* . . . Rodman. Delia Rodman."

"Never heard of her."

"Could you ask whoever is there, any regulars, if they—"

"Look—you want to ask around for some lady you lost, buddy, come down here yourself, okay? I got drinks to serve."

"Wait!" Rodman said. "Don't hang up! Where are you located?"

"Fifty-five Keys Avenue." Then came the click.

Rodman slumped, didn't know what to make of that connection. The police could have made that call, too, and yet the phone he dialed from was the one on Delia's desk, a multilined instrument, and it didn't appear as though the investigators were ever in the room, or even upstairs at all. And why should they have been? Why probe her files, her desk? The wide-eyed neighbor saw the husband, and the dumb-ass husband confessed: case closed. Keys Avenue certainly didn't ring any bells. Was that downtown? The south side?

Rodman thumbed through Delia's bills again, double-checked her credit card receipts—stupid, did he expect she bought everyone a drink and put it on her American Express gold card? But he wasn't really looking for the tavern per se but possibly a men's shop where he suspected she would have bought a special something for this mystery date, a place in which she normally wouldn't purchase a gift for him; or possibly he would spot the name of an unfashionable motel with or without porn cabled in. Delia would be the type of woman to pay the way once in a while (at least she did early in their own lustful relationship, Delia treating for a Saturday night romp at the Dee-Lite Motor Lodge during the days when her sports complex job earned more than his budding real estate one).

Rodman discovered an envelope of Ready Bank cash machine receipts he had overlooked before, but these slips revealed nothing except . . . except . . . that was two, three . . . he found three receipts over the last month that were definitely not from the local machine he and Delia regularly used. Furthermore, the withdrawals registered on these three were significantly more than usual; in fact, one was for five hundred dollars. And all three transactions were siphoned from her private account, not their joint one. So where was this machine?

Rodman cradled the phone receiver under his chin and dialed the bank's twenty-four-hour help line. He read off the cash machine number from the slips to the baby-voiced woman on the other end. She said the Ready Bank Ready Cash unit was on Bailey Boulevard in Point Crescent.

Who lived in Point Crescent? Rodman wondered. Nobody he knew, although he believed he came across the town's name somewhere recently. It wasn't in that Braxton Cole article Howard had given him at the cabin, was it? No, that wasn't it. From what he could recall offhand, Point Crescent was a good day's drive away, twice the distance from his home to Janus Mountain, but at the opposite compass point.

After another perusal, Rodman also noted that the dates on

the bank receipts corresponded to days he remembered either Delia was away on business or he was. Now, all too clearly, Hallie began to loom in his mind like a deformed seer: Point Crescent was where Delia had a lover. *Or*—Rodman countered—where she had a blackmailer. Maybe she was being blackmailed by her lover, or by someone else who knew about her lover. . . . Rodman's head began to ache and whirl and pitch with the storm of possibilities, none of which settled very well in his stomach, churning it, and the one name that churned the most was Sonny Vance. Always crashing back to Sonny Vance like the suck of low tide, the stink of seaweed.

Unable to entwine the living with the dead in some kind of order, some reason, Rodman flushed everything from his head, cleansed his system. He needed a new shirt, pants. (How about a new start?) He craved blankness and both the comforting feel and antiseptic smell of fabric softener. He walked with labored steps to the master bedroom.

It was there where the seepage of torpor, of memory, began its real work. He sat on the quilted comforter to change his rancid clothes, and within seconds her scent seemed to embrace him—her light flowery body powder on her dresser, in her hangered clothes; the tang of perspiration from her hamper, her week-old pillowcase. There are visual memories that spawn distinct, yet distant, feelings. Then there are memories beyond the visual that spawn visceral earthquakes, tactile memories that make you quiver and feel as though you are there completely, now, breaking sweat, back in time, the same touch, smell, *sense*.

Delia was there in bed unseen behind him, turning over, rustling, her red hair unleashed from its ribbons, thick and wild, shadowing a freckle or two. They had just made love before dinner. Or he was just getting up for work. Or she was slipping into bed at night to read her P.D. James, to talk about a snag with some sport celeb for a fund-raiser, to snuggle. A million times done, each a penny's worth of value; never to be done again, a life's fortune lost.

Rodman stood up, wobbly-legged but recharging. He changed clothes as quickly as he could, and sort of held his breath, sort of drew the dense air gradually through his mouth, not wanting to breathe her in anymore, to waken her again.

But as he tucked in a clean shirt, he noticed the rosary hanging over the top shelf of the walk-in closet, the ornate silver crucifix dangling down like a fishing lure, Jesus its bait. Rodman often wondered what Delia had done with the rosary after her toe-step into the still pool of his religion. Following Eric's death, it seemed as though she were willing to try anything for an answer, even a Catholic God. But she could never feel guilty for earnest acts that went wrong, never accepted being a sinner from the start and to the end, never felt the threat of eternal judgment. Her soul was pragmatic; you don't solve life's mysteries with another one, especially one even harder to fathom.

Six months later and she sought out a more secular treatment for her spiritual loss—Caring Friends, a community support group for those who had lost a child to tragedy. But for Rodman, the network of stories these people had lived through seemed all too weblike and entrapping, and he listened and nodded and sometimes talked only for Delia's sake; he owed her at least that much. He would listen to how some parents lost their child to meaningless suicide, some to untimely disease. One couple had a nine-year-old boy who was "car surfing" with a friend, but an accelerated turn threw the friend on a grassy street divider while the nine-year-old struck a corner sidewalk, the head-first impact on the curb renting, shocking dead his brain. Another set of parents discovered their seven-year-old with his toy rifle in a tree he had just climbed. Only they discovered him with his neck caught in the rifle strap, his footing having slipped, his body hanging there in the branches, choked, his face the color of a bruise.

Delia had to tell the group Eric's story. Rodman couldn't, and even then, he had to tune it out with some form of mental static. He had relived Eric's death far too often. That wasn't the catharsis, the flaming sacrifice he needed.

No matter, the group kept trying to get Delia and him to confront themselves about the devastation, talk about it, beyond what the disappointing private investigator's report said that week, and one way to do it, the group believed, was through Eric's room. After his death, Eric's bedroom had been locked up for weeks, literally locked up, as though to ensure instinct didn't take over one morning, one unthinking moment of the day, when you would unconsciously believe he was still alive and you would naturally open the door to his room to talk to him, get him to supper, ask him if he wanted to take a ride to the park. You put a lock on the door so that kind of stupidity, that kind of habit, wouldn't rip your heart to tatters the moment you stepped inside the room's emptiness, its palpable affirmation of loss. Neither he nor Delia could go into that room for nearly a year. Nobody dared use the key.

However, the support group did finally convince the Rodmans to go home and open their son's door, to expose their hearts to the stuffy air, the boy's mess—discarded clothes, loose crayons, comics—frozen in time, got them to sit together on the twin bed and Spider-Man sheets and embrace each other and to think about him, talk about him, laugh about him, weep for him and for themselves. It was one small way of allowing the fullness of their child's life, no matter how brief, to be reconciled. And yet, even with Delia's eyes wet and distant with remembrance, Rodman recalled detecting the anger swimming beneath her gaze, recalled seeing just under her grief her demand and her hope for *the truth*, a truth she died never knowing.

And so it was this influx of feelings and pain that brought him to the front door, to the painting, to a standstill. The house of death had won. Rodman had allowed it to be so, for this was also the room where it stopped, where the search for the truth ended. He could vividly reenvision Delia's pleading expression to him, to her brother Jack, to Danny. (Danny was there, too. That's right.) She wanted to go on with the Barkley people, the investigation into who was responsible for Eric's death. Jack and he thought it useless. Rodman remembered her turning away from the three men left in her life. A fissure was opened, one that would never quite be bonded back into place, no matter how much pressure he applied, no matter how many fund-raisers he started to attend with her, or dependency clinics he agreed to include in his housing development scheme against Braxton Cole. As he had watched Delia march upstairs that night, he caught Jack just shaking his head in disappointment that his sister wasn't being reasonable, that she didn't understand. But Rodman understood: they—he—was depriving Delia of the answer she ached for, although he had it all along.

He was responsible for Eric's death. Rodman wanted to shout it out to Delia before she sadly, bitterly, drifted away upstairs and out of sight, like an angry spirit. *I* am responsible, Rodman wanted to cry out through his tears, and he nearly did. But Jack was there, and he would be too cerebral to understand; would, intentionally or not, play the disdainful skeptic. And Delia would have probably been too agitated to listen at that moment, to care. And Danny . . . Danny was there. And he had never confessed a thing in front of Danny, too damned proud—but he was *there*, wasn't he?

His shadow was spread like an angry stain on the wallpaper, Danny's face in half-light, Danny's eyes on him, burning, for how long? Danny was there—*now!*

"Danny?" Rodman said with a hitch in his voice, a few silent tears having thickened his throat from his recollections. He pushed himself off the door and squinted toward the door frame to the hall, the black stain, shadow, the eyes.

"Danny?" Rodman said louder now as he took a few short steps toward the figure obscured by the room's darkness. The figure began to nod, not in affirmation of the question so much as in a rhythmic oscillation of indecisiveness, of thought, of buildup, like the first flipping of a kettle's metal tongue before the boiling blast of its whistle.

Rodman moved closer, and Danny strode forward, let out a sob, and struck his father with a solid punch to the eye, *thwap*. Rodman, having stepped into the blow's impact, staggered back. His left leg crumpled and he fell to the living room carpet.

"Fucker!" Danny shouted, and jumped on Rodman, swinging wildly. Danny was never much of a fighter as a child. The few schoolyard brawls he had engaged in were gang-up affairs, wrestling gropes en masse. He always avoided any one-on-one face-offs. Now as a young man his inane fisticuffs showed. His fists fell hard like dropping stones from a roof, and with ferocity, but they were poorly aimed and didn't land cleanly, giving Rodman the chance to ward off many of the wilder swats. Rodman kept yelling, "Stop! Stop it!" to Danny's pounding and cursing, but he wouldn't stop and a few punches struck the still tender wounds Rodman suffered at the grueling attack of Louis Dembo and suddenly Rodman began to fight back.

He was still yelling "Stop!" and they grappled each other. Danny was crying and cursing, "Mother fucking son of a—" when Rodman's head caught the crest of Danny's chin, jarring his skull, his teeth, and Rodman tossed him over sideways and punched out, and Danny flinched, dropping limp for that singular stabbing moment of pain. Rodman's hands pushed up quickly, then clamped down on Danny's arms, pinning them to the floor.

"Now, *stop it!*" Rodman shouted into Danny's defiant and twisted face, his body still contorting beneath his, desperate to get up, to struggle free. "Please," Rodman added, begged. Then Danny went dead as though his muscles had lost their lightning current. He was breathing hard; his lip was bleeding badly; his eyes were still wet, his gaze still hard on Rodman.

Rodman, panting as well, looked down at his son, a son he felt familiar beating, striking down. Much too familiar. It was usually followed by a hands-on body search for a vial or a little baggy of white, or just a stolen household item, a Lalique crystal, a Cartier watch, pocketed valuables ripe for resale. No more. He didn't want to hurt Danny ever again. Rodman let their heavy breaths dominate the silence for a moment. Then he swallowed and said, "I didn't kill your mother. I swear I didn't kill her."

Another panting silence ensued and Danny bit his lower lip. His scraped-red nostrils dilated. Then he spat straight in his father's face, the gob catching Rodman beneath the left eye, some on the bridge of his nose. Rodman barely recoiled as though expecting it, deserving it. He just continued to look down as though in mourning at his anguished son, his quivering lip, his loss, their loss. The spit cooled on his face and a slimy string of it swung down to Danny's hot cheek. Then came the approaching siren.

Rodman's face aimed itself toward the sound like a beacon of fear. He glanced down once more at the hatred embodied in his son, then leaped off him and ran toward the back patio door. Danny tried to leap up in pursuit but the blood surged to his brain too quickly, drowning it, and sent him back on one knee to the floor, his head dropping to his hand. The siren wail ceased and the red lights of the police car pulsed through the living room window like intruders. Just like Hallie, Danny thought. She called the cops, but it wasn't their business. Or hers. The encounter with his father, the touch of his flesh, his blood, brought Danny past any more questions. It was none of *anybody's* business. It was family business.

Later that night Rodman stood at the pay phone outside the closed Ninth Avenue Shoe Boutique, propping himself up and fishing in his pocket for change. His breath made frosty clouds in the night air. He thanked—no, not God, never again God—but thanked someone that he anticipated possible trouble before barging in on Hallie and had parked the car two blocks away from his house. By the time the police had addressed Hallie's complaint and came to the Rodman home to find Danny squatting dazedly on the floor, cocooned, unwilling to speak to the officers, Rodman had long since cut past the stone barbecue and through the back gate, free for the moment from capture. Rodman put a dredged-up quarter in the phone and dialed.

He was alone, to be sure, at least in terms of his family. When Danny lay before him on the living room floor, he wanted his son back somehow, the musical child, the boys they both were before the drugs brought them both down. But Danny was as gone from him now as Delia or Eric, another piece of his flesh peeled away. He was down to bone.

Rodman's body demanded rest, but his will demanded more. He needed to get to Point Crescent, even with just a bank slip clutched in his hand, even if just to collar and ask people on the street like a crazed Diogenes if they saw Delia, knew of her, anything. But he needed money. He needed gas. The line was ringing.

Earlier Rodman had taken the few bills Hallie had jammed like crumpled tissues in her handbag, but it wasn't enough. He needed financing, a friend—

"Hello?" came the puzzled voice on the other end.

"Howard, it's me."

There was a long pause. Then words drained from Rodman. Whatever strength left in him sounded them out. "Howard, please, talk to me. You know I didn't do it. I *couldn't* do it. I was with *you* that night. I never confessed. They're lying. My neighbor's lying about seeing me. You know Hallie. This is crazy! I loved her, Howard! Talk to me, *please!*"

Rodman finally stopped and listened for a moment and heard Howard's breathing, then his voice.

"Okay, Carl, calm down, calm down. I know you didn't do it. I—I'm just still in shock from everything—Delia, the police—and now you call—I—God, Carl, what the hell happened?"

"I don't know, Howard. I really don't. That's why I ran when I could. I have to find out who did it. For Delia's sake more than mine. I need your help."

"How? I—"

"I don't want to get you in trouble. I just need some money to keep me moving. I obviously can't get to my bank account."

"Obviously," Howard said. "How much you need?"

"I don't know. A thousand should last awhile."

"But how—how are you going to keep running like this, Carl . . . ?"

"I'm not *running*! I told you, I'm *looking*!"

"Relax, okay? Relax."

"Yeah, sorry, okay? I got some leads, that's all. Small ones, but *something* anyway."

"Okay, keep calm. Where are you? You in town?"

"No, I'm out in my neighborhood. Listen, I shouldn't come to your place for the money. Who knows? The police could be staking your apartment building—"

"What?"

"I don't know this for a fact. I don't even know if they think I'm worth the effort. It's just they know you're a good friend, maybe my only friend right now, and they may have somebody watching."

Rodman already knew that Howard had his phone equipped with a "bug-alert" device, installed a few years ago to ensure privacy when exchanging "trader talk" and deals with other financial whiz kids at the firm while at home.

Howard seemed unsure. "So then . . . what? Make a drop?"

"Something like that. I've been thinking about it. As best I *can* think anyway. I figure we do it publicly but not *open* publicly. They might be watching."

Rodman's weariness was setting in hard, blocking flow, like heavy drapes on delicate rays of thought.

"I'm not following, Carl. You sound awful."

"I *should* sound awful. Look, you still taking Thursday mornings off to visit your mom?"

"Yeah, sure."

Rodman knew that Howard's mother had been convalescing for the past year in a private nursing home in Tarryville, three blocks from the town's train station and thirty-five minutes by rail from the heart of Hollowsport.

"And taking the train?"

Howard seemed hesitant. "Yeah ... the nine-sixteen. Like always."

"Is it crowded?"

"What does that—"

"I'm asking if it's crowded!"

"Okay! Not much. Too late for the nine-to-fivers."

"Then save me a seat."

"What?"

"I'll be there along the way," Rodman explained. "I'll come sit near you. You bring out a lunch bag from your briefcase with the money." Rodman consciously tried to lighten his tone. "So save me a seat ... okay?"

"Okay. Yeah ... sure. Whatever you think. I usually sit in the last car or so." There was a pause. "You gonna be okay for tonight?"

"Yeah, I'll be fine. See you tomorrow, then."

"You got it."

"And thanks, man."

"No problem."

Rodman hung up, his hand lingering on the cusp of the receiver, his energies drained. His thoughts immediately shifted to the exact turnpike underpass he was going to park the car near, and the one-story beachfront motel across the road from it, and the firm, stiff-sheeted bed it offered—mainly he thought of the bed.

There was another bed, too, however, one already occupied and moist and heated from the slide and rustling of bodies. It was on Seventh Street and North Central Avenue, in a refurbished brick condo, post–World War I, in an apartment on the third floor, one-bedroom, hand-carved moldings, small marble fireplace, and parquet floors, the windows open a crack to counter the radiator's constant heat and to encourage some of the city noise to spill inside, to wash up against the exquisite grunts and now to drown out the plunk of the receiver on the cradle next to the bed, the bed where Howard Bernbaum lay sideways, staring at the white phone unit as though staring at Carl Rodman himself or at nothing at all.

Howard was bereft of emotion and semen, as he lay unaffected in the scoop of wetness on the mattress from the recent lovemaking. The sound of the bathroom door opening jarred him from his preoccupation. He squinted toward the harsh light that emanated from the fixture over the sink, but a woman's hand flicked it off, soothing his retinas if not his anxious heart. He sat upright in bed, and a cool feminine hand finger-primped the right side of his hair to reinstate its curly and erect bounce, its having been flattened from the sweat of exertion.

"What's wrong? Who was that?"

Howard looked at Pat Dokes with an impassioned expression, her body outlining the too-small men's robe. Her right bosom was nearly exposed as she leaned in to him; its plump swell was pale white and heaving like a tender living thing snuggling beneath the silky blue cloth for warmth. Howard kissed her there, on the salty-tasting dip of her breast, then raised his head, looked into her inquiring eyes once more.

"It was your ex-boss," he said. And with that he swung away, his feet touching the floor, his vision, too. His body hung there crookedly on the edge of the bed for a moment.

Then like a bitter wisp of air he added, "The son of a bitch," and he extended a blind arm for the phone.

14

RODMAN OBSESSED ON the time-juggling details of his plan. It was a way to deflect the imminent dangers he perceived at any passerby's look that even minutely lingered on him or any idle hand gesture toward him. He especially harbored a stomach-sickening fear of those two men, those brutish thugs who nearly killed him in the car park. They were looking for Vance's drugs? His money? Did that mean they knew where Vance was? Were they holding him somewhere? Were they Vance's saviors? Clearly, he had been fingered by Sonny in some Big Lie—which was Sonny's entire life, as far as he was concerned—so he could thank Vance's longhaired, skinny, and oughta-be-*dead* ass for siccing those mongrels on him.

But the morning's plan kept him busy, preoccupied. He wanted Howard to stay in his routine, not to deviate from his usual schedule, and this, for Howard's own protection. Rodman wanted nothing to look outwardly suspicious. He would meet Howard along his day's normal pathway, and today's happened to include Howard's train ride to his mother. He had driven east to Sappford, which was a handful of train stops away from Tarryville. There, he left the car in a boarded-up dry cleaner's lot which was used by commuters anyway because it was only a block away. From there he took the next train back west two stops to West Lamply. When he got out, he walked a few paces and stood on the opposite side of the platform to wait for Howard's train, due there shortly from Hollowsport. He would board here at West Lamply, stay on through East Lamply, and get off at Sappford for his car, leaving Howard to go on to Tarryville alone. In and out. No trouble for Howard.

The morning was sun-filled, a rarity this fall, and he flipped on the mirror-lensed unisex sunglasses he had found in the car, the ones Delia used to wear. He had always hated them on her, a robotic shield to her bottomless azure eyes, so she would use them only while driving in deference to his complaints. And now the surprising sun gave him an excuse to obscure his own features, to mechanize part of his face into a silvery nonentity.

Rodman stood flush to a platform beam so that he could only be fully seen from the one side. Two teenage boys bouncing a basketball and a troll-like woman with a babushka were the only people on the platform directly before him. He had noticed a few business suits behind, nearer the front end of the platform. Rodman peeked around the beam to see that these men were still there, then checked the time on the massive digital display above First Quality Bank down below at street level. The train should be coming soon. Rodman began shaking his leg from nerves as he pressed himself back against the beam.

Finally, the shimmer of a light could be seen rounding the far curve of the track. Rodman stayed against the beam during the few minutes it took for the train engine to whoosh through and slow and finally stop. Only then did he dislodge himself from his reinforced steel backbone and slip into the next-to-last car behind the troll lady.

Rodman spotted Howard right away sitting in the middle of the compartment on the aisle of a three-seater cushion while reading the *Wall Street Journal.* Before Rodman moved toward his friend, though, he peered through the windowed door at his end of the train to see if anybody unforeseen had followed him on, but through at least three cars' worth of end-to-end door windows he could only distantly discern the spate of business suits he had seen earlier, now just nosing around for a place they could all sit together.

The car Rodman had boarded was only sporadically filled, but not as uncrowded as he would have liked. Two conversing women were taking up the seats across the aisle from Howard, so when Rodman approached the curly-top above the newspaper, he said, "Excuse me," and watched Howard's face remain deadpan in its response. Howard had laid his overcoat on the two adjoining seats beside him, and when he lifted it for Rodman to sit, the middle seat revealed Howard's hard-shell business case with a bulbous brown lunch bag atop it. Rodman nodded to his accommodating fellow passenger and squeezed past Howard's knees in order to drop into the window seat. With his eyes averted toward the world outside the train, Rodman's hand blindly slid the lunch bag off the briefcase and into his own lap. He then focused his attention on the brown sack, as though it had been in his possession all along, and on its two apparent lumps.

With the train departing West Lamply station, Rodman unfolded the top of the sack and glanced inside the opening. On one side of the bag's bottom sat a wad of bills held in a tight roll by a red rubber band; its round twin brother on the other side was an apple wrapped in a paper napkin. Rodman cracked a smile. As he reached into the bag for the lump with the hundred dollar bill stretched out on its circumference, his head turned toward Howard as part of his natural motion.

"Feeding the needy?" Rodman said in a low voice, just under the train's rumble and car chatter.

Howard snapped his paper and gave Rodman a knowing glint. "Even Richard Kimble's gotta eat."

Rodman laughed to himself as he pocketed the roll of money then took out the apple. He bit into it with a snap, its skin cracking off, gushing, its juices exploding in his mouth with a burst of cool sweetness never so appreciated. Rodman felt it was the most sensual and life-affirming act he had performed all week.

"Where to now?" Howard whispered while supposedly reading.

"Going to the peninsula to see—"

The conductor coming by for tickets shut Rodman up, but it gave him the excuse to look at Howard as he reached across toward the aisle to hand over his stub. Howard was pulling down his tie knot from his unbuttoned collar while the conductor punched both their passes, then the trainman gave them both a tight-lipped nod. After that, Rodman settled back, thinking maybe it was better not to talk right now, better to stay strangers. He ate his fruit and gazed out the train window, anxiously anticipating his trip up to Point Crescent as though he weren't going there to find important links to Delia, but Delia herself. For a good while his heart beat steady and hard with that heady deception until the train's momentum slowed with a screeching shift of sideways force. It had started its curve into the final wide bend before East Lamply station.

That was when the flush of Delia's presence left Rodman's face, her irreversible loss took the place of the rushing blood in his skull, and the sudden sight of the distant platform played tricks with his vision. He sat upright in his seat and leaned in toward the glass as though it would magnify what he didn't want to see. Howard noticed Carl's reaction, his twitch of heightened awareness, and calmly said, "Please don't run."

Rodman shot a look at Howard, who had laid the newspaper open on his lap, yet still stared straight ahead, not looking at Rodman at all. "It's over, Carl."

Rodman turned back toward the window and saw more clearly now, no shimmery visions of wife and sunshine mornings, but the concrete-laden platform looming larger, the police car parked below the approaching station, the two uniformed cops standing at the ready on the platform's edge and then another blue uniform and a plainclothesman farther down the landing under the hanging East Lamply sign.

"You turned me in," Rodman said to the window, to himself, to nobody, then to Howard, directly, loudly, whipping the mirror lenses from his face for a better look at betrayal. "You're turning me in!"

Howard didn't move, except for his mouth, which twisted down at the ends in a clenched frown.

"What was that little tie move," Rodman spat, "that little pull on the knot with the conductor? Was that the signal? The go-ahead?"

Howard finally looked Carl's way, but still without emotion, still the deadpan comic, only with nothing very funny left to say. "You set me up, you bastard."

Rodman was momentarily taken aback. Wasn't that what *he* just said? "What?"

"You lied to me," Howard said, his eyes condemning. "You drugged me that night, didn't you? I never sleep that well up there. There was no magic cocoa. After I heard they arrested you, I thought about how my stomach hurt so much that next morning, the kind of pains I usually get with taking killer pills.

But then you said *you* had pains, too, and yet—there you were drinking black coffee, which would have eaten my guts out. Yours, too. That *bothered* me. How come I wouldn't have woken up if, like the cops said, you *had* left the cabin that night, *bothered* me."

Howard paused and looked at Rodman, who had by now shriveled back into the corner of his seat, his vision thrown inward, his head throbbing.

"Delia being murdered *bothered* me," Howard said with exacting enunciation, its accusatory tone prompting Rodman to look at him. "That's called comic understatement," Howard explained, but Rodman didn't respond. What could he say? What could he deny? The train was decelerating rapidly.

Howard continued. "So I decided to appease my doubts about my best friend and had the cops test the cup I used that night. Lucky for the police I'm your typical bachelor dishwasher; I'm sloppy. There was still some residue of the narcotic you put in the mug."

Rodman couldn't look Howard in the eye any longer, felt entwined in emotions, lost in counterpurposes and cross-betrayals. Mostly he felt cornered, ensnared by Howard's incriminating words and the steady slowing beat of the wheels— *ker-chunk, ker-chunk*—as the cars entered the station, the platform appearing to slide alongside the braking train. He watched the two blue uniforms roll by his window then, under their own power, trot toward the door behind him at the far end of the car. The other uniform and plainclothesman merely took two long steps toward approximately where the forward car door was to come to a halt.

Rodman let out a shuddering breath at about the same time the train's brakes hissed and jerked everyone slightly forward with a final nudge before stopping.

"You took Delia twice from me, you fuck." Howard's eyes had filled, and Rodman could only silently stare at his stolid, grieving friend with a sense of acknowledged understanding. But Rodman was now beyond grieving, beyond dwelling on the rightness or wrongness of his actions. He was only acting now, a man twitching through the remains of his life on a survivor's impulse and in quest for truths, no matter how pained, how hurtful, how much the cost. It was all that was left to him, his unraveling legacy.

The doors rumbled open. Rodman immediately snatched the closed hard case from Howard's lap and drove it, full body thrust, into the adjacent window. The glass cracked loudly, fault lines splitting off the smashed-in hole like the legs of a deformed spider. Nearby passengers screamed out, some in shock, some in protest. Howard sat limp, watching, unable to do anything except feel his tears gather in a crested pool at the base of his eyeglass lenses. The two policemen up front were bulling their way, shouting, through the handful of passengers who pushed to get off. Rodman didn't know about the ones who were entering from the other end. There was only one way out. Rodman smashed the case into the window once more and harder. It splintered into thousands of minute fractures, so that when he then kicked out with the heel of his shoe, the entire window, like a finely webbed sheet of ice, gave way almost all in one piece and fell to the track below.

"Stop!" the plainclothesman yelled, stumbling through the aisle, shoving by an elderly man in the middle of a stutter-step attempt to get out of his way. Rodman pulled himself through the gaping window, legs first, grabbing hold of the top of the hole, catching a glimpse of the two uniformed cops scuttling up from the rear of the car then stopping and doubling back to the door they had entered. Rodman slid out as best he could, but lost his balance when most of his body was on the surface hull of the train, and he fell to the platform ledge, bruising a thigh.

However, he knew any hope for escape would not be accomplished across the concrete platform, that is, above the track, but below the train, so with one tumbling motion he rolled himself off the hard gray edge to the stony cushion the steel rails were set in. He squirmed under the passenger car, thankful this branch of the Hollowsport line had yet to be electrified, and came out into the cloudless sunshine on the other side, adjacent the trestle railing. He heard frenzied voices, like muffled orders, from the platform side of the train, and the following footfalls from among the track stones there.

Rodman began to run. Along the entire length of the train,

beneath the curious faces of the remaining passengers pressed up against the windows, he ran, knowing full well that the police had to be running toward both ends also, pondering whether another crawl back under the cars was feasible. The train hissed, as though responding to his mental inquiry, and hummed in vibratory preparation to leave the station. He would be exposed.

Then he stopped short. Beyond the low three-pipe-rail barrier to his right and thirty feet below lay Harley Park Boulevard, the main town road fronting the generations-old shops of East Lamply. There was no possible way to jump down; however, two curving shanks of metal bolted to the lower portion of the trestle like parallel meat hooks caught his attention. He squatted down to confirm, to hope, and—yes—it was the top of a green-metal ladder that had been welded into the green-metal trestle beam to be used by maintenance men. And by desperate fucks like him, Rodman thought. A pistol shot echoed behind. Rodman bolted upright with the concussion and turned. One policeman had rounded the train's diesel engine and was sprinting toward him, while another had his gun aimed upward, having fired a warning shot.

Rodman hustled down the ladder as quickly as his sore thigh would let him. He jumped off and under the trestle's cover just as another hollow-sounding report was heard and a bullet thudded directly down into the blacktop, a few feet from Rodman's fleet heel.

15

T HE WINDOW SHUSHED open with little effort, and it was obvious that any possible alarm had been successfully bypassed.

"Good going."

To the compliment, Marty Dembo responded with a curt nod, not ready yet to expose his chipped front tooth or to forgive his big brother. It certainly hadn't been the first time Louis belted him in anger, but those raps were teenage ventings, the hormone-driven Louis picking a fight with whoever was convenient and over whatever frustration roused his temper—a cold bitch of a date, a run-in with their boozy mother over missing dollar bills from the weekly food fund. Sometimes there was no reason, except maybe to see Marty's twisted face twist up in a different direction and turn red and run to nobody because their mother would have hit him again for being such a "faggot crybaby." In fact, it didn't take much back then to catch a swat from Louis. These days, as relative adults, it was a rarity. And even then, it was *never* at the mouth. The mouth was money.

Marty's tongue slipped eel-like in and around the ragged tooth as a newly formed habit, rubbing the sharp point at one end and then riding the tip along the smooth silver band that now had nothing to brace, a steel span without its section of bridge to bolster. The enamel shard would cost money to restore and caused Marty to make a sucking noise with each unthinking tongue probe.

The two brothers had crawled into the house, Louis dragging along a toolbox. They stood in the obscurity of the Rodman master bedroom for a moment, only a patchwork of moonlight on the dresser. "You go check out the kitchen and living room, like I told you," Louis said. "I'll do the bedrooms."

Marty's small outline nodded again, punctuating the head move with a pointed "you-got-it" index finger and with another loud gap-toothed suck.

This sucking thing was definitely getting to Louis, as his slowly adjusting eyes followed the Day-Glo sneakers in their march down the hallway. But *everything* was getting to him, especially since the zippo results rummaging through Sonny Vance's dump of a hotel room and the foul-up at the parking structure with the bruises he suffered and wore like empurpled medallions of disrespect. Then top the fucker off with the recent phone call to a less-than-sympathetic Sam Ryan and you got one dung hole of a day. "Shit piles up when you don't flush," his father used to say in explaining his mother's troubles. Dembo was letting it all build, too, socking it away in the tense balls of his arm and leg muscles, in the pronglike severity of his cock, everywhere there was a tendon and nerve looking for electric release.

But first he made himself praise the little Marty did right. Breaking and entering was Marty's specialty and had to be acknowledged as such. After all, he did his prison time for it, and that alone gave him license, afforded him title and not just a passing regard. Marty could circumvent any house or apartment alarm Louis challenged him with. (After the incident with Danny and his fugitive father, the police had turned the dormant Rodman security alarm on as a stop-gap in protecting the crime scene. At least, from *un*professional intruders.)

In fact, if pressed, Dembo would say he was proud of Marty's B&E abilities and tried to be fatherlike to him whenever possible. Their own father, Ralph Dembo, was a passive man whose bones seemed stitched together in the lanky, clanky way he walked, though they had the resiliency of iron. He worked in heavy concrete on building sites and had many an accident because of that awkward package of gestures Marty wound up inheriting. But Ralph would always recover sooner than expected, if only to get out of the house where his wife, their mother, Louise, raged in the boiling ferment of her liquor.

For reasons unknown to Louis, his father would let Louise

beat him while she cried dollops of tears, batter him with a mop handle, sometimes a convenient coffeepot, most often with just her fists, which were rough, red, and large, like rolled steaks. She was a big woman, plump but not blubbery, with shapely, meaty legs she pampered with oils and creams as though age-treating a fine dark wood. She had blue flinty eyes that would empower her stares, framed by dense waves of jet-black hair. She had a fair complexion dotted by a chin mole she would darken or not with a pencil at her disorganized vanity. Sometimes, as a kid, Louis thought the mole a kind of barometer of her stormy spirit—the darker she applied the pencil, the rougher that day was going to be to get through. Louis also thought she did time for prostitution once, at least he thought he heard it mentioned, a shrill spear of attack jabbed during a tirade at his father, but Louis had never gotten the facts clear, not granting much priority to historical events on either a worldwide or familial level.

All he knew—all he *saw*—was a deep-voiced, bosomy, boozehound in heat, both in the lustful and tempestuous sense, who, so his father said, was his mother. And she got just about everything she wanted from "her man": gifts, liquor, a big bed, a twenty-five-inch color TV, and his dick on demand.

In truth, the only time Louis Dembo ever respected his father was when Ralph Dembo left them, when he up and walked out on the truant older son, on the slow-witted younger one, and on the bitch with the blade. It took a dinnertime stabbing, Louis watching from the living room while taking off his holey undershirt because of the heat. Above a Frank Sinatra album on the stereo, he heard his mother arguing to no one because his father wasn't arguing back. Maybe he was bracing for a backhanded swat while he tried to chew the underdone flank steak and listen to the Chairman of the Board finger-snap to a Nelson Riddle arrangement. Louis saw a ten-year-old Marty approach Louise with a question and a flinch and get smacked across the head, out of her way. Then she lunged with her steak knife and stuck Ralph Dembo more than half-a-blade deep at the shoulder joint and let go. The knife wobbled in place for a moment like a shot arrow, before his father cried out and jerked himself back against the kitchen chair. Then, trying not to whimper, he delicately eased the knife out with two fingers, Louise watching with a half-lidded smirk.

Dropping the utensil on his cannonball pile of Del Monte peas, he swiftly slapped a paper napkin on the wound and bent over. Louis took a step forward, thinking his father was about to vomit, but his father's folding at the waist was a way to better raise himself without the use of his arms; and with jangly, long legs, Ralph Dembo plodded across the checkerboard linoleum to the front door dripping blood the entire way. Louis never saw him again. More important, it was the last thing his mother ever got to do to his father.

Thus it was appropriate that Louis found her one morning, after his having been gone for a week with some pals on a bar-hopping joyride to Atlantic City and back, found her on her blood-soaked king-sized mattress knifed to death.

At the time Louis could only think of two things. First, he was glad Marty was in the juvie joint on his B&E rap so he didn't see this. Second, he was pretty sure it wasn't his old man who cut her. No great shakes if it was, but it probably wasn't, considering the types his mother had two-week flings with, three-month live-ins with, one-night stands with. Louis never even called the cops. He hadn't been really living there anymore anyway, so he threw together what was left of his stuff and some of Marty's, snatched his father's Sinatra records for good measure, and a month later, after Marty's release, hopped a freight that rolled through the coast towns, to Hollowsport, where Louis "knew a guy" in construction. "The rest, as they say, is misery." Or so Beanpole Ryan would mutter every time it was his responsibility to keep the Dembos on a short leash.

Of late, however, the leash was lengthening: the hits were bigger, the takes richer. Standing amid the expensively tasteful furnishings of the Rodman bedroom, Louis knew his foreman days were dwindling. His "sick days" taken were beyond the union limit, and no one cared. His profession was "muscle," and in a strange way, he thought his mother would be more proud of that fact than his father.

Dembo started his search in the obvious places, though he knew cocaine, or the money it spawned, was usually more craftily hidden. He overturned drawers, flung down watercolor paintings, barreled through the walk-in closet like a child determined to kick up a mess, dumping hangerfuls of shirts and dresses and skirts and ties. He went to his toolbox and removed a handheld razor cutter and sliced through the throw pillows from the bed and through portions of the mattress. After ten minutes of violation Dembo concluded the bedroom was clean.

When he entered the hallway, Marty happened to be coming for him. He shined his flashlight on a black-leather address book he found on Delia Rodman's desk and said, "Whatdaya think?" then sucked his tooth.

"I think that's a good backup," Dembo said, twitching an eye at the sound. "Could be some of Rodman's buyers in there. We could get leads to the money flow and some of the shit that way, but let's concentrate on right here still."

Marty nodded with little emotion and disappeared back into the dark like a wandering spotlight. Then Louis unhooked the hall's only framed painting, and after a momentary deeper look at the chiaroscuro portrait of "some old guy," he found a wall safe. "Ba-bing!" he announced to himself and trotted back to his toolbox.

Carefully, Dembo bore a hole in the tumbler with his heavyweight power drill, then worked the tubular safe handle until it shunted down, allowing the thick metal door to open freely. The light Dembo fed into the walled box seemed to drain the one he had in his eyes. There were only papers inside, insurance material, financial records, sheathed documents, and old ones at that; nothing was dated after 1987. The only item of interest removed was a deed to lakefront property on the east side of Janus Mountain. Dembo shut the steel door and thought a minute. A second home? Stash Central? He moved farther down the hall.

When Louis dropped his tool chest in Eric's boy-filled room of baseball pennants and Ninja Turtles action figures, it brought back memories. Certainly not of his own childhood, but of previous home trashings and booty searches. Dembo knew from rousting gambling deadbeats or union money skimmers that they liked to hide behind their kids, liked to let innocence be a distraction, a shield, from what was dangerous and desirable below the surface. Just like doing a woman, Dembo thought.

Experience said a desperate man often would conceal his cache of money in his child's bedroom, figuring it would be "hands off," the "last possible place." Not so, Dembo surmised, as he once more began his whirlwind razor-wielding tear through belongings and furniture. He remembered once finding a birthday party goody bag full of payroll overtime money stowed underneath what must have been a zoo's worth of stuffed animals living in a little girl's pink toy chest.

Paneling held intriguing possibilities, too. On one occasion he patiently watched a former friend ply open a flush section of basement paneling in his house, which really held a safe behind it, nestled in its own concrete burrow. (Dembo then cracked the friend's skull open with a ballpeen because the chump owed people Dembo had obligations to.) Eric Rodman's west wall was paneled in light oak, so Dembo, as standard procedure, removed the electromagnet from his well-stocked chest, and as though ironing the wall, ran it across the grain, anticipating any hard tug of metal from a sealed-up container.

After the unsuccessful scanning, Dembo stepped over the dismembered bed and kicked away the shattered plastic models of movie monsters in order to toss books off a built-in shelf, thumb through some for envelopes, shake out thick hardcovers for cutouts like square holes in the middle of pages, tucking away a clue or a roll of bills.

Half of a photo extending from one book stopped his fevered hands, an oversized book laying flat in the corner of Eric's desk under a small stack of folded road maps. It was called, *Animals in the Wild, Vol. 2: Forests.* When Dembo turned to the page that the photo marked off, the picture slipped down the spine but was stopped by another road map, this one folded open, tucked back on itself, and well-wrinkled. Dembo picked up the four-by-six snapshot from where it rested upon the book's close-up of a skunk. The half of the photo that had initially attracted him contained Carl Rodman, Dembo's new nemesis, grinning as though just after a laugh, wearing a plush suede jacket and fur collar, holding a log under his left arm. The other half revealed a prone Eric, tucked in the crease of his father's right elbow, being carried like a companion log. The boy was in the middle of a giggle fit, his knit ski cap and the left quadrant of his head blurred with movement. They both fronted a rustic house and an azure sky with pines spiking the blue.

The map, used when Eric played navigator for his dad, had a dark red crayon line, somewhat jagged, but still on course enough to trace a ruddy trail from their home, through Hollowsport, to the precise location of the cabin on Janus Mountain. Dembo slapped the floppy worn map on the edge of the desk in affirmation. "Thanks, kid," he said aloud to Eric's visage before pocketing the photo.

But the moment of good fortune that inflamed and furthered his pursuit was suddenly doused by the sound of talking, *people* talking, coming from inside the house. Dembo instinctively ducked down, as though the surprising sounds were gunshots instead, and switched off his lantern-shaped flashlight in the process. He listened, strained, to hear if they had "street cop voices," had a tone somewhere between lethargic and cynical. No. But no hint of his brother's voice in the mix, either. He also thought he could feel the faint beat of music without the music itself, just the *thump, thump*, like the tapping of a heavy foot, steady and rhythmic.

While Dembo's senses were locked on the intruding noises from down the hall, his hand moved independently, unattended, as though it were part of a self-contained creature, like the head of a snake, winding into the tool chest by feel alone and wrapping fingers around the smooth wooden handle of his electromagnet. Its flat body was now raised to chin level and readied. It showed its diversity and age from what looked like rust-stained patches but was, in fact, unwashed blood, outlines of residue from previous metallic swattings. (Turned on, the device once made a Dembo game-victim scream out and go cross-eyed when run along his pinned-down head containing a mortar fragment from Nam.) It was an all-purpose skull-shaking brain-rattler, and his python-thick arm balanced it nicely upward like a serving tray as Dembo worked himself silently down the hall toward the source of the conversation.

At the corner of the wall before the family room, he only heard the beat and now the music of Dire Straits entwining with it, not voices. But then there was a giggle, a child's, then an older laugh. "Keep up, keep up," said a woman. Dembo noticed a glow, a diffuse blue, emanate within the still unseen room. When he finally stepped inside, his speculation was right. It was the television. And there in a high-back recliner was his fucking brother, bathed in the tepid light, holding a remote control device and frowning.

Louis's first impulse was to yell, then strike out. Maybe just strike out. Man! His mind had eased with the discovery, but not his muscular fibers, his dwelling angers. "The fuck you *doing*?" he said.

His brother just shrugged, still engaged with the screen, unthreatened. The music drowned out a short suck of his teeth. Sulking worked, Louis thought. His little brother wasn't going to make him forget the blow. But it wasn't just that, it wasn't just the nurturing of a hurt; Marty looked saddened, disturbed . . .

"Find anything besides the telephone book?" Dembo asked. Marty shook his head.

. . . *troubled* by what he was watching. What *was* he watching?

Louis moved into the room and stood beside the large sleek black monitor that sat on its futuristically designed stand. It wasn't TV Marty was watching, not programs anyway, but a tape. A videotape. A fucking home movie. The tiny red light of the VCR shone visibly in the dimness.

On the screen was Carl Rodman, a clutch of years younger, clad in a designer sweat suit, hopping around aerobically to rock music in the very room the Dembos were now invading, which, Louis took notice, also contained a complete Denon stereo system. Rodman was alternatingly performing jumping jacks, leg kicks, arm extensions, midair twists, doing whatever his exercising spirit moved him to do at any given guitar lick. He was sweating and heaving and out of shape, but was gamely smiling through fatigue at the little boy, a three-year-old Eric bouncing along with him in, appropriately enough, a jumpsuit, out-of-sync with both his daddy and the music, but energetic just the same. Eric would shriek in joy then laugh at the almost birdlike squawks he made. This reaction would cause Rodman to chuckle and the camera to wobble, as Delia would laugh, too. Then she would abruptly continue her commands to her little son: "No, honey—yes, you are so *won*-der-ful!—but, no, follow Daddy. Follow Daddy, sweetheart. Do what he does."

Which, Rodman had thought, was *so* Delia, so like her to allow her feelings toward deviance and imperfection to color her tone even to a toddler. No, Rodman was glad somewhere deep in his gut, thankful that little Eric would *not* do as his father did, and hopefully never so, he had thought. Hear me, but don't echo me.

Of course, none of this undercurrent was comprehended by the impassive watchers of the Rodmans' video, and Louis Dembo was getting tense again. He realized that the more his brother watched, the deeper his frown, the lower he sank down in the plush black armchair. His torso was already flat upon the bottom cushion, his neck and head barely upright, as though he were gradually melting toward the floor.

So Louis flicked on the electromagnet in his hand and set it upon the top of the monitor. The picture immediately began to twist up and deform. Rodman's head, the little boy's plump body, their homey surroundings, became violent distortions, electrons caught in a tornado of powerful forces. The Rodmans still moved as though nothing in their world was deteriorating, but their essences were mutilated multicolored swatches of hopping, music, bleeding brightnesses, laughing blurs, imprisoned in a cathode funhouse mirror.

Louis looked at Marty, who looked at Louis, then they both cut a laugh and smiled at each other. Everything was straight between them again, Dembo thought. Marty cackled some more as he gazed forward in the ghostly blue light, retaining the silver-striped grin on his face. Apparently Louis Dembo had proven once more that people only liked watching shows they can personally relate to.

16

H E HELD IT as though it were something susceptible to harm, a found object shown, his hand a cup cradling a firefly or a stranded ladybug. Delia's picture, pocketed during the scouring of his home, was hardly that delicate, nor had been the woman it captured in soft studio lights. Yet from a distance Rodman's showing the wallet-sized photo to random passersby looked far more foul an act than it was, as though he were selectively revealing something indecent, proffering a lewd etching. And what was she anyway? Delia the precious victim? Delia the betraying adulteress? Maybe both, Rodman thought disconcertedly, then resumed his questioning: "Excuse me, have you ever seen this woman?"

In East Lampley, Rodman had eluded the police on foot long enough to retrieve the Mercedes from the dry cleaner's lot and drove out of town unnoticed, though clockwork glances toward the rearview mirror punctuated his trip. Nothing was tailing him, except the still jarring sense of what Howard had said about taking Delia twice from him.

One obvious interpretation of Howard's remark was that of Carl having stolen her heart and eventually becoming her husband, and then taking her away once more by murdering her. Another more foreboding speculation might be Rodman marrying her counting as one "taking away," and then, after having a prolonged out-of-town affair with Howard, her deciding to come back to Rodman. Thus even without knowing it, Rodman was taking her away from him again, gaining the prize through incumbency. Or loyalty to the recovering alcoholic. Or guilt over infidelity. Or was it simply true and lasting love first kindled back at the P.R. booth in the sports complex? Wouldn't that kind of severing be motivation for Howard's betrayal, for murder?

And was that story Howard told about the police even true? The chemical testing of the mug? Who was even to say the drug took effect, that Howard had in fact slept all night, that he hadn't driven down to Hollowsport himself after he left, hadn't killed Delia in jealousy, frustration, and had gotten back to the cabin before him? Anything seemed possible at the moment. Anything.

Such were the insinuations, the foundational doubts, that wove like a snaking current in and out of Rodman's mind as his car took the coastal corners of Highway 26 much the same way. Everybody, every *thing*, was suspect, except the moment, his life right now—what he thought, what he was doing—at that vital instant. It was the only way he felt he could survive, seek the answers, every answer; he wanted all the answers. *We want the world*—he was the outsider again, the runner—*and we want it*—but not running "from" this time, but "to"— *NOW!* The Doors played on the car radio, kept him on the road driving straight, kept him ironically sober. Christ, he fucking wanted a drink.

The drive had exhausted all the daylight, and the clouds and sun were in a slow and sinking race to dominate the horizon. Point Crescent lay flat on the peninsula, where no building was permitted over five stories, so the church steeples, like outstretched arms, still held up their brass crosses higher than any glass-faced concrete slabs. It was an old town in the resistant process of renewal, especially since the early 1980s when the Tech Park opened next door in Ridgeway. The town reflected that mixture of the generational and the refurbished, Phil's Pants Store adjacent The Crustacean, a boutique specializing in undersea jewelry and bric-a-brac.

Upon arrival, Rodman cased its schizophrenic grid of streets, and specifically those radiating from his central point of interest: the Ready Bank's money machine, the font of Delia's mysterious cash flow. It operated open-faced above the public sidewalk, and usually accommodated a short line of homebound people, as it did now, waiting their turn to siphon their savings off in twenty-dollar droplets. Rodman had watched it awhile, at first just to see if he recognized anybody who might use it, as absurd as that might sound.

Certainly he wished *he* could use it. The roll of bills, which he had taken from the lunch sack, so neat and tucked, so snapped-tight with a thick red rubber band, proved as false-faced and hollow as every other part of Rodman's life. Only the surface one-hundred-dollar bill was real; the rest was a cylinder of shorn rectangles of yesterday's news. A gas fill-up on the way to Point Crescent left him with eighty and change.

Rodman used that change to buy a local paper to see if his name or picture or story were anywhere, to see if it was safe to question and probe around without recognition. To his relief, he wasn't an item anywhere; it seemed he was only Hollowsport's problem. Thus he began to proffer Delia's photo in earnest. First in the local businesses: restaurants were high on his list, those within walking distance of the cash machine, maybe the place where she and her possible lover/blackmailer/killer rendezvoused. Rodman eliminated any greasy spoons, the red-topped-stools-at-the-counter eateries, and even upscale-looking places that served the glorified hamburger. Only if the menu had fresh salads with endives or artichoke hearts did he bother to show her picture to the phalanx of waiters in the back. Out of three such restaurants, one had a hostess who nodded in recognition at the sight of Delia but couldn't specify when she came in or with whom. Local clothing stores weren't much help nor were the two hotels in town, though Rodman generally assumed Delia had probably stayed with the gentleman she came to see.

It was after the shops had closed that Rodman resorted to questioning the general populace who strolled by or used the bank's cash machine, obviously unaware of the obsessive aspect to his eyes, the etched-in desperation he thought was subdued by his insistent demeanor. People were taking an unconscious step back to his approach, his vectoring questions, his thrusting arm, his slightly trembling hands holding out his dead wife's image. That seekers look scary was a given he never acknowledged.

In frustration, Rodman finally sat at the base of a wall to a closed photo-developing store. After ten minutes of numbing thought, he was joined by another man who sat beside him. He wore a spattered black windbreaker over a shiny pair of chinos that came up very short on him, exposing shin, floppy sweat socks, and dust-colored tennis sneakers. Facially he was all hair; an unwieldy thicket of gray-white covered everything from just below his nose to his collarbone, up his cheeks, over his ears, and under a corduroy cap which sat on the curly tangle atop his head like the tilting cover to an overflowing pot of popcorn.

Rodman looked at the homeless man beside him without surprise. Neither disdain nor compassion colored his expression. The man was equally blank-faced.

"Could use some money for a meal," he said matter-of-factly.

Rodman looked away from the man and smirked at himself. He leaned his head back against the grainy texture of the storefront and in a low voice half sang, half monotoned: *"Yeah, it's a hard ra-a-a-ain's a-gonna fall."* Then he blew a laugh out through his nose, all air.

The man's eyes, brown balls holding fast in a web of wrinkles, showed no change. He had seen plenty of people singing to themselves before. Rodman then shook his head and tilted forward slightly as though to get up. But then he stopped. He faced the man, who was steadfastly watching him.

"You live in this area?" Rodman asked. "Hang around *here*—specifically—a lot?"

"Hang around?" the man responded with a perturbed squint. "Yeah, sure, you could say I 'hang around' here. I *live* here, Jack. I got myself an alley hole over on Keys Avenue. What's that got to do with something?"

Rodman held up Delia's photo. "You ever see this lady before?"

The man leaned in, intensifying the squint, and made a motion to grab the picture for a closer inspection, but Rodman in kind began to pull it back from those dirt-ingrained fingers. Readjusting, the man simply leaned in farther, the reek of him beginning to dominate the air.

"So?" Rodman said.

"Looks familiar."

Rodman's eyes widened slightly. "She does?"

The man righted himself again, sniffing. "A few bucks would make the fog clear up."

Rodman snuffed the spark. "Yeah, right." He tucked the picture away in his palm.

"Come on! I'm not shittin' you, bud. She *really* looks familiar." The man then held his belly like a child's pantomime. "I'm hungry."

Rodman shook his head. "*I* know and *you* know you're gonna booze it away, so don't lay that—"

"I said I was hungry," the man shot back indignantly, "not thirsty. What? You don't trust me?"

Rodman dipped his chin so that his glare would be more effective. "I didn't trust myself, why the fuck should I trust you?"

"Oh, sure," the man said, suddenly enlightened. "You ridin' that wagon, huh? You jokers are the worst of them, did you know that? I mean, didn't you used to eat, for chrissakes?"

"Aren't there shelters?"

"Food!" the man snapped. "Eat *food*! Food you choose, you know, pick out? Get a ham sandwich, you want, maybe a nice pot roast, not Monday slop, which—which looks like Sunday slop."

Rodman didn't say anything. He was still fingering Delia's picture, felt her, what she was before this morass, before this horrific mystery. In her honor, he handed the man a few dollars; in the same motion he reintroduced the picture.

"Way to go," the man said, awkwardly stuffing the bills in his chinos from his sitting position.

"So you see her or not?" Rodman asked.

The man didn't look at the picture again, as he was preparing to stand. "I did. Can't—can't quite place where, but—I swear I've seen her."

Rodman stared at the picture again himself. "Yeah. In your dreams. Go eat."

The man rose clumsily and started backing away in little shuffling steps, an isolated pedestrian or two having to swerve from his blind retreat. "Hey! I'll remember where. I swear. Hell, I'll *find* her!"

Rodman's singular laugh was like a force that pulled him back inside himself. "You do *that*," he mumbled, not talking to the man, barely to himself, "you can have everything." He sensed the blood drain from his head, felt the pain of the moment, of the loss, eviscerate him. "You can have fucking everything." Silently Rodman began to cry.

The scruffy man stopped for a moment and watched the stoic-faced stranger, watched the tears work their way down his drawn and bruised face. He had seen plenty of people cry to themselves, too. He turned and crossed the traffic-burdened street.

A half hour later the nighttime people were few. Some fine-tailored men escorted crisp-suited women with cropped hair and low heels to the nearby restaurants. Some kids roller-skated past with their sweatshirts tied around their waist and one said something smart-ass to him. But the kid was the exception. Most walked by Rodman as though he were a lumpen shadow, a breathing part of the black volume of space he occupied well out of the saintly glow of the streetlight. He finally raised his head from his sadness, his buttocks stinging from sitting on the concrete so long. It was at that moment he thought of the bushy-faced homeless man—for an instant, *was* him. It was also at that moment he thought of Keys Avenue.

Rodman's spine unwound straight, then away from the hard wall. The man had said he lived in an alley off of Keys Avenue. Keys Avenue. The bartender on the phone had told Carl that Ollie's Tavern was at 55 Keys Avenue. Rodman had just assumed that the bar was in Hollowsport—just assumed it! He sprang to his feet as though spasmodically charged, frightening a green-hatted senior citizen strolling with her terrier. The dog barked once at the old woman's sudden flinching, then again at Rodman, but he didn't notice. He was already trotting down the block in the direction he remembered the homeless man had gestured toward, with his head like a blunt pointer, when mentioning the alley. Sure enough, three corners later, Rodman stood under the right-angled street signs designating the intersection of Bailey Boulevard and Keys Avenue. The bright white light of the corner lamp felt good on his face.

Ollie's Tavern was old town, the sort of establishment that accommodated "regulars," defined as those who were born and who died in Point Crescent. (Some even died in the bar.) Step-

ping into Ollie's Tavern was like stepping into the innards of
a thick, ancient oak; a ruddy-hued confine, close, peopled,
smoke-stained, and noisy with talk and the *pock* and *pock*
again of pool ball smacking pool ball to one side of the room,
while on the other side, among round and wobbly tables, a
jukebox played nothing by anybody who dared leave the
womb after 1950. In short, Ollie's was the last Point Crescent
fortification of old-timers, the bastion against hanging plants
and tofu and drinks of any color spectrum other than brown.
And, Rodman concluded, a place in which Delia wouldn't be
caught dead. Then he qualified his surmise: except maybe for
love.

Rodman put himself at an empty table on an elevated platform near a wall-mounted hat rack that, in this place, found
use. A pair of flannel-shirted men in their sixties dominated the
table next to his, drinking boilermakers and amiably disagree-
ing about the price of used Chevy Impalas. Rodman and one
other man, who was lifting a pitcher of beer among friendly el-
ders, were the only two with less than a half century under
their belt and hair over their ears. The bartender spoke loudly
across the room to that particular table, and Rodman immediately recognized the rich granular voice from the phone,
though the British-looking man was surprisingly lean, tall, and
delicately boned, and seemed to have little belly for such dia-
phragmatic volume. People called him "Tommy."

Rodman decided he was going to watch the room, see who
would linger and settle into their liquor versus who was there
for only a nip and a hello. Soon a henna-haired waitress offering a warm but nicotine-ridden smile took Carl's drink order.
Something told him not to pass Delia's picture around like a
bowl of pretzels for all to dip into and inspect and to wonder
why he was asking questions. Thus he nursed his scotch and
soda for over an hour and measured by degrees the heat of the
waitress's smile cool with each tilt of her empty tray toward
him, but ultimately he was glad he had postponed his inquiry,
for there seemed to emerge a center to the room, a focal point
of power, even deference.

It was a man, a strikingly rugged man, who sat alone most
of the time at a square wall-hugging table that would normally
accommodate three. He was dark-skinned and almost entirely

bald. The intense shine of his tanned head made his aspect glisten with respect. His brow was high, his eyebrows grown thick and peppered like his moustache and, by nature, skeptically bent as though doubting everyone, even when he beamed a smile with strong straight teeth at most of his back-patters and stein-wavers. Tommy, the barkeep, would even come out from behind his semicircle of polished wood, the center of his own command, and serve this man personally, sometimes chat awhile; the last time, he left a half bottle of rye for the man to help himself. The divergent lines that creased the man's face offered character and experience to whomever approached him, rather than a telling map of decay. He sat bolt straight, had hairy-backed muscular hands, and, of all things, was reading a hard-bound book—this, in between short conversations with other patrons and long sips of scotch. The table held yet other dissembled hardcovers with some papers trapped beneath them.

Rodman had gotten most of the more exacting details of the man's appearance when he marched up to the flip-top section of the bar in order to ask for a pack of matches he didn't need. While waiting for Tommy to approach, Rodman also closely examined the phone number on the black rotary unit tucked under the bar on the shelf full of shot glasses.

It was time for Rodman to confirm what he sensed in the anxious cavity of his chest. He walked to the open pay phone stationed outside the foyer to the rest rooms, a location that offered an unobscured view of the wooden bar and its immediately surrounding tables. He fed the unit his change and dialed the number of the black phone. Then he watched Tommy snap the receiver up after one ring.

"Ollie's."

"Yeah," Rodman said, turning away slightly and lowering his voice. "I'd like to leave a message for a Delia Rodman when she comes in or calls."

"Who?"

Rodman enunciated the name. "Delia Rodman. I know she comes in your place sometimes or calls, and I need to get in touch with her urgently. There's—uh—there's some money in it for you if you'd do me this favor." The corner of Rodman's eye examined the barkeep's movements, his eye contact, but

Tommy was stock-still, holding a finger in one ear to cut off the music and chatter.

"I appreciate the commission, buddy, but I don't take messages or do windows."

"Okay, but—anybody *there* might know where she is?" Again Tommy offered no suspicious gestures or hesitation. His voice became even gruffer than normal.

"This Delia Rodman person is probably in the phone book. Reach out and touch someone and leave me the hell alone." Then he hung up.

Rodman hung up, too, and turned to see the bartender wipe a damp hand on his shoulder towel, then towel the phone briefly before setting the whole unit back on the shelf. So maybe he was wrong, Rodman thought. Maybe Delia had misdialed from their home phone and never redialed the number she wanted. Maybe her lover's number was a digit off—but which one?

His rethinking reversed itself again when Tommy marched directly to the rugged man and interrupted his read. As Rodman moseyed closer to the conversation, he could read the bartender's face enough to perceive perplexity, read his lips enough to decipher the words "second time." Rodman stopped and gripped the platform's iron railing, allowed the blood to rise up and boil his brain in that instant of affirmation. He stood there, a frozen point in a fluid room, and waited for Tommy to move away, waited for the man, whose reaction to the report of Rodman's second phone call was a concerned nod, waited for him to once more lose himself in his book, to sip at his glass of golden liquor without looking. Rodman then pondered the vacated seat, a void about to be filled, like the answer to a desperate question.

The handsome, rough-hewn man did not look upset when Rodman sat there before him; nothing reacted on him, except the blue-green of his eyes narrowed and those expressive eyebrows floated up his forehead and curled into inquiry. The chocolate-colored sport coat he wore open had officious-looking brass buttons, and his stomach appeared quite flat for a man of his age and proclivity to drink.

"I want to know about Delia Rodman," Carl said.

The man stared Rodman down, his finger flicking the corner

of the page he was about to turn. Rodman noticed the book was *Double Cross* by Sam Giancana, the famous mobster's brother.

"Did I ask you to join me?" the man finally replied, his voice smooth and moderate, notwithstanding a bit of affected crispness to his consonants.

"My choice," Carl said. "I don't have time for invitations, just information. How do you know Delia Rodman?"

The man took another taste of his scotch and looked thoughtful. "Who says I do?"

Rodman leaned in, spoke sharply. "Let's cut the crap. I saw you and the bartender make goo-goo eyes at each other—"

"Goo-goo eyes?" The man started chuckling.

"—when you talked about the phone call just before."

"Tommy doesn't *do* much for my genitals, to tell you true."

Carl wanted the laughter stopped. "What did Delia Rodman do for them?"

"What's that to *you*, anyway?" There it was: the first prick of anger.

"Let's just say I'm a friend of her husband's, and he's asked me to look into it for him."

"That a fact."

"That's right. Since she called you often. Even called you here the other night—"

"That a fact, too?"

"She would come to see you, *be* with you—"

"Hey! Who the fuck *are* you anyway?"

"And maybe she called to say it was all over, and maybe— maybe you killed her for it—"

"What are you talking about?"

"Or was it straight-up blackmail? Over what? Why would she take out all that money from the cash machine?"

Rodman was losing his edge; the conundrums, his emotions, were spilling past the brim of reason.

"You'd better calm down," the man demanded in a loud whisper.

"What did she owe you? What did she *mean* to you?" Rodman paused, the look on his face half mad. "Do you know a sleaze named Sonny Vance!?"

The man's hand clamped down on Rodman's forearm,

which was planted flat on the table. "I said to calm . . . down." The words were spoken with exactness and strength of purpose.

But Rodman would not be appeased, though his breathing eased. "I want you to tell me about Delia Rodman and why she is dead."

The man immediately released Rodman's arm and slowly withdrew to his side of the table. "What was that?"

"Murder. Delia was murdered. And I'm not going to leave here until I know one way or another where you were Monday night through Tuesday morning."

"Murder, you said."

"What? Are you deaf? This a newsflash?"

Rodman couldn't read the man's expression, his intense stare. It wasn't surprise, wasn't the heart-ripping pain Rodman felt at the horrible moment he found out, but the word "murder" did stop the man for a moment, as though a pebble were flicked off that great tanned pate of his. Was it the small hard stone of fear? Fear of discovery? Maybe he had sent somebody to kill Delia and didn't think it would get back to him so soon? Or was Delia just supposed to get a scare and the henchman went too far?

The questions in Rodman's head could not stack themselves too high, as the man rose in a second's time as though at attention, still rigidly locked in thought.

Rodman rose, too. He also took a stride around the small table to block off the man's possible retreat. "Where are *you* going?"

The question seemed to have pulled the linchpin from the man's pensive state. His muscles loosened and he hunched over to gather his books and papers. "Wherever I please," he said, most friendly.

"I don't think so," Rodman defiantly replied.

The man finished picking up his belongings, then straightened and faced Rodman, the trace of a knowing smile on his face. "Think again, friend."

A precisely aimed fist, jammed just under the right side of Rodman's ribs, propelled what felt like every square inch of air from his lungs and bent him over sideways. The descent was quick and oxygen-depleted, so his eyesight was immediately spotted, his head light, vacant. All he glimpsed were the scuffed brown brogues and frayed apron bottom he knew belonged to the bartender. A knee to the side of his temple sent him toward the ground, but not before his skull accidentally rebounded off the wooden chair, sending him into the realm of unconsciousness even before the bulk of his weight dropped to the floor.

Rodman came to only minutes later, a jabbing ache pulsing the side of his head, his body crumpled upon a completely different piece of flooring. The noises of the bar seemed muted and far off, not because of some cottony denseness to his recovering mind, but because they *were* far off. A few rooms removed, at any rate.

By the recuperating strength of his arms, he hoisted his upper body off the roughened planking, his lower half still inert, laying out there somewhere in the gloomy dark. The window above him offered only some illumination, and even that was filtered by a grating of wiggly diamond-shaped wires. Rodman could vaguely discern a few of his fellow occupants: a half-dozen crates (probably booze-lined), cardboard cases of beer, and a shoulder-high stack of metal folding chairs. He lifted himself up in segments, as though testing the viability of his consciousness remaining intact, until finally he was upright, standing by a beveled door frame, steadying himself against it. His left hand held his side the whole time, still tending to the bruise. The pain to his head was inconsolable.

Rodman opened the door gradually, quietly; the life of the bar becoming louder at the first crack of smoky light. Apparently, the storeroom led to an empty brown-hued hallway, which he surmised was in the rear of the building. An open closet was across the way, a mop peeking back out at him. As fast as possible, which was not very fast because of the searing tug at his right rib, he entered the hall and closed the door behind him with a sure click. That's when he heard voices, approaching voices. Without thinking, Rodman dodged into the broom closet, joining the mop in its coffin-sized container. Leaving the door slightly ajar, he heard a grouping of foot steps, then the bartender: ". . . guy was real trouble to Frank. Starting a fight. You know?"

"No sweat, Tommy. We'll check him out," said a youthful voice. Rodman could see three of them: the barkeep and two uniformed police officers. The moment Tommy flicked on the light to the room across the way, he cursed. The young cop said something to him. His partner, a black cop with no cap on, flipped up his radio.

". . . out the back and swing around," the young cop said, trotting around the hallway's bend, then the sound of a metal door, its cross bar pushed in and released, then the door closing with authority. Meanwhile, the black cop had headed quickly back out toward the bar area, listening to the returning squawk on his receiver. Tommy was lagging behind, grumbling to himself. Rodman noted that there was no sign of "Frank."

When just the white noise of crowd talk dominated the hall's echoes, Rodman slid out from the closet and around the far corner toward the rear metal door labeled with a red EXIT above it. He didn't know if the young cop would be standing right outside, but the officer had said "swing around," which to Rodman meant he would circle the building and wind up back out front. He pressed down on the bar and dove into the night air the way he would off his backyard diving board: all hope, no finesse.

The alley was a dirty disarray of small garbage receptacles and scattered rags, amber bottles and beer cans. The husk of a rusted Dodge Dart lay parallel the opposite wall, next to a gray door that said NO ENTRANCE in sloppy white paint right on it. Rodman began to trot down the humpy tarred venue, when a metallic *pong* resounded behind him, and a hundred feet away the young cop was backing out from behind a vortex of wheeled trash bins where he had been searching, only to find an old woman in soiled, layered clothing, huddling there. Spotting Rodman, he shouted, "Halt!"

Rodman's trot became a full run, a hard run, his side burning, the alley narrowing, the air whistling by his ears. He felt as though he were running down an endless tarmac, a plane, a force, about to overcome him from behind. The policeman, giving chase, shouted out again, just before Rodman reached the mouth of the alley. Carl changed direction, *right*, nearly skidding, and churned his shaky legs down the sidewalk, when up ahead a patrol car rounded the corner silently, but with lights flashing. The black cop in the passenger seat pointed at him.

Jarred, Rodman cut down a gap between two buildings, no wider than a large man's girth, the old structure of a neighborhood butcher and the new surface of an office of financial consultants never quite meshing together, allowing him his crack of freedom. He came out another alleyway, the former one's trashy twin. A figure was no more than thirty feet away and spun toward him. Rodman jumped, but another look and it was the bushy-haired man from earlier in the day, hunching over a dented garbage can.

Rodman heard rapid footfalls enter the other end of the narrow valley he had scurried out from. He began to push, shoulder down and with great effort, a wheeled receptacle at one of its ends so as to place it sideways against the opening, effectively blocking the officer's entry into the alley. His side was screaming out at him—or was it himself screaming?—as the bin moved barely inches after each thrust of shoulder, each collision with the flaking hard metal.

Suddenly it moved, not by inches but feet. It rolled as though his efforts were buffeted by a charitable tailwind, God's breath behind him. But the wind was foul-smelling, a putrid helpmate, and not ephemeral at all. Large soiled hands were beside Rodman's. The homeless man was pushing off his sturdy legs and, after another two yards, the combined force of the two men transformed the alleyway Dumpster into an effective barricade.

When the man then looked at Rodman, his eyes were vibratory, like black flies trapped and buzzing in a dark thicket of hair. He was clearly drunk and puffing to catch his breath. Rodman nodded his thanks, but the man had seen the approaching cop as he set the bin in place, heard the cop turn around and run back the other way, so he gestured with his head for Rodman to follow him. Rodman did so.

They hustled about a third of the way down the alley, when they ducked into an open-air garage with cars parked under the overhanging face of a squat brick apartment house. The driveway sloped away from the alley surface as Rodman was led between cars to the wall that fronted the vehicles' grills. Along the wall were rectangular brown doors, far greater in width than in height; many had padlocks on them. However, the door in front of a hood-crumpled black Chevy was slightly ajar, and the man grabbed hold of its edge and swung it open, up to the car's bumper. These were supposed to be storage areas for tenants, Rodman believed, but the one presented to him by the bushy-faced man was clearly his home.

It was strewn with junk, mainly clothes—from what Carl could see in the murky dark—and only five feet deep. Rodman had to squat down to get inside and stay down. However, the compartment was long enough for the men to stretch their legs along its length and sit up against its interior sides. Rodman didn't know what he was sitting on. He thought it was a compost of rags and a torn shard of corrugated cardboard, but whatever it was was wet, and he felt the seeping damp cool his buttocks through his pants. The trapped smells were overwhelmingly potent, a brew of unwashed clothes, unclean bodies, uncooked food, and all decomposing with age. As the man fiddled with something Rodman could not make out, Rodman kept the back of his hand to his nose for as long as he could, the way he did as a child when his father would gut a large trout right under his chin to show him how it was done, but now trying to allow the smell of his own odor mask the guts of another man's entire existence.

Suddenly there was a struck match, then the small sharp flame of a candle and the man blowing out the lit match in the candle's wan glow. Though it revealed a less than scenic locale, visibility was still welcome in the boxlike confinement. But then Rodman's eyes flicked with concern toward whatever might be just outside the now nearly closed compartment door.

"Can't see any light from the alley," the man said with slurred assurance. "I checked."

Rodman nodded, trusted. "Thanks for the help," he finally said. The ragged man squished his face, shook his head. With some difficulty, he twisted his right arm in order to pull a pint bottle of whiskey from his jacket. He burped as though to clear some throat room, opened the half-drained bottle, took a gulp. His outstretched arm then offered a slug to Rodman.

With all the rankness, the darkness, the fatigue, Rodman wanted a hit; his pulsing side wanted it; his painful head wanted it; his painful memories even more so; his legs; his cold hands; and of course, even without any of those real excuses, he would still want it. He always wanted it—probably always would, so they said.

Rodman sucked in the putrid air as though to let it become part of him, to get him used to it sooner. Then he shook his head, no. "Thanks, anyway," he said.

The man shrugged and took another gulp himself.

"You never bought that dinner, did you?" Rodman asked.

The man smiled, then looked away, still smiling, for himself now, keeping the joke in, feeling high. He chuckled. "Yep. I lied." The man stared at the golden brown bottle and the candle's sinuous reflection on its curvature. And he shrugged again.

Then Rodman's second realization, the sadder one. "You never really saw the woman, either? The picture I showed you."

The man made a face and drank again, but Rodman knew a rhetorical question when he asked one. The man shrugged a third time, as though it felt good, loosened him up, shook off the world.

"You do what you gotta do," he said, half-lidded. "Shit. I'm way past apologies." Then he cackled a laugh.

And as he watched the man drift off, Rodman realized he no longer wanted to judge him, didn't want to project his own failures on him, that sullied image of himself he would lay on others like a transparency, then despise what he saw—the disease of the reformed. The disease, he realized, the main symptom of which caused his son Danny so much additional pain on top of his own brutal addiction. Though the ragged man and he were both homeless in all the spiritual complexities of the term, this bum wasn't Carl Rodman, past, present, or future—he was a man, separate, with his own unique desperation, his own moral struggles, his own life's conflicts. Just like Danny.

Rodman said, "I still have a few apologies to go," but the hairy man was asleep. Then Rodman stared at the candle hypnotically and allowed the dark to welcome his own consciousness as well.

17

FEELING AT HOME in the dark, embraced by it, was part of respecting its power, its allure. It was the reason Barbara was there that night—respect. The house before her was dead, was like a corpse whose forlorn spirits hadn't all left the premises. The pool shimmering was one of its signs of life, Delia Rodman's life, most of all.

Barbara stood on the diving board like sculpted flesh, like a part of the garden's Greek statuary, bronzed, poised, exposed to the gathering breeze which cooled her so deep into this dreamy night. Her phosphorescent pink one-piece angled up her slender body, hugged her nearly flat childlike chest, exposed a quarter moon of her cheeks. Her painted toes gripped the edge of the diving board like tender claws on a branch.

She could not sleep, her thoughts too restless. Her anxieties needed a soothing immersion. Danny had refused to visit at the house with Hallie stomping around, and Hallie was always literally stomping around. But Barbara was once more compelled to be a dutiful daughter and had agreed to stay with her mother after the traumatic incident with Mr. Rodman; at least, for a few nights, until the sedatives that Dr. Wilbury had prescribed for her mother became part of her routine, became the equivalent of her daughter's presence, her calming drug. That was the excuse, anyway. Hallie's fears of personal injury, since husband Bertram was still in Montreal, seemed a sidebar motive at best. In truth, any evening Hallie could prevent Barbara's contact with Danny was an evening of triumph, of reestablishing the purity of the Fouche household.

But the nighttime had its own pull. As Barbara lay wide-awake in bed, the warm pool water had a tidal effect, her muscles being tugged, her heart unquenched. The funeral was not enough, she thought. Throwing a rose, no matter how deeply red and full a flower, into the embracing black hole of Delia's grave was not enough, or more precisely, not apropos, not poetic. Barbara wanted to share Delia's true element, throw herself into what Mrs. Rodman felt most alive in.

Barbara was bright and not unaware of Mrs. Rodman's ambivalence toward her from the time she was in high school living her perfect little blond life. But that Mrs. Rodman had always granted her the use of the pool on sultry nights made her believe it was a mark of faith, a spiritual sharing.

Barbara now entered the water, her arms outstretched in the dive, her hands together in the gesture of prayer. Then she swam toward the far side on her back so that her sleepy mind could imagine the firmament drifting along instead of her. The moon was waning, its fullness lost days ago. As she slowly glided along, she peeked toward the so very high octagonal window, imagining another moon, Danny's, at a younger time when she was but a reflection, a hope, a desire. She felt as disembodied as that reflection now, no more than a wavering plume of light riding the blue-green sea of water. That's what love was: weightless promise.

Then Barbara heard a thump. She tensed and her body sank to an upright position, her paddling hands and feet keeping her still and afloat and listening. Her first thought was that her mother had shot an eye open like a touchy shade the moment she had snuck outside at three A.M. for her dip and was now approaching to reprimand her. But there was no further sound, and besides, the sound, she could have sworn, came from the direction of the Rodman house, not hers.

When she heard something knock—like a window-rapping?—she quickly swam for the side and hoisted herself up to the tiled border. She dripped as she scurried toward her towel beneath the diving board, the chill air arraying her browned skin with minute bumps. All the while her ears were alert, attending to the source of the sounds behind her, not the slap of her wet feet or the swish of the snatched beach towel.

She stood for a moment wiping her face and her arms and examining the lifeless house before her as though she expected lamps within to erupt with light, the Rodmans to move throughout, their shadows flowing up and back inside like blood in an organism. But all she heard was a—a squeak? Her face squinted trying to make out the noise. She took some tentative steps toward the darkened glass patio doors, a surface that only reflected her image back to her. She looked hunched over, shriveled and wet, wrapped in white cotton, but her double kept moving forward. It was a definite sound.

Could Danny have gone back to his home again? Could Mr. Rodman? The wind had picked up slightly, enough to make her shiver, but she listened with intensity, beyond the breeze-written song of the silver-tined chimes dangling from the shingled patio. Whatever it was seemed like the squeak of rubber—Danny's sneakers on linoleum—or the peep of a bird, a bird trapped inside the house, perhaps, or stuck in a rafter outside, or injured somewhere in the darkness.

A few feet from the sliding doors the sound became instantly clear, yet still accompanied by puzzlement. It was a kissing sound. Not real kissing from two people, but the sound one person makes when imitating kisses, those tiny lip-smacks as when calling a pet inside. It was in the flush and fear of identifying that sound that the pot-planted tree beside the door moved, jostled, and an arm unfolded from behind, an arcing flat hand, and a blow to her face sent Barbara sideways, off her feet and down, her elbow cracking on the patio blocks, her hip slamming hard, her head bouncing once, and the expression of all this pain being immediately stifled by a sudden hand to her mouth.

A man, with a teal-blue cloth dinner napkin wrapped around the lower half of his face like a bandit, stood above her, the puckering sound still emanating from behind the mask. Another man with a similar disguise was holding her down from behind, pushing her straining head and shoulders to the ground. The disguises were ludicrous; she knew who they were, knew exactly from which fairy-tale nightmare they originated. Not easy to forget a Louis Dembo, his build, his thick sullen eyebrows, his animal noises, his hunger.

Louis bent over and gave Barbara a hard compact punch to her stomach, a punch powerful enough to allow Marty to release his hands from her mouth and throat because the force she withstood left her without the wind to speak, let alone to scream. Marty clamped onto her arms as she heard the thump of the patio door hitting the side wall and was dragged inside the dark house. Marty waited until his big brother closed the patio door again before he attended to the slithering form on the floor. He leaned over her face and said, "You can take it conscious or unconscious."

Her bare kicking legs and feet, and gasps, and flowing tears, were the only response. Louis held the wooden base of a screwdriver in the tunnel-like arches of his fingers and, with a full swing, swatted Barbara across the top of her skull.

"Whatever," Louis said, tugging down the napkin from his face.

Barbara lay before their adoring eyes, bleeding from her forehead and inert, but she was alive. Her body was so alive, Louis thought, dropping the tool, yanking once on his belt buckle to unhook it. He could smell her wetness in the dimmed essence of moonlight. It was hard to believe such riches would befall him in the Rodman house. Like a dream. A yuppie wet dream.

He tore the damp swimsuit from her, lay himself on her, rubbed himself against her, flesh on flesh, flicking off matted blond hair from her cheek with a thick finger. The way he pinned himself to her, it reminded him of Carl Rodman himself, another victim he was destined to abuse, but at least this one had a moist embracing black hole he could stick a dick into.

18

WAKING UP WAS less a coming-to than a disorienting stripping of the senses. They were attacked all at once and with overwhelming ferocity. Rodman's sight was bespotted, his ears ringing, his back knotted. His tongue especially was tasting the husks of degenerating paper food containers piled beside his drooling mouth, tasting the very air that was thick with bodies moldering in the closed confines of this hovel, this home.

Rodman pushed open the door with his foot and squinted at the predawn light as though his eyes were tender wounds. He worked himself out of the storage space, careful of his spine, which straightened one vertebra at a time like dominoes in slow motion.

"What's going on?" the dissolute man said, phlegm-voiced and groggy, seeing his visitor's ass in his face.

Rodman unfolded from his aching toe-touch stretch and turned toward his rag-bag host, who was still scrunched up in the corner of the compartment.

"Thought I'd better get moving. The police seem to be gone. I still got things to do."

"Things, huh?" the man said in what looked like a puffy-eyed sneer. Rodman held the door open as the man shoved his tattered legs, his feet dropping to the floor as though they were just empty, battered shoes attached to the end of his pants. He sat up.

"Yeah," he said after a short yawn, "we all got things to do." He sucked in mucus with his nose, trying to clear the passageways. "You going looking for that woman again?"

"Just people who might have seen her, maybe knew her,"

Rodman replied. Then he paused and wondered and said it anyway. "She's dead."

The man stiffened as though pinched by sobriety's fingers for a moment and gave Rodman a reluctant look, the slightest glimpse of pity. "Mmm," he said.

Rodman didn't notice, didn't need to. "I thought she might have been in that bar, the one down the block there, sometime back."

"Ollie's."

Rodman nodded. "You know the place. How well?"

The man started where he left off a few hours ago: he shrugged. "I don't know. Well enough to know Tommy, I guess. The guy who runs it. He's a good guy mainly. You know he used to be a—a whatayacall—a foot cop here—beat cop, years ago. Used to roust me good when I was a punk kid, hanging out with some of the tough crowd then." The man bulked up and mimicked a thuggish face. "You know."

Rodman nodded and the man's shoulders deflated to normal. "But he was a good guy, Tommy. Like even now, he gives me some leftovers sometimes from the sandwich trays— sometimes hot food, too, he didn't sell. Says he doesn't like seeing me fish the stuff out the trash like some alley cat."

"You know about any of the people who go in Ollie's on a regular basis?"

The man nodded and yawned again. "Some . . . maybe."

"How about a Frank?" Rodman asked.

"Frank?"

"Yeah, a balding guy. Middle-age or older. Good-looking— manly—with bushy gray eyebrows . . ."

The man's eyes widened a bit within the nest of hair. "Oh, sure, Frank—yeah. Looks at me like I was pigeon shit on his shoes."

"You know his last name?" Rodman said, touched by the pulse of anticipation. "Where he lives?"

The man shook his head, raised a snooty brow. "Don't care to know much of nothing about a guy looks at me like I was pigeon shit on his shoes."

"So that's it, then—Frank."

"That's it," the man confessed. Then he said, "Oh!" and his

head shook one way then nodded the other, "No, yeah, yeah . . ."

"What?"

"Yeah," the man said, raising a finger. "That's right. I know where he works. I mean, I guess it's where he works. It don't look like a place you sleep, but—fuck—neither does this hole." The man coughed a laugh.

"Where's this?" Rodman asked.

The man held out a grimy hand. "Give me a boost. I'll point ya."

Rodman stood under the small Romanesque archway of a five-story edifice, a plaque on which proclaimed it the Mace Building. The small octagonal tiles beneath his feet confirmed the appellation by forming a worn brown M in the center of a brown circle. The homeless man had told him he saw this "Frank-joker" come in and out of this building often and at all hours.

Rodman entered the dim lobby and scanned the listing of tenants on the glass-encased board that hung beside the elevator doors. A number of names and businesses had a few of their hand-set white letters either missing or inverted or tilted on the axis of one pin, making the board function more like a word puzzle than a directory. Undaunted, Rodman took the elevator to the second floor and began his door-by-door investigation.

It being barely five in the morning, the hallways were empty and eerie, Rodman's hollow footfalls the only sound offered. The building was clearly prewar, as the length of the doors were framed glass with painted words on them, and the lighting came from single bulb fixtures encased within frosty white globes every fifteen feet or so, the latter giving Rodman the feeling of stepping from one light pool to another—that, and his growing anger and insecurity, and Rodman acted the spiteful kid, deliberately stepping into rain puddles to soil his good shoes.

He also felt the homeless man had told him the truth this time. He felt close to his prey, to Delia's somebody. This building was this "Frank-joker's" kind of building, had his strength, his longevity, his life-worn look of defiance, his earthy brown texture. With each successively higher floor Rodman cased, his anticipation mounted. He looked past the offices of the insurance adjusters, and the marriage counselors, and the personal injury lawyers, and any and all generic business names—Safe-Aid Products, Inc.; Best Boy Clothes Outlets Co.; and on and on. This man would have his name up on the door to pronounce his unassuming singularity, the type of man who could be the rooted fulcrum of a local tavern while reading a book. Rodman was getting excited, flexing his fists as he walked by yet another dentist's office, the last one on the third floor. He took the staircase two steps at a time to the fourth.

And there it was, stenciled on the first glass door to the right, FRANK XAVIER, PRIVATE INVESTIGATIONS. Rodman stood before it a few moments as though he were deciphering a cave painting, reading the name, that title, over in his head to absorb its hidden meaning. It was business, Rodman thought; it was private; it was hers. And it was deeper than any fucking affair.

Rodman heard noise inside like papers being shuffled, though through the smoky glass he could see no light on. He knocked three times and loudly but was ignored, apparently unheard, for the rustle of paper never quelled even a moment to acknowledge there was a knock. So Rodman tried the knob, expecting restraint. Instead it clicked open, allowing him to swing the door slowly inward to his arm's full extension. He readied his reflexes to let fly a punch or anything else he could at the man whose bartender pal blindsided him—but there was nobody there. Not that the sound of flipping paper stopped. The low-silled rear window to the office was open wide to what appeared to be the building's air shaft, offering little light but plenty of bracing air funneling down from the roof a few stories above. It was obviously opened to counter the clanking radiator throwing heat for no good reason, so the room was a clash of temperatures, conflicting pockets of weather.

Rodman took a brisk step inside and shut the door behind him. The room was spacious for a single. A desk dominated one corner, acting as though it were alive, its papers occasionally shedding from it to the floor; those more secure shimmied with the sporadic gusts. The room was book-dominated: one lay on the floor near the window, others were piled near a half-sized refrigerator; most were obliquely stacked on shelves of various cheap woods. They were practical receptacles, not objects of decor.

Rodman took his chances and flicked on the adjustable desk lamp. He bent the neck up toward the file cabinet in order to throw a circle of light against it. A framed newspaper article on the wall nearby reflected its story of Frank Xavier finding and rescuing the kidnapped infant of the wealthy Capstone family after the kidnappers had been shot by an Argentinean gang in a related drug deal. Rodman seemed to remember something about it: the boy had been sold to baby traders . . . ? Xavier's somber rough-hewn face fronted the column with the Capstone child's photo overlapping the lower corner.

Rodman fingered through the orderly files, but a *Rodley* folder abutted the *Roane*; there was no *Rodman*. Delia could have been using an alias, but that seemed unlikely. Still, he tried her maiden name, Able, with no result. Then he thumbed through the more current folders, anything with dates that covered the last week, but most were older cases and he grew frustrated. Maybe Xavier was not the conduit of Delia's business, but of her covert affection, after all. Then what of the money from the cash machine? Her blackmailer, then?

Rodman sat at the desk and scanned the animated paper piles and accessories. Shifting over in the wheeled wooden office chair, he struck an elbow into a Brother electric typewriter on its own thin metal stand. Rodman noticed that the paper rolled about the platen had been typed upon, so he pulled it up a few notches to read it more clearly. It said: "I'm sorry for everything I've done." That was it. No "Dear anybody." No date. Was it an aborted apology note to someone?

Perplexed, Rodman returned his attention to the objects on Xavier's desktop. He snatched up the receiver to the beige touch-tone phone, deciding, If old tricks worked once . . . and punched the redial button. But the phone was unresponsive; there wasn't even a dial tone. Rodman checked whether the line was severed from the wall, but it wasn't. The phone was simply dead.

Somehow, Rodman felt as though he was being plunked with parts, jagged pieces, dropped from a dark sky, doohigs that should fit thingamawhats—dead phones, nonexistent files, private eyes with unlocked doors—something had to draw these disparate things together like a pull string, enclose it, bag it, label it. He spotted a cheap variant of a Filofax and began to digest what proved to be a sparse selection of names, people with whom Xavier drew connections, and perhaps personal, rather than professional ones. Yet again, no Delia. There appeared to be a few relatives listed, a chief of police, government underlings, and there was that name again . . . Mary Dorlack. Rodman put down the address file and once more glanced through a handful of previously scanned case folders. In more than a few the name Mary Dorlack was listed as an assistant operative. Rodman jotted her Point Crescent address down from the index file card. That was at least *something*.

Rodman's hands kept up the chase. They raised the blotter, felt for indentations in the note pad, scoured the drawers, fingering staple boxes and pencil nubs. He lifted the desk calendar, the day-by-day thicket of rectangular sheets you turned over one at a time to get to tomorrow. Only on this one there were no yesterdays; that is, Xavier evidently didn't flip the small sheets over but tore them out, as evidenced by the flecks of white paper adjacent to the metal rings. Rodman immediately grabbed the wastebasket and overturned it on the floor. He fell to his knees and, avoiding the remains of pickle-sweating deli sandwiches, plastic cups, and coffee-stained junk-mail envelopes, he sorted out the crumpled balls and unraveled them. Last Thursday's date: *Call H.—3:00/Dinner? 432-3009.* Yesterday's date: nothing. Last Saturday's date: *Visa—$53/ Bert no show.* Last Friday's date: *Mary D. St. Luke's Rm. 405 flowers?*

Rodman straightened, his rump on his heels. Mary Dorlack! Get well. Last Friday before leaving for work, Delia had handed him a card to mail: Mary Dorlack, St. Luke's Hospital, Point Crescent. Delia had described Mary as a wealthy patron. Delia was lying. Delia was a part of this room, this man. There was no file, but Delia was *there* as palpably as if she was standing erect above him cocking one hip, goading him.

Rodman dove forward, bending, his fingers shaking, fumbling with the next piece of balled-up calendar paper. Tuesday—two days ago—nothing. This past Sunday, the day of the party and . . . Rodman sat up instantly, back on his heels, reading: *D.R. 1732 Tyer Rd., Hollowsport/7:00 sharp gate off of Miller Lane.*

There she appeared, in Rodman's fevered mind, her face tight and freckled by sunlight, her eyes holding the family's burden. And there was Frank Xavier, too—burly, confident. He had come to the affair for Senator Thomas McMann, slipped in the back gate off of Miller, just as Hallie suspected. He gave her something, something he signed. That charred X Hallie unearthed in the stone pit was no departing kiss, but a signatory flourish, like all the large showy capital X's that appeared at the bottom of summary top sheets to folders holding closed cases. With the links joined at last, Rodman knew he had to find Xavier once more, but this time have a detailed talk minus his own emotional storm and subsequent sapping. The route he decided to take, however, was through St. Luke's Hospital and Mary Dorlack.

Rodman raised himself to his feet and grabbed a folder, any folder, as long as it was thick with material so it appeared legitimate. He licked a new file label and thumbed it over the old one; then on it he inked, *Rodman, Delia.*

The wind became especially rambunctious at this time, and Rodman could barely keep the papers from fleeing the counterfeit folder he was working on, let alone the unattended ones he had taken out, some sliding across empty stretches of the desk, the pieces of trash skidding around, colliding. The book on the floor, splayed open near the window, flipped its pages in deliberate chunks as though fighting the urge. Rodman stared at the animate tome for a moment, and the chill air carried with it a fear that tingled and enticed then transformed those slowly turning pages into a beckoning hand.

Rodman stepped toward the book, confirming what had ever so momentarily blipped in his brain when he broke in and blipped out just as fast—it was the Giancana book that Frank Xavier had been reading at Ollie's, *Double Cross.* Rodman picked it up, inspected it for nothing in particular, closed it, then set it on the knee-high refrigerator. He turned to the window and stepped toward the sill, which was the refrigerator's better by only two inches in height. The window displayed the water-stained gray wall six feet across the way as though in an oversized wood frame. It was full daylight now and the sun angled down diagonally into the shaft. Rodman wobbled from his thoughts, gripped the sash and stuck his head out. Four stories below, coiled up like a brown shiny snake, lay the contorted dead body of Frank Xavier, his head dug into his chest from a broken neck, his woolly sport coat seeped in dark burgundy from his bone-split face and cheek.

Rodman backed off, dizzied from the sight. His first thoughts were of the typewriter, the one-line apologia "for everything." Was his informing Xavier of Delia's death the first time Xavier had heard of it? Did Xavier confirm it somehow with anybody? Did he feel responsible? Did he love her?

Rodman dug the heels of his hands to his eyes, having seen too much lately, much too much, and bent at the waist as though punctured by another blindside fist. He wanted to cry out, but he refused and immediately jerked his arms to his sides and stiffened, straightened. Frank Xavier was no suicide, Rodman scolded himself. His own naiveté sickened him. It was the plague of his life, his fatal disease, his mutant lost-lamb gene, his sixties' blinders, his unseen leash which led to Sonny Vance's tugging hand. Rodman tightened his muscles, every muscle; pulled tight by anger; jerked taut by anger; his brain, thoughts, shot through with anger; and anger brought him reason, brought him back to what brought him forward, forward to the window in the first place: the book.

Naive fuck, that's what he was, Rodman thought. What did Frank Xavier supposedly do? Type one line, douse the lights, carry the book with him in the dark just so he could drop it and leap to his death like a drunken Romeo? The book was the linchpin, the teacher, as most books were. Rodman envisioned the more probable black-bordered scenario: Xavier came in, was jumped, dropped the book in a struggle, was struck down, was shoved out the window. The typed note? More bullshit. Generic melancholia for motivation. Brand X, not the one signed with a flourish. Simply put, a cover.

Frank Xavier had been murdered, yet Rodman was past feeling endangered, for through it all he was still only death's harbinger, not its recipient. With loathsome consistency he knew where to find it, engender it, point it out, leave it in his wake. Worst of all, he was getting used to it.

19

HALLIE JUST KEPT yelling something about "violation" over the phone, but it was no more than a tick past six A.M., and the only thing violated at this point was Danny's sleep by this fucking bogus phone call. He sat up in bed holding his forehead with pincered fingers, his chest bare, his day empty, which was all the more reason he wished the fulfilling void of sleep would return.

"Can you crank it down a few decibels," Danny remarked in the middle of one of Hallie's sentences, "and like maybe I'd know what you're talking about." Not that he would fucking *care* what she was talking about. But the statement—it was his first besides a slurred hello—brought about a transitory silence on the other end and allowed Danny to assimilate that which he had aurally endured: the "violation," stridently put forth by Hallie, was that of trust.

"Never mind," Hallie continued glumly and with less volume. "Just tell my daughter I am *ashamed*. That's all I *can* be. Ashamed. I take promises seriously. You shouldn't have to tell her *that*. She knows *that*."

"You take promises seriously," Danny repeated.

"That's correct, mister. They're to be kept."

"What promise is that you're talking about?" Danny asked. And why are you telling me?

"I suppose she didn't tell you she promised to stay here a few nights, *at least*. She still lives here, you know. And after what happened the other night—"

"I know all about the *promise*," Danny interrupted, then enough of his mind had burned away its morning fog. "Wait a minute—she's not here, if that's what you're saying."

"You tell her I'm not in the mood for these games—"

With unthinking defensiveness, Danny decided to up his own volume. "Hey! Listen up! I said she's not here!"

There was silence on the line. Hallie was shaking her head, squeezing the receiver. She finally replied, "Lies out of you— that's like—like talk out of Oprah. You have the gift." Then she hung up, her lips in a tremor.

Leaning on the ottoman arm for support, Hallie nurtured her hurt, let it suckle at her withering bosoms, chew at her; *knew* it was Danny Rodman who forced her daughter to lie, induced Barbara to crack promises like dried twigs, to abandon potential, abandon her and a life of propriety. Hallie knew all their mocking lovers' lies, that is, until Danny was pounding at her door only twenty-five minutes after the phone call.

"She's not with me," came the muted yell through the frosted side window. His blurred appearance, his undefined open mouth, his distant then sudden fist striking the glass again and again, frightened her, but what he was saying frightened her even more, so she let him in.

Danny transformed into a disheveled still point in her doorway, his shirt half out, noiseless, staring. "She's not with me," he repeated in a softly hoarse tone. "Never was. Can we find her now?"

Hallie felt the lines in her face deepen with dread, and Danny thought he saw a shadowed veil of helplessness descend and diminish her fierce piety. It almost made her look like a handicapped person. "Oh, God . . ." she said to herself, her eyes shifting in thought. "Dear God . . ."

Danny arrived at Barbara's bedroom first and accounted for all three of her fall jackets still on hangers in her closet. When Hallie finally limped inside, she noticed, as though by instinct, the bottom drawer to the pink-tinged ash dresser was diagonally ajar. Hallie pulled it open all the way.

"Her suit's gone," she announced. "Her pink bathing suit's gone."

Danny lay down the purple stationery letter pad he was thumbing through and thought of cold pool water and his dead mother.

No sooner had they crossed the border between yards than they found Barbara's beach sandals beside the base of the Rodman diving board. "Barbara!" Danny called out, scanning the rear of his parents' house, the entrance to the tulip garden, the far yard. Hallie picked the sandals up, gazed at them as though this piece of Barbara would summon the other pieces through touch, rubbing her thumb in the worn, blackening indention of a big toe.

"Barbara!" Danny called again as he circled the pool, but there was no response, except for two young wrens he frightened from an azalea bush. The rest of the birds amid this dew-spawned morning chirped their songs regardless of Danny's presence and preoccupation. He gazed up at the famed octagonal window with no expectations. What was he supposed to see there? His younger self? His moonstruck face? His lunar-drenched mirror? The past, its magic, was like a brief reflection on the shiny surface of the mind. Then he squinted toward another one, at least what he thought was a reflection of the bright white concrete bench abreast the pool house wall, but on closer inspection what he saw ghostlike in the sliding patio doors was not on their surface, but *through*, inside the house. He cupped his hand to the glass: it was a discarded beach towel.

To his surprise, then fear, the patio door was unlocked, gliding aside with a steady push of his palm. He stepped toward the teal-striped terry cloth almost gingerly, as though it would awaken otherwise. If that were so, Hallie's clomping approach dispelled any eerie dreamlike quality that embodied the towel, the misty light illuming it, the small shimmering puddles of water on the ornate tile beside it. In fact, Hallie's scream at spotting the smeared droplets of blood coursed a bone-cold reality through Danny's heart.

Hallie lost all control and shook and wept and turned to the frozen young man beside her and smacked him as hard as she could across the face. "Damn you!" she screamed at him. She pummeled his chest with balled-up blanched hands. "Damn you, damn you, damn you, damn you . . ." And Danny let her rage on, even though not a few of her blows caused shocks of pain. However, Hallie weakened quickly, her leaden leg soon supporting a blubbering mass, and she let herself drop wholly to Danny's feet as though deboned.

"What?" Danny asked abstractly, not understanding what Hallie had just said.

". . . to hell," she forced through a choke of tears.

Danny didn't bother to pick Hallie up, his ears listening past the sobs, though her sobs were his sobs, her loss, his. They both expected "the worst"—now and in life; they had that much in common. And Barbara was "the best" they had come to rely on and burden.

Danny looked around from where he stood, and listened, and cursed the House, the structure and the symbol, that which represented his family as would a crest with shield-borne sword and serpent. And in his sickened heart he knew, even with all its scaly twists, he *knew* where the head of that serpent was, *knew* who was ultimately responsible.

It was then Danny finally engaged the courage to push away from the shuddering, sprawling woman and toward the uneasy innards of his former home, where he would search the rooms for what he was most afraid to find.

20

T HE MOMENT IT was ten A.M. and people were allowed up, Rodman stepped on the hospital elevator with the case folder vertically pressed to his chest. As he stood among two nurses, an orderly, and five other antsy visitors, his mouth was hidden by one end of the cream-toned cardboard and his eyes by Delia's mirrored lenses, so if anybody was even remotely about to recognize him, it would have to be from an intimate knowledge of the shape and relief of his nose.

In truth, Mary Dorlack might be somebody to recognize him once he revealed his tired face to her, but it was a risk Rodman believed necessary, balanced against his search for connections, for links in this gruesome chain of bodies. She was in 312, a semiprivate room shared with a lung cancer patient, or so Rodman speculated. An oxygen mask aided a pallid-faced woman whose hardened features showed the edge of an "old-timer" who never once considered shucking her two-plus packs of Salems from life's daily routine. We all self-destruct in different ways, Rodman thought, as if Time itself took too long to do it.

Rodman hesitated near the sleeping woman before approaching the other side of the partition where Mary Dorlack lay. One reason was to straighten himself up, run a hand through his greasy hair, palm-press wrinkles in his pants, hope the aroma of the alleyway had dispelled. The other was the face-flushing realization that this was the first time he was in a hospital ward since—well—he couldn't help re-form the faint shadow cast on the curtained barrier to that of his son Eric.

When he finally stepped around, he saw a woman in her early thirties with dyed blond hair pulled back to its dark roots by a violet bandanna. Only bangs hung down like a yellow comb to her eyebrows. Her lantern jaw featured a beauty mark on its left side, and an ample mouth populated with large teeth which were currently biting down on a strawberry granola bar. She had a wide nose, as though boneless, but her eyes, when spotting Rodman, expanded from their centers and beautified her pugnacious features. Her pupils were also gooey with painkiller.

"I know you?" Mary Dorlack said and lifted herself up on her pillow.

"No," Rodman replied, trying not to sound relieved. "No, you don't, though . . . I could use your help."

Mary's eyes didn't even squint into puzzlement, but stayed wide and open. "What can I do for you?" Her voice had a trace of the South in it, and it furthered the feeling of friendliness she exuded. Rodman felt almost as if he were the sick one and she the supportive visitor. Mary pointed to the green plastic chair adjacent the bed.

"Well, I don't want to bother you," Rodman said, nevertheless accepting the seat, "but Frank Xavier told me I could get a few more insights into the Delia Rodman case from you."

"He did, did he?" Rodman could tell this was Mary's mock put-upon voice. "What's the poor boy too busy to fill you in himself?"

"Well, you know Frank."

"Sure do know him. But I guess *you* don't."

"Not really," Rodman said, trying to dodge, to stay vague. "You see, he just wanted some last minute legwork—"

Mary flailed a hand at him. "His life's a last-minute proposition, that man. Like this phone business. How'd you get to talk to him? At Ollie's?"

"Yeah."

"Very impressive, right?" Her voice came alive, chatty. "I mean, he never gets his phone fixed. Never follows up on the phone company dragging its ass. Excuse my language." She giggled, her eyes half-lidded. "I don't even know you." Her hand made the symbolic gesture to touch Rodman's arm though it was two feet away.

"That's okay," he said. "So he works out of Ollie's now."

"Seems like. He's been parked there at least two weeks. Tommy—you met Tommy?"

"Of course."

"How could you miss him, right? Face right off the potato farm." Mary laughed at her warmhearted insult. "It's okay. My daddy was Irish. He owns the place—Tommy! Not my dad— God, these drugs! Anyhow, Tommy's Frank's cousin—"

"That I didn't know," Rodman commented.

"Good. Yes, Tommy was a Point Crescent cop for quite a while, retired young, fifty-whatever, gets his cousin Frank to come over from Illinois and join the force. But it's night and day, you know?"

"What is?"

"Frick and Frack. The two of them. Frank couldn't stomach police regs. Said it was like being a grunt in the army, only with more paperwork." Mary blushed with self-consciousness. "He tell you this?"

"No, go on."

"It's a long story," Mary went on, "but Frank quit, tried some other kinds of jobs, this and that. He's a smart guy. Loves to read. But, you know? He missed the work. The— the—uh . . . hunt." She looked frustrated. "You know what I mean?"

Rodman nodded.

"Like I do laying here." Rodman watched her eyes get misty, her expressive face undergo sea changes with every wave of emotion. He could tell the dope was suppressing a vibrant personality, someone with a tropism toward movement and direct action.

"I *bet* you miss it," Rodman said, patting her wrist. He was also sensing she missed Xavier, too.

"So Frank gets a license and goes solo," Mary continued. "Private eye. He *hates* that term. Anyway, he's very very good at it."

"Sure, the Capstone kidnapping," Rodman said, recalling the framed article.

"So you know about that?" Mary's cheeks flushed with what Rodman had to interpret as pride. She kept nodding with affirmation after each line of accomplishment. "Got a state-wide rep on that one. Frank was on TV. Didn't want to be, but he's gotten steady work from some really big money people because of that. Yessir, he's the best investigator you could ask for. . . . Of course, don't ask him to do the practical stuff—you know, phone company repairs, visiting people in hospitals—" She snapped off another bite from her granola bar, then saw Rodman looking at what she thought were the yellow and red carnations on her nightstand.

"Oh, he sent those, the brute. Typical tough guy. Loves the rough stuff, but can't stand the results. Looks at doctors like they were cons on parole. I couldn't drag him here."

Rodman smiled and she smiled back, though Rodman did not take notice of the floral arrangement before and had, in fact, been eyeing the card propped up just behind it. He recognized the inky squiggles below the printed Hallmark pap. It was from Delia.

"Ah, but that's Frank," Mary sighed. "Frank is Frank and I love'm anyway. So where is it you've been working?"

Rodman was unprepared for the shift in topic. "Before now, you mean?"

"You an ex-cop?"

"No. I mean, I was in the crime lab over in Hollowsport, but the budget crunch got me, so, you know, I've been freelancing."

"Crime lab, huh? I should get so cushy a job. I wouldn't have wrecked a knee getting thrown down the stairs by a client's crazy-eyed husband—"

Rodman nodded, but needed to get her off him and on track. "Frank was saying . . ."

"He tell you about what happened to me?" The tone of the question was less about information and more about emotion. It was almost as though she were asking if he had brought her up in conversation, discussed her, confessed a dream or two about her.

"Not in so many words," Rodman replied. "He had to leave town. That's why he sent me here for a quick update."

"What case was this again?" Mary asked, her expression fogging up. "Forgive me, hon. I'm having to live off these needles, or else I'd be a killer, I swear. Trail of dead nurses in the hallways. The pain is brutal."

"Delia Rodman." Carl held up the counterfeit file for verification, thick with nothing.

"Hunh," Mary grunted. "Thought he said he was close to closing that one. Said he might go down and see Delia personally if things broke right."

"What do you mean?"

"I mean what I mean. I mean, I think he was close to getting the name of Mattera's client."

Rodman let it settle in, flesh out, before he spoke. "The hit-and-run person."

Mary nodded.

"Which, of course, would have wrapped it up."

"Sure would've," Mary confirmed. "That's what Delia wants more than anything. That's why she hired the best. Frank's an outsider with a lot of inside moves. He knows people. Mattera had the Hollowsport area pretty tight, being the big-shot lawyer he is. Deel wouldn't get anywhere with the local investigators there, but ol' Frank's got ways of poking through from outside the walls." Her face sprang open to a realization. "Say, Hollowsport! *Your* area."

"What?"

"Crime lab . . ."

"Oh, yeah. Right."

"Maybe that's why he's got you doing the work I can't. Maybe he needs that last confirmation. Frank's thorough if nothing else." Mary pointed to the water pitcher. "You mind?"

Rodman rose and poured a cup for her and had some himself, pretending it was something stronger.

"Anything on *Mister* Rodman?" he asked after Mary finished with her refresher.

"Mmm? Whatever we got's in the file." Without looking, she dumped the cup in the wastebasket flush to her bed.

"Sounds like you got to know Delia Rodman well working this case."

"Oh, sure did. One of the real perks of this one." Mary's eyes focused on him, her voice taking on a greater confidentiality, her language becoming more street-talk straight. Rodman imagined her a female police cadet who came up short on the physical, disappointing a father who she knew wanted a son. "Delia and I got very close. She's a trooper with all the family problems she's had shitstorming down. Alky husband. Older boy was on drugs for a time, and poor, poor Eric—well, hey, he's what this magilla's all about, right?"

Rodman could only silently nod.

"Deel even stays with me when she comes down here. It's like high school being with her. Sleepovers. We talk about things. It's more than business. Delia Rodman's not about business. She's all personal. Everything she does is personal. The proverbial class act—too classy for a dipstick like me." Mary laughed at herself. "She's like some older sister I never had who's actually in control of her life. She dives through the muck of it and somehow comes out clean. And strong. And fighting mad, too—no, *better* than some old sister—I know some real dung-hole sisters. Deel's more a real buddy. And when we both kind of needed one, you know?"

Rodman didn't even nod this time, the emotion swelling his throat. It was like experiencing a clock-warping black hole, this talking in present tenses again. Delia is alive. Frank Xavier is alive. It could almost make Rodman feel alive. Almost.

The phone at Mary's bedside emitted a soft trill.

"Excuse me," she said reaching a hand over to the receiver. "Hello, mental ward, inmate Dorlack speaking." She winked at Rodman.

Rodman could hear the entrapped sound of a man's voice, a sobbing voice.

All the sleepy playfulness in Mary's face dissolved, her soft eyes flashing. "Tommy? . . . Tommy? . . . What's wrong, hon?"

Rodman jumped from his chair as though ejected. He waved a hand near Mary's face and looked deferential. "I'll let you go. Thanks for everything."

Mary nodded at him, holding her hand out to acknowledge his departure, but the rest of her—her face suddenly lined and rigid, her tautly craned neck—was forcibly pulled toward the tragic voice inside the receiver, to the wire-charged disturbance.

Rodman's shoulders untensed only after he banged out the stairwell's first-floor door, only after three long flights of spiraling down. He had little tolerance left for his own helplessness, little mental fortitude for witnessing the tilt and fall of another emotional domino.

21

RIGHT FROM THE start of the drive, his mind took its own trip, a wildly speculative one, envisioning the intimate conversations. He imagined a hodgepodgely furnished apartment, Mary Dorlack in a cross-legged squat on her oversized bed, spooning Ben & Jerry's Heath Bar Crunch right from the pint container and facing Delia, locked in her own position, more yogaesque, upturned feet on calves, stretching those swimmer's leg muscles, pulling on a green bottle of springwater, her disciplined idea of dessert. Two opposites sharing, mourning their mutual status in the vague, complex workings called love, Mary expressing her poverty of gains, Delia recounting her wealth of losses. A sum-zero exercise, one might think, but Rodman doubted it.

He nodded to himself at accurately assessing the fact that Delia would never be caught dead in Ollie's Tavern, except possibly for love. Only to his surprise, it was not her consuming love for another man, but for her dead little boy. Eric would not be let go of, just *not*. Her heart had too tight a hold, too deep a wound. Delia demanded closure, not through the healing of time, but through the discovery of the perpetrator. Her surrender that night to her brother and to him was a ruse or just a temporary retreat quickly reconsidered. She would use untold secreted money, continual deception, *any* means, it appeared, to find the one responsible.

And in spite of the pain it caused to think of his son's death again, Rodman had to respect his wife's rebellion. He had always thought that she was the conformer taming his demons, when in fact she was the one willing to go outside of things-as-they-are, to fight the establishment—her husband, her brother, the police, the big-time lawyer Mattera, the church, the support groups. She was the one with the strength to subvert. Maybe that's what he had loved in her all along. Maybe that's why she hated his sixties' storeroom so much. It was all surface paraphernalia, no substance. Like him.

Mary Dorlack was a creature of another kind. No less feisty in nature—he was speculating like mad now—but sorrowful, the unrequited worshiper, the kind of girl who would define herself as optimistic when buying a king-sized mattress "just in case," and yet who never knew where to put her masculinity when dealing with a man, especially one like Frank Xavier. Who was he kidding? Rodman thought. Who was he really envisioning? Mary's smile, the wistful one, the one of lost hope when joking about Frank Xavier, that was just a superimposed reminder of another woman—Pat Dokes.

It was Pat Dokes who had flirted in and out of his thoughts earlier, maybe unconsciously at the hospital, because it was her bag—the travel bag she gave him as a birthday gift one year—that triggered this new journey, the trip up-country.

After deliberately circling around Hollowsport, Rodman finally reached the foot of Mandrake Road and aimed his car toward its dramatic incline. He recalled having left the travel pouch back at the cabin on Janus Mountain, after relieving it of his gun on that distant fucked-up morning he thought he killed Sonny Vance. However, the pouch contained a "secret" side compartment in which he always kept at least two to five hundred-dollar bills. He was in the process of retrieving that much-needed money as well as of avoiding the realization he had no idea where to turn next.

He rose along the mountainside's ledge of road, coiling around the wide bends beneath the creviced rocks, unthinking, like following a giant's strong curving arm to whisper something in his ear the way the wind did through the snow-crested peaks. (His mother's images always came back, always up here.) Seeing Wesley Koontz's cliffside gas stop was a mixed blessing. It usually signaled that the cabin was less than a mile away; now, as it was—it looked as closed up as Rodman's face. The truck was gone. It didn't matter anymore.

Rodman soon pulled onto the bed of bleached-white rocks that served as a driveway beneath the dark bower of birch trees. But he sensed something strange. He thought he heard muted sounds from the cabin, which was twenty feet off, the growth of brush and bark always obscuring the structure from the crunchy drive. As he approached, dusk lay a heaviness to the air and to its sounds in general. It was as though when the visual landscape became blunted and started losing its definition, the aural world attained salience—the restless insects; the scurrying squirrels; the stream, far down the path beyond, crisply fleeing over the stones and intruding branches.

Yet the sound that obscured them all was an unnatural one, that is, one not from Nature. It was muted music. Melodic. Orchestral. At the closed side window, Rodman pressed himself upon the roughened wood and strained to see into the living room area, to see whatever the dimness allowed, for no lights were on. But there was singing; there was grandness of sound, and now the violins. Rodman was afraid.

The encroaching night's dampness made the cross-paned window frame slick, but he managed to raise it up far enough to hoist himself onto the sill. He pulled himself through the narrow gap he made, not worried about making too much of a noise, because once inside, the music truly dominated the blackening space.

When Rodman sat up against the inner wall, breathing in long, deep breaths, eyes fixed on the room's stasis, he concentrated on the impassioned singer. It was Frank Sinatra, declaring that love was no good unless it was all the way.

The only movement in the gray dimness was that of the stylus bobbing up and down on a warped record like a ship in stormy waters. And of all the stupid things Rodman could think of, his first thought was that he didn't *own* this record. Somebody broke in to play their own records on the belt-driven turntable he hadn't used in years, since adding a CD player to his component system.

The song was being played far louder than it needed to be in order to reach any room in the one-story house, loud enough so that maybe somebody outside could hear it, wanted to hear it. . . . Rodman pondered the half-open window catty-corner to where the stereo stack blasted. He scuffled to its ledge, keeping low, then peered above it. Near his boat, the tarpaulin of which was stripped off and crumpled beside, were digging tools and boxes he had stored in the outdoor shed, tops torn open, cardboard shards hanging over like dry tongues. He saw motion in the trees, the music blaring in his ears. He watched a sweaty and hatless Louis Dembo emerge from the thicket in rolled-up sleeves, ripping away at another box, passionately singing out with Ol' Blue Eyes.

Rodman dropped quickly down, balled up in himself below the sill, tucked in a tight penitent bow as though praying. "Fuck, fuck, fuck . . ." he hissed into his chest. Then he sprung out, still somewhat hunched over, his feet moving in small quick steps, shaking free the orchestra's rhapsodic string section now in full lush instrumental, his thinking of where the younger one could be, the skinny one, the Rootie-fucking-Kazootie one with the baseball cap and fucking railroad ties on his teeth.

Rodman ducked into the darkened kitchen and eased a black-handled carving knife out from its wooden block. He trotted to the master bedroom, spotting the travel satchel that leaned up against a straw-backed chair. He slung the strap over his head and across his chest so the pouch lay just under his armpit as though it were loaded with musket ammo. That's when he spun on his heels and then stutter-stepped at the unseen presence of somebody laying in his large hand-carved bed.

The country-blue comforter was bunched as though itself a soft diamond-patterned mountain with its own tucks and valleys, peaks and rounded drops. He saw no part of someone sticking out—no head, no feet, nothing—but sharply sensed a person underneath. Sinatra was singing the final break too loud to hear any breathing.

On the floor beside the bed, Rodman watched a pair of phosphorescent sneakers starting to faintly glow with life, both tipped over, spilling out soiled green socks; it was as though the shoes were regaining an unearthly power in the creeping dark. He took a silent stride toward the bed and raised his fisted knife upward. He trembled while Sinatra was wondering where the road would lead them.

Rodman's free left hand gently grabbed a loose portion of the comforter.

He yanked hard, elbow-locked, toward the ceiling and back,

lifting the quilted covering, while at the same time leaping on the bed, ready to slash down to where he assumed a head rested, to plunge his blade into the ripeness of skulls if need be.

But he wasn't ready for this, this body, this battered and childlike body belonging to Barbara Fouche. He sat straddling her frail naked form, gazing at her as though at a fallen museum piece, at something smashed and irreplaceable, her tan lines demarcating the broken sections, her white breasts and triangulated white crotch blending with the white sheets, fostering the illusion that her torso had been severed in distinct pieces. She lay unconscious beneath him, her wrists bound together with a leather belt Rodman recognized from his closet back in Hollowsport. Barbara was breathing in faint shudders, her face puffy from being beaten, her lean sides displaying dark patches, shapeless bruises; one of her nipples had been bleeding. The top of her head seemed spray-painted green, erratically so, especially around the eyes. She was also marked up by what, at closer inspection, looked and smelled like lipstick, peach lipstick, the kind Delia occasionally used. A tick-tacktoe game, played to a draw, adorned the side of her left breast. On her right rib cage squatted a bug-eyed cat with a tongue extending over a foot long, disappearing into a sticky tuft of blond pubic hair. Her sunken belly button had two widely spread legs and large feet drawn from it with words and an arrow—*insert prick here*.

He didn't want to look much farther below.

"All—the—" Sinatra was hitting his crescendo. *"—way!"*

Rodman stroked Barbara's face, wanted to hold her, tell her to save Danny, save herself, get out of this life somehow, dissolve, shuck this befouled skin and start again, save the children as he had not. You either killed or saved the next generation by how you lived your life. He was trying. He swore, he was trying. The indistinct nature of twilight, the fading string section, the break of hot sweat from revulsion and danger, made everything absurdly unreal and vividly hyper-real at the same time. He touched Barbara's baby-tender skin once more. He had to get her out of there.

No sooner did Rodman put the knife down to attempt undoing the belt on her wrists did he hear the compelling thuds of footsteps—steps *inside* and coming his way. From on his knees atop the bed, he glanced at the window facing the back area, but the gray light offered the density of gray pines, the gray discards of boxes, the gray sweep of grass—any sign of color or of Louis Dembo was gone. There was also no way to exit the bedroom without running into whoever was marching this way. He was trapped.

Louis Dembo had come out of the corrugated metal shack with the last of the cartons. It felt good to do some physical labor outdoors again. His muscular efforts over the past few days were not proving to be as successful as his construction work. However, his "destruction" work, as he thought of it, usually turned out to be more fun. On houses, on people, it was all the same; each had its separate pleasure. Sometimes one offered compensation for the other.

For instance, after having come up empty-handed at the Rodman house in terms of dope or money, he and his brother heard the splish-splash of the pool outside. Sudden apprehension became sudden nourishment. They watched blond wetness rise and dip upon the swaying blue-green surface, first a spread of yellow hair, then gone, to be replaced by the bob of a near-perfect bottom, both in graceful continual succession across the length of the pool, her curves glistening. He made Marty go fetch the pressed dinner napkins he saw in the dining room cabinet drawer while he thumped two knuckles on the patio door to get her attention.

"Dumb," he said out loud to himself, watching her dark brown brow furl and her eyes squint at the still curtains before him.

"What?" Marty had asked, handing him the unfolded blue squares of cloth.

"Nothing," he said. "Keep one. Make like a stickup." He wrapped a napkin about the lower portion of his face in a triangle, and Marty followed suit. Louis peeked back between the curtain folds to see Barbara lift herself from the pool, shiny with water, as if she was buttered. His tongue slid back in his moist mouth and he swallowed.

"What's she doing?" Marty asked, making a knot behind his head.

Louis watched her drip, her muscles flex, her take a step their way then stop. He thought of the Italian restaurant, the name of which he forgot—Torelli's?—the one his dad took him to as a kid. This was before Marty was born, before his father couldn't afford eating out anymore, at a time when his mother would tell Louis to wait in front of the eatery for his father and then disappear and not come back home until after Louis went to bed, sometimes well after. His father would always amble past the restaurant on the way home from work, and if he saw little Louis standing there with his bulky hands sunk in his pockets or drawing on the sidewalks with some stolen street chalk, Louis guessed his father got the hint his wife was not going to be home for dinner that night and took the kid inside to eat. It was there where they always faced the mural—every table faced a white wall with a hand-painted mural by the owner's Neapolitan cousin—but the table they always sat at faced this particular mural of a naked woman coming out of the water. His father said, "That's Venus on the half-shell," like it was something you could order up from the menu and devour—though they always had pasta with sausage whether Louis wanted it or not. Louis thought the woman was kind of "chunked-out," but he remembered that it always made his member tighten, even at the age of seven, and that it was the first time he had seen titties. Probably also the last time he had seen them on a wall—that wasn't part of lewd graffiti, anyway.

"Dumb," Louis said again, peeking out at the good-as-naked young girl approaching them cautiously. This one wasn't chunked-out, he thought, which made him think of the *other* waitress, and now finally he recognized who this golden-haired snatch was. He almost laughed aloud, but cupped his own kerchiefed mouth.

"What did I miss?" Marty said.

"You watch," Louis said, his smile hidden, "You won't miss shit."

Mere minutes later, right there on the tile, Louis fucked her hard, and biting her jawline, her underdeveloped breasts, licking her neck and chlorinated ear hole, she tasted good as long as his tongue avoided the branching lines of blood from her forehead. But it was too quick, a few ram-shots, major heaves and bounces, and he spunked. Louis knew it was all from disuse. It had been a while since the last time, but he didn't keep count of the days or anything because only losers did that. When he rose and zipped up, he thumbed toward the inert nude. "You want it?" he asked.

Marty dropped his head, gave a shrug. "Like it better on a bed. You know."

"Mmm," Louis nodded. "Forgot."

Bullshit, he thought. Then he thought some more. He knew their next stop was this X-marks-the-spot from the kid's map he found in his bedroom, this mountain house. Why not make it a honeymoon cabin?

With a belt they found in the master bedroom, they bound Barbara's wrists, then taped her mouth with a strip of adhesive tape Louis fished from his tool chest. He tossed her limp naked body from the cradle of his arms into the trunk of their Pontiac Trans Am like a rolled-up foyer rug. The ride took more than a few hours but they were both reluctant to admit how mesmerized they were with the deep lush smell of foliage and the freshness of the mountain's color until Louis passed off the remark: "How is it we never got ourselves up here before?"

When they found the cabin, they stowed the car in the underbrush on the side of the house that was away from the road, although the natural country silence that greeted the Dembos also informed them of their isolation. So it didn't bother them that their trunk was alive with thumping and muted fits of weeping.

"Let's bring her inside," Louis ordered. Then pondering how she was obviously conscious and would see their faces, he said, "Get the ski masks."

Marty almost took a stride, then reconsidered. "Can't."

"Why not?"

"They're in the trunk."

Louis's tongue made a singular tsking noise. "Who put the ski masks in the trunk?"

"You did."

Louis nodded. "Right. Get the fucking napkins." He banged a fist on the trunk lid. "Quiet!"

Marty snorted. "I didn't bring any fucking napkins. Why should I bring the fucking napkins? I didn't think we were going to some—some formal thing, some dinner or something—" Then he started to snicker. Maybe it was the country air or what. He started to laugh. He was laughing that his brother was screwing up.

Louis nodded, then smiled. That was okay, he thought, that was good. Cement the bond more. Dembo forced a chuckle, then he felt a real laugh blurt out. His brother made a good joke—fuckit. "Okay, then, you open the trunk and duck out of the way. I'll make sure she doesn't see."

"I mean, where's the fucking candelabra?" Marty said, his arms spread open, palms up, chuckling.

Dembo laughed, nodding. "Yeah, yeah." His baby brother was pushing it. Louis reached down behind the front seat and lifted a can of lime-green spray paint and started shaking the uncapped container. Marty inserted the trunk lock key and turned his face away as the lid sprung open, and Louis sprayed wildly at the flailing head of flaxen hair. She didn't look away in time and her eyes appeared to take in some of the spray.

"Gimme that wood!" Dembo shouted as he dropped the lid down halfway again, before lifting it up and spraying some more. Barbara had her bound hands up near her eyes, protecting, rubbing, grinding at them from the searing pain her left eye especially was experiencing. Her bare feet kicked out, kicked an arm away.

Marty handed Louis a two-foot log from the nearby woodpile, then manned the lid, flipping it up, so Louis could spray then strike the girl once, twice—battering her legs, then her thigh, which forced her sideways, her cries blocked by the tape. Marty and Louis looked like they were erratically opening and shutting a screen door to swat at a wasp wanting to come inside.

Finally, Louis landed two blows to Barbara's shoulders, flattening her down again. "Dumb bitch." He smacked at the crest of her head, a sideways glancing hit, but backed with enough power to knock her unconscious.

"There's nothing to see!" Dembo shouted at her. "Fucking *trees*." He spun the red-stained log into a patch of fern. "Bitch. It's like she never saw a rabbit or something."

Marty was keyed up, shifting from one foot to the other. After breaking into the cabin, they plopped Barbara on the huge bed; her skin was pimpling from the chill. Louis decided with whatever available light left they should start their search outside. They could always do their indoor work at night. But for right then he was tight and turned-on; he needed a hump. He stripped off his clothes in no time and wormed two fingers up Barbara's snatch to see if there was a drop of moisture.

"Dry hole cunt," he said to his brother watching. "First thing you look out for." Louis padded barefoot and naked to the kitchen, removed a tub of margarine and slicked up his now pronged member. Back in bed, he was back in business, Barbara out cold.

Louis liked them motionless. Motion was overrated, he thought. He liked to move the way he wanted and he could move a limp body easier than he could a woman who was so absorbed in her own thing she tightened and stiffened and maybe even shot that ever-so-brief look of disappointment if her clit wasn't being rubbed at this particular happy angle of your cock, but fucking-A—a man's cock should have had a pinky finger attached so you could lick its tip then stick it to a woman's flappy-cocooned mini-dick and a guy wouldn't have to worry. However, if the woman were unconscious, neither party had to worry, so that was that.

This fucking lasted longer than the one at the Rodmans', and he got to roll Barbara up like pastry dough, fuck her like a bowling ball, flip her over, slide along the valley of her valentine-shaped ass, sometimes hang her over the edge of the mattress, dick her mouth. She was nice and light, smelled good, too, if you didn't sniff her painted parts. Her sweat was sweet, honey-thick.

"Come on," he said to Marty when he was done. Got no excuses now, he thought. But even after greasing up his long thin penis, Marty watched it hang there like a deflated balloon. Meanwhile, Louis had brought in a few Sinatra albums from the backseat and put one on the platter. When the music came up, he walked in on Marty, minus his clothes, washing some of the acrylic paint off of Barbara's body with wet hand towels he swiped from the bathroom.

"Just wanted to clean her up a little," Marty said. Louis said nothing. Sinatra said, *". . . hates California—it's cold and it's damp . . ."*

Marty left the green swaths around her eyes and upper cheek because it made her more exotic. To Louis, she looked like a freaked-out tattooed jungle girl, teen-baby Sheena having a bad day at the elephant stampede. Louis had had enough.

"Get your dick up and fuck her like a monkey, you little son of a bitch! I mean it. . . ." He took threatening steps toward his brother, but Marty flung his naked body on top of Barbara before Louis was about to do it. Marty ground himself in her like a flaccid rotary motor, while out of the corner of his eye he could see the disgust on Louis's face deepen. Louis finally had to reach between the useless slap of genitalia and grab hold the base of his brother's penis and pull and squeeze, drive his brother's thickening member into the hole like an ice pick. Marty was crying out, either from the humiliation or the pleasure or the pain of his brother's tight fist, Louis's shadow over him like a breathing canopy, his bulging frame eclipsing the frail corn-stalk hair, the nothing-delicateness, and the girlish shoulders like a wire hanger, until it suddenly happened, it charged, the muscle-shadow, the butter-pull, the yank, the crank, and he came, whooping and smacking his lips, smacking the blond thing, saying, "I did it, bitch."

"That's it," Louis said.

"I did it!" Marty told the savaged body again, as though the delay were all its fault. He began to laugh and roll off of her. Louis was wiping his hand on the bedsheet.

"I'm going outside to start," he said. "Do it up again, you want, without me. You use it or you lose it. Remember. Then come out and help. Maybe you can do the lake supposed to be down there." Louis patted his brother on the shoulder and gave him a closed-mouth smile.

Marty didn't feel up for another lay, so after a breather, he doodled some shit on Barbara with smelly lipstick he picked up from a makeup kit on the dresser. He was feeling good, did his brother proud. He ran outside barefoot and bare-chested in the tingling air, singing with the cranked-up record.

The search wasn't going very well, and it was starting to get dark quickly. Louis had sent Marty down by the lakeshore and into the shallow water with his pants rolled up, looking for sunken waterproof boxes, kicking around the silt for semi-buried booty. Louis was again using thugs' precedent, having previously found deadbeats' stash in sealed containers just beneath the scum of ponds or in seasonally shut-down backyard plastic pools. Meanwhile, Louis was working the more immediate area behind the cabin.

The storage shed was a home for outdoor power tools, an assortment of shovels, and some boat paraphernalia, as well as for a pyramid of boxes, some labeled with Magic Marker, some not, all totally irrelevant for all were potential liars to Louis Dembo's mind and he tore through them like a kid knocking around jumbo blocks. But even within the bullish concentration on his job at hand—his physical self ripping through things, this time cardboard and not flesh; his emotional self entwined with the silken voice and sentiment of a 1950s ballad—he noticed a flicker of movement, up, to the left. It stopped him, his song, his generated energy.

It was at the window, like a bird darkening the sun for an instant when swooping just above your head, this brief shadow beyond the panes, deep within the room, near the bed, the girl! Was she awake? Was she running? Louis was.

Dembo charged up the wooden steps and through the back door. The record was just ending as he took long determined strides to cut her off at the living room, but when he popped his head inside the bedroom, all was still. There was no hint of movement now, or even within moments past. From a concealed leg holster he removed a new toy, one that upped the ante, put the game in the big leagues—a Glock 9mm automatic he had bought for only seventy-five dollars from a street dealer two weeks back and was itching to play with.

Dembo moved inside cautiously, though everything within the bedroom was visible before him, except for the girl; only a bare brown foot revealed itself. Otherwise, the large lump of comforter was still hiding its succulent center, looking bloated like an overindulged stomach. The thought of an intruder blipped through Louis's mind, and he responded by throwing open the closet door and sweeping hangered shirts with his gunless hand across the rack, the automatic at the ready. Maybe the movement he had seen at the window was his imagination, unless the girl was now, in fact, feigning her stillness, pretending sleep. Women could be fucking devious when they wanted to be.

Now, the more he stared at the substantial mound of quilt and the closer he stepped toward the bed, the more that mound looked bigger than before, puffed up higher, too big, too high. . . . Dembo was knee-flush against the mattress now, lowering the gun barrel toward the shadowy relief before him. He reached out a quiet hand.

He snatched and pulled the comforter down, deflating the puff, revealing only the unconscious girl that he and his brother had left there like defiled statuary. If it was her moving before, she was fucking sleepwalking, Dembo thought. In the near dark now, the tan angular body was less appealing to him. Her welts deepened in this light, her whites brightened, her face looked as though she had the mumps. She revolted him. He wanted to fuck her harder and hurt her much, much more. It was a vicious cycle, but what could you do? He stuck the gun in his waist and unzipped his fly.

It was then there was a woodcutter's sound, a thunk, like when an ax sticks itself into the pulpy meat of a tree after a virgin swing. It was also when Louis Dembo let out a scream of unprecedented pain, a pain that bolted up from his shin to his head like a blazened ramrod. From under the bed and with the meager leverage he had, Carl had swung his carving knife the only way possible within his cramped confines. He had hacked in one swift arc, parallel to the floor, and straight into the lower calf, straight into the bone, as hard and as viciously as he could, a squirt of blood splotching his face on impact. In fact, he had sunk the blade so deep that, with his elbow so close to his flattened body, he could not work it loose, his hand slipping the grip after Dembo reacted with a short hop and swivel, pulling the gun from his waist mid-scream, now riveted there to the planking, unable to lift his damaged leg, his torment so great he felt no leg, no foot.

Rodman rolled out from beneath the bed as fast as he could, like a crisply unfurled flag, knocking into both the knife handle and the remaining good leg of Louis Dembo, who pulled the trigger but shot wildly as he was unexpectedly, dazedly falling, toppling backward from imbalance and another jolt of pain.

As he fell, Dembo's lower arm struck the dresser, and the

Glock 9mm sprung from his hand and clattered somewhere in the dark. Rodman was stunned by the sound of the bullet firing, not expecting a gun in the planned equation. He leaped up, squinting toward where he thought he heard the pistol land, trying desperately to see it, knowing the smaller thug had probably heard the shot, heard his older brother's continual wail—when Dembo's sirenlike scream suddenly silenced, as from the floor Louis hooked his left arm around Rodman's leg and hoisted his body forward like a sideways pull-up and bit into Rodman's calf in fulfillment of a need to attack his enemy and quell his agony at the same time.

Rodman yelped and struck down hard with a fist to the side of Dembo's pit-bull-like jaw, then swung his foot into Louis's lower belly, forcing the clamped teeth to dislodge themselves as a whoosh of air came forth as did a renewed release of the thug's cries. Rodman could hear the frantic rustled foliage close by, and then the frightened shout of "Louis!" from just outside the back of the house. Rodman gave up on the gun, irrevocably swallowed by nightfall, and jumped on the bed. He scooped the fragile package that was Barbara in his arms and ran out into the living room, the edge of his vision spotting a shadow enlarging upon the back screen.

Rodman made it out the front at almost the same moment a barefoot and shirtless and mostly confused Marty Dembo reached his agonized brother, who had just finished working the embedded carving knife from the lower shank of his leg. Then, still on the floor, Louis incoherently bellowed in defiance, in rage, and fisted the blade into the wooden planking before him, Marty's toes inches from being freed from their peninsulalike existence on his left foot. Marty had to recoil, to hop back a step at the end of his skidding arrival.

Louis shouted, "Get the fucker! Get Rodman! He's got the girl!"

Marty was frenetic, perplexed, his brother's body in the dark oozing red, his brother's voice a fierce razored note tearing through him. He reached down to help Louis up. Louis smacked him away.

"I said, get Rodman, you asshole! He's getting to his car! Never mind me, *follow* him, *get* him . . . !" Louis was certain the stash was there now. Why else would Rodman have come up to the cabin? Not to hide out. Only, he needed the bastard to make the taking easier. Then he needed to kill him.

Marty raced through the living room and heard the thicket to the left of the cabin rev with motorized life. He sped to the Trans Am and, starting it up, watched the other car spray white stones wildly from gunning in reverse too quickly for the gears to catch up. The Mercedes curved out and backward, screeching onto the blacktop, then sped forward.

It was then Marty smiled—not because he was happy that his brother was hurt (though with Louis down, he was officially in charge of the chase), not because he was happy that the other car had a head start (though Marty was pumping on the pedal of a custom-built 260-horsepower turbo-driven engine, so he knew he could catch that piss-ass yupmobile in no time)—Marty smiled because, yeah, fuck-yeah, because he *was* happy. He had the *power*!

And so the monster engine responded to the Mercedes's wimpy mating call and blew out of its woodsy covering, its mag tires screaming down the mountain road in pursuit.

That the car behind his on this sinuously declining road would eventually catch up to him was not lost on Rodman, however. The way the Trans Am took the sloping curves—its wide tires, its angular low chassis—made the ominous shape that was slowly growing in his rearview mirror seem like a silver shovel with headlights ready to scoop him off the road and down the cliff side in free flight. This realization struck him just a quarter mile into the pursuit. Rodman had laid Barbara across the backseat, and now he heard her body bounce with the car, her legs flopping against the passenger seat. The travel pouch was bouncing against his side, as though emulating his exaggerated heartbeat. He was trying to go too fast. He had nearly scraped the ineffectual wooden guardrail that separated the weedy shoulder grass from the open sky on one hairpin curve already, almost lost his touch on the steering wheel, like when a kite string nearly slips away from you and you're a sudden breath-stopping grab from losing it. But the Trans Am was gaining and would continue to do so if he didn't do something.

There were two significant advantages Rodman had: the dark and the road. *His* road. He could drive this road blindfolded, and on some stupored nights, whether through drugs as the fed-up youth or through liquor as the too-well-fed adult, he might as well have been blindfolded. So it was that just before the bend that led to the wider plateau that housed Wesley Koontz's cliffside general store and gas station, Rodman recalled the overhang, the slot within the mountain that he and Sonny used to tuck their van into if they wanted a toke before hitting the cabin and his father's appraising stare. It was a rocky upward slant of dirt that was just off the road and just big enough for one vehicle, like a bouldered garage.

By instinct and tactile memory, Rodman turned his wheel left as though he were suicidal, determined to smash his car into the mountain's core of stone, but instead the Mercedes slipped into the faithful slot, Rodman having to apply his brakes immediately, considering his speed at the time. He wouldn't have gotten away with this kind of maneuver in the hippie van, to be sure. The mountain's cupped hand held him there, protecting him in total darkness, while Rodman counted—one-one thousand, two-one thousand—estimating the other car's distance behind, guessing really, really guessing, hoping, listening . . . and then at the first slight sound of an engine, Rodman roared out of his secluded confine in reverse, foot flat on the gas pedal, his trunk a sacrificial battering ram—if the timing was on his side.

And it almost wasn't. The Mercedes was almost too late, the Trans Am rounding the bend, so fiercely secure in its blistering speed and grip of the road surface. But Marty flinched when the corner of his eye caught something looming and large with red eyes like a cave monster roar out to his left for an instant of passing, but not quite passing, because the back of the Mercedes rammed the left tail of Dembo's car with enough impact that the accelerating Trans Am skidded out of control, and Marty found himself in a deadly counterclockwise spin. Tires shrieking, his back side splintered through a section of a white wooden guardrail and nearly brought the rest of the car with it over the edge, but Marty was countersteering and pumping the gas so as to straighten out. Thus, the front end swung around into the open air momentarily, the headlights illuminating nothing but misty air at four thousand feet, then came back on the dirt, yet still careening forward.

By the time Marty rotated the steering wheel in the other direction, the car had bounced once on the curve's embankment and flew directly toward the dormant Koontz establishment. The Trans Am then knocked over one sentrylike ancient gas pump and finally smashed grill first into the storefront with a deafening crunch of metal and an explosion of fragmenting glass.

Rodman by now had abandoned his car, which suffered a rear end compression but nothing that hindered its ability to function, and he ran flat-footed, puffing, toward the accident. The cold shock of thin air mixing with the stench of open gas from the unplugged pump hole slowed his approach. He saw nothing move in the front seat, saw the upper semicircle of the steering wheel but no Marty.

Coughing and waving away the fumes, Rodman reached the driver's side of the car to get a closer look, when the door kicked out and the top window frame caught him in the chin and the bulk of the lower door slammed everything from his upper stomach on down flush and hard. He stumbled back and landed on the base of his spine. His head recoiled off the packed-in dirt. Marty Dembo flew out of the Trans Am like a body rocket with a rebel yell, his legs churning, and slipping, his face sliced into a red-lined delta by diamonds of glass. He did not move his left arm, which was obviously dislocated, but he lashed out at Rodman with his right, pummeling his prone victim with a crowbar, luckily just at the legs, since Marty was prone himself and in obvious agony. His bare top was dotted red from his face, but it was the left rib cage that was empurpled and no doubt mangled internally.

On his back, Rodman kicked out like a jostled sand crab, his shoe heel catching Marty in the forehead, then in the teeth. Dembo had long since let go of the crowbar as his side left him nearly helpless, but Rodman was frightened by the surprise attack, shaken by the chase, enraged by the violence, by the crowbar, by the road's racing decline, his life's even more so, that his foot kept on shooting out, kicking the yelping, cursing piece of garbage in the neck, the rib, again in that purple patch of rib, forcing Dembo to roll, Rodman scraping his ass in a crab walk and striking out again and again, like booting away a rabid dog at ground level, only this dog was impotent except for his mouth, which kept yelling *"Motherfucker!"* with each blow, until another shoe to Dembo's side brought him to the brink of the gas pump hole, where his scream suddenly echoed and woke Dembo up from his rolling retreat, his pain-stricken delirium, and he shouted *"No!"* But Rodman kicked him again and the little man fell, baseball cap first, into the gas reservoir hole, his good arm trying to latch onto the hole's edge before the descent, but it was too weak to hold on, so the splash was heard and Rodman's spasmodic attack ceased and he lay his head back on the dirt and coughed and cried out himself, just before he heard the gurgle and resurgent splash from the hole and Dembo break the surface of the stagnant gasoline and scream out for help, sounding like that far-off voice in your head warning that there's something wrong with you.

Rodman raised himself, a somnambulant triumph over gravity. He shuffled into the general store and shuffled out with a flashlight and a pack of pilfered batteries. His hands shook as he ripped the Evereadys from their sealed-up home and force-fed them into the light's tubing. By now the cursing that blared from the pump hole had transformed itself into pleas—wailing, pain-ridden pleas.

"Help me, please, God, somebody! Lou-ie! Lou-ie! Pleeease!"

Rodman lay on his stomach and shined the flashlight down the hole. He spotlighted Marty Dembo leaning up against one side of metal reservoir some four feet down, holding his side so that he wouldn't collapse back into the pool of fuel. The gasoline came up to his waist, but it had already coated his body in a flammable sheen. If Marty were not so injured, he could have sprung up and very probably snatched the rim of the hole and pulled himself out. He blinked in uneven long intervals like a nocturnal creature unaccustomed to the sun, putting up a hand to his eyes during Rodman's silent inspection.

"Please let me out! God! Please! I can't—I can't breathe, my chest, my—oh, God! My ribs—please!"

"Shut up!" Rodman said, his voice reverberating within the chamber. "Who do you work for?"

Marty couldn't stop weeping, pleading. He shivered. "Please let me out! Where's Louis? Louie!"

"I said, shut up and talk to me or I'll never let you out. Who's your boss? Who sicced you two on me?"

"Louie! God, oh, God! Motherfucker! Louie!" Marty doubled over from his last cry and from the strain to his chest and side. He vomited in the inky liquid, the contents floating on the surface like a newly formed volcanic island.

"Listen to me, damn it!" Rodman's voice punctured Marty's ears. "Why did you kill my wife? Why did you kill Xavier? What the fuck is going on?"

Marty straightened up from his retching and tried to speak through his sobs, until he garnered a lungful of air through snatches of short breaths and released it with the cry: "Louieeee! Help me, Louie! Where are you? God, help, Lou, help me!"

Rodman gave up and stood thinking, or trying to anyway, with the banshee wails from the underground cave spooking the night's breeze that slashed his face. Yet those same wails gave him the answer to his dilemma. "Lou-ieeee! Where are you?"

Once more Rodman stepped through the large shattered window frame of the general store and noticed a display of Zippo lighters. He checked his pouch, still belted across his chest, to see if everything was there, then he fished for a quarter from his back pocket. He put it in the pay phone and dialed.

After three rings, Rodman made the connection.

"Marty?" Louis Dembo's voice sounded expectantly agitated.

Rodman didn't respond right away, wanted agitation to shift to anticipation, then to anger. "Who's there? *Marty!*"

Rodman finally spoke. "You hear the crash over there?"

Rodman heard the released air from Dembo's nostrils signal the realization of what had possibly occurred, then: "Where's Marty? What happened to Marty?"

"You want your brother, come to the gas station down the road."

Louis exploded. "You cut my leg open, you fuck! How can I c—"

"It's less than a mile," Rodman responded. "You want him, you'll walk!" Then Carl hung up.

After five minutes of scarfing down a stale bag of Wise potato chips from the clipboard display and shutting out the noise, the damn sobbing screams from the hole, Rodman lifted a pair of binoculars from Koontz's dust-breeding bird-watchers' shelf and peered up the road, across the adjacent chasm, and spotted a cone of light moving down the yellow line, a hobbling flashlight beam heading his way. He dropped the glasses from his worn-out eyes. He had to prepare.

The tourniquet knot felt like an exposed canker against his hacked-up shin, but it was the only way Louis Dembo could stop the flood of tacky red fluid from draining out of his leg. He used a torn-up Nike tee shirt for the job, and screamed out when he pulled the knot tight on it with both hands. However, he allowed the scream and the brain-jolting pain to transfer themselves in the process, in the way such pain can be a form of white noise, just as his hellacious scream was, and in that instant of time, things are timeless, blanked out, all is a shared oneness, and so that pain was not only his, but Rodman's, the world's. He wanted the world to scream. His anger was fueled to the brim now.

He had arm-stretched for the 9mm Glock that lay under the small water-pitcher stand in the bedroom, the gun having slid away from the melee as though wanting to find a peaceful corner of uninvolvement. But Dembo's desperately sweeping blind hand had grabbed on to it, forcing its potency back into the power balance. Now he tucked the barrel into his waist like muzzling the snout of a pet rat and limped out of the cabin, holding a large emergency boat lamp in his left hand, its broad circle of light always his next destination, always just out of reach. That was the only way the pain could be played with, coaxed along. The carrot and the mule, Dembo thought, remembering the image more from animated cartoons than anything else. He didn't like being the ass. And that, too, was Rodman's doing.

Dembo's rage was well-proportioned. It pushed him that ten feet ahead briskly even with a blade of torment running up his leg with each hitch. Then the next ten feet. And so on. Moving faster brought on shorter jolts, better mileage, quicker satisfaction that the end result would be Rodman's torture. He would get Rodman to talk by shooting each joint in his middle-aged frame until he did. Once he found out what had happened to Marty, then where the dope or the money was hidden, he'd shoot Rodman in the joints that were left and leave him to bleed on some bunny rabbit in the hills somewhere.

It took Dembo nearly half a mile and a need to rest before he realized he couldn't feel his toes on his left foot. The slicing knife must have caught some nerves, he thought. It would only make him go faster on this dark downward road. He knew the gas station wasn't too far off because, not five minutes before, he had passed a weathered sign, hand-painted, with a ¼ MI and a fading arrow and a proclamation: GAS EATS, the slash between the words having totally worn away. Gas eats, Dembo had read to himself. "Yeah," he then said aloud, "and life sucks."

He hobbled on not knowing that twenty-plus years earlier, on every drive by the sign, two rollickingly wasted freaks, as though invoking a mantra of brotherhood, would in unison make the same joke. Then Carl Rodman and Sonny Vance would look into each other's phlegmy eyes and chuckle over their shared knowledge.

Not much later, only a few hundred feet or so, a sound came within earshot and made Dembo stop. It was continual in its drone, and though too distant to distinguish, it made him uneasy, made him feel that it was a personal message, a muffled anguish. It came from around the far bend, the last one to the fill-up station, he hoped. The night afforded only black wind-shifting shapes and little else outside the perimeter of the beckoning spotlight he threw ahead of him. But one such odd shape, a balled-up shape, seemed to be stuck at the base of the mountain wall adjacent the curving roadway. Across the tar, Dembo's beam slid and struck the huddled outline. It was Rodman. He was hunched against the rocks, his knees drawn up close to his chin, staring into the yellow cone of light wide-eyed, not like a stunned animal, but a defiant one.

Then Rodman reciprocated with his own flashlight, the two beams crisscrossing like drawn swords.

"Glad you could make it," Rodman said flatly.

Dembo reeled from the surge of rage he released from its

clutching choke hold, no longer needing to tame its brutal essence in ten-foot measures. He loped forward, a huge first step, simultaneously pulling the 9mm pistol from his waist and aiming it at Rodman. "You shit-ass piece of garbage! Where's my brother? What happened to him?"

"I think you'd better stop," Rodman replied, his beam focusing on Dembo's taut, sweaty face, grimacing with each leg-dragging stride forward.

"I said, where's my brother, asshole! I'll shoot your fucking eyes out!"

"Hold it!" Rodman raised his fist, gunless.

Dembo kept lurching toward him, his finger ready to squeeze off a wounding shot. "Where *is* he?"

"I said—*stop right there!*" Rodman's demand was followed by his flipping his fisted thumb and producing a small flame from the disposable lighter he was holding.

And Dembo did stop, almost bug-eyed. His head was bobbing in disbelief. Then he lowered his gun and blurted out a laugh, letting the jolt of humor combat the counterforce of pain from his leg. "Holy shit!" he exclaimed. "The fuck . . . ! What? You flicking your Bic at me? What am I? Fucking Frankenstein? Afraid of fire or something? You've flipped out, guy! You've gone cuckoo, baby!" He raised his gun again. "Now where's my brother, dick-brain?" He was calm now, the laugh cooling him down.

Rodman lowered the lighter closer to his feet and near a puddle. "Listen," Rodman said.

"I don't want to hear nothing from you but what happened to Marty!"

"Then *listen!*" Rodman shouted back. It was only then that Louis realized that it wasn't Rodman who was to be listened to. The sudden silence was broken by the cool breath of the mountain wind coiling up the road and carrying with it the cry, the sound that disturbed Dembo before, the wail of a wounded animal. Louis could almost distinguish his own name.

"Marty?" Dembo said quietly, as though to himself. The distant voice sounded ghostly, echoic. It came from just around the bend.

Then as though this hushed, haunted moment allowed all his senses to disengage from his pulsing wound and embrace the circumstance—the edgy chill of the night, the specter of rock majestically risen behind the little dot of a man with the tiny fire in his fist—he smelled it. Amid the lush aroma of the brushing trees, the intoxicating odor of gasoline touched his nostrils. It was as though the pungent reality of the city where he was born and raised invaded this landscape, rushed up to stab him, the smell of his mother's milk.

Dembo walked sideways now, still focusing his beam on the Buddha-faced Rodman compacted there, walked toward the bend to peer beyond, to listen to the crying become clearer, his name being evoked with the absolute burdening tone of responsibility. He then dropped the flash from Rodman's face and shone it on the puddle near the lighter. He traced the stream down the road and around the bend and to a hole where there sat adjacent to it a silver object reflecting the light, but he couldn't make it out.

"That's a hole to a gas tank reservoir," Rodman explained.

Dembo shot his flashlight back into Rodman's face.

"Sort of like a typical room at a Motel 6, only with volatile fuel up to his waist."

Dembo didn't laugh this time. "What are you? Some kind of sick fuck?"

Rodman had to chuckle at that one. Dembo's response was to once more raise his gun. "Get rid of that lighter."

"You shoot me, the lighter drops in this puddle anyway."

"Douse it or die, God damn it!" Dembo's eyes were lit with hysteria, his brother's incoherent pleas withering him, weighing on him.

Rodman stared the shaking thug down. His voice carried no emotion. It was as though it were already emanating from a corpse.

"You can't outrun the fire, not with your leg."

"Fuck that."

"You can't. You *know* you can't."

"*Fuck* that!"

"Weigh the pleasure of killing me to the consequences of killing your brother."

"I'll shoot you, asshole."

"But you *know*."

"What? Know what?"

"You *know* I don't give a fuck. You can see *that* much, can't you?"

Dembo had no reply. His rigidly outstretched arms, one hand holding the lamp, the other holding the gun, still quivered. He blinked. His eyes felt grainy, weak. Yet Rodman's pupils were as black and deep as the empty sockets in a bleached-white skull and they were locked onto his.

"So lower the gun," Rodman said.

Stiff-armed, Dembo lay the 9mm Glock to his side, looking away as though ashamed.

"Okay," Rodman continued. "Now release the clip and toss it up the road."

Dembo did as he was told, following the commands that now came at him disembodied from behind a glaring light, his own flash no longer on. It was like the voice of God beaming through the night, judging him, his brother's reverberating entreaties already coming from a frightening world below.

"Toss the gun the opposite way."

Dembo wristed the pistol to his right. It clattered off, then skidded unseen.

"Now who killed my wife?" Rodman said.

Dembo snorted. "You did, asshole."

"Cut the bullshit," Rodman warned, the edge back in his tone.

"What? What do you want from me? You're the murderer here, not me. Not my brother. You're killing my brother! He'd better be in one piece—"

"So you're telling me you two didn't kill her."

"Hey!" Dembo said, feeling insulted. "What do you want me to say? The cops are after *you*. That right? I just know what I read in the papers."

Rodman answered with silence.

"Okay," Dembo said, raising his hand then putting it over his heart. "I swear on my mother. We didn't have nothing to do with your wife's murder. That what you want? What's she got to do with anything?"

"I don't know. What?"

"That's what I'm asking you, hotshot." Dembo stuck out his hands in frustration. "I mean, we *told* you our business with you. We *know* you were dealing shit for Sonny Vance. But since that fuck owed us and is—I don't know—gone from the scene, we thought we should get the stuff back from you. That or the cash you took in. That's it. Okay?"

"Us. Who's us? Who's your boss?"

"Tommy. Tommy Ryan. 'Beanpole,' they call him. Okay? He runs the sports bar on Riller's Beach."

"Guess he runs a few other operations, too."

Dembo shrugged and dropped his lids halfway down.

"He runs you two jerks."

"I get paid. I do my job." Dembo said.

"The end justifies the means," Rodman replied.

"Whatever." Dembo shrugged again. "It's free enterprise. Hey! I know I'm paid to fuck people up. I just don't get to do it in a shithole Armani suit like you sports."

"You fuck Sonny Vance up?"

"Sure. That's why he gave you up," Dembo replied, then pointed down the road. "Hey, let me get Marty—"

"Sonny Vance was wrong. He—He's—" Rodman wasn't sure what tense to use. "He framed me. I have no money from the sale of his drugs. *Or* the drugs."

"I don't know. Hard for a man to lie, especially a little turd like Vance with his head sticking out of the sand like a fucked-up little turtle getting kicked around. It would take brick balls to bullshit in that spot."

"Take my word for it," Rodman said, his memories suddenly surging through him. "Sonny Vance could bullshit in any spot. It's his native tongue."

"Whatever you say. You got the Bic."

"When did you see Sonny last?"

"Like I said. He was in a hole in Riller's Beach. We pulled him out so he could get to you."

"He hasn't contacted you since?"

"I suck at letter-writing," Dembo remarked. "It's my worst feature." He shifted his feet, trying not to hear his brother's voice. "Can I go now, Teach? This is the longest goddamn quiz I ever got. My brother—"

"One more question," Rodman interrupted. "You know a Frank Xavier?"

"My brother *needs* me, dammit!" Dembo took a crippled

step forward. Rodman dropped the flame but an inch lower for effect.

"Xavier! A private investigator. Point Crescent."

Dembo was shaking his head. He was still sweating in spite of the cold. "No. No. Fucking no. I don't *know* him. I don't know *any* private dicks." He was panting for seemingly no reason.

Rodman stared at the wobbling bulk before him, listening to his breathing, staring into his shifting eyes. He felt an amazing sense, one he didn't expect considering the threatening situation—it was like when he would get wasted at the cabin with his fellow freakaholics and enter the black heart of the forest and commune with its creatures, hearing their silent stories, feeling as though their sensory lives were his as well— now, somehow, in the same way, Rodman found himself believing Dembo, everything he said, down the line. And his own treacherous naiveté had little to do with it. With inflated cheeks, he snuffed the lighter's flame.

Though woozy, Dembo perked, his eyes becoming alert to the welcome return of darkness engulfing Rodman's hand.

"All right! *There* you go." Dembo began walking backward down the road as he spoke. "It's all done. We're through with each other, right?" Dembo was talking to the hunched shadow-ball again as Rodman had extinguished his flash as well. "It was a misunderstanding. Sonny Vance fucked us *both* good, right? So Marty and me, we got no more business with you. We're square. We didn't do your wife or nothing. That X-avy-something guy—ditto. Nobody. You got no beef with us." Dembo nodded his own confirmation when he heard no reply and turned forward, propelling his painful leg toward the screaming hole, hoping his brother was okay, praying that Koontz's supply store had a large enough boning knife with which to gut Carl Rodman longways.

"Except one thing . . ."

Rodman's sudden shouted retort made Dembo spin around again, hobble backward. "What? Hey! What are you—"

Suddenly, the lighter was again aflame. This time Rodman was standing, back arched straight, his facial contours dimly bathed in the fire's flickering orange glow. His arm was thrust out diagonally as though he were performing some lone tribute at a shroud-dark imagined concert.

"To the derelict dream of the sixties!" Rodman shouted out.

Dembo had stopped completely now, stunned. "What?"

"To the innocents lost!" boomed the wild-eyed and battered Statue of Liberty.

Dembo grew angry, panicked. "What's the matter with you, man?"

"To Woodstock and fuck all chairmen of the boards!"

"What are you *fucking* about?" Dembo bellowed back.

Rodman's eyes and voice lowered, honed in on the indistinguishable hulking shape that stood twenty yards down the throat of darkness.

"To Barbara, you scumbag!"

The words fell upon Dembo like a hard rain because he knew what they signaled, what lightning was about to be unleashed.

"Noooo!" he cried out, only to watch Rodman flip the lighter into the redolent stream like a switchblade, igniting it immediately and sending the ensuing explosion of flame down the trail, a hot snaking message of retribution.

Louis Dembo was beyond thought, compelled beyond his physical capabilities. He hobbled in almost comic fast-motion, the shock produced by his thumping leg on the hard road surface used as a primitive form of cattle prod, self-induced, self-driven. The line of flame was still behind him as he rounded the bend, the dark patch of the hole in sight, the scream of his brother indistinguishable from his own, the silver object. . . . Dembo cried out louder, began weeping and stumbling when the flame caught up to him and passed him like the fiery exhaust to an invisible rocket car, his hands reaching out as though able to reign in its hellish path to his brother.

Up the grade, Rodman watched the actions he had set in motion with amazed detachment. At first it looked like the eternal contest: Man versus Nature, flesh versus fire, with the natural elements always destined to win, the pile of dust to inevitably prevail. But it suddenly became far more personal to Rodman, more meaningful. There was his wife Delia joined in the same race with Louis Dembo, both in the same rush to save when saving was impossible, an unrecoverable past tense, yet both were joined by love—of all things!—thug and mother, brother and baby son. Dembo and Delia both loved to the point of sacrificing all for family. And for it, both burned.

Dembo was ten feet from the hole when the prancing line of fire dipped over the edge, end of the line, and Dembo stopped, and in that split second before the infernal blast, he cried out Marty's name but then saw exactly what that little silver rectangle was and what it was doing there and he physically withered. The explosion sent Louis Dembo through the air fifteen feet, the fire burning away his tears, his cheeks, his sexy bushy brows. His clothes were aflame as was most of his skin. He fell into the roadside scrub and screamed out from his lipless mouth and rolled around in crimson-rich agony while the reservoir's fireball rose skyward, puffing black and gray smoke in a swirling cumulous erection.

Rodman picked up the bullet clip then the empty Glock and fed the pieces to each other to make it whole again. He drove the Mercedes adjacent to the emblazened store—a flash of Koontz's thickly passive face flickered in Rodman's mind and no more—and there he saw Louis Dembo smoldering in the weedy embankment near the cliffside. His head was facing Rodman, and Rodman wondered if Dembo could see him. But that, too, was an instantaneous piece of trivial speculation. Rodman leaned over and opened the passenger door, then literally kicked the broken body of Marty Dembo out of the car. It rolled like a poorly distributed laundry sack, all weighty at one end, empty creases all between, and tumbled out onto the road. His arms had been tied behind him with a heavy-duty electric extension cord, his mouth gagged with an oil rag. Rodman glanced at the mumbling Barbara Fouche in the backseat and pushed the foamy blanket closer to her, tucking her back into the cushions so she wouldn't roll forward.

Rodman inspected his apocalyptic handiwork once more. He felt nothing. No, not true—he wished he still had the silver microrecorder, but it too was sacrificed, though admittedly not for love. It did its job, however. It had taped Marty Dembo's woeful pleas as Rodman prepared his river of gas, and ultimately it had given Louis Dembo—at least so Carl had hoped—a good lasting look at futility, at the essence of gamesmanship, of getting screwed.

Rodman nodded to himself and still believed Dembo, his confessions, what he had said before, about Delia, about Xavier and Vance, about Ryan, and now, most of all, about what he had said about Rodman himself. He *was* some kind of a sick fuck.

PART IV

22

AT FIRST GLIMPSE of their surprise bundle, the two ambulance attendants appeared more amused than upset, but then, as if by instinct, they returned to the ways of their profession. Minutes before, they had just rolled a 5-16 into the emergency room, an elderly spotty-skinned man who had tumbled over his second-story stucco balcony from a sudden stroke while keeping a paternal watch on the white-hot coals of his hibachi. The ambulance attendants were talking pennant race as they returned to their vehicle, but stopped short. Their open back doors revealed another customer. A blond girl was wrapped tightly in a spongy yellow blanket as though it held her parts in one whole, her face swollen and cold, her breathing a steady whine. She lay in their regenerating ambulance like an abused waif who found the most unlikely spot to sleep. The two hospital employees glanced at each other. Then they spun around, seeking her origin; however, Rodman had long since gone.

He knew that Barbara would be in safe hands now, knew that his son would be there for her. Danny loved her, he thought. He could discern that much from the party, but at the time dared not acknowledge his son's inner emotional life. Rodman shook his head at himself. "I'm so fucking responsible. . . ." He laughed aloud. "For *ev*-erybody!"

Rodman wasn't afraid of being heard since he was tucked back in a deserted Kmart parking lot numerous football fields long in the town of Newbury, Hollowsport's poor cousin to the north. The vastness of the tarred landscape conjoined with the pitchlike density of the sky made Rodman feel afloat in the nighttime firmament. And the only thing that shone far up ahead across the vacuum of space was a flickering store light, its neon-energized tubes worn-out from its relentless proclamation. Thus it flashed like a distant star, pink then not, pink then not—LIQUOR. The Mercedes's nose was like a compass needle to that beckoning point on the horizon.

What the hell, said a good part of him, the worn, sleepless part, befuddled, lost. Still lost. He had pulled the four one-hundred-dollar bills from the travel bag he had gone to the cabin for, fanned them out like a poker hand. Life was a myriad of options now. He could take one bill, just one, and follow that star and buy a case of Finlandia and a few bags of ice. That he could do no matter what other decision he made. It all depended on how he wanted to approach those other decisions, wasted or sober, numb or vulnerable.

He could run off to Canada, knew some business people in Toronto, paper manufacturing; had a second cousin in Alberta, too, some town, some name—would have to go back to the house, find the old correspondences—could start again, start drinking again, but then he would have no answers. Could he live with no answers without the paralytic succor of coke or booze? But what did he have left to pursue? Shaking down this Sam Ryan would probably be a waste of time. Obviously Ryan had been duped by Sonny Vance and couldn't have been the one who "saved" him, if in fact Sonny was saved, or else Ryan's goons would have squeezed Vance for the money by now, for the truth, anyway. No. Whether Vance were alive or dead, his mysterious movement had to involve somebody else and for some other purpose than this nonexistent drug money.

And so the same questions resurfaced: Did Delia die at Vance's hands? What did Xavier's investigation tell her about Eric? And why was Xavier killed?

In frustration, Rodman's hand swiped the emptied contents of his travel pouch from the passenger seat, the magazine and business envelopes and files colliding into the dashboard, scattering onto the floor mat. A larger yellow envelope had stubbornly stayed pressed into the bucket seat as though hanging on in spite of the sweeping onslaught. It was melodramatically stamped: URGENT—READ IMMEDIATELY, part of the pile of mail he had collected at the closed office Monday morning. The return address said Haps Security.

Rodman ripped the envelope open and read its contents by flashlight. Usually these reports were routine, without splashy red commands up front; no-news-is-good-news in the security business. But these findings told of an infinity transmitter that had been discovered in Rodman's office by the professional sweeper at 6:02 last Friday evening, the same day of Vance's surprise visit. It was not possible Sonny had planted the bug, Rodman thought, as a similar one was uncovered in the boardroom a half hour later. The device was described as particularly sophisticated but easily installed, a Timbre 3000 model, a quarter of an inch unit that was tucked behind the switch plate of the electrical outlets and afforded more than enough range, meaning that anyone parked on Brussels Avenue outside or renting phony office space within the building could have easily recorded the transmissions. In fact, the unit offered eight channels, so conversations could have been picked up from any of eight locations simultaneously.

The report then concluded with the obvious: that since approximately a month ago, the last time Haps Security swept Triumph corporate headquarters and found it clean, somebody had secured the two "spies" in optimum locations, the information received broadcasted to sources unknown.

Rodman put the report down, flicked off the light, leaned his head back in the restive darkness. Building security at night had been tightened during the past year. During the day, access to both his office and the boardroom was afforded to only a few trusted people.

Instantly Rodman sat up in the driver's seat. He let the erratically blinking sign blur and hypnotize him for a few moments, as though dazed by its cryptic code. Trust. A flickering thing. Pink then not. He started the engine; it still purred like the rich-bitch machine that it was. He was no longer lost. He knew exactly where to go.

23

AND SO, LIFE came down to this:
"I want her home. She wants to *be* home."

"I understand. I will handle it. Do I not always handle it?"

But Hallie would not be appeased—this was not even the right hospital, not *their* kind of hospital—and she badgered her husband, who pinned her meatless arms to her side as though if she were allowed to raise her hands, they would become a separate fury-driven entity to attend to.

"She needs my comfort. Home is her comfort," Hallie implored, pecking her head with each entreaty like a neck-chained hen, her body weight gravitating forward. Bertram Fouche dipped his own head in deference, holding her back, his smile as silken and as finely crafted as his blue suit, hand-made by his favorite tailor shop in the heart of Hong Kong. He played the master appeaser, the conciliator whose crinkled eyes generated star-burst lines about them. (Danny had told Barbara that her stepfather seemed the type of man who said yes to everybody and made money doing it, and of those he said yes and meant no, he made even more.) Meanwhile, the attending physician, a native Pakistani, stood but two feet behind Fouche's right shoulder, scratching a few notes on Barbara's chart as though he were not there at all, which was how Hallie was treating him anyway.

Fouche seemed to be almost singing to his nerve-jangled wife. "Does not Bertram take the reigns? Does not Bertram move the mountain?"

Fouche had been away troubleshooting a customs snafu at the Boston shipyards and coincidentally had returned home the night of Barbara's disappearance. Now he was attempting to pacify his wife, attend to his stepdaughter, comply with the police, and, by spousal mandate, persuade the doctor to release Barbara. Fouche freed his wife only to clasp the perplexed physician by the elbow and to graciously lead him aside as though wishing him as a partner for the quadrille. Fouche explained the situation in no more than a courteous whisper, and though unintelligible at this distance, it had a melody to it and Danny would have sworn the doctor's ears unfurled just a bit, an aural flower attuned to the honey-producing buzz. Hallie, meanwhile, leaned in behind her overweight husband as though he were a thick blue wall and she merely eavesdropping on the conversation taking place on the other side.

And so from the corner of the half-lit hospital room where Danny had sunk deep in the plastic scoop of a molded white chair, he thought, life came down to this: watching a dark farce, a mimed playlet—the money-talks rich, the mummified mommy, the gullible foreigner, the battered victim (they said it was Barbara—he felt he still wasn't sure) . . . and the outsider, of course. *His* role in perpetuity, watching from a distance. The distance made him safe, but also made him other.

He felt certain that he also looked the part, was well-cast. He hadn't changed into fresh clothes since the day before last, his U2 black tee tacky like a tissuey second skin and encrusted with salt rings under his arms. He held his motorcycle jacket as though it were the secret receptacle of all his current strength. His jeans were faded ("and not *pre-washed*," he would bark), with holes torn down the legs like a column of mouths, the pair he wore weeks at a time at his worktable when zoned-in on a guitar restoration. He had forgone a ponytail, so his hair dangled in long matted strings down the back of his neck; slick vines hung over his ears. His facial stubble was prickly, as was his attitude.

Yet in spite of his faraway judgments, which implied a superiority of position, he sensed everyone there was acting the professional. Everyone knew what place he or she had in the scene. The professional doctor, businessman, mother, nurse, the detective who came to question Barbara, even his uncle Jack, whom he watched firmly shake the police lieutenant's hand in the hallway—even he seemed the professional uncle, fronting his aura of class for the family, Danny's side, which right now was just Danny, the wastrel. Meanwhile, his own part in all of this was unclear, ill-defined, not worthy of a script.

So his true impulse was to tear it all down, down to the scenery board, to shake the what-is, change the words, punch through the facade, foil the play, set a gun off in the theater to stop the applause.

That was what his father's problem was, Danny decided. He just now decided. His father's addictive behavior a few years back was not an expression of his radical side, but was in fact the result of his father *suppressing* that side, warding it off, denying it, setting it apart, much like that useless room upstairs preserving all of his time-warp paraphernalia: it was a part of the house, part of *him*, but unacknowledged, rejected, not gone into anymore.

It was always Danny to blame—for his father needing rehab—Danny's habit and the stress of his father's wheeler-dealer job, but certainly Danny, especially Danny, the burden, the druggie son. Dealing with such a boy proved too much for such a man. Bullshit. His father just couldn't deal with the boy-freak in himself, couldn't cope with the other. Danny didn't want to hear shit about being blamed, being responsible. His father didn't have the guts to shake the as-is, to do what Danny was violently thinking—no, was doing, was going to do, and he suddenly thought of his grandfather.

Then Barbara's eyes gradually peeled open, her vision filmy but seeking. She had been in and out of sleep most of the morning and she bore the weight of a headache. Dr. Soondari had informed the family that Barbara was suffering from a mild concussion, innumerable body welts, a hairline fracture in her right rib, and genital abrasions. A staff rape counselor, a Ms. Snyder, had already been assigned and had spoken to Barbara after her bizarre arrival, but only briefly. Mainly the counselor stayed with her, comforted her until the Fouche family arrived, Hallie galumphing past nurses and Ms. Snyder and weeping openly over her daughter as though at a wake, Bertram thanking all who tended to Barbara's needs. Needless to say, Danny Rodman was not on Hallie's short list of people to call.

Danny heard about Barbara only through his uncle, who

maintained priority contacts within the Hollowsport police, who just prior had been informed by Ms. Snyder of Carl Rodman's involvement, that fact emerging from her short conversation with Barbara. Barbara, it seemed, had become conscious a few times when riding in the Mercedes, but could not elevate her head without severe waves of pain; however, she recognized the vehicle's interior and the squared-off back of Carl Rodman's head and caught shadowy back-lit glimpses of his profile.

Danny noticed Barbara's becoming alert and he stood. And did so for a moment. Slowly he shuffled to the bed, to the face that seemed not so much a face as a round and unevenly stuffed pot holder onto which somebody stitched facial features, sewed rows of corn-yellow hair—a mumpy rag doll, not Barbara. Her yearning eyes would have told Danny it was truly her, but he didn't look into them, his line of vision self-restricted to the starch-white fold of sheet tucked under her smooth brown arms. He felt guilty for not protecting her from his family, for letting it all seep out, drip on her like corrosive waste, deform her, them.

But then her hand sought out his, and finding it, her fingertips afflicted with a slight tremor, she squeezed her warmed blood into its cusp, held it as though testing whether it was even part of something alive. At the same time, Jack Able stepped back into the room and was about to approach his nephew, but demurred, awkwardly recognizing the tender circumstance. Uncomfortable, he touched the tip of a potted snake plant to gauge its moistness and listened to Dr. Soondari laughingly say *yes, oh, yes, of course* to Bertram Fouche's melodious monologue.

Danny lifted the slender hand closer to his own face, into the range of his downward gaze, studying it as one would a delicate and unique specimen. He turned it over and opened it up and ran his fingers in her palm, recognizing her map of lines, the cupped sweetness of it, the imprint it had left on his back, his brow, his daily life. He brought his lips down and kissed its center, smelling her skin as he did, knowing it was her, it was still her, and squeezing his eyes in shame. He kissed it again and scraped the back of her hand along his Brillo jaw. He glanced up finally to see her giggle, her index finger curling on his cheek, as though its wallowing in a field of thumb-tacks felt good. He held her hand there to his jaw until her eyes closed again, a smile set on her swollen face. Danny wasn't sure she was back asleep, but Uncle Jack ducked his head near his and said, "A moment."

Danny nodded and quietly rose, following his uncle to the foot of the bed. His uncle's dour expression, though usually the norm, had greater consequence etched into it. Immediately Danny wanted to back off from the look. He was carrying enough crap, thanks, and he glanced away toward Barbara and thought about his grandfather again. Though he had never met Blaine Rodman, he could hear him, through his father's oral recollections of him, told to Danny as though passing down powerful family mythology, but with a tone of bitterness Danny believed his father was never aware of. But what stuck with Danny now was the way his grandfather had supposedly always said their surname: *Rod*-man—

"Something the lieutenant said." Uncle Jack was whispering secretively. Danny brought his attention back to his uncle momentarily, then gazed through him to Bertram Fouche, who was still tilting in to the nodding doctor, he too whispering. Danny felt he was looking into a mirror of conspiracy.

Suddenly a beeper went off, its sound seemingly originating from the empty center of the room's activity. Fouche and Able snuck a quick peek at each other, then both flipped their suit jackets away from their hips, exposing slim black boxes on their belts.

"Sorry," Fouche said to Able, smiling, "it's mine." Uncle Jack took the loss well. Fouche excused himself and strode into the hallway toward the nurses' desk for a phone, pursued by a frustrated Hallie. Dr. Soondari, now out from under his unctuously receptive spell, seemed relieved and left as well.

So, Danny thought, life comes down to this: it's who has the biggest beeper. He snickered to himself. No, too easy. It's who has the biggest gun—metaphorical, literal—take your pick. He couldn't escape thinking about his grandfather, and the long-barrel pistol Danny had gripped in both hands, aimed. It had weight, gave things substance.

"It's your father, Danny," Able said, a little louder now with the room cleared. "He must be involved somehow in drugs again. Only deeper, because clearly he's more desperate."

Grandfather's gun, the missing heirloom his father couldn't find, Danny thought. *He* had it. Danny had copped it. From the cabin that summer right after he used it, shot the shit out of an empty milk carton. He meant to sell it—this back in the pilfering-anything-not-cemented-to-the-floor days for some snort. He could have gotten good, good money for it, too. Not from a pawn—a beautiful gun like that was like a bent clarinet or broken-faced stopwatch to those plebes, everything on the same plane of commodity. No. He knew a real gun dealer, a collector who was also a cokehead.

"The two men who they found up on Mandrake, at the gas station"—Able shook his head—"the young one, he's a mental case, they can't get two straight words from him. But the other man, the one your father burned, he said he and his brother worked for your dad, that they had a deal to help him escape, and in exchange, make a drug connection, some buy, but your father double-crossed them."

But he didn't sell the gun, Danny thought. He stashed it in the concealed bottom section of a tool chest he never really used anymore, crushed beneath a box of used books he had read but was saving. Did he bury the gun for this moment? Was his beeper beeping? After all, like his dad, he *was* a *Rod*-man.

"Your father and these Dembos were supposed to set up something at the cabin," Able explained. "The lieutenant was sketchy, maybe this Dembo guy was, too—in any case, Louis Dembo died of his burns right after, and that's that. . . . And your father's still out there. Somewhere."

Danny nodded at the thought, *Rod*-man, then caught sight of Barbara; she was awake, had been. Distress dominated her expression. Her head pivoted side-to-side through great effort as she mouthed something. Danny squinted to see, lip-read: *It's . . . not . . . him.*

Danny flushed. How did she know he was thinking of killing his father? His *not*-father. His *anti*-father. A devout conviction had sharpened her sea-blue eyes even further, amid the ill-defined and pillowy contours of her face, an insurgent ocean dominating the hilly earth. But she was wrong! Danny screamed. His father may have brought her here. And no, he didn't rape her, he didn't beat her, but it was *him*. With his mother—it was *him*. With his brother—it was *him*. It's always *him*. Always has been. Always will be. And he should not *be*. Will not *b*—

Able jostled his nephew by the shoulder. "Danny, you listening to me?"

24

RODMAN WAS SURPRISED that she had let him in so easily. Instead of ringing the bell, he knocked twice sharply, then after a deliberate pause knocked once again—the insider's signal between them, which meant nothing in particular really, had no recalled origin, but somehow was theirs and only theirs. She must have known who it was right then. She could have ignored it, waited for the disturbance to go away. He wouldn't have stood there all morning, though in Rodman's present state, he would have broken in somehow, the rotting bathroom window downstairs, but she couldn't have known that his psyche had attained such virulence. However, he was *not* neglected. He could feel the peephole come alive, a cyclopic verification. Yes, it *was* him. Now what?

Pat Dokes simply opened the front door to her split-level home and mimed him in with a full-arm flourish. She didn't look at Rodman as he passed her deferential show, but that could have had more to do with the morning's intense light stinging her eyes. It was, after all, a Sunday, nine A.M., and Rodman knew that on weekends she was a notoriously late riser. Over ten years at the workplace with someone tells you *some* things, while almost five years at the cocktail lounge tells you a lot more.

When she closed the door behind her, only her proportionally rounded shape could be seen in her thin corduroy robe, the rooms still sealed, blinds closed. It felt cool in the morning dark, though when she stepped toward him, her body gave off a swell of warmth naturally, unintentionally, for in the dimness her expression was determinedly wooden, varnished.

"So," she pronounced, "did you murder your wife so you

could have me? If you did, you're too late, chum. I'm taken."
She pulled her hand through her unkempt gray-streaked hair.
She had yet to apply makeup, but the smell of liquor adorned
her as she stepped with prideful grace into the sunken parlor
and lowered herself in one motion onto a wicker armchair. It
was only then that he noticed a glass in her hand. It was not
like her. Not in the mornings, anyway.

Rodman took the step down to the gold-and-white-tiled
floor. It needed a polishing.

"Do *you* think I killed her?"

She shrugged, inspecting the contents she was swirling in
her glass. Then she arched back and blindly pulled the cord to
the vertical blinds, letting in elongated rectangles of sun. When
she reached, her right bosom rose from the pink robe to see
who was there, then sunk back into its ribbed bed. Oh, yeah,
Carl.

Half naked or in her cups, Pat Dokes always retained that
regal bearing, Rodman thought. Every chair was a queenly
throne from which she presided, while she listened, empa-
thized. No doubt, this Pat Dokes had taken a royal step down.
She was never a facially pretty woman, her nose too splayed,
her forehead too narrow, so that her hairline crowded her
murky brown eyes. But this morning her eyes looked far puff-
ier than usual, her shoulders bent-in a hair, their first step to
contracting inward, lessening her stature by a fraction. However, she was womanly in the most feminine sense of the
word, and men feared her for it. Feared her lip when she let
loose. She had a wicked tongue for those deserving. It sprung
out most at social gatherings or in their Skyline Club tête-
à-têtes, liquor bedeviling her wit.

"Does it *matter* if I killed her?" Rodman asked.

Her eyes finally, though briefly, contacted his. "Does it matter if I care?"

"You mean aside from your harboring a fugitive by letting
me in—"

Dokes laughed at him and shook her head. "A fugitive. Ooh,
drama! The only person you were ever good at running away
from was yourself."

"Where'd you pick *that* up?" Rodman mocked.

"From you. One of your soliloquies about your life."

"Mm. Had that familiar ring."

Dokes laughed again, though more or less *with* him this time. Rodman walked farther inside the parlor, sidestepped a glass-top coffee table, and perched himself on the wicker sofa. He kept staring at her, hoping for true contact, for the hot wire.

"I always felt you can only pontificate about your life in clichés with people you care about. Because the specifics needn't be stated. They're a given." There was an awkward pause. "I think we shared a lot of specifics."

"I guess," Dokes said, her gaze recast into the whirlpool within her glass.

"But not enough, right? Not everything, that it?"

"You can't *have* everything," Dokes said, tipping her head to the side at him, then shooting down the remainder of her drink. "How's that one register on the cliché-o-meter?"

Rodman was growing sadder by the minute, by what he suspected, and even more by what was truly lost between them. In ways, the Pat Dokes he knew after-hours over the years had become his sometimes shrink, his sometimes flirt, his sometimes tearful needy sister, his ofttimes partner in skewering the world like one more cherry tomato in the cosmic shish kebab. In short, she was his booze buddy, his drinking pal, his copilot during dangerous highs. Many a late night, they would frequent elegant hotel bars with an occasional down-and-dirty pub thrown in for gassy stews and brewskis. He always felt she could outdrink him, but never did. She wasn't really an alky, because she handled it. Any sign of a hangover at her executive assistant's desk was negligible, while Rodman's necessary treatment for those mornings-after was a snort of powder to perk the soul for another business day.

Pat never used and Rodman had never offered. He would sometimes come to their trysts after work already banged if he had the stuff—he tried to keep it to a half gram a day—and Pat would say nothing, would gradually float on her gin and tonics, or shots of Wild Turkey, join him in the clouds, almost like his guardian angel. He felt Pat was looking out for him, and he would do the same for Pat.

In fact, it all started when her husband's sudden heart attack and secret debt crash-landed on her during the fifth year she was employed at Triumph. Probate proved nearly disastrous, as Ralph Dokes had creditors she had never realized existed, all seeking payback on his up-and-down catering business at the Surrey Downs Inn. She had to declare bankruptcy and sell the waterfront establishment, as well as divest some retirement earnings at a penalty just to get the IOU monkey off her back. This detailed tribulation was all exchanged between her and Carl in the space of a four-hour cocktail binge on top of Hollowsport's tallest building, the Skyline Club, overlooking the city. That night, it was *his* treat—not just in the sense of being check-payer, but of finding a compadre, a woman who showed vulnerability yet was sharp-toothed enough to rag on it.

It was the puzzle piece out of the thousand, the one Delia lacked, the frustrating one that got itself kicked under the couch somewhere and would forever be the glaring hole in the middle of the marriage picture. Rodman always felt it hard to unload anything on Delia, who, while silently agreeing to listen, would be somehow distracted, possibly skimming last month's *Beautiful Homes* magazine, catching up, her attention obviously split among unique skylight installations, Carl's soul-searching, and floral arrangements for glass-enclosed patios. Her answers to his fuzzy quests were usually soundly practical while, on another level, imbued with disappointment. Thus, burdens too unseemly for the ears of Delia were transferred to the gin-warm, pillowed heart of Patricia Dokes. Which was when the rumors became more heated, about an affair and such.

True, that as time went on, many evening excursions ended with a nightcap at this house, which became more than familiar to him, the wicker sofa and standing bar a place for discussing her recent dates with losers or her baby sister's single-parent problems with a Down's syndrome child, or his worry over accelerating business pressure, its compromises, its ethics, its *point*, or his son's plight with life and his lack of respect.

Really, Rodman thought he was cheating on his spouse as it was, cheating Eric and Delia of family time, cheating his day-to-day existence with his passion for cocaine. With time, Rodman realized that Pat didn't see *it*, what *was*, as being enough, realized it with finality when Pat began acting very catlike one humid night on the couch, very suggestive within her liquored high. Sick of "the single widow bit," she ran a tongue-wet finger along the entire right side of his face—he was hardly focusing—and suggested, "If Delia thinks you may be cheating anyway, why not reap the benefits?"

Even then, he was thinking, "*That's* not the point," but he was inches away, staring at her two wonderfully globelike bosoms which she somehow released and thrust to him without his realizing, her head bent back, neck arched. She moaned in a whisper, and he hadn't even touched her. Absorbed by the display, he stroked each breast delicately palm-wide; then with just the flesh of his fingertips, tested their firm shape, kissed them both with short gentle pecks, then licks, then suckled on a nipple tasting of alcohol from the bead of perspiration clinging to its hard nub. Then he stopped and looked at her with reverence and admiration, breathing her in. His friend was showing him something beautiful. But it wasn't sex. Pat peered down, wondered what was wrong, but nothing was wrong. He was feeling strong feelings, a sense of wonder and stimulation, like touching the chiseled purity of a Rodin: erotic, but aesthetically so. No doubt, alcohol had been stemming the drives in his life, lustful or otherwise, but that night he did not use it as an excuse. Instead, they lay with each other, dropping off in each other's arms like alternating sentries, but he could tell they crossed over to another dimension of their relationship; their formerly parallel lines showed the first sign of divergence.

They kept seeing each other, as their shared dependency even overcame Pat's wanting a sexual bond. Even after his rehab, it wasn't uncommon for them to go out occasionally and order a "rumless coke" or a "no-gin-fizz" as a goof. Meanwhile, the vague promise of possibility, that netherworld of could-be, had been steadily retreating into the past, at least for him. He still trusted her with many of his truer, uncensored thoughts, and apparently she, him. Then out of nowhere four weeks ago he was told matter-of-factly by Triumph's morning receptionist that Pat put in her resignation to Mr. Whipp and left immediately without severance.

"Hey, sourpuss!"

Rodman's eyes glanced up from the sofa. Pat was leaning

over the ersatz-marble bar, her hands flat on top and turned in, her bosoms inflating out, as though she were awaiting an order, saucy or otherwise.

"*There* you are," she intoned flatly. "I got Stoli sitting here. You off or on? Wait! I'll check the wind." She chuckled at her own joke, took a suck from her finger, then stuck it in the air, her enlarged eyes anticipating a breeze.

Rodman was unamused by the show, feeling caught off guard, still ruminating about the past, but Pat mistook his delay in answering as deliberation.

"I *mean*, pursued by the police, hated by your best friend—I was hoping it was a dumb question." She raised the chilled vodka bottle as though he needed a clearer look.

"Off," he murmured, "I guess. I mean—"

"Yeah, a little pregnant," Pat remarked as she began to pour the liquor into two squat crystalline glasses. "Get with the program, babycakes. Lushes of a feather—"

"Since when are *you* a full-time lush? Drinks at dawn?"

Her voice dropped to a growl. "Don't insult me with concern, Carl, please." She set Rodman's glass forward on the bar toward him with a sharp clunk, like a vindictive chess move.

Rodman released a long breath, feeling defeat, yet he stepped to the bar and watched her take a vocal swallow from her own drink. "You talking about Howard?" he asked quietly.

"What?" she said.

"My 'best friend.' *You* brought him up. You say he hates me."

She maneuvered out from behind the squeezed-in counter, "Ugh," then snorted, "Doesn't everybody?" She was about to take another sip when an overly dramatic veil of dismay colored her expression, as if this were the first good look she had gotten of Rodman now that he shone in relief from the window's slatted glare. "Are you getting any sleep?"

Rodman snapped. "No! Are you?" He snagged her wrist with a smack of flesh, the level of vodka sloshing, but still confined. "Can we cut to the chase?"

"Okay," Pat said, "I'm *seeing* your best friend. About two months now. Did you know that? I'm fucking his brains out."

Rodman closed his eyes, shook his head, let her go. "Jesus

Christ, Pat." Then he turned away, braced his back on the jutting bar.

Pat studied his reaction and finished her sip. "Is this the green monster I see before me?"

Rodman gave her an up-from-under glare that put a chill through her. "Don't mistake jealousy for nausea," he snarled, still staring her down until she withered, moved to the hunter-green wicker chair, but didn't sit. From behind he could discern she was trembling slightly, hugging herself as though she didn't want him to see.

Rodman pressed on, though sadness wove through his remark. "I didn't think you were capable of hurting others, people like Howard, to somehow get to me."

Her shoulders lifted and fell. "You don't know what I'm capable of," she murmured.

In the following silence, Pat could be heard taking long, deep, stabilizing breaths. She drew her hair back with both hands, slowly, then taut, as though stretching off a tight ski cap. Gradually released, her dense shiny locks cascaded down her neck in stiff waves. Then she sat, inclining forward, her forearms supported by her white legs, her hands clasped between her knees. Rodman stood where he was; he didn't want to disrupt her line of vision, her venture into disclosure, wanted to allow whatever she seemed to be fighting to let out flow without judgment, unobstructed.

Pat cleared her throat. "I admit it started out that way pretty much—what you just said. I didn't feel this way or that about dating Howard. But after a while I told myself, you know, I don't know. I thought he was becoming . . . possible, for *real*, maybe. . . . I kept lying to him, though. I wanted him outraged at you. I told him I quit my job because your recent sexual advances were becoming more and more overt. That it was getting intolerable. That I was only thinking of your poor wife, poor Delia . . ." Pat shook her head; a laugh came out as delicate as a distant chime.

"Howard wondered if you and I ever *had* anything before, any *thing*, and I told him, no . . . just friends, which—at least, *that* was true. I *really* wanted him to feel like he was beating you to the punch this time. It was worth it to see him feel like cock-of-the-walk for once, even though the poor guy was in the dark about things."

Pat snuck a peek at Rodman, almost to see if he even cared enough to listen. He felt compelled to say something as a way to say he did.

"That explains his interrogation at the cabin," he responded, and then told how Howard was so insistent in his questioning about the suspiciousness of Pat's resigning—why wasn't she at the senator's party? Why would she leave Triumph like that?

"So I guess he wanted to see if I realized I had forced you out. Thought I might admit man-to-man that I came on to you."

"He was giving you shit about me, then." Pat nodded in appreciation, her gaze adrift in a half smile. "He's a good boy."

Rodman stifled a grunt. That would be the last thing Howard would want to hear, Rodman thought—then he sunk another notch: Howard must have been hating me even *before* Delia's murder.

As though cued by Rodman's inner monologue, Pat added reflectively, "But then Delia died . . . and it was—it was like Howard curled up inside. Like he packed everything away, and left the shell for me to play with. I didn't realize how much . . ."

Then Pat stunned Carl by swiveling toward him, focusing directly on him. He suddenly felt vulnerable to her voice, her revelations.

"He was always in touch with Delia. They'd always talk. He mentioned how she confided in him how angry and upset she was with you about not wanting to look any further into who Mattera's client was, find out who killed Eric. Howard said she would bring it up endlessly in their conversations. His face was always like a red balloon about that, right after she called."

Pat glanced down then up, rejecting then accepting what she was to say next.

"You know, I was there that night when *you* called. A few days back—when you needed money? I was staying over at his apartment. And when he hung up, he told me who it was, then cursed you and called the police. I just lay beside him the whole time he and the cops were plotting. I felt like the double

agent, the mole—read too many le Carré books. . . ." Pat play-
acted. "My hands, I remember my hands"—her arms straight
down, elbows locked, pretending she was lying flat—"they
just kept smoothing the sheets near my thighs, outward sort of.
Listening to a plot, a trap, I saw it snapping on you and I kept
smoothing the sheets, smoothing the sheets. Then after the police, Howard calls your brother-in-law, Jack, to tell him the
'good news,' as he put it. Tells him the family tragedy will be
over, tells him what you said, what the police said, how you're
going to get your ass bounced in jail, and I'm smoothing those
damn sheets like my palms were *fucking* hot irons."

Pat paused and took a breath, inspected her glass, almost
swirled the vodka but decided against it, drank the rest down,
then inspected the glass again as though verifying it was as
empty as she felt.

"Then when he hung up, Howard made some very nasty
love to me. Something not him. Rough stuff. Not good rough,
but hard, mean, and then . . . and then the very moment he
shot into me, he started to cry. He fell on me, bawling. He held
me like I was his grip on the world. Like he was going to fall
into nothingness if he let go. Sobbing away . . . I knew it was
for Delia. I didn't say anything. Didn't hug him back, though.
I found that my hands were still pressed to the bed, smoothing
away. It was all smooth now. I made everything so smooth."

Pat lifted her watery eyes to meet Rodman's. "Surprise, surprise. We were *both* playing the substitution game. We were
both pinch-hitting for someone else."

They let the silence sit awhile like an old cat—heavy, idle,
thoughtless.

"I guess we all play that game," Rodman said finally. He
surrounded the drink she had poured him and inspected it.
"This would substitute for a lot of things. People included." He
poured the vodka in the open ice bucket behind the counter,
then returned his attention to Pat. "I'm not all that sure now
that it was less our bond than our blockage. For all that we
shared, the bottle was more the message in and of itself than
the medium."

"Are you saying we lied to each other?"

"I'm saying we didn't necessarily tell each other the truths that counted, or couldn't because we became so close to each other's pain."

Pat tucked her robe between her legs and furrowed her brow. "You're confusing me—we're close—we're not—"

"I'm sorry, I don't mean to. I came here meaning to be direct." Pat suddenly found Rodman had abandoned his hunkered position at the bar and stood over her like a dark cloud. "I came here to ask you why you left the job—shit—left my *life* without so much as a word."

Pat rose and cocked her head, stared at him obliquely. "*Now* we get to it, huh? We opened her up at one end, let's tear open the other, let it *all* spill out."

Rodman's voice stayed dry, direct. "Why'd you leave?"

Pat moved away, ostensibly to place her tumbler back on the bar. "I was pining over your sinewy thighs too much."

His eyes followed her. "Why?"

Facing the counter, she gripped her empty glass, smothered it, hoping it would shatter in her hand. "I saw the killer side of you. I didn't want to be in the same room when you went off. Too bad your wife was."

She heard two short angry footfalls approach from behind and a brisk hand spun her around. The blush to Rodman's face was spotty like a poorly conductive heating coil.

"Stop it!" he demanded, taking hold of both her arms. "You wouldn't have let me in if you thought I really killed Delia. No sane person would."

"See?" she shot back. "I would have let you in even if I thought you really *did* do it. *That's* what you never understood. My insanity when it comes to you." She sensed his fingers go limp and fall off her like flaking skin. In compensation, she stepped forward and embraced him, clung to him, lay the side of her head on his chest so she could talk with his heartbeat singing to her ear. By instinct, his arms cautiously accepted her.

"I couldn't ever cheat on you," she murmured. "I just couldn't. Yet I did. But I wasn't about to look you in the eye and do it."

Rodman answered, echoing her near whisper. "What are you talking about, 'cheating on me.' With Howard?" Then he understood and, with her arms still about him, angled over far enough to finger his travel sack on the coffee table and slide out just enough of the large report so she could see who it was from. "Or you mean that?"

From just off his chest, Pat had observed Rodman's surprise disclosure, only needing the briefest of glimpses to verify the material.

She let him go and descended back to the chair behind her, poised at its edge. "I couldn't cheat on you, at least not without paying for it, making myself pay for it." A flip of her head indicated the parlor bar. "Twenty-four-hour drownings was partial payment."

"What happened? Why?"

She placed her face in the flat of her hands. She spoke blinded. "Why did I betray you? Why did I put listening devices in your office? In the boardroom?" Her hands dropped; she looked out on nothing. "That's what they finally found, right? I knew they would. Eventually. The monthly sweep. I had a month to wait, but I could only take myself sober for a week knowing what I had done."

Rodman squatted, then lay a knee to the floor, dipping his head, attempting to pry her face up with his look, trying to get her to acknowledge his desperation as she gazed downward. "Please tell me, Pat."

She whipped her head to the side, away from him, but not before a tear that couldn't hold flew off and beaded on his shoe. He gazed at her ear, brushed three fingers of hair from it. "This past week I feel as though I know nothing," he said. "Somebody, something, erased a slate of givens in my head. There's been more death than you know, but I still can't write anything real on that slate. Tell me something real, Pat, please! Tell me what happened."

Pat's head began to move in minute bobs; she sniffed once then began: "You maybe more than anybody know that when people start feeling sorry for me, you know"—her voice turned singsong—"*Oh, she lost her husband, never had children,* I always say, I already have a child, my kid sister, Ann. Never matured. Bouncing job to job. I beat her brains in to get some college training, *something*. If I date losers, this girl *marries* them. You know the rap sheet. Two in, two out. Alimony in a blue moon. And like everything else in this crazy world, her son Billy is half blessing, half burden. Of all the people God gives a Down's baby to . . . I'll never understand. So she finally lands a job at T and G Department Stores, recently—I didn't mention it to you, I don't think—in their main branch, financial office. She sees bags of money every day, Brink's pickup, all that. Pretty soon, the stupid girl starts screwing around with the figures—a friend of hers at the accessory counter register, some finagling there—I'm short on details, just I know she's embezzling money, *needed* money, because the job pays nothing even before taxes and because Billy is costing her a fortune in care. I try to help, moneywise, but she spurns me. The punch line is I find out all this secondhand, not from Ann, but from Braxton Cole."

Rodman dropped from his knee squat, sunk completely to the floor. "Braxton Cole? How the hell—"

"T and G Department Stores is a subsidiary of Cole Enterprises, a small one, but it's there sitting in his big fat-cat paw—" Pat spread out an upward-facing hand then closed it gradually, bent finger by bent finger, like a wicked flower. "—and in no time flat, so am I."

Pat touched Rodman's hot cheek with the back of her cool hand. "He found the chink to your armor, baby," she said in a hoarse whisper, stroking his hair now. "Pat 'the Fink' Dokes. He was going to send my baby sister to jail, let Billy swing in the breeze, social services, who knows? But he knew Ann's big sister worked hip-to-hip with the Man, the obstacle, the grit in his greedy eye. I told him I couldn't get documents about the Aquarius development plan, or copies either. Too risky. He didn't care. He didn't care what was written down, he said. That kind of information could be faked and misleading on purpose. He wanted to hear plans from the source, firsthand, who your links were in the legislature, what angles you were playing on his bond application. He wanted a bug. Said you could always tell if people were playacting if they knew the mikes were there, and if that happened, Ann would be in custody the next day. On the other hand, if I did it, Ann would keep her job, though transferred somewhere safe from temptation, and Billy would be provided for as well. A monthly stipend through a confidential P.O. box. And he's done that. A man of his word, Mr. Cole. America's finest."

Pat's nostrils dilated; her head felt drained. "Needed Benedict Arnold, though ... needed a Judas, a 'dirty-tricks plumber.' Of course, the irony is I think Ann and I hate each other even more than before, but for different reasons. So I'm absolutely alone now and deserve every minute of it."

Pat slipped herself down from the chair to join a dazed Rodman on the braided rug. She broke down, holding his cheeks in her hands, pulling him to her forehead, shaking her own head back and forth, weeping, "I'm so sorry, Carl. I'm so sorry." She sucked in her tears and released another wave of grief, a wail that bent her over as though she were stricken with stomach cramps. Rodman watched her weep doubled over in his lap, as he stroked her back, rubbed it through the thin corduroy, feeling the bumps of her bridging spine, his sudden fatigue from not sleeping for over a day merging with his numbness from Pat's confession. What people did in the name of sorrow, he thought. How far we all will go. How far there still is . . .

They stayed on the floor for a while, until Pat's head rose, her eyes stained red, her cheeks flushed, her hair fanned out like gray-black rays to a crimson sun. Rodman's wounds were moving in, his body relaying all the brutalized bones and strained muscles and unhealed bruises to his sputtering nerve center. "Braxton Cole," he hissed to himself.

Pat removed a yellow tissue from her robe pocket and blew her nose, and with her wrists, wiped the watery sheen from her cheeks. She asked: "What are you going to do?"

"It's better I don't tell you," Rodman replied.

"Why? Can I get in any deeper trouble than I am now, having you here?"

"No. Not that. It has to do more with—with a side of me even I can barely look at."

Pat stared at his placid handsome face. "You've worn some pretty ugly masks in the past. I haven't seen all of them?"

Rodman didn't answer, saw Louis Dembo's torched shrieking head. "Can I sleep here today? I need a rest."

Pat nodded, sniffled. "Of course. You can use my bed." She was about to swing herself up from the floor when Rodman took hold of her shoulder.

"Promise me something," he said. "No more of that for

now." His eyes flickered toward the bar. "You've done your penance."

Pat silently agreed, then led him to the bedroom.

After indulging for a good while in a hot shower, Rodman slid beneath the soft goldenrod sheets of Pat Doke's double bed, took the left side, punched its pillow, and even with his eyes determined to stay shut, could only drift in and out of consciousness ten minutes at a time, hearing the shower beating down on who he assumed was Pat, then sensing her in the room with him, the shoosh of nylon panty hose, the squeak of hangers shifted on the closet rack. He finally heard her leave with the click of the front door—then he thought of his trusting her, of her flushing pink face. Then not. He fell asleep.

The phone ringing next to the bed startled him, caused a short neck-jerk off the pillow, then a slower drop back down into the wrinkled crater. Whatever sweat the sound produced evaporated after a few conscious-grabbing blinks. Following the fourth ring, the voice of the message machine kept his eyelids up in the locked position. It was Howard's. *"There is no one who can come to the phone right now. Please leave your name, the time you called, and a message. Thank you."*

Rodman realized that Howard was trying to sound robotic, the generic male machine voice. Then there was the beep, and Rodman sat straight up in bed, as though on a springboard, when the *real* Howard came over the speaker.

"Hey! I know it was my brilliant idea to put my voice on your tape to keep away the breathers, but it's very weird answering myself. Sorry you're not home. I had to leave town for a few days unexpectedly, so you didn't get my usual Friday night ear-bender. I thought we could get together, you know, rock-and-roll hooch-i-coo. Or whatever you'd like . . . I miss you."

It was a dreamlike sensation, Rodman thought, occupying a strange bed, hearing his best friend's melancholic voice in the powdery-perfumed atmosphere of sun-shimmery yellow curtains and gold-tasseled bedcovers. He felt like the scurvy pirate washed ashore in his B.V.D.'s, bare-chested, taken into a golden palace for succor, and talked to by disembodied spirits from the past. Rodman was extremely tempted to blow his hiding place for shock value alone, to raise the phone and put a lightning bolt through this delicate vision and Howard's ear. But what would he say? *I'm on your side of the bed.* Or maybe, *I've been an asshole all my life.* Maybe, *I'm sorry.* Or, *Fuck you.* He believed all of the above would be apropos.

But instead—" 'Bye," Howard said—Rodman let the answering machine click and whir and beep its last, never touching the interrupt. As it was, his finger had always been far too close to the self-destruct button. No need to push it every time it itched. He stretched over and dipped his hand inside the travel pouch wedged up against the night table. The gun was still buried deep; he wanted the magazine Howard had given him. He read until his eyes begged him for respite. At that point, Rodman gave in, flipped over, and slept most of the afternoon.

Rodman stirred when he heard distant thumping of kitchen cabinets, a bottle-jangling refrigerator door keep opening and closing, and large paper bags being smashed flat. It reminded him of shopping day at the Rodman house, Delia thoroughly checking the list, Eric in the cart's handle seat riding backward, playing with Daddy, the steerer, who was moseying down the aisles, honking Rodman's nose and pinching it, and Carl making a different noise for each press to make Eric giggle. And absurd thoughts descending like: What if some stray grains of powder got on Eric's fingertips and later he puts his fingers in his mouth? Dumb things. But not dumb enough to stop nasal-sucking the shit the next day.

Rodman jacked open his eyes. What house? What Eric? What Delia? His face drained. The muted kitchen clatter suddenly seemed like radio bleeps bouncing back years later from another planet: no sign of life.

Pat popped her head into the room, and seeing Rodman was awake, stepped inside. "Did I wake you with my manic putting-away of food?"

Rodman shook his head, lifted himself up to lay his back on the headboard.

Pat said, "It drives me crazy finding everything its own place. Don't know why. You get some rest?"

Rodman noticed that Pat was looking uncomfortable in her

own bedroom, as though she didn't know what to do with her hands.

"For what it's worth," he replied, now wondering if it was having him in her bed, half naked. Pat, on the other hand, was wonderfully dressed—the consummate professional in a tailored suit of sandwashed silk crepe de chine, caramel-colored. Her hair swirled forward just below her earlobes, its opposing tips pointing to the crinkled edges of her fragile smile.

"What are you looking at?" she said, feeling self-conscious. This was what she could do, Rodman thought. Keep everyone off guard at Triumph by appearing so in-charge and demure after the previous evening's drinkathon with him.

"Where were you besides the supermarket?" Rodman asked.

"Other errands." Pat shrugged, sitting at the foot of the bed, her hand resting on the bump in the sheet that contained his ankle. "I even went to an early afternoon service at my local church. Presbyterian. Don't laugh at me. I've been going this last month between bottle binges. Moving in both extremes, I guess."

She thumb-rubbed the bump, and Rodman didn't move his leg away.

"You hungry yet?" she asked.

Rodman shook his head. Pat felt flushed the way he was looking at her. She finger-pried her heels off, then snuck another look at the hairless chest leaning back in her bed. "Can I come under there with you?"

Rodman nodded.

Pat removed her golden jacket, which had been suppressing the two hard white tips that had come up beneath her blouse even before she made the suggestion.

Her greatest fear during their lovemaking was not whether it was going to be the consummate erotic experience, fulfilling all expectations, but whether Carl, like Howard, would cry afterward, for surely he had an even greater reason to sense the loss of Delia.

His greatest fear during their lovemaking was that he didn't want her to think that he was using her, didn't even want to think it of himself, for his erection was hard with tension and grief and want. He craved her embrace, a need for love and release, and in that delicate dual mix resided the insecurity of whether it was more one than the other. He wanted to please her, but no more than he hurt to please his tightening loins. Pat orgasmed easily, wet and pulsing, which was fortunate, since Rodman, though bent stiff, had little stamina—the toll of the chase, emotionally as well as physically, brought him forth with a screaming gush sooner than he expected, though slower than all his pent-up fears and primal defenses wanted.

They said nothing afterward, both not sure of what to say. Still, their lips were tender upon each other's faces and necks, and their smiles were genuine. Then, as Rodman held Pat from behind, crossing and caressing each full bosom with opposite hands, he felt his heart retreat, beat slow again, like the steady steps toward his purpose, his reality. And she felt it, too. She prepared herself for him never to be there again.

They slept that way for a while, until Rodman grew tired of resting, felt the natural light dying upon the yellow curtain. His stomach growled, but his mind buzzed even louder. He slipped out of bed without disturbance and sat at Pat's antique postal writing desk. He flicked off the blue cap of a Bic Biro and removed sheets of stationery from the wooden rabbit hole beside the rows of minidrawers. It was time to tell it. One final tension-spewing gush.

How to start—all he could think of was *death for death*, a phrase that thumped like a steady fist on a shut door.

Death for death: Rodman had always believed it. If you make death, you breed it. You take a life; a life gets taken from you. The way he had been thinking Delia's death was God's payback for his murdering Vance. The way Eric's death was a definite payback, though Rodman knew that some people truly believed he himself ran Eric down that night after a drinking bout and then never confessed his sin. Probably even Pat suspected. True, he had always convinced himself that he *was* responsible for Eric's death, in spite of the fact he was nowhere near home when his son was victimized by some cowardly driver. Always wanted to tell Delia it was his fault. Tell her it was "death for death." "Eric died for my sins," he wanted to say. "For the death of children."

Rodman reread what he had written, when Pat stirred. He glanced at her, and, as if by cause-and-effect, her eyes opened.

After a few seconds she only gave him a wan smile, thinking the expression on Rodman's face meant he was not conducive to interruption. She was right. Pat sat up then grabbed the morning's cool corduroy robe, which had been flung over a straight chair, and barefooted into the kitchen to cook something.

Rodman by this time had fallen back into his thoughts, into the words, enmeshed in the past. It was late 1970. The still rustic cabin on Janus Mountain was a den of freaks and good times let roll. Eggman 1 and Eggman 2—Carl and Sonny, respectively, who would flop an arm about each other's shoulders like Tweedledee and Tweedledum and sing, *We are the egg men, whooo!* then fall down to the floor convulsed in laughter, coughing hashish smoke. *Goo-goo-ca-choob!*—had been dealing small-time to friends and holding open-ended party scenes that usually started the minute after the buy, no matter if it was twelve noon or four A.M. The fishing boat was left dry-docked, but more than one naked body would usually find itself splashing and goosing and cavorting in the lake before it was all over, howling at a banana moon on their muddied backs and butts, couples rustling thickets of fern in rhythmic waves and giggles. This was Carl Rodman's young dream of a free life. Responsibility was for so-called adults who liked Spiro Agnew, right angles, and self-imposed handcuffs.

But the boys were getting restless, boiling with cabin fever at the approach of late fall and at seeing mountain-drawn flakes of snow begin to stick without ever reaching Hollowsport proper. Chopping firewood to feed the cast-iron heater on the fireplace in the dark of November became the stuff of bad acid trips. We need a winter home, the Egg men decided.

After a few days of newspaper diving, they found one—a white panel truck they low-geared up Mandrake Road, bought from a defunct plumbing service, the Pipe & Wrench Brothers, on Eighth Street downtown, the commercial lettering still on the side of the van. Vance was going to be "Pipe," Rodman "Wrench," but they said, fuck the *Starsky and Hutch* bit, and began spray-painting its entire surface in multicolor swaths and designs, some customers-of-the-day pitching in. Vance hogged the black can, and for every rainbow arching a panel, he would place little devil bats lurking along its chromatic curve. He also contributed one major artwork, a poor rendition of an X-eyed Mr. Natural hung by his own floor-length white beard, its end tied to an unseen giant woman's exaggeratedly long nipple and huge bare breast.

Rodman had wished he had brushes for more delicate work, the kind he enjoyed at St. Joe's. Without them, all he could come up with was many color-blend abstracts and two recognizable artifacts. One was a three-foot-wide eye, blue-centered, with bigger lashes than he intended and a yellow tear coming down. The latter touch made him self-conscious among his rhapsodic fellow painters (maybe it was a bong-downer he hit), so he added a naked man right under the drop, who was ostensibly about to use it to take a shower. His other rendition was that of a red religious cross, the bottom of which curved into the shape of a hook, which had snagged on its end a large golden fish. He tried to think of who would have hated it more, one of the old nuns or his dead father.

The minute the bunch tossed the empty spray cans in the crunch of dried leaves, Sonny and Carl started the engine. In the time it took to warm up, Vance and Rodman had already shut down the cabin and threw the first things that popped into their heads in the back. They careened down Janus Mountain then dropped their guests off in town before hitting Interstate 67 to start their cross-country big-mother yahoo.

The first few weeks, Sonny and Carl snaked their way down the East Coast, hitting the big cities, their van a divining rod to the urban core of tribal hippies and street-smart dealers. They sold Laotian Red and hash, but as the money grew, they bought the Red only for their own pleasure and for bartering with fellow heads. A big chunk of their profits, instead, went for the cheap stuff, the punk grass, the "weed and seed" garbage they pawned off to the mob, the "H.P.," as they called them, the "hoi-polloi"—college-clean boys and girls, townie toughs, geeks who didn't know good grass from strong aspirin, "straights" on the verge of curving but never taking the hairpin, never giving up the brush cut or the Brylcreem. These maroons thought quantity meant quality, so they bought in bulk, and in bulk the Egg men took in the green.

Then Vance and Rodman made a sharp right after North

Carolina, equating the Deep South with the deep-six, had some good fortune in Nashville, skipped Indiana due to its extremely low cool quotient, and headed due north for Chicago, where they hooked into such a wired supplier of Thai sticks and Panamanian weed, they stayed in town almost a month to sop up the cash flow.

By now Rodman had been "keeping books," accounts on a ledger he ripped off at an office supply place in Springfield. He backtracked financially as best he could, back past Raleigh, N.C. He was the numbers guy, and it was like a game, keeping track of the buys, the sells, the trades, seeing what the market was in different parts of a state, different neighborhoods of a city, tracking quality of dope and corresponding prices. Vance was glad Rodman showed such enthusiasm for the project. It kept Carl intense, made Sonny feel that no cocksucker could rip them off, because his man had the figures. They could drop names from town to town to get inside—block to block if they stayed long enough.

By the time they left Chicago to cross the plains states, the trip had revealed the unique shapes of their separate characters quite dramatically, far beyond that which linked them at the armpit while cohabiting the hippie haven on Janus Mountain. Besides involvement in the accounting end, Rodman was a news junkie, read lots of local papers wherever they went, usually with a stolen magazine or two hidden against the inner crease, snuck by the candy counter man. He was fascinated with the political counterculture in print, but as though he were reading history, not living it. He'd visit the main library of many small towns and cop a book when desirable and when there were no antitheft beepers around.

Also, it was about Chicago when he started depositing some of his drug earnings in different banks along the way—a thousand here, a few hundred or so there—for no better reason than he thought he read somewhere that W. C. Fields had done the same thing throughout the states, using the whacked-out character names from his comedies. Rodman also felt that doing this meant he belonged to "the road"; it guaranteed he'd be back to wherever he had just left. However, he couldn't remember any of Fields's funny aliases to present as his own, so he tried out some of Groucho Marx's—Hugo Z. Hackenbush,

Rufus T. Firefly—then, stumped to come up with some more, resorted to second-rung rockers—Al Kooper, Jack Bruce, Leslie West, Ray Manzarek—he figured even a schmuck pig banker in Cedar Rapids would question his using John Lennon or Bob Dylan. These personal sums were not kept in Sonny and Carl's official business ledger, but privately on a Flintstone flip pad that Rodman kept stuck in his back pants pocket. It was his nest egg, he'd claim, and he sat on it every day—"An elephant faithful, one hundred percent." Only the truly stoned on Looney Tunes or Dr. Seuss groupies got that one.

Vance, on the other hand, was the front man in the drug transactions, the talker, the grand negotiator and BS artist. He looked so fucking competent, for a skeeve with greasy blond hair pulled into a ponytail, a beaded headband, and callused bare feet. He laid hands and freak-speak on the women of the flower nation, many more of whom bought his rap more than blew him off. Rodman spent too many cold nights under a scratchy brown blanket in the back of the van, four feet away from a grunt-humping sleeping bag. Mathematically, he figured Vance scored four-to-one, easy, to what he himself got. (What you get for being the "numbers" guy.) In matters above the waist, Vance's reading was as varied as his bagmates, from casino books—how-to's on beating the crap table, guaranteed card-counting theories, poker meditations, and such—to the Sammy Davis Jr. biog, *Yes, I Can*, to the works of Friedrich Nietzsche. In fact, more and more of his business profit seemed to be lost at gambling. Sonny liked to find the action, be it a South Philly furnace room, or a backyard tool shack outside Asheville, N.C. Even the flatheads and hard hats liked his money, if he found a card game through a local bookie he was using at the time. ("These same guys, man," he'd say to Carl, "would tell you how drugs and shit were fucked and immoral-like, but took the hippie's dirty money, no sweat, when they showed me straight flushes.") Rodman sometimes suspected he and Vance left some towns quicker than others because Sonny was stiffing a bookie on a bad bet. Vance, unlike Carl, never planned on ever visiting the same place twice. So Sonny would be tooling away from their last HQ as fast as the panel truck could haul, cranking all their Bob Dylan eight-tracks as loud as he could and singing along. *"I ain't gonna work on Maggie's farm no more ..."*

Business was predictably slow through Iowa and Nebraska, but things gained speed, both literally and figuratively, when they bumped into Denver. It was there that Sonny and Carl met the Mad Russian, a bushy-sideburned rat-runt who always wore a cossack hat of unknown fur and had *the* Rocky Mountain motherload supply of pills, the Alice in Wonderland assortment, big, little, black, green, Eat Me, My Pleasure. Getting into the pharmaceutical branch of the mind-groove became the veritable *chugga-chugga* of their profit machine. It also begat their unraveling.

Rodman and Vance not only sold the uppers and downers, blackies, greenies, Dilaudid, you-name-it, but began consuming vast amounts themselves. Black beauties kept Rodman up for two, three days at a stretch, then he'd come down with a different color pop, but his wiring was getting blistered with the constant buzz and drag, and after a few weeks he just stayed with the smoke, danced on Red, on hash, period. It was on this mellow that Rodman noticed Vance's behavior more clearly, his love of uppers, his wind-up doll movements, one key-turn too many. It didn't take a numbers freak to see Vance + speed = hyperspeed.

Sonny was doing all-night van side runs to other towns for deals, was sometimes gone for days, leaving Rodman to count the paint flakes on the transient hotel ceilings if Vance took most of the supply with him. When he would come back, he'd thumb out wrinkled twenties and hundreds from his tight jeans and let them tumble onto the bed, sometimes wake Rodman up by letting a bill or two hit his dormant face and laughing. After a few doses of that mind-fuck, Rodman made Vance divvy up the stash, halve-zees, from then on, so he wouldn't be caught short if Sonny suddenly decided to disappear to *Gilligan's Island* and sell downers to the Professor and Mary Ann; at least Rodman would have his own stuff. Clearly, the Egg men were showing cracks.

When *finally* they rocked out of Denver, rolled down the mountains and toward the California coast, they were well-stocked in pills. Still, Vance was brooding over losing contact with the Mad Russian, Sonny showing a baby's sour aspect after being detached from his mother's-milk-sweet teat, and he took his anger out on Rodman. To appease his fellow Egg, Carl made sure the van veered toward Viva Las Vegas, whose desert lights reflected off the glaze on Sonny's strung-out eyes like an Xmas display, Santa Roll Seven; Vance was fucking home!

Once in town, Rodman was selling his load in a steady flow, just outside the Strip proper, around its periphery, to its peripheral populace—to the live-theres, not just those here to gamble—as was Vance. Only Vance's next stop was always the neon-acid trip lineup of gaudy Gomorrah establishments, the actual wearing of shoes and socks, the using of copped hotel soap under the arms, the elbow-rubbing on green felt tables. Rodman got Vance to promise they were just doing a weekend in Mafiaville—promised with a sneer—because Carl started feeling scared by Sonny's feverish antics, his excuses for losing, his proclaimed mastery when winning, when in fact Vance was really pissing away his pill profits, living hand-to-casino.

The Vegas visit lasted most of a week instead of a weekend, but Vance's pill-dry supply was the impetus for splitting rather than Carl's bitching. Rodman still had a healthy batch from his half of the load, so when they set up shop in Los Angeles, he gave Sonny blackies as he would One-A-Days, just enough to give Vance his U.S. daily minimum requirement of nutrient speed and no more, enough to energize him to find more product.

Sonny being Sonny, he quickly latched onto a few dealers who had Pan-Pacific pipelines to the best head-banging smoke this side of Da Nang, the kind the Cong swung through the jungles on like slit-eyed Zippys. He also found himself an artist with whom he teamed up to sell tee shirts, a quasilegit enterprise that Sonny thought would be a great cover, as well as profitable. Sonny had made up a mock saying months before that he always wanted emblazoned somewhere (preferably the firmament), but somebody's chest would do: *Suppose they gave an orgy and nobody came.* Below the slogan, the freak-o artist, who took his cut in hashish, drew a pseudo–R. Crumb character looking bummed out, eyes bugged, holding a limp yard-long penis in his hand like so much flaccid garden hose, while encircled by faceless and prone naked bodies with splayed legs.

And Vance was right-on: The Tee Shirt of the Month crowd dug it and thought it hip, though there were some freaks who didn't find it funny, mainly Nam vets-cum-hippies who thought it put the mock on the original antiwar slogan and on the peace movement overall. But Vance would smile and nod and say, "That's cool. That's cool," and shuck around and sell them a few dozen tabs cut-rate, then glance at Carl cockeyed when the weren't looking, and when they left he'd say, "Converted vets, man. Worse than born-again bozos stickin' J.C. in your face every friggin' minute." Once Sonny was pulling the blue jeans off a Melanie look-alike, only with a zitty face—maybe she was fourteen—and he saw her pubic hair had been shaved in a peace symbol. He gazed down at her and said, "Fuck peace. Don't mind if I do." Such was Sonny Vance's take on causes.

So when he heard that there was going to be a big-kahuna Vietnam Peace Moratorium the following month up in the flower-power capital of the universe, San Francisco, Sonny suggested he and Rodman cruise up the highway, pop in a few towns, sell their wares, then in the City by the Bay make the biggest one-day pot 'n' pill score in modern history.

"What about Woodstock?" Rodman had asked, mid-toke.

"That was *three* days, man," Vance said, "and it was mostly communal shit, you know, commie-time grass-sharing. I'm, like, talking capitalistic opportunities, the heart of Rockefeller-and-roll."

"Bankroll," Rodman added.

"Bankroll." Sonny laughed. "That's right, man. You got it."

Then Rodman sobered and asked, "But, like, *what* pills?" because even Carl's supply had run out that week, and Denver was not the second exit on the Ventura Freeway.

That's when Vance raised his finger, signaling a plan. "Operation: Placebo," he announced.

Operation: Placebo was the selling of bogus uppers and downers, a scam to be aimed at grade-schoolers because even the older straights might guess that the sugar capsule in their mouth was doing zip. But nine-year-olds bounce up and down like Silly Putty naturally anyway, so they assume they're high.

Vance said he had seen it work in Hollowsport, that he knew some kid was sucking on a month-old linty Certs, but the kid thought it was a form of acid, and he was telling Vance and the dealer about all the wow-colors he was seeing. Vance figured this kid must have been watching the world in black-and-white all his life if a breath mint gave him rainbow vision.

Operation: Placebo was a lock, Vance told Rodman. A hit-and-run sell-and-go all the way to Frisco, "Then we use the money to buy the real thing up there and work the big Nam freak parade." It sounded okay to Rodman, since they had no real pills left to sell anyway, and he would never sell real ones to little kids even if he did. However, what Carl wasn't aware of was that the infamous Mad Russian had, in fact, moved his pill factory operation from Rocky Mountain High to the City of the Angels, and that Vance was in the know, and that Vance had bought a whopperload-plus from the Mad one, and that Vance was really about to implement Operation: Double Cross.

Rodman didn't suspect much at first. It took almost to San Francisco proper for him to feel like some shit was happening just out of sight, some dark blotch moving too fast from the corner of his eye and gone. It was just that in every van stop up the state—Santa Maria, Paso Robles, King City—Sonny and he would split up. Rodman would work a number of schoolyards, public playgrounds, parks, and he assumed Vance was doing the same on the other side of town. Yet Sonny wouldn't unload his take once back at the van or hideaway hotel. For him, it would be a pit stop, then out, doing his usual scan for a gambling man, he would say. Which wasn't uncommon. Rodman was used to his partner's disappearances by now. What *was* uncommon was that time-after-time Vance would bop back home with a wad-and-a-half, claiming Dame Fortune was finally getting him off. And Rodman would make attentive faces and laugh and listen to the stories, while something in his guts said it was all a double-pump goof, a light show, a perfumed shit-shower. Yet he said nothing, bogarted his joint, finally rode into San Francisco like a lamb, not to slaughter, but casually slaughtering other lambs as naive as he.

Pat Dokes squeezed Rodman on the shoulder, and he stopped writing.

"I thought you might need food," she said almost apologetically.

Rodman touched the top of her hand. "Thanks." She placed a plate of broiled chicken with lemon sauce next to the stationery on her desk. It looked pretty on round blue-speckled ceramic with a green sprig, garnished potato skins, and the sweetly sour smell from the yellow sauce coating the robust breast. It looked like a self-contained house and yard, orderly, neat, a patch of suburban nourishment. He devoured it, not realizing how hungry he truly was. Pat wordlessly ate beside him, her sitting up on the bed, listening to WROC soft music through a Walkman headset. Secretly, she would glance over or perk her ears above the sounds of a Whitney Houston single to hear whether Rodman muttered something her way. But with his head back hovering over the paper, and the pen top wavering, Pat put the dirty dishes on the rug, lay back and closed her eyes to a schmaltzy love song she knew would rip her heart out.

On paper, meanwhile, Rodman and Vance were truckin' down the streets of San Francisco with a few megabucks worth of righteous dope. They watched as schoolbus loads of college students, magic-bus loads of longhairs, and what seemed to be half the under-thirty (i.e. the only ones you could trust) populace of the planet pile into downtown for the long moratorium march west to Golden Gate Park, where there was to be a rally of speeches and oneness.

They worked the march, though Rodman began spectating more than spieling, fascinated by the sheer numbers; the waving to clapping spectators as though they had all just come back from the moon like scruffy astronauts, moon-children on the march; the signs to stop the war—NIXON'S THE ONE, with a hand, the middle finger of which designated the number; a poster of J. Edgar Hoover with oversized ears; a *Mad*-magazine style drawing of Alfred E. Neuman in a U.S. Army dress uniform with a name tag reading "Calley" and a subtitle that said: *What, My Lai?*—the singing in the streets; freaks with guitars strapped to their chests like M-16s playing whenever someone wanted a song and would join in; TV crews and sudden spotlights on a bizarre group of Mao-jacketed kids who took their fifteen seconds of fame and marched in hurried syncopation while "hut-hut"-ing with each jerky step; the chanting of "Ho-Ho-Ho-Chi-Minh"; a family on a park lawn with naked dashing toddlers, the father trying to erect a tepee; American flag hats askew on afro–Uncle Sams; wheelchaired vets shouting and hugging people; a girl with four-foot-long pigtails and tiny square-framed glasses blowing bubbles the size of basketballs and offering them to people as if the bubbles wouldn't pop to the touch, though that didn't stop her from joyfully offering someone else the next one, and the next, and the next, Rodman seeing something symbolic there somewhere, a kind of counterculture's Sisyphus.

One shoeless teen angel with a flute and a paisley smock looked Vance in the eye and said, "You are an eternity."

"No, babe," Vance said, "this parade is," though she just nodded and took it the *right* way.

"It's a *march*," Rodman corrected, and Vance shot him a quick up-and-down, Rodman not realizing the sharp snap in his tone.

But it was all this, this community, that affected Rodman a different way . . . that and the old woman. Especially the old woman. It was when their section of the march was in the process of turning the last corner, nearing the entrance to Golden Gate Park, when amid the songs and chants and applause and yells and chaos, Rodman spotted an old woman on a nearby curb, a cliché of an old woman at that. She was in a babushka and slumped, with a sucked-in face from having no teeth. She wore clodhopper black shoes, had a Slavic old-country air about her, and she was weeping, deeply, passionately. She would dab her eyes at one moment with what looked like a handmade handkerchief and wave it at the passing crowd at the next, and for Rodman she became the center point, the mind pivot, making him confused, frightened. She *was* an eternity, he had thought, beautiful and sad, someone crying for the dead, for her lost sons in other wars, for lost sons in the Vietnam War. She became all mothers crying for the children going to all wars, for the children marching these streets not being heard, for Rodman himself. She was his mother crying over what he had become, for his fucked-up head, for being outside it all and preying.

Rodman suddenly became flushed and embarrassed by his

self-serving greed, his being so alone, so apart from the brotherhood. He wore the tribal garb of the social outsider, but he was even outside the outsiders. He was their exploiter, the hash-for-cash man, harboring a soul closer to Nixon's than Hoffman's. Part of him had always seen these kids as losers, flunkies, or at best, naive, but he himself was lost, without purpose. Though thoroughly wasted to begin with, Rodman downed some blackies, wanted to feel high, buzzing, happy and with the people, but instead he started to feel sick, and left the park to the complaints of Vance, who saw their profit margin nosedive and drug-dealing history pass them by.

It was during this time, when Rodman became physically ill and stayed in his clammy, stained hotel bed days afterward, not eating, not sleeping, playing out a come-down scene, being sullen, mum, reading, hiding out, letting Vance do his thing, Vance barely acknowledging the ghost-freak in the room whenever Vance *was* in the room, which was close to never—it was then that Rodman came upon an article, pages deep within an old *Chronicle*, a column nearly only glanced at by thousands over breakfast coffee, flipping past to the TV time schedule for that night, but caught, hooked by Rodman's casting eye: BOY DECLARED OD VICTIM IN SCHOOLYARD. The article was datelined San Jose and six days old, just about the time the Egg men nested in Frisco. It told about eight-year-old Jesus Marco popping a bottleful of "greenies," all in one hand shovel, and having his heart explode. His friends said that Jesus bought a fistful worth of the pills earlier that day from "a stranger, some hippie cholo," and Jesus had said they were okay but nothing special, so when he got some more later, he downed a whole bottle "to feel the big one, the macho mind wave," they said. There was a photo of Jesus alongside the article.

Rodman let the newspaper fall to the floor and ran to vomit in the damp hotel's porcelain bowl. He had recognized the boy. And himself: he was that hippie cholo. He knew for a fact he sold the kid only phonies—he *knew* it! He was certain! He had made them up himself, using green capsules and baking powder. But the second sale . . .

Rodman ran nearly all the way to the public library, spotty-eyed. He used some loose change and bought a hot dog from a street vendor in order to supply him some form of strength, snuck it into the newspaper stacks and sought local papers that intersected the Egg men's route upstate. He mustard-stained one article right off from Santa Maria, second page, another boy, eleven years old, dead from a drug overdose, from greenies bought at a local playground. And another in King City, "Amphetamine Killer," and a third in the valley north of L.A. The *Times* reported a month back of an Oxnard child's death in his bedroom, a lone "greenie" found in his little brother's Batmobile, one he stole from his big brother before the fatal dosage.

And that was the thing, he thought. The fatal dosage. They were all killed by ridiculously high amounts of pills no sane person would take. But Rodman read on about how many ODs stemmed from addicts, who, after having used batches of cut or watered-down dope, then overcompensated and took more the next time, and if the stuff was potent, it laid them out. To be a kid *is* to overcompensate, Rodman thought. And he may have been selling them no-dope, zero-fiber, a bubble's worth, but the next guy was hitting them with the real thing. Double profits. Death by one-two punch. Rodman faked the jab; he knew who supplied the right cross.

Sonny Vance had barely licked the petite Grateful Dead skull tattoo that festooned the upper portion of a dyed-blond stone-mama's rump when the van's side panel shot across and banged its announcement of a visitor. Rodman leaped at the sleeping bag as the girl shrieked, was grabbed by the forearm and tossed naked outside the vehicle. Her clothes followed and the door slammed behind.

"Fucker!" she cried out, banging the side panel, bleeding from scrapes at the knee and shoulder from her fall.

Inside, Vance was scrabbling backward out of the bag, his soiled underwear nearly rolled across the middle of his crack from his sliding retreat.

"What the fuck did you do?" Rodman was screaming, nearly in tears. "What did you do to us?"

"What are you *doing*, man?" Vance screamed back, pulling up his shorts, leaning on the back of the driver's seat. "Cool out!"

"You killed kids, man!" Rodman shouted, nearly on top of

him now. He flung across the articles he had ripped out of the library stacks. They floated down like failed aircraft halfway to their target. "They're dead. Our dope. Or it should've been *our* dope, but you got a pill supply somehow and kept it yourself, didn't you, fuckhead?"

Vance was mentally dancing now, his brain fried and fruging, the truth, a skip-step. "I was gonna eventually cut you in, man, but, like, the way you get with this kid shit, not selling to minors or some crap—"

"We set them up for a fall, don't you get it? I sold them nothing. Then when you retraced my steps behind my back, you sold them enough to kill them."

Vance looked shocked. "What? All of them?"

"No! Not *all* of them!"

Vance shook his head. "So what's the problem?"

"What's the problem?" Rodman cranked his imitation up a notch. "You mind-blown turd! Four kids, that I *know* of, are dead, maybe more, because you led them to OD."

Sonny tucked his legs under his rear end and rose up to a kneel in a posture of counterattack. "Hey! I didn't do *shit*, man! Sure, I figured there'd be a few kids who would think what you sold them earlier was a 'just okay' buzz, and I'd give them a heavier taste. But I wasn't sellin' it pure. I wouldn't waste *good* stuff on them."

"So you cut the stuff—B.F.D. It didn't matter! They swallowed a truckload after me to compensate."

The curtain of control shaded Vance's face, a sneer crept up, and he sat back on his heels, his head cocked, his voice cold. "So what am I? Their fucking father? I'm not responsible for where they piss or what they eat or how much shit they swallow. I can't help it if their daddies didn't teach them their Tim Leary right."

The steadfast fuck-you posture stunned Carl. "What?"

"If they go 'Tune out, turn off, drop dead'—what are *we* supposed to do?"

Rodman lost it. There was no responsibility. He couldn't find it anywhere. Not in this panel truck, not in his life. What was the difference, he thought, between radar-bombing Vietnam villages filled with women and children from thousands of feet away in a cloud bank and drugging to death kids from a rainbow-van hundreds of miles away on Highway 1?

Zippo, zilch, nada.

He wasn't sure how the monkey wrench got in his hand, didn't even know they had any car repair tools along on the trip, but he found himself taking one, two, maybe five, six full-swing raps to a suddenly balled-up Vance, pummeling his side, hearing a rib crack, his screaming out, beating him again, then suddenly stopping short of a straight-down blow to the back of Sonny's head.

In retrospect, maybe it would have been better then, better to have caved in the little fuck's brain right there and avoided the tragic show playing out now—the farcical murder in the slum lot, Eric, Delia—maybe they would all have been saved if he had crushed Vance's skull then and there and served his time, then stayed an ex-con drifter, an alias in every small-town bank he could find. But instead he threw aside the wrench before the fatal blow and nearly broke down; then without a word, he fled the van.

So he became the drifter anyway, a cross-country runaway. At the hotel, he had hundreds in the satchel he'd hid behind the dresser mirror. He worked his way east alone, hitching rides, selling smoke, hitting the banks he had sequestered money in, collecting it all in bank checks, his nest egg now ostrich-sized. By the time he got back to Hollowsport, he had enough money to clean up his act, at least for a while, and then to buy into the Janus Mountain deal with Howard's assist, with Delia's prodding. The sixties had drifted off, its ideals, its excesses, but they were replaced. After establishing himself in the seventies, Rodman's recast sense of "being free" in the eighties had little to do with the sixties, with its proviso of living without the rules, but much to do with using those rules to take, to acquire, to empower. In some ways, Rodman felt he went from one form of exploitation to another, more legitimized, one.

And, as Braxton Cole had just proved, it was still filled with danger and dirty tricks. The dirtiest one was Sonny Vance's first letter a few years back, just after Eric's death and after almost two decades of noncontact, the one that recounted "your saturation bombing of grammar school kids," (Vance's emphasizing *your*) and the proof he would bring out, show the press, send to enemies—Carl's drug account ledger. No, Rodman did not take it with him when he abandoned Vance and his broken rib that day, never even crossed his mind in twenty years. (The dead children were always too vivid a picture there for him to notice a notebook.) Vance had sent a Xerox-copy sheet of a torn-out page showing a circled record of one transaction of many in Rodman's handwriting, Rodman selling "greenies" at the San Jose schoolyard, cholo to Jesus. An easy entry for Vance to find since Rodman deserted the flung articles in the van, too. Vance then asked for an obscene amount of money since the ledger book showed Rodman, and Rodman alone, would be implicated.

Did Vance truly have the whole account book or just that page? Did it matter? Why didn't he show up in his life sooner for money? Did *that* matter? Physical evidence was real, but psychological evidence was more so, and Rodman paid out of guilt that first time as automatically as a cash machine being poked in the belly by a bank card.

He would have thought he'd already paid. Eric's death for Jesus and the rest. Children for children. *Death for death.* That's what he had always believed. Then Vance's second letter brought about Rodman's killing Sonny. Which was paid back with Delia's death, a fateful murder that happened at roughly the same time, thus eliminating any alibi Rodman could have. But how "fateful" was it? It wasn't God-punishing irony that had him killing Vance while his wife was being killed. It was *known* where he was going to be at four A.M. that morning. It was on audiotape, listened to. If it was Fate, it was named Braxton Cole.

Rodman quoted from the article about Cole he had just read in the magazine Howard had given him at the cabin: "The only luck you should have is the luck you can control. It's called good fortune when you're empowered; it's called bad luck when you've lost. Life's that simple." That bug in his office was empowerment—over Pat, over him, over the whole development project. Rodman was ready to place his heavy thumb on that balance of power like a nickel-thieving butcher.

Rodman ended the letter with an emotional plea, an apology,

and signed it. He sealed it up inside one of the stationery envelopes within another hutch.

Pat Dokes felt disconnected and fuzzy when Rodman shook her, evening naps the worst to resurface from. In fact, she thought the moment dreamlike, his near-naked figure before her on the sheet. The body-shadow spoke to her and handed her something.

"Could you please deliver that personally? It means everything to me."

Pat nodded and took the letter, and the cool chest of his body squeezed next to her bosom, his skin enveloped hers, and she felt sadness in this dream because she knew that when she closed her eyes again, he would be gone.

25

THE EDGES OF her dream were silly: tiptoeing that produced modest thumps in syncopation with silence causing the bed to jar as though expressing a tremor of fright. She thought of those hippos in *Fantasia*, all big and orangey and light on their feet—thumpity, thumpity, thump—grand jeté, plié, arabesque—she thanked God ballet school ended in the third grade with a bad ankle, the wiping off- of at least one sweet pastry decor on her birthday-cake life. But Barbara's haze and shifting borders between the real and the not didn't prevent her from knowing it was her prima donna mother, the balletic beast Hallie, trying to be quiet, moving with frenetic stealth about her bed in her Sunkist-hued robe, making sure the medicines and prescriptive pills and ice water and towels and all the Clara Barton amenities were laid out within the room for her daughter's bedtime.

Hallie was her official fluffer of pillows, her hairbrusher, blanket tucker, and Barbara felt the paper pile on her chest, the receipts, the tallies, what she owed, the debts piling in her mother's martyrdom monetary account, Barbara's unlimited credit in that area, any area, her credit card fund courtesy of Big Bertram, Wheeler-Dealer of the World, buying into the family, Hallie able to play house, her dolly in her dolly bed— How her hair shines with each stroke!—and those judgmental eyes, her mother's retributive pity.

Barbara was getting close to the core; the dream edges, the cartoon nature of her grogginess, slipping, imploding, the center was darker, had teeth. A different kind of beast, not plump but narrow, slithery then suddenly stiff in attack, the snake tattoo—the strike, the strike, the strike—its bite and blows, the pain, her wanting to get past the numbness and the dark.

She opened her eyes wide and saw a light, a hall light, through the doorway; as long as there was a light, she could get past the core of the dream—these stupid pills screwing with her head!—her head pumping blood like a pulsating cock, those teeth, pull from the core, pull out from the core, pull it out from the core—

Barbara jammed her eyes shut but faced the light and let it seep through her lids' edges, out of the core, closer to the circle of white, to the fantasy, the playfulness, and yet there were still teeth even here nearer the border. She remembered seeing the hippo from the movie dancing with green, the alligator, tugging in two-step, but from the real, the green jacket, Army fatigue. Danny.

Danny was arguing, Hallie pulling on him, trying to get him away. They had been talking. Barbara and Danny. She had been talking to him and seeing his dark core. It was in his pants.

Barbara shot up in bed and cried out. She didn't know what.

"What is it? What's wrong?" Hallie shouted, pile-driving into the room from the hallway, eclipsing its light. "Are you all right? Was it a dream? Does something hurt?"

"Okay, okay, okay, okay," Barbara said with each short breath sweating, thinking, trying.

Hallie was already at the medicines like a confused but driven scientist believing he was on to something. However, the moment she spun toward Barbara, balancing a spoonful of bloodred liquid in a tablespoon, yellow pills cupped in the same hand, and a tall glass of cold water in the other, Barbara cried out.

"No! *No!*" And she swung her right arm out, flipping the spoon from Hallie's grip, the medicine drawing a crimson line like a slashing diagonal cut across Hallie's chest. The sedatives dropped straight to the floor and bounced under the bed. Barbara snatched the glass from Hallie's other hand and started gulping. The wave of tipped water spewed from the sides and onto her collarbone.

Hallie was shaken. "What—What in God's name, do you think—"

Barbara brought the glass down, nearly panting. "You don't understand! I need to . . . I need to . . ."

. . . *Think!* The alligator, the teeth, the core, *tonight*—it happened tonight, didn't it?—Danny fighting Hallie in order to talk to her. Succeeding. Barbara mumbling things to him. He loved her. He said he loved her. She said it, too. He was asking about the men, the snake, the core was black and . . . the men, where she might have seen them, the men who did this, did *this!* And Danny was holding her hand—

"Lie back, baby," Hallie said, trying to pressure each of Barbara's shoulders down to the pillow, but Barbara shoved the gesture away, her brain, her mind, her dreamy sense digging, why are you digging? Was that what she asked Danny tonight? Or was that only what she was thinking now? Because—yes!—because she told him, she told him about seeing those men, the Dembos, seeing them with Ryan one night, seeing them talk, knowing each other, had just remembered that, when Danny asked, had forgotten it, but she remembered when Danny asked, and Danny nodded and said, "Then Ryan may be the one who knows where my father is."

"I'll have to call the doctor again, missy, if you keep acting this way," Hallie warned, precariously standing up from her perch on the bed.

Then Danny kissed her, Barbara remembered the heat, the burn of his lips, dry, as though parched from exposure, his eyes two suns of purpose, but dark, the core was dark, he was showing his teeth—yellow—No! that was the beast—*Danny's* teeth, nice teeth, smiling, but Barbara saw the madness in the grin, the core in his pants, dark, black—

"Oh, my God!" Barbara exclaimed, her throat contracting, her face growing pale. "He has a gun!"

"What?" Hallie said, readying to grab hold of her delirious daughter again.

"I saw a *gun*—he was hiding a gun," she said, sitting straight up now, tucking her legs, kicking out from the sheets, rising, her faulty vision giving everything its own lurking double just behind.

"Who?" Hallie said, snatching at her. "Get back in bed!"

In avoidance, Barbara rolled over to the other side and slid from under the sheet, her feet touching the cold floor. "I have to call the police. He's going to kill him."

"Who's going to kill who?" Hallie asked frantically, hitching her heavy leg toward the foot of the bed to cut Barbara off.

"Danny. He's going to do something terrible. He's going to shoot his father."

"That's crazy," Hallie snapped. "It's crazy if you think that. It's your concussion, the medication—and *he's* crazy, if it's true. No police. We've had enough police."

Barbara and Hallie met at the bed's footboard, where both wobbled for different reasons, both breathed silence when their eyes engaged each other.

"Don't lower yourself to it," Hallie whispered in a hoarse, angry voice. "We've already been stained. . . ."

Barbara didn't answer, instead tried to body her way to the phone; however, Hallie used her leg as an anchor this time, her hand wrapped about Barbara's wrist, mooring her.

"Don't!" Hallie said defiantly.

Barbara glared back. "I hated it enough being put on a pedestal, but I wish to God you'd get down from yours!"

Barbara clenched her teeth and swung her arm in a circle, an impromptu windup to twist away from her mother's handcuff. The sudden forceful arm turn and Barbara's barreling through bent Hallie's upper body back over the corner of the bed, her leaden leg too far up ahead of her, skewing her balance, and she toppled backward onto the floor. She blurted out a cry of anguish not because she was in pain from the fall but because of what Barbara had just done. The whelping sob stopped Barbara mid-stride. She looked at her mother as she would a fish flopped onto the planking of a boat.

"And *stay* down," Barbara said, trembling. She dialed 911.

26

T HE PIER WAS quiet; the dunes of sand like sweeping
clouds, a hazy white in the offshore gusts and half-moon
brightness. It was almost too bright, Rodman felt. It gave an
extra dimension to the dormant machines, an aura of inner life,
especially when he had crept past the burrowed bulldozers and
sky-fisting cranes as though he were tiptoeing among dino-
saurs. Too bright because of his feeling exposed, right *there*,
now a hundred yards from the Mariner's Restaurant and Beanpole's sports bar, flat on his stomach atop the discolored planking, waiting. He might be seen. The reptiles might awaken.
Braxton Cole might see it coming, be that deadly step ahead.

It was all Cole's, this land, this ocean kiss, Cole and his
kingdom by the sea, developed through his well-applied effort
in securing the city council vote, the dark rumor circulating
that Cole had hired an independent investigator to unearth a
few council members' subterranean bones, so to speak, some
bones proving to be from a homosexual or two, a true arche-
ological find.

But wait! Rodman raised his head ever so slightly over the
pier's edge to get a better perspective. Blue dots on the hilly
white horizon appeared in bobbing sync like bouncing sand
fleas. Rodman dropped his head back down, the moon not his
friend, more like a night watchman's flashlight. No more exposure. He would try to listen for them somewhere above the
whistle of breeze and rolling ocean breakers, listen for their approaching footfalls; more so, he would time them, a stride a
bob, a second a stride, one-two, one-two, judging their distance, estimating their exact moment of approach.

After a few hour-long minutes, Rodman's body pulsed with

too much energy, his timing mechanism off, sped up, antsy—it wouldn't work. He had to risk being seen. His head rose pneumatically smooth and exactly so high in order to see it *was* them—yes—just the way they looked in the magazine. The duo was close enough to be somewhat recognizable in their march-formation run, yet vague enough to seem ethereal, untouchable in their ever-forward movement. That was Braxton Cole to a tee. The magazine article had told of a nearly blind, energetic man who bracketed all the door frames to his estate with marble so that through each archway he entered, his hands would touch flanks of cool stone, as though they were his guiding eyes. The smooth surface, the room-to-room passage, were elegant transitions of the day.

And here it appeared much the same. Burton, Cole's longtime companion and bodyguard, a lean and looming man of thirty-five, was jogging ahead of his precious benefactor, as though pushing the air itself aside, allowing Cole with his shock of glowing white hair to slipstream in his vacuuming wake, to make his run more effortless, make it another smooth passage.

As they ran beneath the pier and disappeared into its dank shadow, you could have sworn they were chimerical, a two-headed four-legged beast or simply Barbara's chariot with its snorting muscular horse and silver-maned king behind. At the same time, you could have also been struck by the moon's vibrant gleam off the empty, yellow waste drum that Rodman had raised with both hands high over his head at the pier's edge, could have thought there stood a raging wounded cyclops ready to dash his boulder at the passing ship of industry.

The drum was hurled downward the moment Rodman saw the frontal curve of Burton's skin-domed head appear out of the pier's dark netherworld. The dream was over. The barrel cracked Burton on the top of his skull, driving him forward into the sand, instantly unconscious. Cole, still in a reflexive rhythm, nearly trotted over Burton's body, his foot catching his companion on the calf of the leg, causing Cole to stumble, then jerk straight with fear. Rodman leaped on Cole, a full-weight drop, nothing athletically graceful or timed, the equivalent to a cannonball in an emptied pool.

Rodman pulled off his prey and stood quickly. Cole was

about to shout when Rodman gun-whipped him to the side of his cheek: "Quiet."

But Cole rolled over and mumbled, "Burton?" through his swelling jaw. Rodman glanced at the long-boned man, Cole's stallion, still breathing, his terry-cloth headband soaked red above his right eye.

"He's alive," Rodman said with a tone that was far from reassuring, then shot out his hand and snatched the goggles from Cole's face with a snap of elastic and flung them somewhere behind.

"They're prescription! Please!" Cole cried out, groping a piling to pull himself up.

"I know."

"I can't see!" Cole shouted, finally straightening up, his spine reinforced by the cylinder of sea-worn wood.

"I *know*!" Rodman repeated, then pressed against him, the 9-mm gun touching the magnate's quaking lips. "I know a lot of little personal things about you, Braxton. The *V.I.P.* article was quite thorough. I found your one A.M. jogs down the beach most beneficial to discover. Your punctuality is obviously another misunderstood aspect of people perceiving you blessed with mere good fortune. Luck is what you make. Isn't *that* your point? Responsibility for the self?"

Cole was breathing in stutters; a rivulet of urine cooled his inner thigh. "Who—what do—"

Rodman jerked Cole's head away from the shade and into the moon's spotlit view, then his own head as well, and looked him deep into his eyes from inches away.

"Rodman!" Cole shouted in a whisper.

"We've met once," Carl said, gripping him harder. "We had jackets and ties on then, but I think we were doing this dead man's grope underneath the business suits anyway, so I've just cut away the accoutrements, got us down to our essences."

Rodman released Cole and shoved him, the fearful man staggering backward, holding his knotting stomach. "Why are you doing this?" he pleaded. "I'll give you anything. Burton needs help. What is it? What do you want?"

"What do I want?" Rodman snarled, then flushed, feeling tears—wrong time for tears!—feeling the swell of possibility and impossibility beat in his chest. "I *want*!?" he shouted, then quiet, eyes lost: "I want my wife. I want my little boy. I—I want the Aquarius development, the new rehab, my bed— I want it *all* back; can you do that for me?—I want my life. I want my stinking perfect life!"

Cole could only drown in the silence, shake his head, not knowing what to say.

Rodman finally muttered: "I know about the bug."

Cole shook his head more vigorously.

"Is that supposed to be a denial?" Rodman asked.

"No, no, not that, I . . . So you know. I don't know how that changes anything. Please, a doctor for Bur—"

"Where's Vance? Is he alive?"

Rodman watched Cole's tucked-smooth face reform into anger. "You *shot* him, for God's sakes! You threaten me and hurt Burton for a question like that?!"

Rodman remained, not cool, but cold, his innards tense. "So then you must have had me followed to the lot. You knew from hearing my conversation with Sonny I was to meet him at four A.M. on Tuesday morning—"

"A blackmail. Yes, yes," Cole said wearily. "We knew you were being blackmailed, so I had Burton ready at the point of your meeting to take pictures. As it happened, unforeseeably, he was delayed, but in time to see you pump bullets into that weasel-friend of yours, saw you put the body in a Dumpster and leave. Burton phoned me and asked what he should do. I told him to put his gloves on and extract the body, leave it in a safe place, until I could call you later that day and kiss your ass good-bye on competing for the Aquarius racetrack land. I didn't care you killed that scum, but you had to pay *me*, if you weren't going to pay society. Burton also found a bloodied pin with your boy's name on it in Vance's fist. So we wouldn't even need his eyewitness testimony. Wouldn't need him to be within miles of that lot. Your dead son's pin would point you out the minute we let the body be found through an anonymous phone call to some friends on the force."

Carl watched Cole nod at what he himself had just said, absorbed in the web of his own spinning, admiring the intricate design. Like all powerful men, even while trapped in subordinate, moreover threatening, positions, you give them the floor and they slowly evolve into the power player again, speak as though they were the ones with the insider's knowledge or, more relevant to this circumstance, the loaded weapon. Rodman felt this cocky-assed fuck needed to be reminded about which direction the muzzle was pointing.

Rodman took an aggressive step forward, showing a wild-eyed readiness to shoot. Cole flinched bodily, but Rodman surprised himself as well. He *was* ready to shoot, more than ready.

"So you *had* me, you son of a bitch! Why murder my wife, too? And Xavier. Were *you* Mattera's client? Were *you* my boy's killer?"

Cole seemed dumbfounded. "What are you raving about?"

"My *wife*! You *killed* her. You knew I was going to be at that lot and you had her murdered, knowing I would have no alibi—"

"That's absurd!" Cole protested. "I had you cold and out of the Aquarius deal just by your association with that Vance fellow, even if you were merely paying that lowlife off for whatever he had on you. Your killing him was like a Christmas bonus. Why would I kill your wife, too?"

"Because she knew something. Something through her macho Point Crescent P.I. Frank Xavier, something about Eric's death. You had them both killed to save your ass, or maybe Burton's—he's your *driver*, too, isn't he?—and then you pinned me for it."

Cole's brown round face changed during Carl's last summation as though he were starting to realize something, something muted clicking in his head. Then an expression of true sincerity swept over him. "I swear! I *swear* I don't know any Xavier. And I *never* had your wife killed."

Rodman was losing patience, losing the touch of the real in this fuzzy moonglow. "Then who did it? This wasn't luck; this wasn't fucking fate or bad fortune. This was planned. This was known. What about those Dembo boys?"

"Who?" They were so good at it, Rodman seethed. He had gotten the hang of it himself, learned it, used it, but for these guys it was inbred.

"The scummy twosome your ex-jock friend Ryan employs to strong-arm deadbeats and rape girls."

"I know nothing about that." Cole's voice had the ring of court testimony to it. Rodman gripped his gun tighter and shoved it closer to Cole's stomach. Cole put his hand out as though to ward it away. "I *know* Sam Ryan has his shady side, I know that, but I see nothing, so I know nothing."

"Severe nearsightedness comes in handy in big business, I'm aware. That still doesn't solve my problem."

"I can't help you," Cole said flatly. "Please, think of Burton—" The feeling had left his voice. Burton was no longer a faithful injured employee, but a convenient bargaining chip.

"How about the tape?" Rodman pressed. "Who else heard the tape?"

"We must get Burton to a hospital. Immediately."

Rodman felt the stonewall, the deadpan deal-breaker, the deaf and dumb power move. "Who else heard, dammit!?" Rodman was sweating; a fall ocean breeze, the cold heart of night, and he was sweating, building heat.

"Look, you must stop this," Cole insisted. "For your own good."

"Who else knew!?" Rodman began stepping forward, Cole back.

"You're still a very well-off young man," Cole reasoned in his retreat, like a squinting dark sage. "You'll have the best lawyers. You'll be able to get off lightly with the right persuasion. We can work some arrangement. I swear. Just stop everything now."

Rodman's grip on the gun tightened, as though cramping, his patience wrung out of him, moving forward. "I swear I'll shoot you if you don't answer me."

"You have too much to lose by doing this—"

"I have *nothing*, God damn you! So I have *nothing* to lose." Rodman's face twitched with recognition, and he snorted a laugh to himself. Then his trigger finger spasmed. Cole yelled. A sharp crack. And a bullet slammed into Cole's right shoulder.

"How does it feel?" Rodman shouted in rhythmic cadence. Cole's palm slapped the wound quickly as he cried out, his

hand acknowledging the tearing impact, his expression not. He started panicking, lurching backward, eyes no longer cold with calculable solutions, but bewildered and begging, locked on the weapon that pierced him.

Rodman stepped forward for every step back that Cole took. He shot again. The snap of a stick on a tight-skinned drum. A purposeful miss near Cole's other shoulder. The bullet paths were deadly walls squeezing Cole's options. He made no sound, his heart experiencing a stasis of shock.

Cole's voice was suddenly hoarse. "Please, no."

Cole searched, but there was nothing in Rodman's cratered eyes for him; nothing there to save him. Rodman raised the gun to eye level, set a bead on Cole's forehead.

"No!" Cole cried out.

Cole's last ducking step backward set him unknowingly at the top of the dune and he lost his balance, the smell of his own blood, sweat, and feces suddenly confronting him like a final humbling prod, and he tumbled down the other side of the embankment.

Rodman stood at the crest watching the wounded man roll. Cole got the idea. As Carl foot-slid down the steep side of sand to the shivering heap that was a real estate magnate on better days, he realized that Vance wasn't dead at all. Vance was alive in him. Was always a part of him, the part of himself he denied, the "sick fuck."

Cole's tiltawhirl down the slope landed him abutting an oversized tire on a bulldozer. His face was bespeckled now, granular, as though his brown skin were really coarse sandpaper. Cole moaned, then barked out in pain as Rodman sat down on him full-weight, straddling Cole's jumpsuit at the abdomen. Rodman thought he saw more thick blackness surge from Cole's wound like toothpaste from a fist-slammed tube.

"Now!" Rodman said. "Again. Did anybody else besides you and Burton hear the tape?"

"Doc . . ." Cole gasped, ". . . tor. Please call a doc—"

"The quarter's in the slot, but I asked did anybody else—"

"Yes!" Then weaker: "Yes . . ."

"Who?"

"Just a few—few members, that's all, members of the law firm I employ." A breath. "Winetraub, Dryer and Magee."

Rodman suddenly looked away, staring out, not wanting to go on, waiting, waiting for the next foamy roll of waves to suck him in, for the night sky to explode in a star shower, for the general to become the specific. "Jesus," he said quietly. He knew. The bastard was there and he *knew*.

Cole grabbed at Rodman with little strength or threat. "Help me now. Please. Help me."

"Jesus, God," Rodman said, not paying attention, plucking Cole's clinging fingers off him the way he would after walking into an unseen spiderweb in the dark. He rose and Cole's upper body rose partway with him, as though attached.

"No!" Cole screamed, falling away as Rodman marched off slowly, trudging up the dune, gathering himself, letting it all reheat and vitalize the core.

"Please!" came the voice behind, beyond the swirl of high sand now, like a faraway voice, a trick of the wind and sea. "Rodman! Help me!"

With each kick of sand, Rodman moved faster and faster, building speed, breathing harder, stuffing the gun in his waist, trotting now, focusing in on his own shadow before him, the shadow leading him.

"Rodman!" sang the wretched water.

He was running now, aiming for the parking lot.

"Rodman!" whined the cold brutal wind that now gusted, pushing him. "Rodmaaaaaaaaan!" He was running as fast as the shifting smooth granules would allow, his feet sinking with each stride, puffing, strained by the treadmill game the sand plays.

Then came the shots, two of them. The one sprayed a bloom of sand five feet to his right and ahead, so he knew the bullet must have come from behind. The second buzzed by his ear, a rocketed bee whose fatal sting landed past him unseen. He dove to the ground. Probably Burton, he thought, but didn't look back, didn't dare, didn't want to see a groggy lug with a gun, but he never stopped churning, scrambling on all fours for a while, moving, still moving, lifting himself on the move, then running crouched, then running full-bore again on harder sand this time, moving faster, and another idle shot from behind came nowhere near, and he finally reached his car and he stopped and he panted and he stopped panting. And he listened. No sirenlike melodies of his name in the wind. It was approaching police cars.

27

I T WAS ONE damn embarrassment after another. He was just picking his gun up, too, like lifting something to feel its weight, its *there*-ness. Had it in his hand not ten minutes ago. He liked his little .32. He could almost hide it in the fold of his long-fingered hand as though harboring a small black bird. Fuck, Sam Ryan thought, he could grip a basketball with one hand, swing it around, toss it to a teammate like an apple you share at lunchtime. Used to grip his little brother's fat head in high school that way, too, and threatened to squeeze hard enough to pop his shifty eyes out if he caught him in his room. Teddy. In and out of how many bankrupt mail-order business ventures. Lives in a trailer park. Kids out his butt. Another loser, another embarrassment.

Not that the gun was that far away now, just behind the office's file cabinet crammed with inventory papers, but too risky. Like relying on anything with a Dembo name tattooed to it to do anything straight and neat and *right*! Fuck-asses self-destructed before he could lay his big hands on the drugs or drug money Sonny Vance squealed about when he was buried to his nostrils just outside. They couldn't even find that fuck Vance! Ryan figured they found Carl Rodman, though, or he found them. Either way, those muscle-dicked losers were now meat—one well-done; the other, the IQ of Salisbury steak. Played games. Slam-dunked some rich tramp. And so the Beanpole sat in his office with nothing, pulling his pud at one o'fucking clock in the morning. Then Death Valley got even deeper.

Ryan had just turned around from a bite of a leftover and too-dry turkey club sandwich, holding up to his mouth one of the bar's paper plates designed with the stitching of a baseball, and from nowhere there was this punk in front of him, quiet as sea fog, his having floated in the office like that, scruffy sort, wannabe hippie type only good-looking, wearing a rumpled green Army jacket. Didn't seem like he had shaved for a while or slept for more than three seconds the whole week. But there he was holding one sonofabitch ugly long-barreled gun up at him, some fucking Marshal Dillon model that looked like it weighed tons the way the kid needed two hands, tipping him forward slightly, and him trying to keep his heels grounded, back off the balls of his feet. And so Ryan stood there dumb-founded by fate, by his beleaguered station, holding an undermayoed hero instead of a loaded pistol. His life was one fucking humiliation on top of another.

Danny Rodman, of course, didn't see it that way. He saw a lean giant of a man with a drawn peevish face in the center of block-long shoulders who looked as though he could reach out with a cranelike arm and snatch him up at any moment. That's why he approached Sam Ryan with the gun already out, knew it would take eons to raise the thing, let alone aim. His blood suddenly shot through his face with the flushed hope that it still worked at all.

"Let's talk," Danny said, feet spread for stability, arms out, one eye down the muzzle.

Ryan managed a day-long blink of his eyes, then, his mouth having lost all pockets of moisture, removed the cakey ball of overchewed sandwich with his right hand and flicked it into the empty trash can in disgust. It *thucked* as though glued. "Let's," Ryan sighed, "What's the topic? Personally, I wanna play, 'Who the fuck are you?' But it's your call."

"I'm Danny Rodman. I'm looking for my father, Carl. Carl Rodman."

"Oh, please," Ryan said, rolling his eyes, moving closer to the file cabinet, to maybe a better shot at the .32, maybe a 4-to-1 he could—*zip!*—snatch the heater and, before the long-hair knew what finger to pull, he'd plug the little queer. Too long a bet . . . for now. "What? Did he swipe the joints you had stashed under the Axl Rose throw pillow in your room? You know where Sonny Vance is?"

"Stop moving!" Danny said, shifting a few degrees left, following the big man, who seemed to be inching in that direction like a bone wave, his head first, then his chest, then waist, then knees and feet. He was tall enough so it looked as though his body was almost rippling slowly west.

Ryan put his hands up in innocence. "All I want to know is if you and your father deal the stuff together. He run out on you, too?"

Then there was a shot.

It was distant, outside, could have been anything, but with all the guns around, in perspiring young hands, in the mind of business-weary jocks, it was the first thing that was assumed when Danny's and Ryan's eyes suddenly met.

"What was that?" Danny said anyway. Ryan shrugged. There seemed to be a wail, a human voice, attached to the back end of the noise's echo. Then another shot.

"It's coming from the construction site on the beach," Ryan said matter-of-factly, able to shift that much nearer the cabinet with Danny somewhat distracted, that much nearer the dark gap behind, just about close enough—give it 2-to-1 odds now—not bad, but about two inches more and they would be even money and worth a lucky spin.

Then there was the most amazing sound of all.

Danny's eyes widened, his head vibrated slightly; even the disaffected Ryan reacted with curled brow.

"Was that my name?" Danny asked.

Ryan made a face. "Your mommy calling?"

Danny didn't like the crack, and his emotions showed it, but once again, like the ghost of a drowning man, came the eerie incantation of his last name, desperation entangling the elongated last syllable.

Danny couldn't just stand there anymore. He bolted out of the back room, and it took a second of dead space for Ryan to realize that Danny had done so, and with such speed. Ryan lunged for the file cabinet, jamming his shoulder into the top edge—fuck!—snatching once, twice, at the gun and finally grabbing it, hoisting it up one-handed like a prize fish unsnagged from a scooping net.

Danny had already clamored outside, craning his neck, his ears, trying to listen, trying to see, and amazingly he did see, see a man trotting, then breaking into a run toward the far car lot. The man's back was almost flush to him, but he knew that run, knew the gait from many a memory's rerun, from a kid's game of "chase," from tossing a high and deep Frisbee and watching him try an over-the-shoulder snag as though it were a touchdown pass from Joe Montana. It was definitely his father. His blood told him; his hatred listened.

Danny streaked forward, pursued him for fifty feet then stopped, realizing he would not be able to catch him with his having such a formidable lead, so he dropped to one knee and pretended his family's destroyer was a bobbing, syrupy fruit can, and he squeezed off two rounds, the second nearly piercing the back of his father's head. But nearly was not good enough.

Meanwhile, Sam Ryan had lumbered determinedly out of his office, fisting his baby .32, ready to take on the kid or whatever else was out there fucking up his night, but within moments he saw the danger sign of telltale red, which caused him to falter and stop: the scarlet flash of a police car's whirling roof light was painting the wall in the hallway from the wide front window of the bar, so Ryan whirled around himself as well, just as adroitly as he used to when feigning a jumper then making a spin move to the bucket. He dropped the unlicensed .32 into a white push-in waste can for later pickup, buttoned his double-breasted blazer, and nonchalanted himself back into his office to finish his taste-free sandwich before the cops arrived.

Up the beach, Danny had run a few more yards or so and fired again, though he knew it was hopeless at that distance and visibility. His father had reached his car and was ready to drive away. Danny cut back to the side of Beanpole's where his motorcycle had been tucked between a Portosan and a seawall. A policeman walking out to the boardwalk caught the corner of his eye as he revved his engine, and the cop's older partner shouted something at Danny that he couldn't make out because of his insulating cycle helmet. But what could the cop say to make him stop now? What could anybody say? Not a thing.

Danny kicked off and throttled down the other end of the unfinished boardwalk, away from the approaching fuzz, spun wide through a scoop of sand, spewing grains out from the back tire like scattershot, then out to the highway, narrowly avoiding another approaching police car that abruptly skidded, swerved, and nearly back-swiped a parking lot lamp post.

Danny watched his mother's Mercedes flying down the coastal highway, which had only sporadic traffic at this hour. He tried following a safe distance back, screened behind a surfer-decaled sport van that was busting the speed limit with enough horsepower to keep up with Rodman for many miles. However, Danny would dip in and out of concealment at approaches to highway turnoffs to make certain the Mercedes wasn't exiting. It took great willpower on his part not to thrust himself out there, rocket up to his father's car, knock on his window and wave, zoom past, spin around a quarter mile up, then come barreling down like a human bullet, straight on, the death dance, a final fiery meeting of the minds in oblivion.

The sign for another exit flashed past, and Danny was stunned out of his clouded fantasy. He ducked out from behind the van on instinct and heard a piercing beep, a short squeal, and throwing a sidelong glance to his right, saw a black Vette from hell, which must have been bombing a century's mph, blasting up the right lane, veering to avoid staining its tires with Danny's ass. Danny swung back left, tried to brake gradually, but the torque was too great. His bike struck the curb of the highway's grassy divider and flipped. It hopped once at one end then smashed sideways into the metal barrier, a wheel breaking off. Danny was luckier, most of his body landing in a large bordering shrub, except for his left arm, which snapped the moment it struck the packed-in ground beneath the bush. He cried out more in frustration than pain, more in anger than in need of help, as with one scratched and bleeding hand he unstrapped his helmet and pushed it off his head.

Getting to his feet, Danny made sure of his balance, sure that his light-headedness would still allow him to run, for run he did, avoiding a honking Volkswagen and across the three-lane highway toward the exit ramp. The sport van he'd been following had pulled aside a hundred feet away, its teen driver shouting after him, "Hey, bro', you okay? Hey! *Hey!*" Out of breath, and clutching his broken forearm to his body like a dying baby, Danny stopped and caught a final glimpse of the red taillights to the unswerving Mercedes, which had departed the highway at this point, Exit 12, and took a right on Domino Road a few blocks away.

Danny knew Exit 12, knew Domino Road, knew what was less than a mile up that road, and who. He sucked in some air, and after clenching his teeth, began striding forward.

28

HELEN ABLE, JACK and Delia's mother, had some Woolworth's plaque that one of her grammar school students must have given her when she was hospitalized once with a dysfunctional kidney, and it said something about knowing what can be changed and knowing what can't be changed and knowing the difference being the most important. God was in there somewhere, too, as though He was supposed to help to sort it all out somehow. Jack Able himself was very clear about what could not be changed, about what wasn't in his immediate control, so as a child, he would use that as a rationale for wishing people ill fortune and for particular events to go very wrong, like his aunt Grace should have a minor car accident on the way to his house so as to prevent her from babysitting. He figured, so what if he wished an opposing ballplayer, especially a New York Yankee, to strike out or even be injured to a degree (or at least for the duration of the three home games against the Red Sox, maybe longer if necessary), because his sitting at home and watching it on TV and just wishing it clearly had no effect on what was going on at Fenway Park miles away, or with Aunt Grace's Ford, for that matter, unless you believed in ESP or bad karma or ridiculous things like that, and Jack didn't.

In fact, Jack Able felt free of guilt when hoping the worst for others throughout his growing up—because he hated feeling guilty for *anything*, especially pure fantasies like praying that certain people in high school would drop dead, teachers and fellow students alike, or that certain friends or relatives keep meeting the "wrong" girl or guy and remain unmarried, all of course for purely selfish reasons, sometimes envious

351

ones, but again, to what end? What possible effect could he
have? He would never deliberately sabotage a relationship—
except once in college for his sister's own good. He would still
give a person objective advice about the paramour in question.
He *was* able to distinguish these self-serving wishes from un-
biased evidence. That's what made him good at law, after all.

When he grew older, the practice was just as ineffectual: no
matter how much he wanted his chief rival at the firm, Henry
Cowl, to hook his driver into the lake at the country club in
front of senior partner Langston Weber, it rarely happened, at
least never corresponding to the exact time of the heartfelt desire. Even wishing people hurt or dead as an adult, so what?
Who hadn't wished some public figure dead? Some young lib-
eral wishing a President Nixon dead? Some white-sheeted
KKK wishing Jesse Jackson dead? Some high-culturist wishing Madonna laid out on a slab? Would Henry Cowl die if he
wished hard enough? No. But what if he *knew* Cowl would die
if he wished hard enough? Would he? A hypothetical. Ridiculous to answer, usually, but he would say *no* in this case and
say it resolutely to himself. Able thought he would stop wishing for such a destructive fate if that were the case. But again,
rationally, he had no effect on Cowl's health, or Saddam
Hussein's or his brother-in-law Carl's. He could wish them all
homeless, toothless, and stricken with AIDS, and with what
real results? None. So Able logically concluded from childhood on that he could hate anyone or anything with impunity
since the hatred affected no one.

Of course, this was a lie.

That it affected no one in public life was true; that it had little
effect on his friends could be said to be true, too, though former
friends were always wary of petty retribution; that it never disturbed his relationship with wives, or sisters, or family in general was debatable, especially in the area of feeling free to
sharply criticize at will. Obviously, the one it most affected was
Jack himself. He harbored free-wheeling hatred and wished for
self-aggrandizing goals with little regard for how it soured his
outlook on life, his spiritual well-being, his subconscious
makeup, how it became darker, boiling with arrows and spears
of critical distrust. It allowed his ego to grow, his voice to bite,
his general aspect to appear even more distant with each passing

year. Distrust became disregard; a happy inner doom-wishing fronted by a false face. He had made the split between his empathetic spirit and cool rationality as wide as a ravine. And maybe it was his soul that fell in. Maybe the thought became the deed, the act just a natural follow-through like swinging a golf club. What other explanation could there be?

The shocking sound of shattered glass could not be more disturbing. And with it, Jack Able leaped out of his bed, blinking furiously, his heart palpitating. The sound had come from downstairs. His ears primed, his eyes attempting to adjust, he quietly slid open the night table drawer and fumbled for his handgun; then he rose and one-armed a green silk robe over his pajamas, still listening with a kind of stunned ferocity. He stood and gathered himself, feeling his muscles stretch then tighten, ready themselves, and he left the room, armed and primed. He slowly padded downstairs.

Dim moonlight cut through the front door's high-perched panel of sunburst glass and shimmered on the blue foyer tile, creating the illusion of water, a small sea within the hallway, an ocean to cross in order to discover what was waiting on the other side. Able moved cautiously into the study and saw the curtains flapping like rubbery arms in a panic caused by the large jagged hole in the frame window. The window was still closed, however. Then, in half shadow, he saw a rock laying amid diamond-shiny shards on the blue throw rug. An act of vandalism at Hamlet Hills Estates? Christ Almighty! Able put the gun to his side, stooped and picked up the stone, examining it as though the ruffian's return address were printed on it somewhere.

Suddenly, his wrist exploded with a jolt from being swatted with something hard and metal, his gun falling, then being kicked from behind by a sliding foot, not his. As he turned, the metal rod (which he immediately recognized as one of his fireplace utensils) was thrust into this stomach, jabbing him just above the waist, driving him down into a wind-depleting fold and dry retch. Then it was up again, against his stomach muscles' will, this time yanked up by the neck, the poker across his throat, pulling him back, two strange hands on either side and a knee sharply driven into his back. He fell into a forced kneel, and Rodman's maniacal face appeared just over his left ear from behind, jarring him further.

"It's me, Jack," Carl said with clenched jaw. "Just your fugitive brother-in-law playing his tricks. You see, first you throw the rock, then you reach in and open the window lock, raise the window, let yourself in, shut the window behind and wait. Then the jerk who owns the house comes in, thinks it was some passing punk who likes to smash parts of pretty houses, and the jerk drops his guard. Then he becomes like you now. You know where I learned that? I didn't. I made it up tonight. I can't tell you how resourceful being wanted for your wife's murder can make you. Or how angry. Or how hungry for revenge."

Able was nearly choking but his own hostility kept him tense, alert. "I had the house alarm set, you know. The police will be here soon."

Rodman nodded and spoke directly into Able's left ear. "Yeah? Tell somebody who gives a shit. Now move!"

He threw Able's face to the floor, though Jack managed to buffer the impact with his hands, both of which then gripped his own throat in response to its release. He coughed and sucked in the stinging night air funneling through the glass hole. Rodman motioned him up with his hand, and Able complied slowly, his eyes secretly searching in the dark for his spun-off gun, but Rodman produced his own and this sped Able along.

"Let's go to your office for some business," Rodman said. "That's what we're supposed to be good at, right?"

Able trudged up the curving stairs, still rubbing his Adam's apple, sensing the weapon and its seething bearer at his back. Inside the oversized luxurious room, Rodman switched on a small silver table lamp that stood opposite the black triptych desk, which in the stark singular light grew blacker still, its physical spread that of a manta ray. The Gothic-arched window behind was uncurtained and allowed the cool moonlight to illuminate the other parts of the room with just enough sharpness. Nothing had a true edge, except maybe Rodman's voice.

"I want to see your appointment ledger," he announced.

"It's over there," Able said, still raspy from the choke hold. With his chin he indicated a small stand-alone lectern opposite the front of his desk, almost as though guests to this grand room should sign in. In fact, a feathered ballpoint arched out of a phony ink well, trying as hard as it could to look like an ancient quill. With his gunless hand, Rodman picked it up, glanced at it, then back at the man he was pointing a bullet at. "Gives that feel of importance to the day ahead?"

"Whatever you say, Carl," Able replied, Rodman not certain the remark sarcastic or surrendering.

The book itself was large and weighty, hardcovered with a hand-stitched leather overlay and binding. The pages were woven and tinted light gray, each day edged in gold trim. Rodman flipped to the previous Friday and scanned down the page, his peripheral vision still attuned to the impatient Able. Nothing. He tried Saturday, and in the one P.M. slot he found it: a meeting—Able and Collin Magee, the junior partner—at Cole's offices.

"God," Rodman said aloud, though faintly, sadly. Like most things you know but only *feel* after they are confirmed, the actual evidence gutted him; Rodman's face drained. He pictured the tape playing, Cole nodding to himself, sensing the Aquarius development slip silently into this billfold, pictured Magee probably pleased that his biggest client looked pleased, and then there was Jack. Happy Jack. Or was Jack just puzzled at that point? Or was he relieved? What *was* he, anyway?

Rodman looked to his brother-in-law, whose eyes showed fury in one blink and fear in the next.

"Let's do this right," Rodman intoned. "From the beginning, then."

"Beginning of what?"

Rodman grimaced. "You really want me to shoot you *now*, don't you? You don't want to live these extra ten minutes. Is that a sense of guilt or stupidity, or are we still doing the hubris thing, motherfucker, because if it's *that*, I'll make you watch each bullet hit you, I swear. This isn't meant to be a civilized conversation. I jumped out of the evolutionary cycle—I don't know, yesterday, maybe before—anyway, we're out of the loop. So when I say the beginning, I mean, the night you ran my little boy down, fucker. I mean, the night you left him bleeding there and sped off. *That's* the beginning of the story. It was the start of the end for me, but it was the true beginning of your kind of evil, wasn't it, Jack? *You* killed him. Tell me. I know you did, now *tell* me!"

Able flushed. "I didn't mean—"

"You didn't *mean* to run him down, how very noble. I respect that. But backing up or stopping or helping or owning up, well, you had to *think* about it. So tell me, you were just coming to drop by—"

"No!" Able snapped. "I mean—I was in the area, down the street really, at another client's home, a little gathering of forces, and—"

"Were you drinking?"

Able looked as though the interruptions were making him lose his train of thought. "I think so."

"You don't remember? You're not drunk now, are you? How can you not remember?"

Able began rubbing his temples with the flat of his hands as though manipulating his thoughts around. "I had my share. But—look, I thought I was okay, I was loose, I was going to drop by, surprise Delia—"

Rodman laughed. "You must have been very loose to want to drop by. So instead you *sped* by. Changed your mind? What?"

Able's hands dropped to his side. "I changed my mind." The reply had a numbness to it.

"And you sped by," Rodman repeated, but there was no response. Rodman looked down and tried to contain himself a few minutes longer, yet his tone was as direct as a bullet's trajectory. "The experts said Eric had to have been hit by someone going over sixty miles per hour on our little neighborhood road—now let's use the proper descriptive *terms!*"

"I sped by," came the robotic reply.

"Good."

Seeing Rodman's acknowledging nod, Jack felt he had to explain. "I—I didn't want anybody at the house to maybe see my car. I would have felt obligated to stop."

Rodman smiled a wicked smile. "Now *that* sounds like you, Jack, drunk *or* sober. And you hit Eric."

"I swear I didn't see him!"

"We've already established, counselor, that this wasn't premeditated bullshit."

"I didn't even know what I hit let alone who, except—" Able's pupils flitted up as though reexperiencing the moment. "—except when I slowed, I looked in the rearview mirror, I recognized the body."

"You mean the parts of my son that were still not meshed with the tar."

"Please, Carl," Able insistent now, "you *must* understand my position."

"Must I?"

"I couldn't go back. I couldn't tell my sister I just ran over her youngest child. I had—I—"

"You had your ass to cover," Rodman said.

"I had too much too *lose*," Able countered, his fist clenched. "I was on my way. My lines were connecting with powerful people. I would never be what I was supposed to be if I was found drunk and guilty of hit-and-run."

Rodman stepped forward, scaring Able for a moment, until he saw the puffiness in Carl's eyes, the depth of hurt there. "What were you supposed to be, Jack? My boy's loving uncle? Oh, no, sorry. High school class president. That it? Politics?"

Able knew that Carl, like Delia, didn't, wouldn't, understand. He pursed his lips. "Something like that."

Rodman let the bitterness of the moment pass like a deserted boat, drifting. Then he snapped on again. "Scene two: the hospital. Thomas Mattera, attorney to the gods, shows up representing his mystery client—you. Eric dies. The case is closed and so is Mattera's mouth. Lawyer-client privilege and all that good legal stuff. Then Delia trusts you to take care of hiring a private investigative firm *for* us, in order to find out who his client, the child killer, is. In short, with my suffering wife's heart and soul in your hands, you volunteer to help find *you*." Rodman dilated his nostrils. "Do I smell irony here or is that just your toilet backing up?"

The question was met with a brooding silence.

"What did you tell Barkley Investigations to do? Supply phony reports . . . ?"

"I told them that my sister was a hysterical woman who wanted answers she would never have," Able barked out. "So I paid them twice their fee to supply you two with something every month—dead-end leads, run-arounds. . . . I told them it would help ease her pain. They worked for our firm before—"

"So they owed you a favor. You scratch my balls, I cut off yours. Politics. I know it. Don't need to hear about it." Rodman started moving around, restless, yet his gun steady in its purpose. "But we move our story now, up a few months. We tell Delia that you and I decided to call off the dogs from Mattera—you, for obvious reasons; me, because I'm a shit who didn't want to face it anymore and was insensitive to my wife's desperate need. So Delia, without telling me, or *you*, obviously, goes to an out-of-town solo P.I. with a growing rep and excellent skills—Frank Xavier. He digs and he digs and he digs. Delia takes trips under false pretenses up to Point Crescent to see him, pay him, hang out with her newfound friend, Mary Dorlack, Xavier's right-hand gal. Then one day Xavier hits on something. It's Eureka time in Sam Spadeland. He knows who done it, won't tell Delia on the phone, probably considering who the fuck it *is*. Wants a quiet place. But Delia insists he come down ASAP. So he meets her on the sly at my party for Senator McMann. Gives her the report. Crushes her with the news about her dear, only brother. Xavier cuts out the back gate, to Hallie's dismay, and Delia burns up her copy of the report in the barbecue pit. My guess is she said something to you at the party. . . ." Rodman's eyes lit up and his hand pretended a lightbulb snap of the fingers. "Hey, I got an idea, Jack. Why don't you take the story from here? Nobody can tell a story the way you can. Not a good old-fashioned murder, anyway." Then noticing his brother-in-law's passive reluctance: "*Tell* it!"

Able complied. "She approached me close to dark when I was alone near the pool. She said she knew. She didn't have to tell me what she knew. I know my sister. I know that face. I made some attempt to talk to her, and all she said was, 'Come see me tomorrow morning. Early.' That was it. I had appointments that Monday, but—"

"But you canceled them! A trooper. A-number-one, J.A."

Jack was too absorbed in his own life's history to react to the slings. "I came down. She was cold toward me and yet bursting into tears every five minutes. I didn't know what to do or say. She made me drive her to the auto shop with the

Mercedes for service, as if she refused to let what she knew shake up her day-to-day life."

Rodman nodded to himself, thought: that explained Benny DiLauro's thinking he'd been with Delia when she dropped the car off, having seen a man with her.

"I kept trying to tell her why I did what I did," Able recalled. "I knew she knew what I wanted to do with my life, my career. I was hoping she would understand. But Delia . . . well, Delia would look through me as though waiting for the real explanation. There was no *real* explanation. It's what happened."

"So she was going to tell the police? She certainly didn't tell me."

Rodman suddenly remembered his sense of Delia's harboring something before going to bed after the party, like a child hiding a deformity from someone who might tease her. Why didn't she *trust* him with it? Rodman began to feel the growing wound after each pinprick of discovery.

Able shook his head. "She didn't say *what* she was going to do. She said she hadn't told anybody, and I knew that was true. It was what she *would* do. 'But whatever I do,' she said, 'I'll do what's right by Eric.' Then she froze me out the door. That's when I knew—"

"You knew you would kill her and frame me."

"No," Able said resentfully. "I mean, not right away. That's when I knew she would tell somebody, eventually. Maybe the police. Maybe you. Maybe somebody I needed *for* me, not against. She was unstable."

"Says Mr. Bedrock."

An otherness now modulated Jack's voice, a dead calm. He turned his back to Rodman. "I knew you would be tied up with Vance and not wanting to admit to being there at some blackmail payoff when you were supposed to be at the cabin. So I drove to your house about the same time as your meeting that Tuesday morning. I parked far from the house, but I got hold of an old denim jacket, the kind I saw you wear on our own little cabin outing, the kind you always wear up there. And I banged on the sliding door at the kitchen. Loud. I was hoping your neighbor Mrs. Fouche was as nosy as Delia always complained she was. I saw a curtain jiggle out of the cor-

ner of my eye so I figured I was spotted, or really, *you* were.
I shouted I forgot my keys. I don't even know if she heard
that. I don't think Delia did. She came sleepy-eyed to the glass
door. I could see she brought the gun she'd said she had gotten
for protection on your trips away. I was glad I didn't have to
use the one I brought. When she let me in, I took it from her
and pushed her down. I couldn't see much in the dark. It was
like it wasn't her and yet it was. I told her I couldn't trust her.
She was . . . she was too good."

Rodman bit his lip, forced back the tears. "Now *there's* a
negative," he mumbled.

"I left the gun there. I was wearing gloves anyway, so
there'd be only *her* prints, though I guess you had a few on it,
too. Caught a bigger break when I found out you shot that
Sonny Vance. There was no feasible way you could use *that* as
an alibi. I thought, unbelievable, things are really falling my
way."

"And all you had to do was run down your nephew, shoot
your sister, and frame your brother-in-law. It doesn't get any
better than that."

Able exploded, spinning around, tensing, but he stood back
from the gun. "I didn't *want* to do it, you wise-ass piece of
shit! You were always dirt; she was class. I *loved* her!"

Rodman shook his head at Able, almost shot him right there
for blaspheming, pushed down the feelings, made sure the
flood in his eyes retreated—no water show for Jack, no way—
took a breath. "We're losing it there, Jack. 'Cause, you know,
like your big beautiful desk here, there are three parts to this
story. Chapter Three: Loose Ends."

Able had again turned away when Carl started talking, Jack
hating himself for showing emotional weakness, hating Rodman for prodding it, stoking any sense of guilt or remorse.
"Xavier," he muttered almost without realizing it.

Rodman acted surprised, playing the puncturing showman
again. "Xavier, yes! Now we're rolling! Now we're picking up
momentum! Everything was breaking your way at that point,
right? The cops had me by the nuts. The Aquarius deal was a
lock. Cole was ready to anoint you and your associates the Fat
Cat Firm of the Year Award. But then I went and escaped.
Fuck me. Though in and of itself, it wasn't much. I mean, this

solidified my guilt, right? *The Fugitive* was a helluva show, but this was real life. The only one-armed man I knew was Zack, my friendly postal clerk, and I think he was on night shift that morning and could prove he was postmarking a birthday card at 4:02 A.M., so I was fucked anyway. Except—" Rodman raised a finger. "—except Howard, Howard who hates me the way only a best friend can. He calls you one night after hearing from me. He tells you I'm needing money, but he's setting me up for the cops, and says that your family's misery will be over with my recapture. But it fucks up. I'm a slippery S.O.B. Yet something bothers you even more. It's what Howard said I wanted the money *for*. I was going down the coast to the peninsula. Something like that. What peninsula could that be? Florida? 'Hey, Carl Rodman, you just escaped from the clutches of the cops and your betraying best bud and are wanted for murdering your wife, where are you going?' 'I'm going to fucking Disney World!' No, not Florida. Ah! Point Crescent. Oh, my! Could I have gotten wind of Frank Xavier in all this hubbub?"

There was no response from Able, who faced the wall bearing his degrees, his honors, his worth, weighing them, drawing from them, thinking that this was all right, this was okay, this was a way to stall for time, he needed time.

Rodman continued expounding his theory. "Before, you figured Xavier wouldn't hear about much of this. The case was closed, slammed in a cabinet drawer. He was never going to see a Rodman again. But now. Who knows? He had a file. A former client was killed. Maybe they were connected, maybe not. But you couldn't afford that, could you?" Rodman noticed Able's trancelike look toward the shiny framed artifacts on the high-ceilinged wall. "Hell-*o*!"

"No, I could *not* afford that!" Jack spat over his shoulder at Rodman. "I just wanted his copy of the file. I knew Delia burned hers with the evidence. She told me. So I went to steal it. I found out Xavier just about lived at that Ollie's Tavern almost twenty-four hours a day, especially with his phone out. So I broke in, took the file."

"Then I guess my move at Ollie's forced him away from the bar."

Jack turned completely around this time and paused, staring

Rodman down for a moment with sour puzzlement. "Was that you? Thanks for nothing." Then he shook his head, relived the scene. "I heard somebody come. I waited behind the door, and after he walked in, I just wanted to knock him out, but when I hit him, his head was like stone. He hit me back and nearly broke my ribs. We struggled, but I rolled us near the window, and when he kind of rose up to punch me while I was flat on the floor, I kicked out into this stomach and he fell back. Out the open window. I didn't think anybody really heard. The place was deserted."

"Then you typed up some bullshit suicide note. Generic variety."

Able seemed peeved. "Listen, I didn't know the man. How specific could I be? Anything to stall the police. Confuse things. Things were pretty confused already."

Rodman shook his head, the effects of having swallowed the entire tragic, comic, fucked-up story in one sitting making his skull pulse. He ran his fingers up through his hair as though to steady the blood flow. "Man. You're a regular fucking death squad. And you're still wondering why I've come here tonight to kill you?"

Able sneered at Rodman, his back straightening in spinal superiority. "And what are *you*? What did Vance have on *your* sweet existence? I heard the tape, remember? What did Vance mean by calling you a 'child killer'?"

"Hey, this isn't confession. And you're wearing the wrong-colored Italian robe to be a priest."

Able snickered, cinched up said robe with one taut tie-pull.

"You're more like me than you want to admit," he said. "You cut the right money corners way back when—once Delia and Howard got you rolling in the right direction—skirted the right laws, lubed the right wheels on the wrong tracks; only you were some hippie, peace-and-love schmuck before, and I was always this way. Maybe that makes you worse than me. Think about it. *You're* the one who's changed. *I* didn't."

Rodman was enraged. "You want points for *always* being ethical scum? Fuck you, Jack!"

Both men suddenly cocked their heads. A faint wail of sirens could be heard emanating from down the hill near the gates of the multi-estate development. Jack strode behind his winged desk and peered out the arching window to see if he could discern the glow of their red lights, too. Then he turned to Carl, feeling more confident, saved.

"So what did Vance mean?" Jack said, allowing the sound of the approaching police cars to slowly infuse him with strength, a revitalization of the system, the checks and balances, social stability. This scene would need no explanation to the police. There's a man with a gun over there.

Rodman studied his brother-in-law's half-lidded expression of disdain, his wife's noble face perverted by years of loathing and manipulation. If Sonny Vance was all that was dark and destructive about the sixties, the overt killing of children—the haphazard bombings in Vietnam, the pedaling of drugs to grammar school kids—then Jack Able was the personification of evil in the eighties and nineties—the death of the family, the buying and selling of the soul in the marketplace, *for* the marketplace. Not self-discovery through chemicals, but self-fulfillment through greed and reputation. Rodman had rid the world of Sonny Vance. He would rid the world of Jack Able.

Carl raised the automatic with both hands in order to aim it at Able's heart. Jack stiffened, his eyes flashed wide.

Rodman said, "From one child killer to another, Jack."

A cry rose and echoed off the cathedral ceiling: *"Stop!"*

But the plea wasn't from Able; in fact, it wasn't a plea at all, but a command, and it originated from Rodman's right, the doorway. It made Rodman flinch, whip his locked arms in a quarter arc, still on dead aim, and there stood his son at the nub of his sights.

"Drop the gun . . ." Danny said, and like a spat-out grape pit, added, *"Dad."* The long-barreled pistol was tucked in the V-crease of his left elbow so that his left hand could grapple his right forearm in support of the split bone. His cheeks were chalky; his eyes were erratically blinking. Even Carl could see the only thing holding him up was a sense of purpose.

"Thank God," Able said breathily and took an almost-step forward but swiftly took it back when Rodman swung the gun over in his direction again, shouting, "Don't move, damn it!" Then Rodman swung the gun back on Danny. "You don't understand, Danny. Your uncle—*he* killed your mom, not me."

Able injected, "He's desperate, Danny. He's hateful!"

Rodman could see that his son's eyes were bored-in holes of fatigue, yet flicking energetically, manically, left to right from father to uncle, uncle to father. Carl tried to get as much emotion in his plea as possible. "Listen to me, son. He's murdered us all. We're all dead because of him."

Able's intonation came from on high, the clear lucid sound of reason. "You *know* your father did it. The police know. *You* know."

Able backed closer to the uncurtained Gothic window and took a furtive glance below. He raised his hands to heighten the effect of what was taking place inside and shouted as loud as he could over his shoulder through the fragile glass, "I'm being held hostage! Don't come up!"

The police, who were originally alerted by Barbara's phone call to go to Beanpole's, where they heard shots, saw Danny roar off on his motorcycle, and found the wounded Braxton Cole, had asked for backup at the beach when Cole told them where he thought Rodman was heading. Cole's conjecture appeared to be true when they found Danny's bike smashed against Route 15's divider and a motormouth seventeen-year-old telling them about the awesome accident and how the biker was jammin' toward Exit 12. So now here they were, Officer Lansing pulling a baby bullhorn out of his trunk, hoping the batteries weren't dead, while his partner, Officer Key, watched Jack Able's back at the high window on the second floor. The cops from two other units unracked their car rifles and prepared themselves for the possible long night and for the arrival of the special crimes unit hostage team.

Lansing pressed the red button on the horn. "This is the police. Do not do anything foolish. Throw out your weapons and come out peacefully with your hands raised."

Inside, Rodman was ignoring the exact words, but the police presence brought the pressure level up, his neck knotted, slick with sweat. "There isn't much time left, Danny," he said tenderly, calmly, responding to the suffering that marked his son's face, his life. "Please, you have to let me shoot him. He ran over your brother. He killed your mother when she found out. He framed me, duped you—I'll explain everything. Only *after*. It has to be after."

Able bore in from the right. "He's *mad*! He's out of control. He wants to *kill* me, you *see* that!"

The Rodmans' guns still confronted each other, muzzle on muzzle; no matter how trembling, neither grip lessened.

Danny kept closed up in his numbness, knowing his heart would only twist things around, make him crazier than he was, split him in two—stop splitting me in two! His cheek was twitching, his finger hurting, his arm— He closed his eyes to push it all back. His voice came from nowhere. "I can't let you kill Uncle Jack, too. Please drop the gun, Dad."

"That's no good!" Able suddenly shouted to his jangled, scrungy nephew. "If the police come, he'll get off. He has connections, you *know* that. Your father is the establishment at its sickest."

Rodman was shaking his head at this son, deliberately, as though in a trance. "I have to kill him before the cops let him get away."

"Don't—" Danny said in a whisper.

The bullhorn blared from below: "I repeat. Throw out your weapons. And come out quietly. Nobody will be hurt."

"He'll get away," Rodman pleaded to Danny.

Able stated bluntly: "Your father is all that's dirty in the world today."

"He can't get away. . . ." Rodman's voice faded into nothing.

Danny started shaking his head, his voice getting louder. "Please, don't. Listen to me. *Please*—"

But Rodman swung his gun back toward Able, his finger already applying pressure to its trigger. A shot went off and a bullet pierced Carl Rodman's side between two ribs, its impact thrusting him against the ledger stand as though rammed by an angry gust of wind, his own gun firing a split second after, his own bullet veering from his aim, blasting a hole through the Gothic window up and to the left of the jolted Able. Then, with his gun having rocketed from his hand upon impact against the podium, Rodman began sliding to the floor, grabbing for support, knocking the ledger down to him, adding weight to his fall. His blood erupted and bathed the leather in a rich burgundy. Rodman landed on his ass with a small thump, sitting up, his eyes transfixed on his son, who was still locked in his shooting stance, his face drained of all hope, his grandfather's gun, hot from use, now a burden in his grasp. Danny flung the pistol aside—it clattered near the front window—and bolted to his father, squatted to him, shaking his head, grimacing in the pain he felt, the questions he had: all that hate exploding with one bullet.

At the shots, the police outside were on the move. Two officers were starting to batter down the front door, the two behind them ready to dash through, to race upstairs with loaded weapons shoulder-high and at the ready.

Meanwhile, Able had picked up Danny's gun from the floor. As he cocked the cumbersome pistol's hammer, he made sure he was out of sight from the remaining task force outside when he yelled to them: "It's okay. They were just trying to scare me. No one's hurt."

Officer Lansing waved the door-ramming team away from their duty for the moment, so as to listen.

"But they told me to tell you they have demands you must follow. Or they're going to kill me!"

Danny stopped helping his severely wounded father stand, his head snapping toward his uncle. *"They?"*

Able's face burned red, his determination hardened like lava rock, his necessities demanding feeding. "Sorry, Daniel. I'll have to tell them I was defending myself," he said, standing just to the other side of the desk, holding the archaic weapon at his waist. "Self-preservation," Able lamented. His eyes were touched with dazed madness. "It's gotten . . . so messy. Always having to clean up." He shrugged. It was as logical as he could get at the moment, raising the gun toward his nephew, Jack Able secure in his actions, at home in his platinum-shiny world where wishing made it so.

Rodman watched with rage the leveling barrel of his father's gun directed at his son. He embraced the throbbing, blood-pumping gash in his side, the pain—a thrust outward, a scream forward, a dark core to act upon.

"No more!" Rodman cried out, pushing his son away with his right arm, then springing up, gripping the ledger with both hands before him like a shield of armor. The first shot was absorbed by its thickness as Rodman leaped upon the desk. Able backed off, panicked, crumbling back toward the window but

getting off another shot, this one below the book and into Rodman's left thigh.

But it didn't matter. Rodman had already sustained enough momentum, gathered up enough ferocious energy for him to lunge downward with a gut-tearing bellow and dive onto the shouting Able, propelling them both backward and shattering the arched window behind, sending their headlong bodies in free fall. The stunned police below stared paralytic at the two men in flight.

The midair trip seemed endless, Able's mouth emitting an open song of despair, while Rodman dropped in a cocoon of silence. He had lost the ledger to the rushing air and had his two hands clasped onto the front of Able's robe in a last swirling dance. He saw his brother-in-law's pallor whiten even further than its natural tone, the fear in his face almost making it youthful, a child being frightened of the unknown. It brought a momentary glimpse of Delia in that brotherly countenance; there, even amid the terror, the beauty of innocence.

When they first landed, Rodman was compressed on top of Able, and he could hear, and most definitely feel by osmotic contact, Jack's back crack in many places, then saw his head split apart from behind, open flat, making his face a grotesquely spread-out mask of agony. But that was an instantaneous vision, as Rodman then bounced off his brother-in-law, flipped over, and hit the driveway. He felt his internal organs twist and slam and nearly snap off their connective tissues.

At first he just heard buzzing and commotion, people shouting at people, saw lots of blue, cop blue, lined brows and strange hands, and the pain started seeping in and he wanted to float away from it, from them, but then he saw a face he needed to see. It was Danny. Danny was stooped over him, close, breathing hard, a sad, frozen, handsome face. Rodman sensed himself far away reach out something, a hand, and press his son's chest, his fingertips and palm. Everything so still and breathless in his own body, he could feel and hear Danny's, feel the pulse of Danny's heart through his own palm, the steady tattoo of life, his life, his one redemptive life.

Danny embraced his father's hand with his, held it against

him, tight, then tighter. A droplet fell from Danny's watering eyes and landed on his father's cheek. It was one tear, but it was as good as an ocean, and Rodman smiled inside and sunk beneath it forever.

29

I T RAINED THAT day at the funeral, not in discreet drops or parallel sheets, but a spritzing in-your-face kind of rain. Danny remembered it raining in some form or another for every funeral he had ever attended, his mother's recent one included, and he remembered friends and guitar store customers remarking the same thing. It couldn't rain at *everybody's* funeral, but people must remember the times it did rain and put that setting in their book of memories for all of them, in order to enhance the brutal sadness, to paint it all as gray and dreary, and in some ways to establish a constant, a tragic thread through all our lives through death, a communal cliché.

His father was buried beside his mother and his brother Eric at Greenwall Cemetery, to the dismay of Danny's grandmother, his mother's mother, who resided in an upscale senior citizen complex in Arizona, and who would not attend the services.

In truth, the number of people at the church and gravesite were few. Aside from those paid to be there, including a local priest whose name Danny forgot, there was only Danny, Barbara, and Pat Dokes. After all, as far as the public knew, the police files were closed. History showed Carl Rodman to be a murderer and near madman. He killed his wife Delia and, according to the arresting officers, openly confessed it. Later, he burned to death an ex-con construction supervisor, Louis Dembo, and seriously wounded the real estate magnate, Braxton Cole, with an unregistered Glock 9mm. Finally, he pushed Jack Able, his brother-in-law, out of the second-story window of Able's own home.

All of these were strong reasons why Howard Bernbaum, or anybody from Triumph Corporation, or certainly Hallie and

Bertram Fouche, would not attend the funeral. State senator McMann considered it, but only as a political gesture to secure Triumph's hold on the Aquarius land. However, with Braxton Cole hospitalized in unstable condition, McMann felt that maybe he didn't have to go that far. He simply stumped to the press, saying that "whatever tragic end Carl Rodman may have come to, possibly stemming from his abuse of cocaine, it is all the more reason to push through the Triumph plan which includes a state-of-the-art rehab center to help fight this horrible disease that destroys the heart of this country." McMann would prove an even greater benefactor to the Triumph plan than once thought.

It seems that after the confrontation at the Able house, Danny was trying desperately to tell the police about how his uncle was about to kill Rodman and him, about how his father found out that Able had murdered his mom and brother and somehow framed his father. The police listened to Danny's rant with testy courtesy, at best sensing the boy was traumatized by the piling on of tragic events, at worst wondering if the kid was "doing" again.

"The point is—you're his son," they said. "Why should we believe you?"

Danny shook his head and nearly let out a pained laugh. "No," he said. "I wasn't. *That's* the point. That's why you should." But the police didn't believe, didn't understand, didn't have time to absorb the family history, the past few years of mutual resentment, the sudden brief bonding after the fall.

The next day, Pat Dokes sought Danny out, found him at his apartment. In the doorway, Pat appeared stunned and couldn't speak. She was too busy staring at Danny, inspecting his face, watching his father in it, seeing Carl's agonies live there, but also Carl's fortitude and rebellious drive.

Pat finally took the sealed envelope from her purse and handed it to Danny inside. His look asked a question.

"It's from your father," Pat said. "He said I should give it to you. He said it meant everything to him that you get it."

Danny took the envelope and saw his name written on the front in his father's hand. His throat locked and he could only glance at Pat and give a curt nod of thanks.

"Who was that?" Barbara asked from the bathroom. Danny

wanted to say, "My father" as his hand slightly quaked, holding the letter. He sat at his repair desk and flicked on the overhead lamp. He read it once, then read it again. The glare of the stark light on the white stationery hurt his eyes. But that wasn't why they were tearing. "I have to go," he shouted to Barbara, throwing on his jacket, and he placed the letter within its warmth at the place his father last touched him.

"Where?" Barbara said coming out of the bathroom. But she said it to no one.

At the police station, the letter revealed much more than a tragic story of cross-country drug-dealing in the sixties. It detailed the entire series of events leading up to Rodman's confrontation with Cole, including a confession to killing Sonny Vance in a certain lot, his body placed in a certain trash bin at a certain time, the same time Rodman was supposedly murdering his wife. Later, a blood test of Rodman's jacket would match the blood spots found in the bin. The investigation of Delia Rodman's murder was reopened and the life of Jack Able was being probed based on what Danny had said. Even Rodman's epistolary mention of the Frank Xavier "suicide" brought the Hollowsport and Point Crescent homicide divisions together to ruminate.

That was when state senator McMann received confidential information and reentered the fray, complicating the murder picture, asking for a complete investigation of Braxton Cole's operation and proclaiming the existence of a certain audiotape obtained through corporate espionage. Nobody knew at the time, but the information had been leaked by a Cole defector, one Henry Cowl, Jack Able's chief competitor at the law firm and prime object of his many internal mantras of hate. Cowl was angered by his lack of advancement at the firm of Winetraub, Dryer and Magee, and especially of Jack Able's quick rise and close dealings with the Cole project. He was working for the Triumph Corporation now and was the mole McMann had needed to push the Aquarius project and the Rodman Rehab Center over the top.

After the dark, drizzling funeral, Danny was standing inside the front foyer of his parents' home, his helmet bowing his right arm, hugged to his side. He was waiting, his weight shift-

ing from leg to leg every few minutes with impatience, yet
there was no sign of it in his face. Pat Dokes had come back
to the house with the young couple, brought in some lunch she
had made for them, knew they were leaving town, needed to
see them off. She had promised to take care of things, the probate, the lawyers. She owed the family that much.

"Where are you guys going to go?" she asked.

Danny shook his head. He wasn't being sullen or incommu-
nicative or withdrawn. He really didn't know.

"What do you want me to do with the house and things?"

Danny appeared to have never considered the question
until that moment, yet it didn't bother him that he hadn't. His
tired eyes briefly scanned the immediate vicinity. He looked
toward the dining room at the imported Danish chinaware he
once started to sell piece by piece when he was hooked and
hateful. He looked toward the kitchen, where only the best
appliances—from juicers to German ovens—made their
home, and where the cleaning service couldn't get the blood-
stains out. He looked at the far wall, at the bright painting of
the shepherd and his flock, which to him was always imbalanced, always forced the viewer to look beyond the beauty of
the natural surroundings and focus in on the loss, on that
which was missing. . . .

"Danny?" Pat prodded.

"Burn it," Danny said. "Just burn it all."

Pat half smiled, not sure how serious to take him.

They stood in silence for a while, when Danny furled his
eyebrows. "Where did Barbara *go*, anyway?" he asked.

"Upstairs," Barbara replied, coming down the steps slowly,
awkwardly. She had changed from funeral attire into a pair of
blue jeans with a baggy chambray shirt hanging out. One of
Danny's big old jackets covered her, the sleeves tubing up to
her finger joints. Her hair sported no ribbons and she had forgone her makeup: lines etched into her tan, arching up from
under her eyes.

"Be careful," Danny said, watching her falter. "We have to
go. What were you doing up there?"

Barbara grinned coyly, and from behind her back she lifted
that which had made her move clumsily—the circular mirror
from Carl Rodman's storeroom, the reflective peace symbol.

"I wanted to take the moon with us," she said softly, gazing at Danny.

Danny gazed back at her. His viscera had been shaking for the past few grueling hours, *still* shaking, flashes of wanting, craving a taste, a line, just one, always just one, which is always before the next, but just one for now, to get by. Barbara looked even thinner now than ever, less brown and healthy now, too, bonier since her ordeal. Older. They hadn't made love for some time with all that had happened to her physically, emotionally. Most nights he would have to hold her, comfort her, after she'd awaken with crying jags, fits of sweat. She was having nightmares in the middle of the day if left alone, and her vaginal damage was yet undetermined in terms of having children. . . . Still, she wanted to take the moon with them.

To Danny at this moment, Barbara was all at once a child and his mother, retaining innocence and power in a simple gesture. He wrapped Barbara in a long hug after she descended from the last step, then smiled at her and kissed her lips tenderly and her forehead softly and pressed her to him again. "I love you," he said. "We'd better go, okay?" Barbara nodded, teary-eyed over his declaration. But also from confronting their departure for real. When she was just upstairs, she had taken a long look out at her parents' house and saw a small still head between curtains at a window, peering out, like the last tiny white dot on an arcane TV picture tube just before vanishing.

Barbara sniffled and stepped back to Pat, who had been watching her and Danny embrace. "'Bye," she said, leaning over to kiss Pat's cheek.

"Bye-bye," Pat said, giving her a one-armed squeeze.

Danny nodded at Pat. "Thanks for everything you've done for us."

She touched his cheek, Carl's. "Yeah," she could barely say, and turned her face aside.

The sun was cracking through the gray clouds, elbowing them away, shooting holes in the dark, spiraling light into the day. Danny revved up his repaired motorcycle, donned his helmet, and made sure Barbara and their moon were safely clasped to him.

Gathering herself, Pat Dokes stepped outside, surprised by

the sudden shafts of brightness, and shading her eyes, watched the bike pull away, Barbara sending her a blind wave. They swerved left at the driveway and disappeared down the tree-thick suburban street, the motor's rumbling echo still faintly alive, though the children themselves could no longer be seen. Pat felt envy and joy and sadness and hope—everything you are supposed to feel when looking toward the future.